PEARLS

Spirits of the Belleview Biltmore

Book One

BONSUE BRANDVIK

For the Crescent Oaks Book Club —
Thanks for caring about
local history!
Bonsue Brandvik

Belleview Biltmore

Then:

And

Now:

Acknowledgements

This novel is dedicated to: My husband, John, the hero in my real-life love story and also to the Belleview Biltmore Resort, the inspiration for this novel, which is currently in desperate need of a hero of her own.

My sincere thanks to: My friends, family, Beta-readers, fellow authors, and the Clearwater Writers Meet-Up Group, who have read drafts, critiqued the storyline and cheered for my characters for years. Thanks especially to my mom, Mary Buehrig and to my dearest friends, Deborah Corbett and Cathy Casteleiro, for their on-going help with editing and cover graphics, and to my editors, John Brandvik, Cara Lockwood and Colleen Rogers, for their amazing eye for detail.

Additional thanks to: Diane Hein, Rea Claire Johnson, the Historic Preservation Board of Belleair, the National Trust for Historic Preservation, and the thousands of local residents and past hotel guests, staff and preservationists, who continue to do everything within their power to preserve the 820,000 square feet of the historic Belleview Biltmore, currently known as the largest occupied wooden structure in the world. Developers are trying to demolish Henry, Margaret, and Morton Plant's magnificent hotel, originally built in 1896 (wings added in 1901 and 1924), but this dedicated group of individuals continues to resist, understanding the historic significance of this awe-inspiring building and recognizing that many spirits might still call the hotel 'home'.

I hope: You will enjoy this novel, which intertwines historic fact with fiction, and that you will be inspired to find out more about the Belleview Biltmore's rich history & famous guests. Please peruse my website: www.SpiritsOfBelleview Biltmore.com, for more facts, photos and interesting stories shared by past hotel guests and staff. I remain hopeful that one day, you will be able to visit the restored Belleview Biltmore Resort, known as the *White Queen of the Gulf*, and come to understand why so many are dedicated to her preservation.

PEARLS

Spirits of the Belleview Biltmore

Book One

Chapter 1

"Rat Bastard!" Honor Macklin slurred between clinched teeth; her green eyes flashing with alcohol-infused anger. "How could you?"

The conversation she had overheard earlier that evening wouldn't stop echoing in her ears. She had been just outside the conference room door when she heard the handsome new client ask, "How did you let Honor slip away from you, William? She's gorgeous and her software designs are brilliant."

Honor had smiled at the compliments and continued to eavesdrop, expecting her ex-husband, William Guard, to give their agreed-upon response: *We developed different interests over time and although we are still close friends and excellent business partners here at Soft Fix, ending our marriage was in both of our best interests.*

Instead, William snickered. "Trust me, her looks are deceiving. A blow-up doll would have been more exciting in bed than her."

The client laughed. "I figured she was too good to be true."

Mortified, Honor hadn't stuck around to hear any more. It was already past normal working hours, so she slipped out of the office and into the chilly autumn night, fleeing for the solace of her condo in northern Chicago.

By the time her personal cell phone rang, she was well into a second bottle of wine and submersed in a tearful pity-party, wondering what other humiliating tidbits William had been sharing with their male colleagues and clients.

She tucked a wayward curl of dark brown hair behind her ear and eyed the caller ID. Rolling a single pearl back and forth on the gold chain she always wore around her neck, Honor contemplated whether or not to answer. Normally, she wouldn't be that eager to speak with Charity, but tonight, her younger sister's palpable contempt for William appealed to her.

Just before the call went to voicemail, she flipped open the cell phone.

"Hi, Cherry."

"Why do you sound so weird?"

"It's been a bad day."

"Are you sick? There's a bug going around at the girls' school. I've been spraying antibacterial on everything, but I think Mercy's coming down with it anyway. You know, at times like this, I envy you for not having kids."

Honor ignored the jab, already beginning to regret answering the phone. "I don't have the flu. And you didn't call to tell me one of my nieces has the sniffles. So what's up?"

"Well, I hate to bug you, but we really need to get down to Florida to get Mom's house cleaned out and fixed up, so we can list it for sale."

Honor knew that by *we*, Cherry really meant *she*. When could *she* go? It was an annoying habit and tonight, *she* couldn't let it slide.

"Okay. When do *you* want to head down there?"

"Come on, Honor. You know I can't get away while the girls are in school." Cherry paused, lowering her voice. "Listen, I know it's been a tough year for you, but I honestly believe it would do you good to get out of Chicago for a while. Besides, don't you want to finish your list of executor duties?"

Honor realized Cherry was pushing her buttons and hated that it was working. She had chosen her words to trigger Honor's slightly compulsive desire to complete checklists. Honor habitually maintained lists for everything from what she needed to purchase at the store to what steps she would have to take to achieve her career goals. So of course, following the death of their mother, Honor made a list of her executor responsibilities. And she was itching to finish it.

She had already divided most of their mother's assets between her three sisters. To complete the liquidation of the estate, Honor needed to go to Florida and oversee the sale of their childhood home.

The wine was making it difficult to remain focused.

Unbidden, Honor's 'Lifetime To-Do List' popped into her mind. She wondered how much of her decision to marry William Guard had been based on her desire to check an item off that list.

At least she had kept her maiden name. Though truth be told, she hadn't done that out of any strong sense of maintaining her individuality, but because her name would have sounded ridiculous if she had changed it to *Honor Guard*. She shivered at the thought and returned her attention to the conversation with Cherry.

"I have responsibilities, too," she protested. "William would be lost if I just took off for Florida."

"Who cares?" Cherry shot back.

Honor had been making excuses for William's behavior for so long, it had become second nature, but tonight a conflicting desire - to get even - was raging dangerously close to the surface. She struggled to remain in control, to take the high road.

"My engineering staff would eat William alive if I left town."

"And what - you're worried about the poor engineers getting indigestion?"

Honor smiled at her sister's show of support. "Don't hold back, Cherry. Tell me how you really feel."

"You want me to lie?"

"No, but tonight I overheard William say something that

made me wonder... if I had just tried harder..."

"H-E-double-hockey-sticks Honor! That man has been a lying, cheating son of a-you-know-what from the start. Nothing you could have done would have changed that."

Honor's thoughts drifted to the beginning of her relationship with William. Even then, there was no fairy tale ambiance. Their romance, such as it was, blossomed out of their tremendous business success together. Honor thought they made a great team, so when William proposed marriage, she accepted.

"I think maybe our personalities were just too different to make things work."

"Yeah, you guys are 180 degrees different. You make money; he spends money," Cherry sniped.

Honor considered this. William did love the trappings that came with their acquired wealth. And he always wanted more. More fun, more parties, more friends, more trips...more space.

"Yeah, it used to piss me off when he acted like there was something wrong with me because my idea of fun was lounging in front of a fire with a good book and a glass of wine."

At the mention of wine, Honor remembered the open bottle and refilled her glass.

"*That's* what made you angry?" Cherry's sarcasm was unmistakable. "He didn't spend his evenings reading books with you? Give me a break."

Honor flinched; her sister's comment dredged up painful memories.

While their business, Soft Fix, thrived, their marriage spiraled downward, with neither of them paying too much attention to the fall. William took frequent trips with 'the boys' and Honor suspected he wasn't being faithful to her.

Cherry's voice grew shrill. "William showed his true colors when he was late for Mom's funeral service and then..."

"Can we change the subject?" Honor pleaded. "My day was

lousy enough without rehashing this."

"I know, but what kind of a blankety-blank does something like that? Frankly, I don't see how you can stand to continue working with the a-s-s."

"Don't spell, Cherry. It makes me crazy. If you're going to cuss, do it like a grown-up." Honor took another long drink, trying to gather her thoughts. "I know what William did sucked, but I don't want to be bitter about him finding happiness with someone else."

"Listen to you; trying to be all stoic and modern about the whole situation."

"It's just that our relationship is complicated. I mean, our company is really important to me and he's important to the company. It's hard."

"Of course it's hard. He took advantage of your trust and made a fool out of you. It's not normal to pretend that's okay, Honor. You're going to make yourself sick if you continue trying to act so saintly."

"Yeah, I know. I thought I could handle it, as long as we kept our personal lives separate from work, but I just found out he lied about doing that, too."

Honor took a large gulp of wine. She considered telling Cherry what she had overheard earlier tonight, but she was embarrassed. And a part of her wondered if William was right about her lack of prowess in the bedroom.

"Wow. William lied—that's a shocker," Cherry deadpanned.

The simple comment was so on target it was as though a light bulb switched on in Honor's brain. Of course William lied. He always lied. Why had she ever believed he would uphold their agreement? With another long drink, her fury returned.

"You're right. He's the one who ruined everything. What gives him the right to screw me over time and again and expect me to just keep going along with everything?"

Cherry perked up. "That's more like it. He's had you under

his thumb for way too long and until you take charge of your life again, he's going to keep making you feel this way. I'm telling you, a trip to Florida will be good for you."

Honor sneered. "You just want me to get the house on the market."

"Well, as executor, it is your job."

Honor bristled. "She was your mother, too. You guys should help."

"The rest of us have children. We can't just pick up and go the way you can. Besides, Patty, Chase and I already emptied out most of the house."

Honor fumed silently as Cherry lectured. "Mom chose you to be the executor. You've done a great job so far, and once the house is liquidated, you're done. You know Mom would want you to finish this and move on."

Honor and her mother had been close, though they didn't share many common interests. Faith Macklin had been an accountant who loved baking and enjoyed living in a small town. Those interests didn't appeal to her, but Honor did possess certain similarities to her mother. She looked more like her mother than her sisters did - tall and lanky, with thick, curly hair. And like her mother, Honor could use her methodical logic to solve problems and get things done. It was the characteristic that allowed her to be so successful in her work... and the reason her siblings expected her to handle the disposition of their mother's estate on her own.

"Are you listening to me?" Cherry's piercing tone jolted Honor back to their conversation.

"Yeah," she grumbled.

Honor polished off the second bottle of wine and stared at her empty glass. Suddenly, she knew what to do to make her sisters happy, and avoid the humiliation of facing everyone at work tomorrow. It was simple.

Two birds; one stone.

"You're right," she announced, "I'll fly to Florida tonight

and stay there until I check everything off that damn list."

"Really?" Cherry was ecstatic. Before hanging up, she reminded Honor, "Don't forget the house is empty. You'll need to make a hotel reservation at the Belleview Biltmore."

Honor dropped her cell phone into her purse and began throwing clothes haphazardly into her suitcase. She grabbed her business Blackberry off the charger to call Julie Wells, her assistant. After instructing a sleepy and confused Julie to clear her calendar, Honor tossed the phone aside to close her suitcase. Then she stumbled downstairs and into a taxi headed for O'Hare—accidentally leaving the Blackberry behind.

Chapter 2

Honor drove her rental car over the little bridge and pulled up next to the guardhouse at the entrance to the Belleview Biltmore Resort. "I'm checking in," she whispered, her head pounding.

The stocky guard smiled and handed her a bright yellow parking slip for her dash. "Well, then, welcome to the largest wooden hotel in the World. I hope you have an enchanted stay, miss."

She thanked him and eased her rental car along the curving, palm-lined drive toward the mammoth white structure, with nearly a hundred gables dotting its sprawling, green-shingled roof.

Despite the hangover and reason for the trip, Honor was enjoying her adventure so far, feeling a bit like a kid skipping school to take an unplanned holiday.

She had sobered up when security at O'Hare singled her out for a full-body scan; the penalty for making a last-minute, one-way reservation for the red-eye flight to Tampa.

Regretting her hastily made commitment, she was about say she changed her mind about the trip, when one of the security guards made a wisecrack about his girlfriend to a chuckling co-worker, reminding her of William. She stalked off to her gate without even looking back.

Now, her car glided to a stop at the hotel entrance and a cheerful valet opened her door. "I'm checking in," she repeated—grinning despite the headache, as she suddenly remembered William's dumbfounded reaction when she called him after landing in Tampa, to let him know she was going out of town for several weeks.

The valet signaled to waiting bellmen and extended his hand to help her from her car. Honor breathed in the salty air, enjoying the warm Florida sunshine on her bare arms. Quick to action, one bellman placed her luggage on a wheeled cart while two more pulled open the large double doors, welcoming her into the majestic, domed lobby of the grand hotel.

Her sneakers squeaked on the richly colored mosaic-tiled floor as Honor crossed to the massive mahogany registration desk. While the clerk processed her reservation, Honor gazed up at the arched ivory beams supporting the light pink dome. She marveled at the carved details on the cornices decorating the wide crown molding, and recalled how her mother had treasured this historic hotel. Even though they lived only a few blocks away, Faith Macklin had spent countless weekends here over the years.

A young bellhop took Honor's key to the Presidential Suite, and led her down a long, broad corridor, which smelled of aged pine. Every twenty feet, an ornately carved beam arched across the towering hall, with a crystal and brass chandelier suspended from each ivory-painted peak. Between the beams, burgundy and forest green wallpaper covered the lower half of the walls beneath carved wainscoting, and these colors were echoed in the thick carpet runner. Huge, antique photographs hung on the cream wallpaper that covered the upper portion of the walls, depicting the hotel in its early days, along with many of its famous guests.

The enthusiastic bellhop entertained Honor with trivia as they walked. "This is known as the hotel time forgot. You know, they built these walkways wide enough that two women wearing hoopskirts could pass one another comfortably." He waved a hand in the direction of the intricately patterned crimson carpet. "And check out the floor. Of course, the carpet has been replaced lots of times over the years, but most of those pine floor boards you see on either side of it are original 1896 construction."

When he noticed Honor admiring the photographs, the bellman quipped mysteriously, "People say a few of those guests are still here with us."

"Well, as long as ghosts don't hog the covers, they won't bother me," Honor joked wryly.

The bellman laughed and pushed the button to call the elevator. "When the hotel first opened, it didn't have elevators. I would have had to drag your suitcases up to your suite through a hidden staircase." He winked, "Some changes are good."

Despite the grand hotel entrance, Honor was not prepared for the antique elegance she encountered when the door to her suite swung open with a comfortable squeak. The rich mahogany furnishings, flocked burgundy wallpaper and ivory lace curtains made her feel as though she should have arrived with steamer trunks and an entourage of housekeeping staff.

The bellhop seemed to echo her thoughts. "Yes, ma'am, this suite is amazing." He carried her suitcases to the master bedroom and laid them on the magenta floral bedspread that covered the enormous four poster bed. Then he gave her a tour of the apartment, starting with the separate master bedroom parlor, private balcony and large bath. He explained, "This part of the resort was remodeled several years ago. They pulled out the claw-footed tubs and replaced them with replicas that are actually state of the art Jacuzzi baths. Like I said before, some changes are good."

Down the hallway were two bedrooms, a bath, partial kitchen, huge dining room and another small parlor. When he finished the tour, the bellhop wheeled his cart back into the hallway and wished her a nice stay. Honor gave him a generous tip and closed the door.

Her inner child wanted to continue playing hooky and explore the grounds of the hotel, but she knew she should unpack. She compromised by imagining what kinds of clothes she might have seen in the walk-in closet when the hotel first opened. No doubt it would have been filled with long, lace and satin dresses, feathered hats and ruffled petticoats. She could almost visualize them on the rod where her tee shirts and jeans now hung.

After settling in, she decided to take advantage of her private balcony, where she could enjoy the warm air and colorful landscape while writing a list of tasks she needed to accomplish during her stay. She listed only a few items before her eyes grew heavy.

On the lawn below, two Victorian ladies appeared, chatting lightly as they strolled casually under the balcony. One was stocky and wore a long, pink dress with a full bustle in the back. She carried a white, ruffled parasol. The other woman was thin and dressed in a high-necked white blouse, a long black skirt and held a simple black parasol. Both wore large hats, decorated with satin roses and several long feathers.

Honor gasped and jerked her head up; her eyes wide open. The lawn was empty. She shook her head, confused. She had never had such a realistic daydream before. She could still remember the sound of the ladies' pleasant chatter and every detail of their attire.

"Whoa. I must be more tired than I realized. I'd better grab a bite to eat and turn in early."

Honor wandered down to the hotel's restaurant, where she elected to dine outside, overlooking the water. While waiting for her bowl of shrimp bisque and salad to arrive, she turned her personal cell phone on and frowned. Sixteen messages, all from William. With a heavy sigh, she began listening to his angry blasts, most of which started with lectures about her being unbelievably irresponsible and ending with questions for which he should already know the answers. What projects are in the works? Who is handling the various work orders? When do you meet with the technical staff? Why the hell did you leave town without your Blackberry?

She sighed, pressed his speed dial number, and braced herself for his angry tirade. She still wasn't sure what she would tell him when he demanded more details about her sudden departure. Several times during the flight to Tampa, she thought about catching the first flight back to Chicago. And each time, she restored her motivation by remembering the afternoon William asked for a divorce.

It happened immediately after her mother's funeral, while mourners were still gathering at her family's home. He pulled her aside, saying he needed to talk to her about something important. Once they were out of earshot, he began an obviously rehearsed speech.

"There's no easy way to say this, and I apologize for the timing, but it can't wait. I still respect you and value you as a business partner, but I've fallen in love with someone else and want a divorce. Please try to understand. Sometimes the desires of the heart just can't be denied."

"Gag," Honor uttered sarcastically at the memory of the conversation. She still believed he had followed the desires of an organ much lower on his body than his heart.

It turned out *Miss Barely Legal*, as Honor liked to call the pony-tailed blonde, was pregnant with his child and the reason William couldn't wait was that she demanded a ring on her finger before their baby was born. This had been the most painful part for Honor because William had always said he didn't want children—that their company, Soft Fix, was their baby.

Honor breathed a sigh of relief when William didn't answer his phone. She left him a long message, answering all of his work-related questions and then, with uncharacteristic bravado, turned her phone off again. She glanced up just as the waitress approached her table and swung the serving platter deftly from her shoulder without spilling a drop of Honor's sweet iced tea or bisque. The meal was delicious, but once her stomach was full, Honor could barely keep her eyes open. She found her way back to her suite, took a quick bath and settled into bed for the night, with her most recent checklist lying next to her unfinished.

She dreamed of the same ladies in long dresses, their parasols now closed as they conversed in white rocking chairs on the wide veranda porch. When they rose, Honor followed them leisurely down corridors smelling of freshly polished wood and orange blossoms, back to her own suite. There, they sat at her parlor table, contentedly sipping tea. "Such simple times. Such opulence. Such a well-ordered existence," she voyeuristically observed.

The alarm clock woke her with a start.

Honor was momentarily confused - not only about where she was, but about what year it was. When she turned off the alarm, her surroundings came back into focus, but she couldn't shake the eerie sensation that she wasn't alone. It wasn't like her to let her imagination run wild, but as she dressed, she shot glances over first one shoulder, then the other—half expecting to find the Victorian ladies at her parlor table.

Despite her unusual dreams, Honor felt very well-rested. She decided the bath before bed must have been the key to a great night's sleep. "But from now on," she chastised herself, "No more late-night meals to fuel crazy dreams!"

As she walked down the main corridor towards the restaurant for breakfast, Honor again noticed the old pictures hanging on the walls and stopped to read the brief captions below many of the photographs. She still didn't understand why her mother spent so many weekends at this hotel, but Honor was beginning to grasp what she meant when she explained, "Staying at the Belleview Biltmore is a little bit like *traveling back in time.*"

Honor's gaze froze on the photograph of a lady dressed in Victorian attire. The woman's hair and facial features were so similar to Honor's that she could have been mistaken for her sister, had the picture not been taken over a hundred years before. Moreover, she was sure this was one of the women she had seen in her dreams. "I must have seen this picture and subconsciously incorporated it into my fantasy because we look so much alike," she rationalized.

Suddenly a little ball of dark brown hair with a red tee-shirt and blue jeans whirled into her, grabbing at her knees to keep from falling down. Instinctively, she reached for the little boy to catch him. "Whoa there, little guy! Where are you going in such a hurry?"

Chapter 3

Honor searched the corridor for the child's mother and saw instead, a tall, gorgeous man approaching her.

"Sorry," he muttered as he scooped up the little boy. "See what happens when you run in the hallway, Cody?"

The child squirmed in the man's arms, attempting to break free. "Put me down, Daddy. I won't run anymore. I promise," he cried. But the man held on tight and smiled at Honor.

"He's been pretty wound up since we got here yesterday. I'm hoping he'll work off some of his energy at the pool after breakfast. Are you okay?"

Honor smiled back at him, trying not to ogle the well-developed muscles in his arms. "Sure, I'm fine. Thanks for asking."

She turned to continue walking toward the restaurant. She hadn't gone but a few steps when she heard Cody call out, "Daddy, look - it's the pretty lady from the picture." She glanced back and saw him pointing at the photograph of the Victorian woman.

The man looked from Honor's face to the photograph and then back to Honor. "You know, there really is a strong resemblance."

"I noticed that, too, but it's just a coincidence."

Awkwardly, they proceeded down the hallway, with Cody continuing to try to talk to her from several steps behind. They reached the Reservations desk and stood there together a few moments before the Hostess noticed their arrival and came over to seat them.

"A table for three?" the Hostess asked.

"Yes, please." Cody immediately responded

They both looked at the little boy in shock and then back to the Hostess. "No!" they blurted in unison. Together they tried to explain they didn't really know one another, which became an embarrassing montage of broken sentences.

"So then, separate tables?" the clearly puzzled Hostess asked.

Cody stubbornly insisted, "But why can't she eat with us, Daddy?"

Now quite pink and sheepish, the man turned to Honor and grinned. "Hi. My name is Josh Lancing and you've already met my son, Cody. Would you like to join us for breakfast, miss? I mean, I would completely understand if you would rather be seated on the other side of the restaurant, but we would enjoy your company."

Honor smiled, noticing Josh and Cody had the same bright blue eyes—and that Josh wasn't wearing a ring. She didn't enjoy eating alone, but was still surprised to hear herself respond, "Why, thank you. That would be nice." She extended her hand. "I'm Honor Macklin, and I'm pleased to make your acquaintance, Josh and Cody."

Cody beamed at her when she shook his tiny hand and kept smiling at her all the way to their table.

"So... Honor, huh? That's unusual. Is it a family name?" Josh asked in an attempt to break the ice.

Honor nodded. "My great-great-grandmother started a tradition in my family, naming all the baby girls after admirable virtues or traits. My sisters are named Charity, Patience and Chastity, but we call them Cherry, Patty and Chase."

Josh's smile was friendly and genuine. "Well, what do you know? We have something in common already. My parents had a weird baby-naming thing, too."

Honor arched her eyebrows in an unspoken question,

waiting for details.

"Because my Mom's name was Jeanette and my Dad's name was James, they decided that all of their children's names would start with a 'J', too. Of course, when they decided that, they didn't realize they were going to have eleven children and all of them would be boys," Josh chuckled.

Honor gasped. "Eleven children? And all boys? That's incredible! What are your names?" Amused, she listened to him rattle off the names in rapid succession.

"Well besides me, there's James Jr., John, Jacob, Jeffrey, Jeremy, Jesse, Jerrod, Justin, Joseph, and Jason. We call each other the 'Js'."

"Why don't I have a 'J' name, Daddy?" Cody asked.

"Well, because your mom liked the name Cody and when you were born, the name fit." Cody seemed to accept this explanation and went back to coloring in his Spiderman coloring book while he waited for his breakfast to arrive.

Josh leaned toward Honor, lowering his voice. "When he pipes up like that, it reminds me that when he is within earshot of a conversation, he is *always* listening to it."

Without looking up from his drawing, Cody nodded in agreement and said, "Yeah, big ears." Honor's eyes flew open wide and she looked at Josh for confirmation that she heard Cody correctly. Josh just shook his head and smiled at his son.

Honor and Josh's conversation flowed effortlessly.

"I'd forgotten how wonderful the weather is down here. It makes me regret that I established my company in Chicago."

"You own your own business." Josh admired. "Tell me about it."

"Really?" Honor crinkled her nose. "What do you want to know?"

"Well, how did you get started?" Josh rested his chin against his fist, waiting patiently for her to find a place to start.

Honor blushed under his handsome gaze. "I was working for a computer software company in Chicago," she began hesitantly. "Management was happy because a piece of software I designed was selling like hotcakes, but I was bored and wanted to start working on something new. Unfortunately, the Board of Directors decided to focus on marketing our current software instead of funding research and development."

Honor paused, pleasantly surprised to find that Josh was still paying rapt attention to her. Encouraged, she continued, "I knew that was a bad idea, but I couldn't make them listen to me.

William Guard ran our marketing department, and he agreed with me about needing to stay on the cutting edge of development. These days, William is my ex-husband, so to make a long story short, he convinced me to quit my job, sell my stock, and start a software business together. We christened our company 'Soft Fix' and we've managed to carve out a comfortable niche for ourselves, designing specialty software for small businesses."

"Impressive," remarked Josh.

Honor shrugged. "A lot of it was dumb luck and good timing."

"It doesn't sound like dumb luck to me. It sounds like you're good at what you do." Josh flashed a brilliant smile.

Honor smiled back. "Maybe it was both. It turned out I sold my stock just in the nick of time. As I predicted, a competitor released a superior software product, and my former employer's 'cash cow' software was instantly obsolete. It was a nightmare. Almost overnight, their stock value crashed and the company was dissolved." She shook her head sadly. "Most of my former co-workers lost their investment and their employment. It was heartbreaking, but like I said, we're blessed with good timing. They lost their jobs just as we were ready to expand, so we were able to hire several of them."

"And now they work for a woman who's a lot smarter than their old boss," Josh interjected.

"Only about some things," Honor confessed. "I can design software, but that's about it. William handles all the marketing and business stuff. Our skills mesh together beautifully. I guess that's why I once thought our union was destiny. But then..." Honor hesitated.

Josh leaned toward her, compassion filling his eyes. "But then you learned destiny has a way of throwing curve balls?" he suggested.

"Curve balls. Hmmm... yeah, that's one way of putting it. I learned that we didn't mesh together very well when we weren't working. So now my business partner is also my ex-husband, and he is remarried to a bubbly blonde with a baby."

"Ouch. That's got to have its unpleasant moments," Josh observed.

Honor laughed at the gross understatement. "Yep, downright unpleasant."

"You've got a great laugh," Josh grinned. "So, tell me, what brings you to Florida? Vacation?"

Moved by his tenderness, Honor opened up. "Actually, I was raised in Belleair. I'm back here because of another one of those nasty curve balls. My mom was killed in a car accident last year and I'm here to get her house ready to be put on the market."

Josh's smile quickly faded. "I'm so sorry. Wow, you've been through a lot."

"Please don't apologize, Josh. I was beginning to think I'd forgotten how to laugh. I should be thanking you for reminding me not to take myself so seriously. But now it's your turn. Tell me your story."

Honor rested her chin against her hand, in an obvious imitation of Josh and waited.

Josh sat up straight. "Okay, fair is fair, I guess." He shot a glance at Cody, who was busy using his fork to trace designs in the syrup on his plate. "Well, I'm a general contractor and have been living in North Carolina for about six years now. I'm here in Florida because all of my brothers live here and now I'm thinking about joining them." He paused, trying to think what else to say. "Ummm... Cody's my only child and he's four years old. I guess that's about it for me."

Honor protested, "Come on... I told you a lot more than that! Give me the details. You're not wearing a ring... divorced?"

"I'm sort of a widower, I guess." Josh replied, as though the question didn't come up very often.

"Sort of a widower," she repeated. "I don't think it's technically possible to be *sort of* a widower, is it?"

"Yeah, you're right. But Cody's mother, Amy, died following a car accident that had left her in a coma for the last month of her pregnancy."

"A car accident," echoed Honor in a near-whisper.

"Yeah. Something else we have in common, I'm afraid. Amy and I weren't together very long, but we planned to share joint custody of Cody." He paused. "I think she would have been a good mother." Attempting to lighten the conversation, Josh joked, "You know, people said having a baby would change my life; but they didn't warn me a baby would alter every single aspect of my world!"

Cody looked up from his plate, indignant. "I am *not* a baby," he informed her. Honor smiled, remembering Josh's warning that Cody was always tuned into the conversation. A moment later, he added, "My Mommy can't come to Florida, but in North Carolina she sings me Happy Birthday and tells me stories."

Josh met Honor's puzzled expression. "I know. Cody has an extremely vivid imagination, but I've been told that's a sign of creative intelligence." He turned to Cody. "Stop talking for a while and eat some of your pancake so you can grow up to be big and strong, okay, pal?"

Obligingly, Cody picked up his sticky fork in his chubby fist and took a stab at a bite of syrup-laden pancake.

Josh turned back to face Honor. "As I was saying, my brothers have been after me for years to move down here. With Amy gone and construction booming in Tampa Bay, I think I've run out of reasons not to. Besides, it would be nice to have help taking care of Cody when he starts school."

At the sound of his name, Cody chimed in. "We should move to Florida and live in this hotel, Daddy. There are lots of nice people here to play with and they make good pancakes."

Honor and Josh laughed again and again as their sometimes three-way conversation rolled on in this manner. Too soon, they finished their breakfast and reluctantly rose to leave.

Josh ventured, "I really enjoyed meeting you, Honor. Would you mind... I mean, if you want company for another meal... Could I get your phone number?"

"Sure," Honor replied, rifling through her wallet with butterflies in her stomach. "I don't seem to have any business cards with me, but I could enter my number in your cell phone if you want me to."

Josh smiled and handed his phone to her. While she was busy entering the number, Cody stood on his chair to watch. "This is good. True love doesn't grow on trees, you know," he quipped.

Both Josh and Honor stared at him; not sure they heard him correctly.

"Where in the world did you hear that phrase, Little Buddy?" Josh queried.

Cody pointed at the empty chair at their table. "That Fuzzy Man told me."

Honor felt the hair rise on the back of her neck, but Josh just laughed it off. "I'm sorry, but in addition to Cody's endless stream of invisible friends, he has a penchant for memorizing things he hears on TV and repeating them back whenever the urge strikes him."

He tousled the child's hair and lifted him to the floor.

Honor recalled her weird dreams and the feeling that she wasn't alone in her hotel room that morning. She wondered if Cody's invisible friends were the normal imaginings of childhood or something else altogether.

Chapter 4

As they left the restaurant, the Hostess smiled at them, apparently pleased that her assumption when they arrived had turned out not to be a mistake after all. "I hope the three of you come back to see us again real soon."

"Sure will. And thanks for fixing me up with such a beautiful lady," Josh joked.

Her ghostly concerns temporarily forgotten, Honor quickly glanced away, hoping to hide the fact she was blushing over the compliment.

In the lobby, two bellmen pulled the heavy doors open and Honor exited the hotel into the perfect November Florida sunshine. Not wanting to spoil her good mood, she decided to leave her cell phone off just a little while longer. Besides, visualizing William freezing his butt off in Chicago, frustrated she wasn't instantly available, gave her a sense of guilty pleasure.

Minutes later, she pulled into the driveway of her childhood home and turned off the engine. Honor stared at the two-story, light yellow Queen Anne with white gingerbread trim, pretending her mother was still inside, alive and well.

For the first time since the funeral, she thought about her mother's burial. Faith Macklin had always been adamant about being buried in Florida, where "her bones wouldn't freeze in the dirt" and years ago, she showed Honor the small cemetery she had chosen as her final resting place. Honor had been incredulous. The cemetery, located just outside the town of Belleair, had probably once been charming and quaint, but over the years it had become crowded by commerce on all sides and divided by a busy road.

Aghast, Honor questioned, "Why in the world would you want to be buried here?"

"Because I'll be with those who remember when these surroundings were peaceful and glorious," her mother explained. "And I can enjoy listening to their stories throughout eternity."

Honor still didn't understand, but she made sure her mother was laid to rest among the old headstones, with the urn containing her long-dead husband's ashes tucked securely at her side.

Honor swallowed the lump in her throat and unlocked the front door. The foyer was empty, except for the Grandfather clock that her mother had insisted Honor, as the eldest daughter, was to inherit.

After the funeral, Honor encouraged her sisters to divide the antique furniture and other keepsakes among themselves. But she hadn't realized how peculiar the house would look without its furnishings and the valuable collectibles that used to line the shelves and fill every corner of the home.

Honor walked from empty room to empty room. Her sisters had taken everything except some miscellaneous dishes, their mother's clothing, old bedding and large stacks of miscellaneous paperwork. They hadn't bothered to throw away their empty soda cans or vacuum the carpet before departing, which irritated Honor. It struck her as being rude. After all, their mother had been such a fussy housekeeper. She decided to make a quick trip to the store to purchase some cardboard boxes, cleaning supplies and a shredder.

As soon as she returned, Honor sat on the living room floor and forced herself to call William. Braced for his heated tirade, she couldn't believe her good fortune -- she got his voice mail again. Like a child hiding from an angry parent, she left him a short message and quickly turned her phone off before he could call back.

Next, she rolled up her sleeves and got to work cleaning, sorting and packing what was left of her mother's possessions, starting with the kitchen. This had been the heart of their home throughout her childhood and even without furniture, the familiarity of the kitchen was comforting. After packing a few cabinets, Honor took a break and sat on the floor in the bay-windowed nook where the round maple table had always been.

She pretended she and her mother were chatting over a cup of coffee and a cookie. "Gosh, Mom, so much has happened in the short time you've been gone, I don't know where to begin." Her eyes welled with tears. "William cheated on me and accidentally got a girl pregnant. Well, either it was an accident or he didn't care enough about our marriage to take precautions. I guess it doesn't matter. We're divorced but still working together, which is every bit as awful as it sounds. And the cherry on top is that I just learned he's been telling people our marriage failed because I wasn't..." She paused and bit her lip. "God, my life sucks!"

Honor imagined her mother listening sympathetically, offering her another cookie. It was a consoling thought. When she was growing up, her mother had used cookies like emotional Band-Aids. She smiled, wondering what size clothing she would be wearing today, if she had eaten every cookie her mother ever offered.

"Mom, I sure do miss you," she mused. She rolled her pearl back and forth on its chain, remembering the day her mother gave her the necklace.

The gem was said to have come from a stunning triple strand of natural pearls that once belonged to Honor's widowed great-great-grandmother. She had taken the necklace apart during lean times, selling several of the pearls to help pay for her only child's upbringing and education. That child, Honor's great-grandmother, Hope, had raised four daughters of her own. In her will, she decreed the remaining pearls from the necklace were to be divided equally among her daughters; a symbolic connection to their ancestors.

Subsequent generations continued the tradition, so when Faith Macklin's daughters reached the age of sixteen, she gave each of them one pearl on a gold chain, and added another pearl each time a daughter was born to them. Honor was the only sibling still wearing a single pearl. She idly wondered how many pearls her mother was still safekeeping at the time of her death, hoping Honor would "earn" them someday. She sighed, "Mom, I don't think this pearl is bringing me the strength of my ancestors like it's supposed to."

She clambered to her feet and went back to work, packing-up mismatched dishes and old glasses. Over the years, Honor had tried several times to convince her mother her dishes were no longer stylish and offered to go shopping with her to buy replacements. Her mother tolerated her criticisms and sometimes added a few new dishes to the cabinet, but she never replaced anything that wasn't broken beyond repair. She said the dishes reminded her of when Honor and her sisters were little girls, eager to help-out in the kitchen. Honor had scoffed at her silly sentimentality... until now. She smiled and set aside a favorite glass to keep for herself.

From one of the lower cabinets, Honor began to unload cookbooks. She was fascinated with the yellowed and tattered pages, contemplating fondly how her mother, grandmother and even her great-grandmother used these recipes over the years. They had been wonderful cooks and their gourmet cookies were almost legendary.

Honor smiled. The internet had changed the way she found, exchanged and stored recipes, so these cookbooks were headed for Goodwill. Still, she had a hard time dumping the whole pile of them into a box. Instead she combed through the pages of the old books, reading little notes written in the margins by her ancestors and unfolding and reading several hand-written recipes.

An hour later, she looked up and was surprised to discover that she had absently set aside a little pile of handwritten cookie recipes she didn't want to let go. Somehow it was as though the words written on those scraps of paper kept the people she loved with her.

On the floor of the deep cabinet, buried beneath the mountain of cookbooks, Honor discovered an old soda cracker tin. She lifted it out and carefully opened the lid. Inside she found an old journal, written by a woman whose name Honor didn't recognize: Darcy Loughman. The ink was quite faded on the yellowed pages and the verbiage was difficult to decipher, but she could make out the date:1896. She wanted to read the entries, but recognized she would never get her work finished at this slow pace. She opted to set the journal aside to serve as bedtime reading material, and went back to work cleaning the kitchen.

Late in the afternoon, she took her checklist list out of her pocket and with a triumphant flourish, checked off the item "Clean-out Mom's Kitchen." Then she gathered up the day's *treasures* and put them in her car. Remembering her hotel room had seemed quite chilly the night before, she went to her mother's closet and grabbed an old-fashioned flannel granny-gown to sleep in, and then drove the short distance back to the hotel to order room service.

Belly full, bathed and dressed in her mother's old flannel gown, Honor snuggled under the goose-down comforter, against the oh-so-soft pillows and began to read the faded text in the old journal. It began, "I long for a world so different than the one I inhabit..."

As she began to drift off to sleep, Honor became aware of a chill in the air and she heard voices coming from... coming from where? The hallway? Her suite? She tried to focus on the conversation.

"She has the journal. It's time for her to know everything," a woman's voice said.

Honor rose from her bed to investigate and was amazed to find two women sitting in her parlor, clothed in full Victorian dress. Then it slowly began to sink in. They weren't exactly what you would call *solid*.

Chapter 5

"Who... what..." stammered Honor, startled almost beyond words.

"Good evening, darlin'," the larger of the two women greeted her. "I'm Margaret and this is...well, this is Darcy. We see you've found her journal, gone from sight these many years."

Margaret turned to face the thin, older woman. "It's time, Darcy. You know it's the right thing to do."

"But what if she doesn't understand?" The older woman looked worried. Her anguished eyes locked on Honor.

"She comes from good stock. She'll understand," the plump woman replied.

Suddenly, Honor found herself inexplicably fading from her hotel room, into a fog. She floated through the mist, enjoying the sensation. When the fog lifted, she was sitting at a cast-iron garden table with a cool breeze caressing her face.

She felt dizzy and a bit sick to her stomach, as if she had just stepped off a roller coaster. Desperately, she tried to orient herself to her new situation by focusing on a pink hibiscus bush nearby. She heard someone call out from a nearby path.

"A grand afternoon to you, Madam Darcy."

Honor turned toward the voice and saw the heavyset woman who had called herself Margaret, waving at Darcy, who was seated across from Honor at the garden table.

Honor's mouth hung open as she gazed beyond the courtyard to the original Belleview Hotel. She felt Darcy's eyes upon her, pulling her attention back across the table. Darcy spoke as though they were still in Honor's hotel room, seemingly unaware their location had changed, or that she appeared to be several decades younger than she had been only moments ago.

Darcy offered no explanation for the changes. "You must understand. I grew up in a world very different than the one I found when my husband brought me to this place," she said, waving her hand in the general direction of the garden. "My father was an honorable man, but he was not blessed with a keen business sense and his dire financial situation caused his health to fail." Darcy took deep breath, as if the words revived painful memories.

"My mother bore no sons to help support our family, so by the time I reached womanhood, my family's name had become its most valued asset. I was forced to put away any thoughts I may have possessed about spending a glorious debut season in New York and face the reality that my marital prospects were quite poor. With no dowry, I was no longer viewed as a suitable match for young gentlemen of good breeding and wealth."

After another long pause, Darcy continued, her voice a flat monotone. "And so I was given in marriage to Reginald Loughman in my fourteenth year. Reginald was thirty five years my senior."

Darcy flinched, as if remembering the feel of the old man's wrinkled touch on her tender, young body. After a moment, she lifted her chin. "My parents tried their best to secure my future, but..." She shook her head.

"I was Reginald's third wife, he having been sorrowfully widowed twice before. He had already sired and raised his heirs; so thankfully, he didn't come to my bed very often. My wifely duties were mostly confined to providing my husband with social companionship and running his household," she murmured.

Without warning, the fog returned and Honor fell away

from the garden. She tried desperately to fight the sensation and return to her chair at the garden table, but to no avail. Eventually, she relented and floated in the fog for what felt like a long time. Finally, a musty smell began to filter through the haze. When the mist cleared, Honor was standing alone in the small, dark entryway of an old home. Despite being nauseous, she focused on voices coming from one of the nearby rooms. She thought one of them belonged to Darcy, but she wasn't sure. It was the voice of a child, stammering, attempting to explain something.

The other voice belonged to an angry man. His voice boomed, chastising the girl for failing to... for failing to do what? Honor shook her head, struggling to understand where she was and what was happening. As her stomach began to settle down, she moved closer to the dimly lit room, not sure if the occupants were aware she was witnessing their exchange. She listened closely, wondering if she should make her presence known.

"You are no longer a child; you are the mistress of this household and you must begin to act like it!" the man shouted. "If you let the servants have their way, they'll use your household budget within a fortnight, and you'll have nothing left for the market," he snarled. "I'm not surprised you learned so little, given your father's poor aptitude for managing finances, but you must do better. Now ready yourself for bed. I'll be up to join you shortly, as soon as I've dealt with this mess you've made."

The young girl rushed from the room in tears. It was Darcy; but now she appeared as the child bride she had been. She didn't acknowledge Honor, even though she scurried by only a few feet away from where Honor was standing.

Honor followed her up the dark stairs to the master bedroom chamber. Despite the fire burning in a large, stone fireplace and the glow of two gas lamps, the room was cold and foreboding. Darcy was so tiny, her body barely made a dent when she sat on the edge of the embroidered ivory bedspread and leaned against the footboard of the dark mahogany sleigh bed.

Once settled, Darcy spoke to Honor in much the same manner she had done in the garden setting—again, with no explanation for the changes that had taken place.

"This is my world. My husband will be here in a few moments, having bolstered his sense of manliness by dressing-down the servant girl that bade me spend too much of my monthly budget on new linens," she sulked. "He will expect me to be ready for him. To welcome him between my legs, even though he believes I am daft and not worthy to bear his name. I am expected to accept his critiques without resentment; lo, even with gratitude for taking the time to teach me to become a better head mistress for this house."

Darcy looked so miserable, Honor wanted to take her hand and lead her away from here. To return her to her childhood that had been stolen for lack of a dowry.

Church bells began to toll in the distance, drawing Honor's attention. There was something strange about their sound. Without warning, the fog enveloped her. She fought to return to Darcy's side, but again, her efforts failed. The bells became louder and then changed into beeping sounds. Honor's eyes flew open. She was lying in her hotel room bed, the alarm clock ringing on her nightstand.

Chapter 6

Honor shut off the alarm, closed her eyes and tried to return to her dream. Nothing happened. She rolled over, covered her eyes with a pillow and tried to focus. When she realized her efforts weren't going to pay-off, she sat up and looked around her suite.

What was it about this place? She had never experienced such bizarre dreams. They were so real. Unlike normal dreams, she was able to remember even the smallest detail long after waking up.

She glanced at the old journal lying on her bed and rationalized she must have incorporated the journal entries into her dreams. Feeling a bit silly, she shook off the eerie sensation and dressed for another day of packing at her mother's house.

She placed the old journal into a box of keepsakes she planned to ship home to Chicago and picked up her cell phone. The moment she turned it on to check messages, it rang. William was calling. Reluctantly, she answered. While the phone was off, she had imagined confronting William about his despicable behavior and demanding an apology. But faced with the reality of his anger over her "desertion", she cowered.

She apologized repeatedly for her impromptu trip, but stood her ground when he ordered her to return to Chicago immediately.

"Please, William. Try to understand. I postponed my family responsibilities until our divorce was finalized, but I have a legal commitment to liquidate my mother's estate."

"Why can't you just hire someone to clean out the house?"

"No one else would know what papers and pictures are important to my family. Listen," she lied, "my phone has been off a lot because I was too emotional about being back here to talk to anyone. I'm doing better now."

William grudgingly acquiesced. "Okay, but hurry and get back here as soon as you can. Remember, you have important responsibilities here, too. And you didn't even take your Blackberry with you, for God's sake."

Accustomed to biting her tongue to avoid William's angry tirades, Honor mumbled goodbye and hung up. She got dressed and put on make-up, hoping to run into Josh Lancing at breakfast.

She was musing about her unusual dreams when her phone rang for the fifth time that morning. Exasperated and still remembering Reginald's overbearing behavior in her dream, she barked, "What now?"

"Don't get snippy with me!" William snarled. "I have some questions about setting up the new Wooden Rose account."

His tone was so reminiscent of Reginald's that Honor snapped.

"Come on, William. Even my assistant, Julie can set up a new account and assign engineering personnel. Please stop interrupting me with such routine questions. You know, I *never* call you when you're on vacation or out-of-town on business."

Honor reveled in William's stunned silence at her uncharacteristic bravado, knowing it was only momentary. She decided to push her luck. "We're supposed to be equal partners, and this is the first time I have ever asked you to cover for me. You've got to step up, William!"

Angry and confused, William hung up without responding.

Honor was shaking with exhilaration. "Men haven't really changed much during the last century," she observed. "But women have, so husbands are no longer a necessity."

She strolled downstairs for breakfast and, again, stopped

in front of the photograph of the woman whose likeness was so similar to her own. While gazing at the portrait, she remembered it was Darcy Loughman's journal she had been reading when she fell asleep.

"Of course!" she beamed, smacking the heel of her hand against her forehead. "In my dream, I combined Darcy's name with the face in this photograph."

The whole thing made perfect sense in the light of day. She felt silly for allowing herself to become spooked by an overactive imagination. She ate breakfast alone, wondering how Josh was spending his morning.

When Honor's phone vibrated, she hoped Josh was calling, but it was William again. "I swear I'm going to block his number!" she hissed as she flipped open the phone. This time, he was concerned about an upcoming meeting and his ability to present some technical concepts Honor had sketched in the client's file. Honor tried to explain the design she envisioned, but William couldn't understand.

"Dealing with the technical minutia is supposed to be your job," he complained.

Honor was exasperated. "Who's the team leader?"

"Pete Cross."

"Okay, have him call my personal cell number - once. I'll go over the design with him and then he can handle that part of the meeting for you. And please, William, don't give my number to anyone else."

William agreed immediately and hung up.

Honor finished briefing Pete just as she unlocked the door of her mother's house. Without thinking, she called out, "Hi, Mom," as she had done throughout her childhood.

Pretending to talk to her mother was comforting, so she continued. "Sorry I'm getting such a late start today. William keeps calling me for help, if you can believe that. He's always said I don't know crap about running the company."

She walked into the kitchen and sat cross-legged on the

floor. "You know, when William and I first started out, I loved the way he took charge of everything, but so much has happened since then. I was kidding myself to think we could keep our personal lives separate from work after the divorce. Things have got to change somehow." She sighed.

Chapter 7

Honor carried her packing supplies into her mother's bedroom, where large piles of papers, pictures and bedding were stacked along the walls—items left behind when her sister, Patty, claimed the bedroom set for use in one of her guest rooms.

She opened the closet door and stepped inside. Her mother's light, flowery scent still clung to some of the clothes, and as Honor folded them neatly into a cardboard box bound for Goodwill, the reality of her loss hit home. There would be no more hugs and cookies, no more cheerful pep talks when things were going badly, and no one to brag to when things went especially well.

Honor sat down with her back against the wall, closing her eyes to hold back her tears. "Mom, I'm sorry I moved away and didn't include you in my life more often. I didn't know we would have so little time together. I hope you know how much I loved you."

Honor could almost hear her mother cooing, "Don't be silly. Of course I know you loved me; it just wasn't your style to say so all the time. Now, come on into the kitchen and have a cookie with me."

Honor smiled and dried her eyes. Glancing up, she noticed an antique hatbox on the floor directly across from where she was sitting. Honor guessed her siblings had overlooked this piece of their mother's antique collection. She scooted over to the box and examined it carefully before gingerly untying the silk bow that held it closed. She expected to find an antique hat inside, but instead, she found a Victorian Era blouse, skirt and petticoat, along with a small velvet bag. She turned the bag upside down over her open palm. Four pearls and a small brass key spilled out.

In an instant, Honor realized these were the last of the pearls from her great-great-grandmother's necklace. The ones her mother had saved in the hope that Honor, like her sisters, would have daughters of her own someday.

Honor contemplated this tangible connection to her ancestors. She unfastened her necklace and slipped the new pearls onto the chain, giving her a total of five pearls. She refastened the chain around her neck, and then carefully tucked the clothing and key back into the hatbox and retied the silk bow.

She went into the master bath to admire the pearls in the mirror above the vanity. "This feels right; one pearl for each generation, starting with me and going all the way back to Great-Great-Grandmother." She fingered the pearls, enjoying a sense of unity with past generations.

Her cell phone rang, interrupting her contemplation. She pulled it from her pocket, hoping Josh was calling, but it was just William - again.

Disappointed, she rolled her eyes and answered. "Hello, William. What now?"

William hesitated a moment at her unfriendly tone. "Pete Cross has more questions. Can I have him call you again?"

Honor felt sorry for Pete. He was more of a colleague than an employee and she didn't want to put him in the middle of this situation.

"If I say 'no,' then I'm the bad guy. So, yes, have him call me. But after this, try not to call unless there's a major *crisis* at Soft Fix, William. If I keep talking to you and working on software designs all day, I'll never get finished here."

"Come on, Honor... it's not like you're on a hot date or anything."

"Go to hell," she countered, as she flipped the phone closed. She remembered William's cruel comments she overheard the night she left for Florida. "Maybe that's why Josh hasn't called. He doesn't find me attractive, either."

She sighed and went back to work in the closet.

A moment later, her phone rang again. Annoyed, she flipped it open. "This had better be a major crisis!"

It wasn't William.

"No crisis, but did you know there are seven different area codes in the Chicago area?" the friendly male voice countered.

Confused, Honor glanced at the caller ID, but didn't recognize the number. "Excuse me?"

"When you entered your number in my cell, you didn't include your area code. This is the fifth one I tried, but there were seven possibilities."

"Josh?"

"Hi, Honor. I figure you left the area code off on purpose so I couldn't call you, but I really enjoyed meeting you, so I had to be sure."

Stunned, Honor fumbled for words. "It was an accident! I hoped you would call. You really looked up all the area codes in the Chicago area? When you didn't call, I thought... I'll shut up now."

Josh laughed. It was the most wonderful sound.

"It seems like you're busy and I'm heading over to meet some of my brothers in a few minutes, but now that I know your entire phone number, I'll call you later, okay?"

Honor's knees turned to jelly. "Sure," she squeaked.

Perhaps it was the new-found confidence she gained from Josh's phone call, or maybe it was the additional pearls, but a new goal began to form in Honor's thoughts. It might take years, but she was going to dissolve her business partnership with William.

Honor's thoughts drifted back to Josh. "Mom, I've met a wonderful man. His name is Josh Lancing and he's a contractor.

He has a four-year-old son, named Cody who is just plain adorable. And Josh... well, Josh is incredible. He's funny and charming and interesting and..."

Honor pictured Josh's body. Below his wavy dark hair, blue eyes, and brilliant smile, were wide shoulders and a v-shaped torso. She recalled how the muscles flexed in his arms when he picked up Cody, wondering how it would feel to be wrapped up in those arms. "Mmmm..." she murmured, blushing at her lustful thoughts.

To take her mind off Josh, she tried to bring her new business goal into focus. Soon her mind was racing. It was William's job to court customers and in the process, he formed close friendships with many of them. Honor wondered if she could convince any of them to stay with her if they simply split Soft Fix in half. Could she run a business without William?

She thought about the changes she would like to make in her life until finally, her desires crystallized.

"Mom, I know what I want now. No matter how long it takes, I want my own business. I want to enjoy life with someone who appreciates me. I want a home like yours - that's filled with things that are important to me," she paused. "And yes, Mom, I want a daughter of my own."

Chapter 8

After emptying the bedroom closet, Honor decided to tackle the stacks of paperwork balanced against the bedroom wall. Sorting and shredding documents would be tedious, but at least the work could be done in the comfort of her hotel suite. She filled a cardboard box and put it in her car, along with the antique hat box, the new shredder and a compact luggage dolly from the garage.

As she left, she called out, "I'll be back tomorrow, Mom!"

In her hotel room, Honor found it hard to concentrate on sorting paperwork. Images of Josh's hard body kept creeping into her thoughts. She finally caved into temptation, but just as her steamy fantasy began to take shape, her cell phone rang. She felt an instant rush of guilt. Certain it was William, she reached for the phone, reminding herself that they were divorced and he was the one who cheated in real life, anyway. She answered, hoping William wouldn't notice she was flustered.

She glanced at the caller ID as she flipped the phone open. The fact the display didn't show William's number registered a millisecond after she said "Hello." Guilt instantly morphed into embarrassment. The number belonged to Josh. She desperately tried to clear the sexual fantasy from her mind and regain her composure.

"Are you okay? Did I catch you at a bad time?" Josh asked

"I'm fine. I was just... um... going through some of Mom's things and was thinking about her—you know, sad... so my voice probably sounds strange." Hoping Josh couldn't already tell she was a terrible liar, she took a deep breath and added, "I'm glad you called, Josh."

Josh relaxed, his confidence restored. "I was hoping to see you this evening, but if Cody isn't in bed by eight o'clock, he'll be cranky all day tomorrow. Could I talk you into hanging out with us at the playground for a little while? I'd be willing to spring for a homemade ice cream cone."

Honor glanced at the box of paperwork, dismayed by her lack of progress. Still, she didn't want to pass up an opportunity to spend time with Josh. "I guess I can take a break for a quick 'play date'. I'll meet you at the ice cream parlor in five minutes."

Sitting at a table near the playground, Honor and Josh munched rich black-cherry ice cream cones, while watching Cody dig in the sand. Honor noticed Cody appeared to be talking to someone. "What's he doing?" she asked Josh.

Josh shrugged, "I guess it's another one of his make-believe playmates. He's been doing that a lot since we've been here. I think it's his way of adjusting to new surroundings."

Honor spoke without thinking. "Maybe he's talking to ghosts."

Josh cocked his head. "What makes you think this place is haunted?"

"Probably my imagination is just working overtime because this is such an old hotel, but I've had seriously weird dreams about ghosts every night since I've been here."

"Really? Then maybe I should come to your room tonight to stand guard," Josh teased. "Hey... that would make me an Honor Guard!"

"And who would guard my honor from you?" she shot back.

Josh pretended to be offended by Honor's insinuation, but a moment later, they were both laughing. When their smiles faded, they gazed at one another with unmistakable desire.

The breeze was picking up and blowing Honor's curly hair

around. Josh captured a stray lock and tucked it behind her ear, allowing his hand to rest against her cheek for a moment before moving it away. Honor gulped. Her heart was racing. She licked her lips and took a deep breath, never taking her eyes off his. The only word she could muster was a quiet, "Wow."

Josh nodded his head in agreement. "Yeah. Wow."

Cody had grown tired of playing in the sand and ran toward them, interrupting the tender exchange.

"Daddy, come swing me!" he pleaded.

"Okay, mood wrecker." Josh mumbled. When he rose to walk over to the playground, Cody took hold of his hand.

"Come on. You too," Josh coaxed Honor. "You're never too big to let someone push you in a swing."

Honor smiled and stood. Cody immediately grabbed her hand and lifted his feet off the ground, so that he was suspended between the two adults. His laughter was infectious. They walked together, swinging him forward in giant leaps until they reached the swing set. There, Honor and Cody sat side-by-side, as Josh pushed first one swing and then the other, back and forth.

Cody cried, "Higher, Daddy! Push harder! Faster!"

Honor blushed, imagining she was saying similar things to Josh, but under a very different set of circumstances.

Soon it was eight o'clock: Cody's witching hour.

"You could hang out with me after I put Cody to bed," Josh suggested.

"I'm tempted, but I still have a lot of paperwork to go through before I can call it a night."

Josh nodded, trying to conceal his disappointment. "I understand. No pressure. I'll call you tomorrow."

They parted ways on the elevator, with Honor's only kiss goodnight coming from Cody. She closed the door of her suite and leaned against it, allowing a soft moan to escape her throat. The chemistry between her and Josh was undeniable.

And she had told him more about herself in two days than she had told William throughout their entire relationship.

Honor took a cool shower and slipped into her granny-gown; then began sorting through the paperwork. Once she focused, the job went quickly. She fed old check stubs and ancient tax forms to the shredder, but near the bottom of the box, she found a few pictures of herself and her sisters when they were very small. In one shot, they were sitting side-by-side on a swing set, with their father pushing them, each in turn. Perhaps because she had just been on a swing that afternoon, Honor clearly remembered the moment captured in the photograph.

She leaned the picture against her bedside lamp, lay back and closed her eyes. She could smell the grass and hear the delighted squeals of her sisters and her father's booming laughter. He said his arms were too tired to push them anymore and they begged for—and were receiving—just one more push. Her mother was smiling at her family from a picnic blanket when she took the photograph. Afterward, her father had walked over and laid down with her, resting his head on her lap.

The fog rolled in while Honor was wondering how much more she would have cherished days like this one, if she had known how few of them remained. At the time, it had never occurred to her that her father wouldn't always be there with them, but a month later, he died when somebody else's dad fell asleep at the wheel and veered into oncoming traffic, sending her father's car careening into a tree. His death broke her mother's heart.

Honor's reflections were interrupted by a voice within the fog.

"Tisk, tisk... it's a shame love requires risking great pain. But I know your mother wouldn't have changed anything about her life with your father, even if she had known exactly what would happen in the end."

Chapter 9

Honor was more indignant than frightened. She marched into her parlor and found the Victorian woman, Margaret, sitting exactly where she had been the night before.

"How would you know how my mother felt about anything?" she demanded.

"Because she told me so," Margaret replied.

Honor was confused, but tried to make sense out of the situation. "Are you trying to tell me you're a ghost and that you've seen my mother since she died?"

"No, darlin'- I expect your mother took the lighted path as soon as she died. She wasn't interested in hanging around this world after death, but when she was alive, she used to come visit me every month or two and we talked for hours at a time."

Honor sat, even more confused. "I don't understand," she mumbled.

Margaret poured her a cup of tea and slid it across the table. "It's a long story, but one that's worth hearing, if you want to know."

Honor nodded.

"Since my death, I spend most of my time in this hotel. There are many spirits here."

"I didn't know so many people died here. Did something happen so that you weren't able to go into the light?" Honor asked.

Margaret scoffed. "You may not believe you favor your mother, but you are her spitting image. She couldn't sit quietly and listen to a story either -- always interrupting me with questions. But eventually, Faith Macklin and I became good friends and I enjoyed her visits. I'll miss her."

Honor was incredulous. "You mean my mother talked to ghosts when she stayed here?"

"Spirits, dear," Margaret corrected.

"There's a difference?"

"Certainly. Ghosts are the fragments that splinter off some spirits as they travel the lighted path. Spirits, on the other hand, still have all their faculties about them and have chosen not to take the lighted path when they die."

"You mean the path to heaven or hell?" Honor asked.

"Actually, I'm not sure where it leads. I do know that spirits who travel the lighted path never return to this realm. From what I've observed and learned from other spirits, most take the path before they even realize they have died. They just become aware of the light and are drawn toward it. But some hesitate and decide not to take the path right away. Most stay behind only a short while -- to say goodbye to friends and family and offer comfort, if they can. Some stay longer, usually either out of fear about where the path will lead or to resolve some important matter. And a few, like me, stay because we like it here and find this existence fascinating."

Margaret sipped her tea. "If a spirit is torn about taking the path, a small piece of his energy might escape from the cloud of his form while the rest of his spirit journeys down the path. I suspect the energy fragments that stay behind are what you call ghosts. As partial beings, they're confused and often become angry when they come into contact with spirits or the living."

Margaret raised her teacup to her lips, blew on the steamy contents and took another sip. "Personally, I delight in establishing relationships with other spirits. I also enjoy interacting with the living and learning about new inventions. I can't think of any existence that would be more interesting than the world I inhabit right now, so I won't be making that one-way journey down the lighted path anytime soon."

Honor was fascinated. "Did you know you were dead when you stepped off the lighted path?"

"No. I thought I was experiencing a remarkable dream. But then I began to notice things like changing seasons and modifications to the hotel that I couldn't explain. My natural curiosity forced me to analyze my situation. Finally, I came to the conclusion that I was observing time well beyond my living memory. Once I accepted my new reality, I read the dates on the Belleview Hotel register and determined ten years had slipped by since I had been a living person. I learned to establish contact with many spirits, but with the exception of a few children and one or two young adults, the living remained unaware of my existence."

Margaret smiled and lifted her chin. "But I kept working at it, and now very few spirits are as capable as I am of communicating with living beings."

Honor narrowed her eyes. "What changed?"

Margaret chuckled. "I discovered how similarities can provide a bridge between spirits and the living."

"A bridge?"

"Yes. When entities experienced a similar event, suffered a comparable trauma or share an interest, that connection makes it easier to communicate. It forms a bridge of sorts."

Honor nodded to indicate she understood.

Margaret poured some fresh tea. "Bridges can also be formed between blood relations. A spirit recognizes a familiar voice or notices similar physical features, personalities, characteristics, passions... you would be amazed at how easily one can spot a blood relative."

Margaret smiled. "Occasionally, the bridge between the living and dead is so strong the spirit is able to share its memories with the living being." Her smile faded. "Unfortunately, the living usually can't comprehend what has happened, so bridge connections are often attributed to strange dreams or imagination."

Honor recalled how Josh had explained Cody's behavior in the sandbox and his conversation with "*the Fuzzy Man.*"

"But don't ghosts—I mean spirits - have to stay where they died or in the cemetery?"

"Another myth," Margaret protested. "I'm able to roam my burial site as well as every location I visited while I was alive. I used to enjoy spending time at the Tampa Hotel, and my summer home on Fifth Avenue in New York City, but those places have changed so much over time, I hardly recognize them anymore. The exotic Tampa Hotel has been transformed into a University, and my summer home in New York is now The House of Cartier Jewelers."

She sighed. "I still travel to Europe now and then, but I spend most of my time right here at the Belleview. Of all my favorite places, it has changed the least over the years and it provides an endless array of interesting people to watch." Margaret winked. "And when I'm here, I can help guide the living and other spirits, to make the most of every bridge connection."

"How?"

Margaret sipped her tea before responding. "A bridge between worlds is a delicate phenomenon. I teach spirits the most effective way to communicate with those on the other side is to wait until the living person is either very relaxed or sleeping. And because it's difficult to prove the experience wasn't just a dream, I teach the living to accept that their bond with the spirit realm is a personal matter. If the bridge connection is successful, the living benefit from the knowledge and experiences of those who have gone before them."

Honor nodded.

"Something about this hotel seems to draw spirits and the living together. Perhaps that's because spirits here..." Margaret was interrupted mid-sentence by a knock at the door.

Irritated by the interruption, Honor whirled around in her

chair, toward the knocking sound. The instant she turned, she realized she wasn't really in the parlor, but rather in her bed, with her eyes closed. Startled, Honor bolted to a sitting position and stared at the empty table in the adjoining parlor.

A voice called out, "Housekeeping!"

"Please come back later!" Honor cried.

She lay back down and focused on her dream of Margaret, but she had no more success than when she had attempted to return to her dreams about Darcy. Frustrated, she showered and got dressed.

Honor decided to write down everything she could remember from her dream before the details faded from her memory. Reaching for her small notepad, she quipped, "I'm definitely going to need a bigger notebook. Maybe even a journal."

She stopped short, remembering the day she found Darcy Loughman's journal in her mother's kitchen. Was the old diary strengthening a bridge between her and the spirit realm?

She could feel the hair on the back of her neck stand, as goose bumps rose down the length of her arms and legs. "This is crazy! I'm an adult. Adults don't believe in ghosts."

But what had once been comfortable, rational thoughts on the subject, were pitifully lacking this morning. Her experiences since checking into the Belleview Biltmore were simply too real to be denied.

Chapter 10

When her phone rang, Honor jumped, still unsettled by her ghost musings. Josh's voice had a welcome, calming effect.

"Cody and I are headed downstairs for breakfast. Care to join us? Afterward, I could follow you over to your mom's house and haul some of the packed boxes to Goodwill for you."

"Two dates for breakfast and free labor afterwards sounds great to me! I'll meet you guys at the Terrace Restaurant in fifteen minutes."

As she passed by the old photographs adorning the walls of the main hallway, Honor studied them from a new perspective, wondering how many former guests were haunting the hotel.

The troubling thought disappeared when she caught sight of Cody, waiting at the restaurant entrance. As soon as he saw her, he wiggled free from Josh.

"Honor, Honor! Look at this, Honor!" he called as he ran toward her.

She caught him in her arms and laughed at his excitement over his new Spiderman action figure, complete with a "realistic action spinning web accessory."

She greeted Josh with a light kiss on his cheek. "Good morning," she exclaimed over Cody's chatter. "Have you already learned how to operate the 'realistic action spinning web accessory'?"

"I most certainly have," Josh assured her.

Cody continued to gush over the new toy until their food arrived.

"Time to put Spiderman away and eat your breakfast," Josh

instructed.

Cody pouted, refusing to eat.

Honor naively tried to persuade him, "I'm certain Spiderman always eats his breakfast."

She saw Josh shake his head and wince, but it was too late. She had forgotten Cody was an authority on everything about the superhero.

"Spiderman doesn't eat. Only Peter Parker eats food," Cody informed her.

"Peter Parker is Spiderman's alter ego, right? Well, I'm sure he always eats his breakfast."

"Lots of times he doesn't eat because there's an emergency and he has to be Spiderman really fast."

Honor was amazed by Cody's advanced vocabulary and powers of reason. She decided Josh was right. In addition to being adorable, Cody was brilliant and creative. She switched tactics.

"Let's make a deal. If you eat your breakfast now, I'll let you and Spiderman swim in my mom's heated pool this afternoon."

Josh winked and gave her a subtle *thumbs-up*.

The new approach worked, and soon Cody's plate was empty. The three of them stopped by Josh's room to pack a few essentials for the afternoon, like Cody's Spiderman arm band floats, and then went to Honor's suite to collect her things.

When Josh came through the door, he blew a low whistle of appreciation for the elegance of the Presidential Suite. "Great digs! Are these rooms furnished with real antiques?"

Momentarily forgetting to censor herself, Honor replied, "Not the furniture, but it's furnished with a few authentic ghosts."

Josh snickered before realizing she was serious. "Really?"

Honor shrugged, not sure how much she wanted to reveal. After all, she didn't want Josh to think she was, as her mother used to say, "a few sandwiches shy of a full picnic."

"You'll have to tell me more when little ears aren't listening," he encouraged.

"Maybe," Honor teased. She couldn't remember ever feeling so in sync with another human being. She held up her car keys. "Do you want to take separate vehicles, so you won't be stuck at my mom's house all day?"

"Why would I want to leave if you're still there?" he grinned. "I'll drive."

In the parking lot, Honor climbed into the cab of Josh's shiny black truck. It felt more like they were going on a date rather than driving a few blocks to her mother's house.

When they arrived, Josh whistled. "I wasn't expecting a Queen Anne. Did I tell you my construction specialty is restoring vintage properties?"

"Really? Would you mind looking it over for me, then? It belonged to my grandmother before my folks bought it, so I'm sure it needs work."

Despite the short drive, Cody was sound asleep in the back seat. Josh smiled. "Nap time. I should be able to carry him inside and lay him down without waking him up, if there's a bed or couch we can use."

"I'm sorry. I thought I told you my sisters took all the furniture," Honor apologized. "Should we go back to the hotel until after his nap?"

"No way! I treasure his nap time and I'm not giving up a minute of it." Josh winked at Honor. "I must have forgotten to tell you I was also a boy scout."

He unlocked the truck bed cover and pulled out a fully inflated air mattress. "Cody and I camped out a few nights on our way down here. He got a real kick out of it. If I toss this on the floor in one of the bedrooms, he should sleep for a couple of hours."

Honor unlocked the front door and helped Josh maneuver the uncooperative mattress into a bedroom before fetching Cody. Just as Josh claimed, Cody barely opened an eye throughout the entire transfer process.

"This used to be my room," Honor confided as she tucked a blanket over the sleeping child before quietly, closing the door.

Honor gave Josh a tour of the house. He was quite impressed with the heart of pine construction and pointed out several features of fine craftsmanship that Honor had never noticed, such as the intricate crown molding and the expertly carved Yule post on the banister leading to the turret loft.

After touring the entire house, Josh suggested they carry the boxes headed for Goodwill out to the truck. Honor agreed and led the way back to the master bedroom.

"It was hard to pack up Mom's clothes," she choked. Honor envisioned her mother bustling around the kitchen, whipping up snacks and fussing over Josh and Cody. "I wish you could have known her. You would have liked one another," she paused. "But if she hadn't died, I might not have met you."

Without a word, Josh took her into his arms; gently cradling her head against his muscular shoulder.

Honor felt her eyes well up with tears and made no effort to stop them as they spilled over and ran down her cheeks. Until now, she hadn't realized how much the empty house underscored her loss.

"It was just so sudden and unexpected," she stammered. "It isn't fair. I lost both of them in car accidents and..."

"Shhhhh, I know it's hard. You don't have to explain," Josh whispered. "I understand."

And she knew he did.

Josh tilted her face up and brushed her tears away with his fingertips. He kissed her forehead with soft, warm lips. When she looked up at him, he was gazing at her with such compassion she almost started to cry all over again. He bent to kiss her cheeks and then her nose before pulling away to search her eyes for permission to kiss her mouth.

In wordless response, she closed her eyes, parted her lips slightly and leaned toward him.

Chapter 11

When Honor felt his lips taste hers for the first time, they had grown much warmer than they had been only a moment ago. Their tongues eagerly explored one another; their bodies pressed close together.

William's words echoed in Honor's head, "An inflatable doll would have been more exciting in bed." She hesitated, worried Josh would agree.

Unaware of her self-doubt, Josh pinned her against the wall, reining kisses on her as his hands found their way under her blouse and cupped her breasts. His fierce passion ignited hers, eliminating first her concerns and then her inhibitions.

Rubber doll my ass, she hissed to herself. She moaned and threw her head back, arching her spine toward him.

Honor pulled Josh's shirt up and ran her hands over his impossibly hard torso; then reached for his belt buckle. Once his jeans were unzipped, she slid her fingers inside to continue exploring his body.

Josh gasped for air and groaned, his voice thick with desire, "Oh my God, Honor." He pulled her hand away. "That feels way too good and I don't know that many baseball statistics. You're going to have to give me just a second."

She smiled, enjoying the fact he was as turned on as she was. Honor couldn't decide which was more exciting: the rush of power she got taking what she wanted from him, or the thrill of submission.

Josh pulled his shirt up over his head and dropped it to the floor.

Honor pressed herself against him for a moment, wickedly licking his neck and slowly sliding her tongue down his body. He groaned with pleasure.

She stepped away from him and pulled the neat stack of bedding from against the wall, quickly spreading blankets, sheets and pillows onto the floor, while Josh closed and locked the bedroom door.

Honor pulled off her blouse and bra, then lay back on the pillows, holding her arms out to Josh. He removed his jeans without taking his eyes off her. She couldn't even breathe as she feasted her eyes on the living Greek statue standing before her. Never had she seen anything so beautiful. And never had she craved anything the way she craved him right now.

He dropped to his knees and pulled off her jeans and panties, kissing her belly and inner thighs as he did so. Honor was writhing now; unable to stop or even think of anything except how it was going to feel to have him inside her.

He continued to hold himself back from her, kissing and licking her until she felt the electric shocks of a climax and began shivering uncontrollably. She reached out her arms for him again and this time, he obliged her, allowing the full length of his naked body to rest on top of hers, calming her tremors.

Breathless, Honor moaned, "Perfect. You are perfect!" as her hands ran freely over him, wanting to explore every inch of his body. Her hips began to move in a slow circle under him, as she whispered urgently into his ear, "Now, please... *now!*"

He rolled away and quickly pulled on a condom before sliding back on top of her moist body. Without hesitating any longer, he pushed himself all the way into her. "Jesus, Honor, you feel so good... so good!"

He moved in and out slowly, until Honor thought she was going to lose her mind. When she could stand it no longer, she pleaded, "Faster... please... faster!"

"I can't... last much longer!" Josh warned through gritted teeth.

She panted with aching need, "It's okay. Come with me. Do it now... faster...now, Josh... now!"

Josh responded with an animalistic growl and plunged himself into her hard and fast, causing riveting sensations she had never dreamed possible. Together, their groans of pleasure culminated in a frenzied climax. Seconds later, they melted together, breathing hard and whimpering with exhausted satisfaction.

Honor was the first to speak. Shy now, but still holding him close, she whispered, "I never knew it could feel like that."

Josh raised himself up on an elbow and looked into her eyes. "You and me both, Honor."

"Really?"

Josh nodded. "You were amazing."

He rolled to her side and began touching her naked breasts, as if really seeing them for the first time. He lowered his mouth to her hard nipple and began to suck and gently nip on first one and then the other. Honor's body began to move beneath his hands as if it had suddenly turned into a marionette and he was controlling her strings.

He used his fingers to excite her; his eyes riveted on the motions of her body. Under his intense scrutiny, Honor's feelings of inadequacy began to creep in, threatening to spoil the moment. She closed her eyes tight and surrendered to his touch; every nerve of her body sharply focused on each new sensation. She thrashed her head back and forth and arched her ribcage, her stomach muscles tight as he coaxed her body to a fever pitch once more. Soon her body convulsed with another orgasm.

Honor collapsed against the pillows, her eyes still closed. "No more..." she begged, panting. "Oh, Josh...there are simply no words for how good that was!"

She didn't know Josh was continuing to watch her glistening body relax as her breathing returned to normal. Nor did she know that in that instant, Josh realized he was falling in love with her. He loved that she could be confident one moment and vulnerable the next. She was beautiful, intelligent and possessed a great sense of humor. But she lived a thousand miles away. He would probably never have the chance to say the words out loud, so he silently mouthed, "I love you."

A moment later, Honor's eyes fluttered open and she smiled at him. "You know, you've been a great help so far, Josh," she teased. "At this rate, I should be able to have this place totally packed up in a year or two!"

Josh grinned and kissed her. "I think you're underestimating the value associated with a release of tension."

With work to be done and Cody waking soon, they forced themselves to get up and dressed. But they found it difficult to keep their hands off each other as they loaded the truck with the boxes of clothing and other odds and ends headed for Goodwill.

When Cody woke up, he was full of energy and immediately remembered Honor's promise that he could go swimming. Josh helped his son change into his Spiderman swimming trunks and put on his Spiderman arm floats.

"Cody," Honor teased, "Is there any Spiderman stuff you don't own?"

The little boy grinned and jumped in the water, calling "Come on, everybody!"

"What if I dangle my feet in while you swim?" Honor suggested.

Out came Cody's bottom lip. "It's no fun by myself."

Josh winked at Honor. "I guess we should go inside and change our clothes so we can get in the pool with him," he said, attempting his most innocent voice.

Honor giggled at his not-too-subtle suggestion and wagged her finger at him.

Josh admitted defeat. "I guess we better take turns changing, so one of us can stay out here with Cody - damn it."

Honor laughed at his pitiful expression. "Don't be such a baby."

The trio played in the water the rest of the afternoon. Honor laughed at Cody's squeals of joy, while simultaneously ogling Josh's sexy body, his well-defined muscles wet and glistening in the sun.

Honor always believed William cheated because she couldn't satisfy him. Now, replaying the images of Josh and her tumbling wildly on the bedroom floor, she knew she wasn't responsible for William's wandering eye, no matter what the men back home believed.

Thoughts of Chicago spoiled the fantasy Honor had unwittingly conjured -- that they were a family and could enjoy afternoons like this one forever. She forced herself to remember that Josh and Cody were vacation friends, not a part of her permanent reality.

When Cody got tired, Honor helped him towel off.

"Did you have fun, Cody?"

"Yes!" he chirped. "Did you have fun too?"

Honor lifted her eyes over his little head to gaze at Josh. "I've never had a better time in my whole life."

Josh smiled warmly. "Me neither."

"Then let's do this every day!" Cody enthused.

"I'm not sure I would have the stamina to do that every day," Josh joked.

"Why not, Daddy?"

Honor giggled at Josh's sexual innuendo and quipped, "Yeah, why not, Josh?"

Chapter 12

The trio ordered some Chinese food. While they waited for their delivery to arrive, Honor leaned across the breakfast bar toward Josh and shared some memories of her family and the good times she had growing up in Belleair.

"I wish I would have visited more often, but my company kept me busy. I guess I thought there would be time…"

Josh covered her hands with his, his empathy for her radiating silently.

"And now that I'm finally back here, weird things keep happening that I can't explain." She paused. "Sometimes when I'm alone here in the house, I can feel my mom's essence so powerfully I could swear she's right beside me."

Cody walked over and hugged Honor around her legs. She reached down and picked him up, cuddling him close to her.

"She said to tell you she loves you too," Cody whispered in her ear.

Startled, Honor stared first at Cody, then at Josh. She wasn't sure she had heard him correctly, or what to say in response.

She sat Cody on the counter and took a step back. "What did you say?" she choked.

Cody hesitated, then repeated, "She loves you too." He stuck out his lower lip, wondering what he had done wrong.

Josh stepped close and hugged his son. "That's okay, Buddy. You're absolutely right. Honor's mommy loves her very much."

Josh turned toward Honor. "I taught Cody that mommies

keep on loving their children even if they die. I think that's what he was trying to say - right, Cody?"

Cody nodded his head in agreement and Honor relaxed a little, feeling somewhat ridiculous.

Josh offered Cody a distraction. "I brought your portable DVD player along. Would you like to watch a Spiderman movie?"

Cody lit up. "Spiderman *Two*, Daddy."

Josh smiled, "Okay."

He scooped Cody up and carried him out to the living room to start the movie, leaving Honor alone in the kitchen to ponder what had just happened. She tried to convince herself that Josh was right. Cody was just trying to comfort her. But if that was the case, why had he whispered, "*she said to tell you*"?

When Josh returned to the kitchen, he asked, "are you okay?"

"Sure," Honor replied with an unconvincing shrug.

His perplexed expression persuaded her to tell him everything. Opening a couple of beers, she suggested, "let's talk outside by the pool, out of Cody's earshot."

Once they had settled into a pair of chaise lounge chairs, Honor confided she had been talking out loud to her mother and believed she was listening. She also told him about finding the journal and without going into too much detail, explained her vivid dreams about people she didn't know.

"At first I dismissed the dreams, figuring they were tied to me being back in Florida for the first time since Mom's funeral." She shook her head. "But that's not working anymore. They're too real. And then Cody..." she trailed off, without finishing the thought.

Josh listened to her without interruption, but now he gave a low whistle.

Honor was relieved everything was finally out in the open, but she couldn't tell what Josh was thinking. She asked point blank, "Do you believe in ghosts?"

"Truthfully, I haven't made up my mind on the subject," Josh answered in the non-judgmental style Honor had come to expect from him. "I want to believe, when people I care about die, they go to a wondrous, pain-free place and that I'll join them there at some point in the distant future." He paused, "On the other hand, there are too many reports of people interacting with ghosts for me to just write off their experiences without giving equal consideration to that possibility. I guess the jury's still out as far as I'm concerned."

"I think we're more or less on the same page," Honor concluded. "I try to keep an open mind about things that can neither be proved nor disproved."

"And we both agree you've experienced some pretty weird stuff lately, regardless whether it stems from your imagination or ghosts." He grinned suddenly, raising his eyebrows suggestively, "I'll tell you what. I volunteer to stay in your hotel room all night long, just to see if I experience any eerie phenomenon."

"I can see through you like saran wrap," she laughed. "You're just trying to get into my bed!"

"Well, I never said I wouldn't enjoy certain aspects of ghost hunting," he joked.

Chapter 13

While Josh was out dropping off boxes at Goodwill and Cody was busy coloring a picture, Honor placed a call to her assistant and trusted confidant, Julie Wells.

"Hey, Julie," she began, "I want to toss a few ideas at you, but I only have a few minutes to talk."

"What's the rush?"

"Well, I met a man and I'm watching his little boy while he's out running a quick errand for me," Honor explained.

"A man? Okay, who are you and what have you done with my boss?" Julie wisecracked.

Honor giggled. She had forgotten how quickly she and Josh had become a couple. Before she could reply, Julie started firing questions at her. "Is he hot? Have you kissed him yet? Tell me, tell me!"

Honor flushed, embarrassed. She wasn't ready to confess how quickly she had become intimate with Josh.

Julie misunderstood her hesitation. She moaned, "Oh no. You're going to tell me you two are just friends, right?"

Honor collected herself. "We're more than friends, but that's all I'm going to share about him for the time being. Now, are you alone? I want to discuss something with you in confidence."

To Honor's utter amazement, when Julie heard she was considering breaking her partnership with William, she exclaimed, "It's about time you figured out you're the brains of this outfit!"

Honor brushed off the compliment. "Are you sure I'm not out of my mind, thinking I can run a business without William?

I mean, I don't know the first thing about finding new customers or keeping the books." She faltered. "Maybe it's a crazy idea."

"Of course you can do it! Most of our new business these days comes from referrals, and you can hire people to do the accounting. Besides, I need to tell you something." Julie lowered her voice. "I overheard someone in the ladies' room say she thinks William *cooks the books.* It's probably nonsense, but since William has demonstrated he's capable of deceit with a capital '*D*,' it might be a good idea to check into it before revealing your plans."

Honor was caught off guard by the allegation. "That sounds like good old-fashioned office gossip to me, but it wouldn't hurt to investigate. Any ideas?"

"I can start snooping around a bit."

"All right. But be careful. I don't want to stir up trouble over a rumor."

"Okay, boss."

After hanging up, Honor sat staring at her phone. She didn't want to believe gossip, but one thought nagged at her. *William proved he was capable of cheating on his wife, so why not his business partner?*

Cody interrupted Honor's thoughts to show her his finished drawing. Forcing a smile, she took it from his outstretched hands and examined the circle of squiggly lines, secretly hoping she was holding the picture right-side-up.

"This is terrific, Cody. A real, um... work of art. I think we should tape it up on the fridge."

"It's Spiderman's web," he beamed, as Honor pulled a roll of tape from her box of packing materials and applied it to the corners.

Honor enjoyed seeing Cody's pride in his accomplishment, but was still preoccupied with the disturbing phone call. She bent down and hugged him. "You're such a good little boy. Don't change when you grow up, okay?"

"I'm going to grow up to be like my Daddy," Cody responded.

Honor cooed, "That's wonderful, Cody. Your Daddy is a very good man."

Cody turned back to admire his picture, now hanging on the refrigerator door. Over his shoulder he said, "Don't worry, Honor. The lady said you'll be happier without that bad man."

This time Honor was certain she had heard Cody's words correctly. She struggled to remain calm. "What lady said that, Cody?"

"The nice lady who lives here."

Honor's knees turned to jelly. She slid to a sitting position on the floor directly in front of the child. "Cody, is the nice lady's name Faith Macklin?"

"No."

Honor tried not to let her disappointment show. "Did the lady tell you her name?"

Cody nodded. "She said from the looks of things, I should probably call her *Grandma*."

Honor gasped and tears sprang to her eyes. She gave Cody a big hug.

"You're squishing me!" he complained.

Honor let go. "I'm sorry, Cody. Listen, would you consider making another picture for the refrigerator art gallery?"

"Sure!" Cody ran back into the living room.

Honor was still sitting on the floor when Josh returned, her mind pouring over the events of the afternoon.

As soon as he saw the look on her face, Josh was worried. "What happened? Is everything okay? Where's Cody?"

Before Honor could answer, Cody yelled from the next room, "I'm making works of art, Daddy!"

Despite her introspective mood, Honor giggled.

Instantly less anxious, Josh sat on the floor beside her. "So talk to me, Honor."

Honor told Josh the highlights of her conversation with

Julie and how the rumor about William paled next to what Cody revealed about her mother's spirit.

When she finished, he joked, "So you're telling me my son sees dead people?"

"Don't kid around about this, Josh. Even the words he used... I could almost hear my mother saying that exact phrase."

"Okay, at the risk of pissing you off, I'm going to suggest an alternative theory," Josh countered.

Honor folded her arms, listening.

"First of all, Cody is very sensitive to other people's feelings and he really likes you, so he doesn't want you to be upset. Second, Cody has the hearing of a hawk on steroids. Third, he knows you're hurting about your mother and he empathizes with you, since he lost his own mother. Now, given these facts, isn't it possible he was just trying to say something that would make you feel better?"

"So you're going to use logic on me instead of simply jumping on my ghost bandwagon?"

Josh was visibly relieved she wasn't angry. "Afraid so," he chuckled. "Do you agree my theory is at least a possibility?"

"Well, I agree I've been through a lot this year, which obviously caused me a boatload of stress. I was just starting to come to grips with the fact my mom is gone and my marriage is over, when I learned my ex-husband is more of a Rat Bastard than I originally thought. And then I met you and began this whirlwind romance..."

Josh interrupted, "Whirlwind, huh? I like the sound of that." He reached out to pull her closer to him.

"Yes, whirlwind," continued Honor, playfully pushing him away. "So I'll admit it's possible my imagination could be getting the best of me. Still, you've got to agree there are some pretty weird happenings afoot."

With mock seriousness, Josh replied, "Yeah, weird. You're even starting to talk funny."

Chapter 14

Honor longed to feel Josh's naked body next to hers again, but she knew she needed to be alone tonight, to sort out the day's events. After dinner, she announced, "It's getting late. I think we need to call it a day and go back to the hotel."

"Yeah, I know," Josh grumbled.

They hung up another piece of Cody's abstract artwork, packed a box of paperwork for Honor to review and then climbed into Josh's truck. Again, Cody promptly fell asleep.

They trudged to the hotel elevator, with Cody sound asleep on Josh's shoulder and Honor pushing the box of paperwork on a luggage cart.

When the elevator doors closed, Josh begged, "I don't want to say goodnight, yet. Come stay with me a while."

"That's not a good idea. What would Cody think if he woke up and found me in your bed?"

Josh pretended to be shocked. "It's just an innocent invitation to watch TV. Wait a minute...did you think I had ulterior motives?"

"Innocent, my butt. I know exactly what you had in mind!" Honor shot back.

Josh broke into song, "I *am* an Innocent Maaannnnn... oh yes, I am..."

Honor rolled her eyes. "Yeah, right. Keep your day job."

When they reached Josh's floor, he stepped halfway off the elevator, holding the door open with his back. "Last chance!" he declared, trying to disguise the longing in his voice.

"Not tonight. I mean I really want to, but I'm going to stick to my guns. I need to sort through this paperwork and get some sleep. Call me in the morning, okay?"

She gave him a quick kiss and a gentle push the rest of the way out the door. As the elevator doors closed between them, Josh's exaggerated pouty expression made her laugh.

Alone in her suite, Honor filled a hot bath. "I can't believe I slept with a man I've only known a couple of days," she moaned. Feeling a bit sleazy, she began to rationalize. "If I count our breakfast as one date, and ice cream at the playground as our second date, that means today was technically our third date. Having sex on a third date isn't *horribly* promiscuous."

Honor closed her eyes and pictured Josh naked. She replayed every luscious moment of their rendezvous over in her mind, still amazed by the intensity of the experience.

Until today, she had always thought sex was overrated. After all, making love with William had been so repetitious that Honor created a mental checklist of steps in the process and often checked off items while William panted on top of her, oblivious to her dissatisfaction with his rubber-stamp performance.

Thinking about William reminded Honor about the rumor that he was, as Julie put it, "cooking the books". While toweling off, she decided to contact Leon Goldstein, their corporate attorney, to confirm there was no reason for concern.

Honor sat on her bed while sorting through the box of paperwork. Soon, her thoughts drifted to Cody's assertion that 'a nice lady' told him to call her 'Grandma'. Was it possible her mother's spirit said that after she saw them having sex on the floor this afternoon?

Honor threw herself back against the pillows to consider the horror of this possibility.

"Yuck!" she wailed.

After some uncomfortable visualization, Honor finally concluded her mother's spirit would have respected her privacy just as she had done while she was alive.

She relaxed and drifted off to sleep as the familiar chill settled over the room.

Chapter 15

As if she were floating onto a foggy movie set, Honor took in her surroundings. She was seated at a worn, wooden table. A young girl sat next to her, scrubbing something foul-smelling from a man's jacket. Honor peered through the haze to the opposite side of the small, dank cottage. An older woman sat by the fire, speaking in hushed tones with a middle-aged man. Honor returned her focus to the child. She appeared to be about twelve-years-old and wore a plain black dress, covered by a dingy white apron. A ribbon kept her dark brown curls from falling into her face.

When the last of the mist cleared, the girl turned her almond eyes to Honor and began talking to her as though her sudden appearance in the room was the most natural thing in the world. Despite being dizzy and nauseous, Honor recognized the beautiful child. She was Margaret.

"That woman over there is my mother. Though her blood is bluer than most, her life has been difficult since my father died and his loathsome brother became patriarch of our family. My uncle deserted us, but not before he gambled away our savings and our home."

Honor listened, intrigued that only Margaret seemed to notice her presence.

"We were in a miserable state of affairs for a while. Fortunately, out of respect for my father's memory, his gentlemen friends and business associates called on us frequently, bringing meat and household goods from their surplus. Mother is a compassionate woman and good listener, so they felt quite comfortable talking to her. They often sought her advice on marital issues and in return for her counsel and discretion, they became more charitable with their gifts. Their generosity helped us immensely in our darkest hours."

Margaret finished scrubbing the jacket and took it to her mother. When she returned to her place at the table, she folded her small hands in her lap and resumed her narrative. "One night, an agitated gentleman stopped by and asked if Mother could help remove the smell of spilled whiskey from his jacket to save him from suffering the ire of his temperamental wife. Mother did such a fine job that the gentleman recommended her services to several like-minded acquaintances. You see, a gentleman must maintain a good reputation to preserve his stature in respectable society. Mother removes evidence of missteps that might otherwise tarnish this valuable asset."

Margaret glanced in her mother's direction. "Sometimes, she just cleans their clothes or provides a quiet place for gentlemen to sleep-off their whiskey. But when necessary, she can make the love bite of a prostitute look like a poison ivy rash, or transform bruises from a barroom brawl into injuries received in an accidental fall from a horse. When an injury or ailment is more serious, she hires a discrete physician and then sends a servant to the gentleman's home with a reasonable explanation for his extended absence."

Margaret smiled. "Mother has received so many payments from gentlemen for hiding their debauchery, our kitchen pantry is now filled to overflowing!"

Margaret and Honor watched Margaret's mother walk the gentleman, now freshly attired, to the door.

Margaret folded her arms across her chest. "My mother is prized for her skills, candor, and intelligence. Gentlemen thank her for saving their reputations on a regular basis. But the ungrateful wretches no longer think of her as their equal in society. Married gentlemen don't invite her to attend their galas and widowed gentlemen don't contemplate asking for her hand in marriage." She paused. "And they pay no attention to me whatsoever. But one day they will show me the respect I deserve." An impish grin teased the corners of her mouth. "After all, I know their darkest secrets."

Without warning, the fog rolled in and Honor began to experience the unsettling roller coaster sensation as she floated through time. When the haze cleared, Margaret had transformed into a stunning young woman. Honor closed her eyes to ward off a particularly strong wave of nausea.

Margaret waited for her to regain her composure. "I'm sorry for your discomfort, but the memories I'm sharing with you are important. They weave together with your own ancestry."

"You mean we're related?" Honor sputtered, frustrated by the vague reference.

Before the last word of her question faded from Honor's lips, she was pulled abruptly into the fog. When the mist parted, she was sitting at the parlor table in her own hotel room, facing an irritated and much older version of Margaret.

"It takes a tremendous amount of energy and focus to recreate the details of a memory and share it with you. When you speak, the illusion shatters," Margaret scolded.

"Why can I talk when we're in my room?"

"It takes less concentration here because the surroundings actually exist, but it's still difficult to maintain my form. It's easier when you sit quietly and listen, trusting you will understand everything in time."

Honor started to apologize, but opted instead to nod her head and remain silent.

The gesture was not lost on Margaret, who returned the nod and continued. "Determined to regain my proper place in society, I began to formulate a plan. My mother's objective had always been to get the gentlemen cleaned up and out of our home as quickly as possible, but my approach was different. Sometimes I would continue to pour them drinks even after their clothing was clean, just to keep them talking about a particularly interesting business venture. When a gentleman left my home, I quickly wrote what I learned in my journal, and I studied the entries as though they were schoolbooks. Over time, I became well-versed in the steps of building capital, making financial investments and other business matters. I also learned many secrets—like how some businessmen adjusted their bookkeeping records to hide some of their profits. I learned who they paid off to obtain favorable rulings from the magistrate and what favors could be granted to persuade a local sheriff to overlook transgressions. Most importantly, I came to understand how gentlemen managed their circle of associates to expand their influence. I learned how to skillfully parlay friendships and family relations into financial allies and political connections."

Honor nodded again, encouraging Margaret to continue.

"Following my mother's death, I began to dress and act in a manner consistent with what should have been my proper place in society. I continued to greet troubled gentlemen at my door and assess the particulars of their situations, but instead of handling routine cleaning tasks or errands myself, I delegated these assignments to a trusted staff of employees. While my employees worked, I chatted with the gentlemen. Soon I was ready to utilize the valuable investment information my customers so willingly provided, but it was improper for a single woman to openly participate in business matters. That's when I created my dear Uncle Ulysses." Margaret's eyes grew bright, remembering her clever ruse. "My new uncle lived in London and had money to invest in the States. By means of messengers bearing "official letters of authorization," bribes and other deceptive practices, I pretended to make investments at the direction of my Uncle Ulysses. Most people didn't question my actions or increasing wealth. They assumed my doting Uncle Ulysses was providing my support."

Margaret paused to refill her teacup, adding a generous portion of cream and stirring slowly, as though delighted with the memory of her hoax. She tapped the spoon on the rim of her cup and laid it on her saucer. Then she gave Honor a stern look and ordered, "This time, do not speak."

Honor took a few deep breaths and swallowed hard when she felt the clouds of fog enveloping her, hoping to ward off the nausea. It helped, but when the fog cleared, Honor was still somewhat woozy.

They were in the parlor of a lavish Victorian-style home. Margaret, dressed in finery, sat reading a book. Just as Honor's dizziness subsided, there came a knock on the door. Margaret turned to Honor and confided, "This night will change many lives."

Chapter 16

Without explaining the mysterious comment, Margaret opened the door. A distraught gentleman stood on her stoop, struggling to support the weight of a younger man - his son - who was drunk and bloodied. Margaret quickly ushered the men inside and called for her workers. Once she determined the blood was not his own, her staff took the inebriated young man into a water closet, where they removed his soiled clothing and began bathing him.

Meanwhile, Margaret sat in the parlor with his panic-stricken father, as he explained, "In recent months, my son became involved with a prostitute who allowed herself to become pregnant. She must have been deranged, because when he visited her tonight, she claimed the baby was his and demanded that he wed her. When my son told her he had no intention of marrying a whore and rearing her bastard child, the girl became livid." The man grimaced, his words slowing as if difficult to utter.

Margaret feared the worst.

"The trollop attacked my son and he was forced to defend himself. He slapped the girl hard and unfortunately, her head struck a table as she fell." The older man choked out, "My son tried to render aid but the fall killed her. When he realized she was beyond help, my son fled. He hid in our barn so as not to upset his mother and then he sent a trusted servant to fetch me."

"And you brought him directly to me?"

He nodded. "You have a good reputation for handling

matters requiring discretion. I want to hire you to remove the evidence of the dreadful encounter from my son's clothing and dispose of the harlot's body."

Margaret understood the father's concern. After all, such a grave mistake with a woman of ill-repute could bring shame and ruin to the family name. Still, she was struck by the man's lack of compassion for the poor, wretched girl who had died.

"The cost for such services would be substantial."

The gentleman handed her a small sack filled with gold coins. "I'll pay twice this amount if you can manage to keep this unfortunate situation from coming to light."

The young man joined them in the parlor. Clean and wearing a robe, it was hard to imagine he was the same person who arrived at the house in such a dreadful state less than an hour ago. He glanced with envy at the glass of whiskey in his father's hand, but accepted the cup of coffee offered to him. Margaret obtained precise directions to the girl's room.

"It would be best if you both remain here and rest while I assess the situation and determine if the girl's body has been discovered."

Honor wasn't sure if she was invisible or simply being ignored by everyone, but she followed Margaret as she instructed her workers to pack a basket of herbs and bandages and then called for her driver.

Honor was impressed by the way Margaret's mind flew, as she considered her alternatives. Slowly it dawned on her that Margaret was no longer speaking out loud. Rather, she was allowing Honor to read her thoughts. Fascinated; Honor paid closer attention.

"Until I know what I'm dealing with, it would be dangerous for any of my workers to go to the girl's room, least they become suspects in the crime. If I am seen there, it might raise some eyebrows, but I would never be suspected of such wrongdoing."

As she walked to the waiting carriage, Margaret explained

to a concerned worker, "The young man was so drunk, it's possible he believes she is dead, when she is merely stunned."

As they clamored along in the carriage, Honor longed for her warm, safe bed at the Belleview Biltmore. A sense of foreboding danced on her nerves as she contemplated the unfolding events.

As if she could hear Honor's unspoken concerns, Margaret laid out their plan of action. "If the girl isn't injured too badly, she will most likely be willing to move to another town and give the baby up to an orphanage in exchange for a tidy sum of money, thereby closing the matter. On the other hand, if the girl is dead and her body had not yet been discovered, I'll look through her room to determine if she is in contact with her family. If so, I'll position her body at the bottom of a flight of stairs and slip money into her pocket, to pay for her funeral and any other expenses she might have left unpaid. On the other hand, if the girl is dead and appears to be alone in the world, I'll arrange for her body to be buried quietly."

The brothel was dark and still; closed for the night. She instructed her driver to wait outside and crept to the back door, carrying her supplies.

With her heart pounding in her chest, Honor followed as Margaret stepped inside. The offensive odor—a mixture of smoke, alcohol, sex and perspiration - turned Honor's stomach, but Margaret didn't seem to notice. She lit a small candle and slipped down the corridor to the room number the young man had provided. She entered without knocking and closed the door. After locating and lighting a gas lamp on the wall, Margaret blew out her candle and gazed around, stunned by the destruction.

The man had obviously lied to her and to his father, regarding the amount of rage he had unleashed upon the poor girl. Blood smears and spatters seemed to cover the tiny room, leaving trails across the bed, the floor and even the walls. Margaret could tell the girl had tried to fend off his savage beating. An especially dark pool of blood in the corner of the room appeared to mark the spot where the girl had succumbed, but there was no body. Confused, she searched beneath the bed, but the girl wasn't there, either. Margaret stood, trying to think. Suddenly she felt someone watching her and whirled to find a frightened girl in a nightshirt, staring at her from the now open doorway. Thick, dark braids framed the girl's gaunt, freckled face and her mouth hung open in amazement, revealing crooked teeth.

It was hard for Honor to tell which of them was the most startled. Margaret smoothed her dress to regain her composure and then, with far more authority in her voice than she actually felt, asked "Who are you, child? Do you know what took place here earlier this evening?"

The girl stammered, "Josie. My name is Josie." She pointed a trembling finger toward the bloody corner. "After her man left, I found Hannah curled up on the floor, in real bad shape. I was a-feared he was comin' back, so I drug her to my room. I expect she'll be meetin' her maker before daylight." She lifted her chin in defiance. "But at least he ain't never gonna hurt her no more." Margaret followed Josie into her room, with Honor continuing to shadow along behind her.

Margaret and Honor were appalled by the sight of the battered girl. Margaret wasted no time. She knelt and examined her wounds. Hannah's face was bleeding and grossly distorted by swelling. The entire length of her body seemed to be covered with cuts and abrasions she suffered during the beating. Her skin was as pale as the linens upon which she rested. When Honor noticed the pool of blood between Hannah's legs, she exchanged a knowing glance with Margaret. The baby was gone.

"This was not a momentary loss of control," Margaret hissed. "That bastard meant to beat this girl to death for becoming pregnant with his child."

Josie nodded her agreement. "Boss Man shoulda' stopped

this, but he was passed out drunk again."

Margaret sniffed, her distain for the brothel proprietor evident. She turned to Josie. "Run, girl. Tell my driver to fetch my physician at once."

Margaret opened the basket of bandages and silently began wrapping Hannah's injuries. Honor watched, thoroughly puzzled. "What connection could I possibly have to these people?" she pondered. Then, remembering Margaret's promise that she would eventually understand everything, Honor refocused her attention on the details of this memory.

Chapter 17

The doctor arrived quickly. He too, was sickened at the amount of abuse the poor girl had suffered. Without speaking, Margaret let Honor know this physician could be trusted to keep quiet... for a fee. While the doctor worked, Margaret began formulating a plan. It would be dangerous to move Hannah in her weakened condition, but it would be even more risky for her to remain in the brothel with people who were willing to look the other way while she was brutally victimized by a wealthy, powerful man.

Honor watched from the shadows, impressed by Margaret's actions. She paid the doctor to take Hannah to his home and tend to her there. Once he and her driver had carried Hannah out, Margaret and Josie got to work on Hannah's room. They washed down the walls and floor, with the exception of the one, blood-darkened corner. Next, they wrapped some partly filled feed sacks tightly together inside the bloodied sheets and bound the bundle securely with ropes. The finished product closely resembled a body, both in shape and weight. Margaret sent Josie to fetch the undertaker to come and remove the 'body' for a quiet burial, claiming Hannah had fallen, suffered a miscarriage and bled to death. Margaret knew the undertaker was a particularly callous man, concerned only with obtaining the largest fee possible for his services. Assuming Margaret was acting on behalf of one of her wealthy gentleman clients, he demanded enough money to cover the cost of a maple coffin, a burial plot, grave diggers and a marker. She agreed to his terms, as long as he would provide the information about the accidental death to the local church and newspaper.

On the back of one of the undertakers' calling cards, Margaret penciled the name *"Hannah Johnson."* He shoved the card into his pocket along with his payment, then hoisted the bundle over his shoulder and walked out. Margaret knew there would be no coffin or proper burial. The bundle would be dumped in a shallow hole somewhere to save the undertaker the expense of digging and marking a proper grave. But she didn't care. The charade was complete, and that was all that mattered.

Before leaving the brothel, Margaret pressed money into Josie's hand. "Child, I think you might be safer working elsewhere."

Josie thanked her and closed the door behind them.

At Margaret's home, the young man and his father waited anxiously for her return. When she finally arrived, Margaret glared at the young man, barely able to hide her disgust. "The girl bled to death," she announced. He shifted uneasily in her icy stare.

The older man didn't notice the contempt in her voice. "May god have mercy on her soul," he murmured. "You saw to her final arrangements?"

Margaret gave the older man a curt nod. "Your son's name is preserved."

The corners of his mouth turned up slightly; his approval evident. "Splendid. It will be as though this ugliness never occurred."

The younger man chewed on his lip, hoping Margaret wouldn't tell his father the truth of what he had done.

Margaret addressed the young man. "You must never return to the brothel. Someone may have overheard the argument and blame you for the girl's death. In fact, I recommend you take an extended trip abroad immediately."

His father agreed and handed Margaret a stack of folded

bank notes. "We are in your debt. My son's reputation would have been sorely tainted, had the news of this unfortunate accident been made public."

Honor heard Margaret's unspoken thought. "I'm sure that evil monster has no remorse and will eventually commit other such crimes. I just pray our paths never cross again."

The fog appeared suddenly, pulling Honor back to the parlor table in her hotel room. Margaret still sat with her cup of tea, but appeared more transparent than she had earlier.

Pleased that she hadn't awakened from this dream, Honor asked, "What became of Hannah?"

"I've shared all I can for now," Margaret whispered, her fatigue obvious.

An instant later, Honor woke with a start in her bed. The room was cold and dark. She turned on the bedside lamp and jotted down a few of the names and events from the dream before falling back to sleep.

Chapter 18

Once again, Honor woke to the sound of the phone in her hotel room, but at least this time, the sound wasn't pulling her away from a dream.

"Good morning, gorgeous" said Josh. "Are you ready for breakfast?"

"Not really. I had another of my wild dreams and truthfully, I just woke up."

"Well then, why don't Cody and I come up to your room and the three of us can order a room service breakfast? Cody can watch some cartoons while you fill me in on your new adventures."

"Okay," Honor agreed. "But you have to give me some time to get cleaned up a little bit."

"I've already seen you all mussed up and you have nothing to worry about. You always look great."

Honor laughed. "There's a big difference between how I look when I first wake up and how I look just after having mind-blowing sex," she teased.

Josh let out one of his low whistles. "I can't really respond to that with a four-year old in the room, listening to every word, but I think I'm going to have to judge for myself. We'll be right there."

He hung up.

She yelped and leaped out of bed, racing to the bathroom to brush her teeth and wash up before they arrived. She was still undressed when Josh knocked on her door, so she pulled an extra-long T-shirt over her head and let them in.

Josh licked his lips and let his eyes move over her body, obviously liking what he saw. Flustered and self-conscious, Honor reached down to pick up Cody and give him a hug before brushing Josh's cheek with a quick kiss.

"Find a TV station for Cody while I get dressed, okay?"

Josh grinned. "Now Honor, don't you go to any extra effort on my behalf. You look fine wearing just what you have on. Trust me."

She set Cody down on her bed and gave Josh a dubious look. "Uh-huh. Right. The TV is over here." She smiled over her shoulder at Josh as she stepped into her walk-in closet and closed the door.

She had just pulled on her jeans when Josh opened the closet door and stepped inside, taking her into his arms. "Now how do you expect me to behave like a gentleman when you open the door wearing barely anything?"

"Cody is going to wonder what we're doing in here," she warned.

He smothered her protests with kisses. "Don't worry. The gods are smiling on us this morning. Spiderman's on TV."

His lips felt so good, she gave up and melted against him. But when he reached around to unsnap her bra, she stopped him. "Hold that thought until later, when we're alone. Now, let me finish getting dressed so we can order breakfast."

Josh groaned, knowing she was right, but he held her tight and kissed her once more before pulling himself away. He started to open the closet door, but hesitated. "Honor, I want you to know that when we met, I wasn't looking to fill a void in my life or anything. I mean, I thought I was doing just fine on my own. But now I can't stop thinking about how right it feels to be with you." Suddenly embarrassed, he grinned. "I hope that doesn't freak you out." He stepped out of the closet and closed the door behind him before she could respond.

Honor steadied herself, realizing she was holding her breath. She exhaled, wanting to rush out and tell Josh he had taken the words right out of her mouth. To think, she could have lived her whole life thinking her relationship with William was the best she would ever know. She pulled a sweatshirt over her head as her mind raced. Could Josh be *the one*? Her soul mate? The kind of love they write songs about? "Get a grip!" she hissed under her breath, shaking her head to clear her thoughts. "It's just lust. No one falls in love this fast."

In the span of a heartbeat, the closet grew frigid. Honor felt someone standing over her shoulder and heard the voice of a woman whisper, "We fell in love the first day." Honor spun around, Goosebumps covering her body. Whatever had been there was gone. Spooked, she flung the closet door open and rushed out.

The look on Josh's face told her that he completely misunderstood her actions. Honor stammered, "No... wait... it's not..."

But Josh had already turned away from her, pretending to concentrate on the room service menu in his hands. "Cody here wants pancakes again, but I'm not hungry after all, so I think I'll just have a cup of coffee." He struggled to sound nonchalant. "What about you?"

"Josh, I need you to come over here right now!"

The urgency in her voice broke through to him. Josh tossed the menu onto the bed and walked over to her, his arms folded tightly across his chest.

"Go in the closet and tell me if you hear anything," she pleaded.

He glanced at her curiously, but did as she asked. After a few seconds he began to examine the closet in earnest. "Honor, I don't hear anything, but it's a heck of a lot colder in here than it was a minute ago and there's no air conditioning vent in here." Perplexed, his voice trailed off. When his eyes met hers, they were filled with confusion. "Okay, what just happened in here?" he demanded.

Honor stepped back into the closet, relieved she hadn't

imagined the strange occurrence. "Congratulations, Josh. You just had your first encounter with the spirit world."

She suppressed a giggle when his mouth dropped open.

"Josh, I have no idea why this is happening to me. I'm not psychic. In fact, I never even believed in ghosts. But ever since I arrived back in Belleair, I've been a magnet for weird stuff like this." She bit her lip. "I know this is going to sound crazy, but I think these spirits are connected to me somehow, and they're trying to tell me something important."

Josh glanced down, avoiding eye contact. "When you came out of the closet looking so upset, I thought you were reacting to what I said a few minutes ago and..."

Honor moved closer to him. "No. That wasn't it at all. I love spending time with you, too. But I do think we need to be realistic about our relationship. I mean, you live in North Carolina and I live in Illinois. I don't want to spoil our time together worrying about what happens when it's time to go home."

"Me neither," he grudgingly agreed.

Honor decided to change the subject. "If you're game, I'd like to tell you everything I've experienced since I've been here and enlist your help figuring out what's going on." She crinkled her nose. "Of course, after you hear everything I have to say, you might decide you want to get as far away from me as possible and stay there!"

"Not likely." He lifted her chin, his lips only inches from hers. "I'm pretty sure I'll want to be with you, even if you really are being haunted." He kissed her and then murmured, "I think my appetite returned. Can we order breakfast now?"

Honor's laughter filled the closet.

They ordered breakfast and discussed theories at the table on her balcony; then they sat outside by the pool, watching Cody play and talking over the details of her dream visits to the past. While Cody napped between them in Josh's suite, they wrote down all the names and places she could remember from the encounters. When they moved back to her suite, they looked up information about ghosts on the internet, and ran searches on the names, with little success.

Late in the afternoon, Honor gave up trying to read Darcy's too-faded journal and smiled over at Josh, who was still busy looking for clues that would tie everything together.

She tried to imagine how William would have reacted if she had told him she was being haunted. She winced, visualizing his familiar look of disapproval and could almost hear him scoff at the ridiculous notion. Thinking about Darcy's husband, Reginald Loughman, she realized, though the two men lived a century apart, they were quite similar. Intelligent, successful, and self-confident, both wore their dominant demeanor and sense of entitlement like a mantel around their shoulders. And both men had the ability to make their wives feel inferior in every way. Perhaps that was her connection to Darcy -- their mutual subjugation to powerful men.

Honor stiffened in her chair, repulsed by the thought. Defiance rising, she stood and strode purposefully to the closet. She felt Josh watching her from across the room, but she didn't stop to explain her actions. She opened the closet door and went inside, closing it behind her.

She took a deep breath, then whispered, "Darcy Loughman, are you here?"

She paused, waiting for a response. None came.

She raised her voice slightly, in an attempt to sound authoritative. "Darcy Loughman, I summon your spirit to come forth."

She felt ridiculous. "God, I sound like a teenager leading a slumber party séance."

Honor wasn't sure what she had expected to happen, but she was positive that—at least for now - she was alone in the closet, talking to her clothes.

"I don't really know how the spirit world works, but Darcy, if you're listening, I just wanted you to know that I will always remember the memories you shared with me. Maybe you couldn't change your situation, but I'm sure going to try to change mine."

Chapter 19

She opened the door and stepped out of the closet to find Josh eyeing her with curiosity.

"I thought I'd try talking directly to the spirits, but it was a waste of time." she explained.

"Well, it was worth a shot." He gave her an impish grin. "Maybe the ghosts only come to visit when you're half naked." He raised his eyebrows while fingering an imaginary cigar, in a poor imitation of Groucho Marx. "Want me to come in there with you to check out my theory?"

Honor rolled her eyes with amused sarcasm. "Thanks, but I think I'll decline that generous offer. Seriously though, I'm ready for a break. How about you guys?"

"I thought you'd never ask" Josh replied.

Cody had finally gotten over his fascination with the shredder and was keeping himself entertained on the floor, playing with a few of his Spiderman toys in a nest of shredded paper. He jumped to his feet. "Can it be an ice cream break?" Then, remembering the magic word that sometimes made the difference in the reply, he added, "please?"

Honor glanced at Josh for approval.

"Cody and I don't usually have dessert before supper, but... I guess we can break that rule this once."

Honor turned to Cody. "I'll race you to the Ice Cream Parlor!"

"Whoa," called Josh, stopping their race before it began. "How about we only break one rule at a time? No running in the halls, okay buddy?"

"The last time he was doing that, he almost knocked you over, remember?" he reminded Honor.

"Oh yeah," Honor quipped, recalling their first meeting and realizing that seemed like a long time ago. "But don't forget, if he hadn't broken that rule, we might never have met."

"Point taken," Josh conceded. "New rule - he can run in the halls whenever I want to meet new women."

Honor laughed and shook her fist at him.

***

On one of the hotel's many secluded porches, Cody sat at a small white table, happily gobbling the last of his strawberry ice cream cone. Nearby, Josh and Honor cuddled together on a wide, wooden glider, quietly enjoying its comforting squeak, while watching sparrows hop in and out of several hanging flower baskets, overflowing with a variety of brightly colored impatiens. As dusk began to settle, a great white egret landed on the grass by the porch steps, watching them carefully; perhaps hoping they would toss some food his way.

Almost purring with contentment, Honor tilted her head back, nibbled on Josh's earlobe and reined little kisses on his neck.

Josh closed his eyes. "I'll give you a couple of years to stop that," he whispered.

She whispered back, "Why don't we get the little guy bathed and into his jammies and then go back to my room and order a pizza? If Cody falls asleep, we can, uh... watch TV in my bed."

Josh gazed at her, licking his lips. "I sure hope you mean what I think you do."

She smiled and nodded, doing her own Groucho Marx imitation.

Clear about her intentions, Josh jumped to his feet so fast, the startled egret took flight. He turned to Cody. "Okay, buddy, it's time to head back inside now. Let's go!"

Although the large apartment had two empty bedrooms down the hall, Honor and Josh were concerned Cody might be frightened if he woke up too far away from them, especially if spirits were around. They decided it would be better if he slept on the little bed in the parlor that opened into Honor's bedroom. Cody was excited about the proposed sleeping arrangements, and beamed when Josh agreed to hang one of his spider web pictures over his cot.

As Josh predicted, the ice cream spoiled Cody's appetite. After picking at a slice of pizza for a while, he asked if he could go to bed early. No one argued with him.

Honor tucked an extra blanket around the little boy, to keep him warm if the spirits visited. She kissed him goodnight and cooed, "sleep tight."

"And don't let the bed bugs bite," Cody responded.

Josh bent down and kissed his forehead. "Good night, buddy. Sweet dreams. And if you wake up, don't forget we're right outside this door, okay? If you need anything, just call me, and I'll come right in."

As he closed the door, Honor asked, "do you want any more of this pizza?"

He eyed her body. "Nope. I have a taste for something else."

Honor held him at bay. "Not yet. I want to be sure Cody is asleep before things, umm... get heated. Besides, I want to change into something more comfortable."

She giggled self-consciously and stepped into the bathroom, wishing she had packed some sexy lingerie in with her practical clothing. Then she recalled the effect the long T-shirt had on Josh that morning and decided it would work just fine. She changed and freshened-up; then opened the door.

In her absence, Josh had turned on some romantic music, dimmed the lights and folded down the comforter. Lying in bed wearing only his boxer shorts, he looked as though he might have just been ripped from the pages of a beefcake calendar.

When she neared him, Josh reached out for her and Honor tumbled into his arms.

They took their time making love, exploring every inch of each other's bodies. Honor thrilled at the way his muscles tensed with pleasure when she teased him with her tongue. He brought her body to a climax time and time again as she moaned, struggling to keep quiet so as not to wake Cody. When their sexual appetites were finally spent, they basked in the afterglow of complete satisfaction, so tangled together that it was hard to tell where one body stopped and the other started.

Josh smoothed Honor's errant curls back from her face, staring at her so intently that she finally demanded, "what?"

"I'm trying to memorize everything about this moment because I want to remember it for the rest of my life."

Touched by his romantic explanation, she murmured, "I love you, Josh," catching them both by surprise.

Josh beamed. "I'm glad your heart finally caught up with mine. I think I fell in love with you almost at first sight." His expression grew serious. "Honor, I've never felt like this before and I swear to you, I'm going to do everything in my power to keep us together, even if that means moving to Chicago."

Honor's eyes welled with tears as she tried to absorb his declaration. She wished she could come up with a poignant response, but for now, the only words that came to mind were, "I love you." which she whispered over and over again.

Exhausted, Honor rested her head on Josh's shoulder and fell asleep with a smile on her lips. As the air chilled, she reached for the comforter, pulling it up over them both. A moment later she was floating through the haze.

When the fog cleared, and she tried to orient herself while taking deep breaths to lessen her nausea.

Margaret was busy working at her desk. Without looking up, she said, "My 'Uncle Ulysses' is preparing to invest the money I was paid for handling the 'Hannah issue.' Poor girl. I often think about her plight. Those in the lower ranks of society are considered to have little value beyond that of a commodity - to be used and discarded by wealthy men."

Margaret rose and began pacing. "It's dreadfully unfair that women are judged, not by their abilities, but by the station in life to which they were born."

She stopped directly in front of Honor. "These recent experiences have steeled my determination to do what I can to outfox the men who created the rules of this unjust system."

Without thinking, Honor said, "Good for you, Margaret!" Instantly, she floated from the disintegrating memory, cursing herself for speaking.

When the fog cleared, Honor was sitting with the older Margaret at the small parlor table in her hotel room. Honor's eyes shot to the small bed under the window. Sure enough, little Cody was sleeping there. She shifted her gaze to the closed parlor doors, wondering if she opened them and called to Josh, if he would become part of this experience.

Then she remembered she had gone to sleep naked.

Chapter 20

Honor glanced down self-consciously and was relieved, though surprised, to find she was wearing a Victorian blouse and skirt. Margaret offered tea and once again, Honor accepted. Then, without any reference to Josh or Cody, her previous visits, or explanations of any other sort, Margaret settled back in her chair and began telling her about Hannah's recovery.

"I knew I should stay away, but after a few weeks, I couldn't resist paying a visit to the doctor. He told me that not only had Hannah lost her precious baby, but the severe beating had left her unable to bear more children. Still, her face was healing without too much scarring and her broken bones had recovered to the point that she was beginning to move around a little bit. The doctor told me Hannah wanted to meet the woman who saved her life." Margaret smiled, recalling the moment.

"On the night of the beating, Hannah's room had been relatively dark. Perhaps that's why I was shocked to discover how young she was. Resting on her little cot, bandaged from head to toe, she appeared so small and helpless." Margaret paused to dab a tear from her eye. "I began visiting regularly and learned that she was an orphan who had been sold into prostitution the year before, when she was thirteen years old. I couldn't help wondering how different the girl's life might have been, had her parents lived."

Honor could tell these memories were painful for Margaret.

"I had originally planned to move Hannah to a new town,

where she could resume her former occupation. But when I discovered how young she was, I changed my mind. Besides, her injuries left so many scars, the brothel proprietor would most likely have offered her to men whose perversions wouldn't be tolerated by his more desirable-looking ladies."

Honor gasped at the thought of the horrible fate Hannah so narrowly avoided, but managed to remain quiet.

Margaret paused again to dab her eyes with a handkerchief. "The poor little thing was so miserable. It was obvious the treacherous young man who had done so much damage to her body that night had also broken her heart and crushed her spirit. I took such pity on the wretched child that I decided to take her in and offer her employment at my establishment."

Margaret shook her head, a modest smile fleeting across her face. "It was truly a small gesture, but by the way she reacted, you would have thought I had offered to dress the girl in spun gold!"

Honor smiled, pleased Hannah was no longer alone.

"Hannah was shy and quiet by nature, and her life experiences thus far had taught her to be careful, if not completely distrustful of everyone, so keeping her hidden wasn't too difficult. Also, I knew that as soon as the rest of my staff learned about her predicament, they would become willing accomplices in the conspiracy to keep her identity secret."

Honor nodded her understanding, encouraging Margaret to continue.

Margaret took a sip of tea. "I thought Hannah might earn her keep by learning to clean and repair clothing and other such tasks, but she far exceeded my expectations. When I discovered she knew how to read and do simple math, I began to teach her the art of bookkeeping. To my utter amazement, the child became a gifted accountant, able to expertly manage the books for my Uncle Ulysses' investments, my business, and the entire household."

It was obvious to Honor that Margaret was proud of Hannah's accomplishments.

"Over time, Hannah became a trusted confidant. I knew her heart was broken over the loss of the unborn baby, but I admired the way she seemed to accept her lot in life without complaint. Watching her become a skilled accountant also opened my eyes to the fact that intelligent women with heads for business were not as unique as I once thought. Since the two of us were capable of handling business affairs in a manner equal or superior to that of successful men, I concluded the likelihood was that many other women could do the same, if given the opportunity."

Honor nodded.

"I made a vow to seek out intelligent women and assist them in overcoming the obstacles placed in their paths by a society which granted them no power."

The fog closed in and soon Honor was floating through time again. When the haze cleared, they were still at Margaret's home, but Margaret was dressed in an extravagant pink silk gown, with white lace overlays at her neck, wrists and bustle. Her hair was piled high, and accented by a small tiara of pink stones. She spoke immediately.

"When I was a child, one of my mother's best customers was a railroad tycoon that I greatly admired. He always talked to me as though I were worthy of his attention."

Without warning, the fog rushed in and spun Honor around into an earlier scene at the old house. Margaret was about ten-years-old and was chatting with a man who was easily thirty years her senior.

He laughed. "Ah, Margaret—you are a dear child. My son, Morton, is about your age. I can only hope that when he marries, he will choose a girl with your sensibilities and wit."

Margaret ventured, "Is your wife like me?"

"When she was younger, she was. She supported my

ambitions and enjoyed traveling. Sadly, now she suffers with consumption." He shook his head. "She has become so fragile that even the smell of liquor or cigar smoke on my clothing can trigger severe bouts of coughing. That's why I stop by here so often. Your mother works magic with my clothes."

"Well, I'm glad you come here," Margaret beamed. "I adore spending time with you and hearing about your adventures."

He laughed again. "God willing, I'll have many more adventures building a railroad that will conquer the wilds all the way down to the coast of Florida. Imagine—the entire Country will be open to even the most delicate, female travelers. Then you'll be able have adventures of your own."

"Tell me about Florida," she begged.

"Maybe during my next visit. I need to see myself home now."

As she watched the man walk to the door with her mother, Margaret turned to Honor. "He's an extraordinary man. He recounts his fishing and hunting exploits in such thrilling detail, I imagine I am at his side. And his business associates are among the most important people on earth. More than anything, I long to be a part of his world."

The fog engulfed Honor, hurtling her back to the previous scene, her head spinning wildly. Margaret didn't notice Honor's distress, but instead spoke as though she never left this memory.

"When my mother died, I took over her business, but I also continued my education. Soon I was able to discuss a wide range of topics with equal confidence - everything from business matters and horse racing, to the works of master artists."

Margaret turned to a free-standing oval mirror and smiled at her reflection. "The gentleman continued to visit over the years, even after his ailing wife died and he no longer needed cleaning services. I remained enchanted by his courageous spirit and his remarkable business acumen. Eventually his visits became a courtship, and I traveled to Florida as his social companion on several occasions. We even sailed to England for a summer."

She reached for a lace veil and carefully tucked it under the tiara. "And now finally, eleven years after the death of his first wife, Henry Bradley Plant and I are getting married."

Chapter 21

This time the swirling fog returned Honor to the table in her hotel parlor. The older Margaret smiled, her blue eyes misty. "Henry and I enjoyed a wonderful and adventurous life together. I became an avid hunter and expert fisherman. His railroad and shipping empire thrived, making him one of the richest men in the world. Near his railroad lines, he built several hotels to rival the finest royal castles in the world -- and I furnished each of them with treasures we collected from our travels."

Margaret took a long sip of tea. "But I never forgot my pledge to help elevate the status of other women whenever possible. Because of that vow, I didn't hesitate to come to Darcy's aid on the dreadful day that almost destroyed her." With an air of mystery, she added, "But that story is not mine to tell."

Margaret stopped reminiscing and turned her gaze toward Cody. "That one is a special child. He's very sensitive to the spirit world, and though he didn't come from your belly, I believe he could be a fine son to you." She pointed at the spider web drawing. "Who taught him to use a dream-catcher? That web pattern seems to repel splinter-spirits—what you call ghosts - but they have no effect on complete spirits."

Margaret's comments about Cody startled Honor. She was consumed by an overwhelming urge to protect the child, but as she turned toward him, the thick fog overtook her.

Honor woke with a start in her bed, Josh's arm draped loosely across her chest. Carefully, she slid out from beneath his arm, slipped on her long tee shirt, and went to check on Cody.

What was it that Margaret had said? A dream catcher? Honor studied the picture, taped to the wall above the little boy's head and wondered if Amy's spirit had taught her child how to protect himself from ghosts so he wouldn't be tempted to block out all spirits, including her.

Honor wasn't sure how long she was standing over Cody pondering the situation, when she heard Josh at the door. She turned and smiled when he rubbed his sleepy eyes—a delightful similarity between father and son. He lumbered up behind her and wrapped his arm around her waist.

"Did he wake up?" he whispered.

Honor breathed in his musky scent and opted to wait until morning to go into the details of her most recent experience with Margaret. "No... I just woke up and wanted to check on him. He looks so peaceful and relaxed...not a care in the world. Did you know he smiles sometimes when he's sleeping?"

"Yeah, he's done that ever since he was a baby. Makes you wonder what he's dreaming about, doesn't it?"

He gave Honor a tender squeeze. "Come on back to bed. It's freezing in here." Then, understanding seeped into his consciousness. "Uh-oh...it's cold. Does that mean you had more company tonight than just the two of us?"

Honor nodded. "Let's talk about it tomorrow. Right now, I'd rather get back into bed and cuddle up with you."

Josh grinned at her. "I like the way you think."

They slept soundly, wrapped in each other's embrace, until the sound of cartoons playing on the TV in the parlor woke them several hours later.

As soon as Cody discovered they were awake, he started babbling about his morning. "I woke up a long time ago! Look, I drew some pictures. This one is for you, Daddy, and this one is for Honor. Are you guys hungry yet? Did you see I turned on the TV all by myself?"

With her eyes half closed, Honor turned toward Josh to see if he was concerned about Cody's erratic behavior.

He smirked, "Welcome to my life. Now you understand why I treasure his nap time!"

"Yeah - he looked so angelic when he was sleeping," Honor moaned and pulled the blanket over her head. Just then, her cell phone rang and she blindly reached out from underneath the comforter to answer.

"Hey, Julie—No, I was already awake. What's wrong?" Honor mumbled, as she sat up in the bed.

Julie struggled to keep her voice down. "It's been crazy here today!" she wailed. "William is acting like a dictator, and it's become glaringly apparent to the software design teams that he doesn't have a clue how the technical side of the business operates."

"Is it really that bad?"

"Well, this morning, Mark Sutton called our technical support department in a panic. When I interrupted William's new, mandatory staff meeting to ask if one of the engineers could be excused, William refused to allow anyone to leave. I tried to tell William that Mark is an important client and he needed help with his primary operating system, but William said the department was shorthanded with you out of town, so Mark would have to wait until you get back to fix his problem."

Honor gasped, "Mark can't wait that long for his computer operations to be repaired! It would cripple his company."

"You're preaching to the choir," Julie cracked. "Mark was furious and the engineers were, too. Seriously, Honor, if you don't intervene pretty soon, the technical staff might mutiny."

"Okay, listen. Ellen Christianson worked with me on the design of that operations software. Give me Mark's number and I'll call him to smooth things over. I'll bet Ellen and I can design a patch and download a fix to his file server by the end of the day."

Julie hesitated. "About Ellen..."

Honor groaned, wondering what William could have done to upset Soft Fix's most valuable software design engineer.

"William told her she can't bring Mr. Peaches to the office anymore."

Honor bowed her head and shook it with disbelief. Ellen was a single woman who had two passions in life. The first was designing software and the second was her pink cockatoo, Mr. Peaches. Honor had been able to steal Ellen away from a competitor by allowing her to bring the bird to work.

"Julie, you tell Ellen to ignore that directive and if William gives her any more flak, call me immediately."

"Okay, I'll take care of it. But there's more, Honor - lots more. It's kind of like...well, like gossip has become a sport around here. Everyone is trying to figure out what's going on behind closed doors. On the bright side, people have started including me in some office gossip, so at least I know what's being said."

"Like what?" Honor coaxed.

"Well, they're speculating about the *real* reasons you left town so suddenly and wondering if you're ever coming back. Rumors are circulating that William owns Soft Fix now, and that you just work here."

Honor felt her face flush with anger, but kept her voice calm. "Well, we should be able to quash that rumor pretty quick."

"I guess so." Julie paused. "But one of the guys in the finance group told me he's getting fed up with William's *'questionable business practices.'* He's worried about criminal liability and said he's looking for another job. Could William be putting the whole company in jeopardy?"

"Julie, that's probably just a bunch of BS, but I need a little time to think about everything you've told me. Don't tell anyone I know about the rumors just yet. If William really is doing something illegal, I don't want him to panic and start shredding the proof."

"Understood. I'll call you right away if I learn anything new."

She gave Honor Mark's phone number and hung up.

Josh watched as Honor sat motionless - her mind obviously racing. "So, no floating around in the pool today?" he ventured.

Honor glanced up. "I'm sorry, but I have to design some software, and then I have to see what I can do to prevent William from destroying my company while I'm out of town."

"Is that all? Say no more. I'll grab Cody and get out of your hair. Maybe we'll go hang out with the 'Js' today, since I've been kind of ignoring my brothers the last few days."

"How about it, pal?" he called to Cody, "You want to go visit your uncles?" Cody was thrilled with the prospect and ran for the door, ready to go, now that a good time with his uncles was in the offing.

Honor's brain was shifting into work mode, but she still took her time saying goodbye to Josh, despite the fact Cody was trying to push him out the door.

"As soon as I can wrap-up for the day, I'll call to see what you guys are up to. Hopefully it won't be too late and we can spend the evening together."

She kissed Josh one more time and then stooped down to give Cody a hug.

"Have a good day, Cody. I want to hear all about it this evening."

Cody squirmed away. "Okay. Bye, Honor," He dismissed her, trying to push his way out into the hallway.

She laughed at his blatant brush-off.

Josh chuckled. "Deep down, I'm sure he's going to miss you today."

"Uh-huh...no doubt. Bye, bye now." Still giggling, Honor closed the door behind them, then turned her attention to work.

Chapter 22

She called her client, Mark Sutton, and assured him she was already working on a software patch to correct his issues. "While I have you on the phone, I wanted to apologize for William's behavior this morning. With me out of town, he's under a lot of pressure and I'm sure he just didn't understand the seriousness of your issue."

"No kidding. Now that I've seen William in action, I think I'd ask that blonde receptionist of yours to work on my operating system before I asked him. To tell you the truth, Honor, I really enjoy doing business with you, but I would appreciate it if you could arrange it so that I never have to interact with William again."

Honor was confused. "But I thought you two had a great relationship. I mean, you guys play golf together so often..."

"Whatever gave you that idea? William calls me about once a month and asks me how things are going and I tell him everything's fine. That's about it. Whenever I need anything, I call you."

"Really? I guess I must be confusing you with another customer." But Honor knew she hadn't made a mistake. She had frequently seen Mark's name on company expense reports for client appreciation rounds of golf, lunch and drinks. In fact, she was certain Soft Fix helped sponsor a charity golf tournament Mark had supposedly organized last summer.

Honor was stunned, but hid her reaction. "Well, I better go now. I'm collaborating with Ellen Christiansen to figure out what's wrong with your system."

"You and Ellen are both working on this problem? Great! I can relax now that I know the dynamic-duo is on the job."

After they hung up, Honor tried to convince herself that William simply entered the wrong client name on his expense reimbursement reports, but her mind kept posing troubling questions. How could William make the same mistake over and over? And if William wasn't entertaining clients like Mark, then where did the money go? She decided to focus her attention on designing the software patch and add these concerns to her discussion with the company's attorney.

Ellen Christianson was in rare form by the time Honor called. "Good God, Honor—you have to do something about William. The imbecile doesn't possess enough business sense to run a bake sale and yet he's trying to micro-manage the technical operations of a software design company!"

It took a while, but Honor finally refocused her colleague's attention on resolving Mark's operating system issues. Once they got started, their work processes were so harmonious, the project felt less like work and more like a challenging puzzle for them to solve together. The day flew by, but by late that afternoon, the software patch was finished and downloaded to Mark's operating system. Honor was ecstatic when Mark called to happily confirm their solution worked.

Smiling with satisfaction, she hung up and immediately called Josh.

His voice sounded oddly hushed, but his words warmed her all over. "I've been missing you like crazy all day long."

Honor could hear a chorus of men's voices in the background, heckling Josh.

"What's going on?" she asked.

He laughed. "Hold on, Honor. I can't hear you. I'm going to walk outside so these idiots can't hear our conversation."

The laughing and good-natured taunting faded into the background.

"What's that all about?" Honor repeated.

"It's nothing, really. The 'Js' are just acting like a bunch of twelve-year-olds, teasing me about you."

"Why?" Honor felt her insecurities beginning to surface.

"Well, I guess I was talking about you more than I realized and they aren't used to that coming from me. They're harmless, though. I remember treating Jeremy the same way when he first fell in love with his wife, Cathy. I think it's our way of finding out how serious a relationship is. If you care about someone enough to accept all the abuse the 'Js' can dish out, then it must be the real thing."

"How are you holding up?"

"They can tease me all they want. It runs off my back like water off a duck."

Honor sighed with relief. "Do you still want to get together for supper?"

"I sure do," Josh exclaimed. "I was afraid you were calling to say you had to work late. I'm glad I was wrong. Give me and Cody a few minutes to say goodnight to my family and we'll be right over."

***

When Josh knocked on her door, it was Honor's turn to be surprised. Dressed in an open-necked black shirt and tailored gray sports jacket with dress jeans and boots, Josh took her breath away. It took Honor a few seconds to realize he was alone and holding a vase filled with fragrant, pink stargazer lilies.

Grinning at Honor's speechless reaction, Josh set the vase on the entry hall table. "Cody was having fun playing with his cousins, so my brother James and his wife volunteered to keep him for the night," he explained. "I thought I'd take you on a proper date."

Honor slid into his outstretched arms. "God, you feel good," he whispered. "I was planning to take you out for dinner, but suddenly room service sounds more appealing. What do you think?"

With some difficulty, Honor resisted his attempt to seduce her. "We have the whole night to enjoy the things that are on your mind," she purred. "I want to savor the anticipation for a little while. Let's have a romantic dinner out and, if you're an exceptionally great date, I can guarantee there will be champagne, a bubble bath and maybe even a massage in your near future."

Josh groaned at the thought of waiting, but obediently released her from his arms and opened the door. "After you, my lady."

After selecting a nice, full-bodied chardonnay at the E & E Stakeout Grill, Josh told Honor the Js and their wives were anxious to meet her. "Of course, getting to know the whole gang at once can be a bit overwhelming, so I told them I would introduce you to a few of them at a time." He smiled, his blue eyes sparkling. "I thought for starters, you might be willing to ride over with me to pick up Cody at James and Lisa's house tomorrow afternoon."

"Sure, as long as we can spend the morning working at my mom's house. If I don't start making better progress over there, I'm never going to get finished," she lamented.

"No problem. I can even check out the house to determine what repairs need to be made to get it ready for the market."

"Great!" Honor gladly accepted his offer. Then, between bites of succulent steak and lobster, she told Josh about her discussions with Mark Sutton and her growing suspicions about William's financial dealings. But despite her concerns, Honor remained in high spirits, due in no small part to being able to talk things over with Josh.

Before long, they polished off a second bottle of chardonnay. Honor glanced around and noticed that only a few tired-looking employees were left in the restaurant. "Yipes!" she said with mock horror, "we'd better get out of here. If looks could kill us, we'd be goners."

The restaurant hostess did her best to stifle a yawn as they walked past her on the way to the exit. "I hope you come back and visit us again soon," she mumbled automatically.

As though reading the thoughts behind her polite expression, Josh joked, "But next time, we should make our reservation for earlier in the evening, right?"

The hostess just smiled.

Back in Honor's hotel suite, they ran a bubble bath in the deep, Jacuzzi tub and opened a small bottle of champagne from the mini bar. It was fun to be naked without worrying about Cody walking in on them and so they stayed in the bath until the bubbles were long gone and their fingers began to wrinkle.

Eventually they both wanted to be dry. Josh helped Honor from the tub and wrapped a towel around her. He pulled her close, intoxicated as much by the scent of her as by the wine. When they began to caress one another, the towel dropped to the floor between them. Soon their kisses gave way to the thrill of passion. They tumbled into bed, inhibitions abandoned, each seeking to please the other as much as possible. Afterward, exhausted and completely sated, they fell asleep, absently pulling tangled blankets over their naked bodies as the chill began to fill the room.

Chapter 23

Honor peered through the fog, hoping her nausea would subside quickly. She focused her eyes on a teenage girl curled in the corner of a high-backed settee. Besides Honor, the girl was alone in a dark library, the only light coming from a small fire at the center of a huge, stone fireplace. Honor recognized Darcy Loughman even before she spoke.

"I've been married two years now. I should be adept at managing the household, but try as I might, I'm afraid I'll never be able to handle the post in the manner Reginald expects. Today he instructed Ella, the head housekeeper, to teach me how to better handle my responsibilities. Imagine. A housekeeper given the authority to instruct her mistress about what is expected of her! It's humiliating." Darcy wrinkled her button nose at the thought.

When Honor's eyes adjusted to the dark, she gasped at the magnificence of the room. Tall, dark bookcases lined the wall on either side of a heavily draped window. An enormous desk and seating filled the opposite wall. Along with the settec, several chairs and small tables were set in a semi-circle in front of the fireplace. Through the open door, she could see several men gathered in the well-lit room across the hall, enjoying a spirited discussion.

Darcy caught her gaze. "Those are Reginald's sons. They are each several years older than I. They're ashamed their father remarried a third time and they're mortified about my age." She narrowed her eyes at them. "They treat me like a flea-infested pet that must be tolerated as long as their father lives.

My own father died this year and my grieving mother has gone to live with my aunt's family in New Hampshire, so I am truly alone here. Heaven only knows what will become of me when Reginald is gone..."

Darcy rubbed her eyes. "This house is situated in the bustling metropolis of New York City. The wives of most men with Reginald's social standing maintain a busy social calendar, entertaining and visiting others on a regular basis. But Reginald says it's unseemly for a married woman to go out in public without her husband. The truth is he believes my upbringing lacked sufficient training in proper social etiquette. He fears if I went calling, I would make blunders that would reflect poorly on him. Reginald travels a great deal, and when he's home, he rarely accepts invitations out. So I sit in these rooms alone. *I might as well live in a cave.*"

Darcy hadn't said her last words out loud, but Honor heard them as though she had. She also felt the depths of Darcy's misery, trapped in the opulent surroundings of this gilded cage.

Darcy began concentrating on her favorite daydreams and Honor floated through her thoughts, fascinated, as though watching several picture shows all at one time. In each of the dreams, Darcy imagined herself living a very different life: one in which her father was alive and wealthy, and her family was socially prominent. She envisioned shopping for beautiful new gowns and traveling to far-off destinations. She pictured attending extravagant balls, where her dance card was filled with names of handsome suitors, each hoping to win her approval. She dreamed a young man of her choosing would gaze at her with longing, and that a simple touch of his fingers would ignite passion. Most of all, she dreamed her marriage was based on love, rather than financial necessity.

When Darcy's green eyes fluttered open, the daydream visions ended. "My imagination does naught but torture me. It is high time I put away my childish dreams and accept the reality of my life with Reginald," she said.

Honor could still feel Darcy's agony burning deep within her soul. But when she reached out to comfort the girl, the swirling fog engulfed her.

When the mist parted, Honor was with young Darcy in the same library, but now it was well-lit and excitement crackled through the air like electricity. Reginald had been invited to spend the fall and winter in Florida, and had decided to take Darcy with him. Honor smiled, listening to Darcy's unspoken thoughts.

"Florida! Such an exotic name! Flooo-riii-daaa." Darcy repeated the sweet word over and over, letting it roll through her mind like a butterscotch treat. "Florida. Florida. We'll be wintering in Florida!"

Although giddy with anticipation, Darcy tried her best to sit still and focus on her husband's monotone vernacular, as he outlined their itinerary.

"None of the household staff will be traveling with us, so you will be expected to care for my needs and contend with the servants at the hotel," he droned. "I've instructed Ella to spend the next few weeks preparing you to handle these responsibilities."

Despite her efforts to remain calm, Darcy's enthusiasm bubbled over. "Do you think we might encounter alligators or wild Indians in Florida?"

Honor almost laughed at Darcy's innocence, but Reginald glared dolefully in her direction and continued his perfunctory presentation as though she hadn't spoken.

"We'll travel by rail to Florida and stay at the Tampa Hotel, as guests of my third cousin, Margaret, and her esteemed husband, Henry Plant."

Honor raised her eyebrows at the connection between Margaret and Darcy, but continued to listen to Reginald.

"Just after the holidays, we'll take part in the opening ceremonies for Henry's new Belleview Hotel, and we'll reside at the Belleview throughout her inaugural winter season."

Reginald scrutinized Darcy to make sure she was paying attention. "I plan to join business associates on numerous hunting and fishing outings throughout our stay. Whenever I am away, you will continue to reside at the hotel. Fortunately, the social morays are not as strict in the south as they are in New York, so your ineptitude should be less noticeable there."

Not even Reginald's obvious lack of confidence in her abilities could dampen Darcy's soaring spirits. When the familiar fog began to overtake the room, Honor couldn't stop grinning.

As the library faded away, Honor could hear Darcy's disembodied voice speaking to her from within the swirling fog. "In the weeks before our journey, I found it difficult to sleep, let alone tend to my household responsibilities."

Time was flying by just at the edges of the fog, causing Honor to experience a sensation similar to carsickness. She focused her attention on Darcy's words, hoping to lessen the effect.

"The housekeeper, Ella, was a fly in the ointment. She tried to instill in me the importance of my domestic duties, as though my being able to perform them flawlessly would render life or death consequences. But it was difficult to concentrate. Each time I read the advertisement for the Belleview Hotel, my imagination ran wild. Of course, I knew the only reason Reginald was taking me with him was because several social events were scheduled throughout the season, and he was anxious to show off his youthful bride to his business competitors. But I didn't care. I was going to be away from this house for several months and that is all that mattered."

The passage of time began to slow and when the mist cleared, Honor and Darcy were just outside the parlor door, candidly listening to a conversation between Ella and Reginald.

"Sir, I believe you're making a grave error leaving me behind. The girl is dimwitted and will be incapable of tending to your needs properly."

Darcy shook her head in disbelief. "I was aware Ella considered herself to be the *real* mistress of the house, but this behavior is outrageous. Reginald should fire her on the spot for demonstrating such insubordination to his wife!"

Instead, Reginald consoled Ella. "There now, good woman, don't fret. The only reason I want you to stay home is because my sons, Robert and Edgar are planning to spend the winter in New York with their families, and I need you here to care for them." He patted her shoulder. "Don't worry about me. I'll be alright on my own."

Darcy hissed at the insult, disappearing as the fog rolled in. Again, Honor could hear her voice inside the mist. "On his *own!* This is the moment when I understood Reginald never expected me to become a capable mistress for his household. Nor did he expect I would be able to rise to the occasion in Florida. It was as though he had clipped my wings just before setting me on a ledge and asking me to fly."

Gratefully, Honor noticed time was slowing down again. She gulped air to settle her stomach as the fog began to dissipate.

Darcy was sitting on the edge of her bed, near three steamer trunks. She spoke immediately. "Ella has been instructing me on how to pack, as though I'm an addle-minded wretch. She has developed the annoying habit of clucking her tongue while looking over my shoulder, which for some reason, seems to make my hands turn to all thumbs and my mind go blank! It's infuriating, but there's little I can do about it."

Darcy pointed at the open trunks. "I've realized with some dismay that everything I own fits into a single trunk. However, it takes two trunks and several special carrying cases to accommodate all manner of sports equipment and apparel for Reginald."

Darcy rose and started to pack a fishing pole into a long,

leather tube when, much to Honor's amusement, she suddenly began pretending she had hooked a large fish on the rod. Darcy fought hard with her thrashing, imaginary prey, as though trying to land it the way she had heard the feat described. Soon, she tired of the game and dropped the pole into its carrying case. Then she picked up one of Reginald's golf clubs. Just as she took her first swing, Ella slinked into the room. When Darcy heard Ella cluck her tongue, she instinctively whirled around to face her and in doing so, managed to knock an unlit candle from the table with the golf club.

"Tsk, Tsk," Ella clucked disapprovingly. "Master Loughman wouldn't be too pleased to learn that you are treating his valuables with such disregard."

Darcy's mood instantly shifted to gloomy. Honor narrowed her eyes with contempt for the domineering woman.

Terrified Reginald might change his mind about taking her with him to Florida, Darcy righted the candle and muttered, "I'm sorry. I meant no harm. I beg you... please keep silent about this brief indiscretion."

Ella snapped, "Master Reginald knows of your many shortcomings without my pointing them out. You best give that golfing stick to me before you do more damage." She took the club from Darcy and laid it gently in one of the nearly-full steamer trunks. "It's time for bed now. I'll finish the packing myself in the morning." Honor noticed a look of smug satisfaction flashed over Ella's cruel face as she stalked out of the room.

Darcy sat back down on the bed and stared at her hands, clasped tightly in her lap. "Perhaps she's right. And if Reginald thinks I'm hopelessly incompetent, he'll likely demand I remain in our room at the hotel unless he is with me. If that happens, my life will be little different in Florida than it is here."

Chapter 24

Helpless, Honor watched Darcy toss and turn in her sleep, filled with apprehension about her ability to handle her domestic responsibilities in Florida. When she could stand it no more, Honor whispered, "You might surprise them all and be extraordinary."

Darcy didn't wake, as Honor feared. Nor did the fog return. Instead, Darcy's pensive dreams gave way to visions of beautiful vistas and the peaceful sensation that wonderful experiences awaited her in Florida. In her dreams, she caught a giant fish and hit golf balls far out of sight. She reveled in the looks of amazement she saw etched upon the faces of Reginald, Ella and her step sons as they watched her flawless performances.

For Honor, the entire night elapsed in minutes. Darcy woke refreshed and with renewed excitement about her upcoming adventure. She donned her traveling clothes and nearly skipped towards the dining room.

When Darcy entered, Ella scoffed, "Master Reginald said to let you know he'll meet you at the train station. I mentioned to him that I woke early to finish your packing and then I arranged for the men to load the luggage onto the coach, to make sure it was done properly. Goodness knows, he'll miss my dedication to detail throughout the coming months."

Honor's dislike for the woman was escalating by the second. Darcy ignored the jabs and ate her breakfast.

Ella raised her voice to make sure the rest of the kitchen staff could hear her. "I'm just so worried for Master Reginald, having no one capable of attending to his needs while he's in Florida. If only I..."

Without warning, Darcy slammed her balled fists on the table. The months of suppressed hostility had surged to the surface, transforming feelings of inadequacy into rage. She roared, "Enough!"

The intensity of the single word was so forceful, the shocked housekeeper stopped talking mid-sentence. Fuming, Darcy stood, turned on her heel and strode to her waiting coach. She bid a quick farewell to the staff, glared at the still-stunned Ella, and stepped into the carriage.

Just as the driver closed the door, the mist rolled in. Honor relaxed into the fog, smiling. She expected to wake up in bed. Instead, she was pleasantly surprised to discover she was at the train station with Darcy.

The station was a beehive of activity. Darcy heeded the conductor's call to board the train. He punched Darcy's ticket and helped her up the stairs, pointing her in the direction of her private compartment.

Once she found her seat, Darcy's mind began to race and self-doubt reared its ugly head.

Honor remained silent, listening to Darcy's thoughts.

"I'm expected to take care of my husband's needs from the moment we leave the station until we return in the spring, and already I have no idea where he is."

Reginald said he would meet her at the station, but she hadn't thought to ask for an exact location or specific time for their rendezvous. Darcy wrung her handkerchief while searching the crowd outside the train window. When she finally observed her husband boarding the train, she frantically waved her handkerchief at him until, almost imperceptibly, he nodded at her. She collapsed into her seat, relieved.

The fog rushed in and time began to race by, offering glimpses at memories. Darcy never tired of rocking in her seat, listening to the rhythm of the train on the rails as she watched the scenery change from busy towns, to hills covered with trees that were already beginning to turn bright yellow, orange and maroon.

Reginald was pleased that Darcy adapted to rail travel so easily and required no special attention. He busied himself reading or sitting in the smoking car, discussing politics and other matters of interest to men. Darcy watched the other travelers with curiosity, but never engaged anyone in conversation for fear a social etiquette slip-up might remind Reginald of her shortcomings. If that happened, he would surely confine her to their hotel room whenever he was unable to serve as her escort.

As the train continued south, the rolling landscape began to flatten out and become green again with thin pine trees so tall they seemed to touch the clouds. Finally, Darcy spotted her first palm trees. They looked just like the ones pictured in the well-worn Belleview Hotel advertisement. She drank in the fragrance of the air as though it were fine wine.

The train whistle blew, signaling it was coming to a halt at yet another station. They stopped several times along the way to pick up and drop off passengers, supplies and mail, but Darcy never disembarked, fearing the train might leave without her. Through the window, she watched several young men on the train platform amuse themselves by hitting small stones into a nearby field with a golf club.

Darcy focused her attention on a man who was hitting the stones much farther than the others in the group. Even at a distance, she could tell he was devilishly handsome with thick, dark locks and a square jaw. She couldn't help ogling at the way he moved his body with such grace and agility. She stared transfixed until he turned and smiled in her direction.

Ashamed, she spun her head away, aware her cheeks were scarlet. She clenched her hands in her lap and prayed her husband would never find out about her brazen antics. She didn't lift her eyes again until the train pulled away from the station. As the engine picked up speed, she shot a glance back toward the platform. The young man was gone. She relaxed, confident her brief indiscretion would be forever known only to herself.

The journey to Tampa was scheduled to take three days, but on the second day, the train experienced engine trouble. The conductor encouraged the passengers to disembark and rest in the shade of some large oak trees nearby, until the engineers corrected the problem. At first, Reginald and Darcy remained in their seats, but when the heat inside the train became unbearable, Reginald decided they should join the other passengers. Honor followed them, grateful for the breeze.

As they neared the shade, Darcy froze in her tracks. The handsome golfer she had ogled on the train platform was not only here, he was approaching them! She dropped her gaze to the ground, hoping he wouldn't recognize her.

"Good Day! I'd like to introduce myself," he announced, presenting a calling card to Reginald. "My name is Rory Collins and I'm a professional golfer, hired to provide lessons for the guests staying at the new Belleview Hotel. I understand you will be staying there and wish to offer my services." Then he turned to Darcy. "I'm also teaching ladies to play, if you have an interest in the sport."

Darcy gulped, terrified he was going to mention he had noticed her watching him play.

Reginald seemed oblivious to Darcy's discomfort and to her utter amazement, replied, "Yes, I believe I would enjoy playing some golf with a professional. And perhaps my wife would like to learn to swing a golf club while I'm away on business."

With a smile and a tip of his hat, Rory departed.

Darcy's heart was pounding as she followed Reginald to where a few of his business acquaintances were gathered. Their conversation bored her, so she wandered a short distance away and sat on the ground under a broad tree, with her back resting against its trunk. She closed her eyes and contemplated Rory Collins, first wondering whether he even recognized her, and then pretending he made up the entire story about being a professional golfer, just to get near her.

She dozed off and dreamed her favorite fantasy. As always, she stood at the top of a white marble staircase, wearing a blue silk ball gown, and when the butler announced her arrival to those attending the gala in the ballroom below, all eyes turned to watch her descend the stairs. But this time, Rory was there, offering his arm to her.

Just then, Reginald shook her awake. "Come along, wife. The train has been repaired. It's time to re-board."

Darcy stood and followed him back to their compartment, feeling guilty and praying Reginald couldn't read her emotions. Honor knew Darcy needn't worry. As usual, Reginald hadn't noticed a thing.

Chapter 25

The depot in Tampa bore little resemblance to the organized rail station in New York. Here, cowboys prepared to move livestock from pens into railcars, while men of every description busied themselves loading and unloading wagons, and drivers urged carriage horses closer to the train, calling out for passengers to hire their services. Wooden crates filled with oranges, grapefruit and limes were stacked in neat rows, like colorful tin soldiers. Barefooted children clustered nearby to gape at the disembarking northerners, while large, odd-looking birds sat atop every flat surface, overseeing the commotion. In the distance, huge ships, docked at the Port of Tampa Bay were tied to pilings with ropes as thick as a man's arm. The air was saturated with dust and pungent odors, but when scent of the salty bay wafted through, it was invigorating.

Here, Darcy didn't stand out as a novice traveler. She reveled in warm sunshine while overseeing the transfer of their luggage to the carriage Reginald hired. The temperament of the hired help was more relaxed than workers in New York, putting her at ease and making the task less difficult than she had imagined.

Seemingly invisible, Honor climbed into the carriage next to Darcy for the short trip to the Tampa Hotel. Darcy gawked in amazement at everything from the lush foliage to the large, white birds perched along their route, which flapped their wings when the carriage passed, as if to welcome her. She pointed to the silver turrets of the hotel shining high above the trees and gushed, "It's as though a castle from a child's fairytale has been magically transported here!"

Soon the white, crushed shell road gave way to the paved brick entrance of the hotel grounds and the red brick, Moorish castle came into view. Even Honor was breathless at the sight. The hotel covered six acres and its roof line resembled a crown, featuring six minarets, four copulas and three domes, each covered in silver steel. Jauntily clad bellmen, wearing matching red jackets and pillbox hats, helped Darcy and Reginald disembark and ushered them into the grand hotel lobby. No one noticed Darcy had become quite dazed by the incredible experience. She stumbled along behind Reginald, trying to maintain her composure while taking in her intoxicating surroundings. The décor was a combination of European elegance and wildly exotic furnishings. When Darcy looked straight up into the high, ornately carved ceiling, she became lightheaded and swayed, increasingly unsteady on her feet.

She felt a strong arm catch her waist and, as if from a great distance away, she heard a soothing voice say, "There, there, Mrs. Loughman. You'll be fine. Just sit a moment."

With great effort, she bent her knees and sat as instructed. When she tried to clear her head, she heard the disembodied voice again. "She'll be fine. Sometimes the rapid change of climate takes a bit of adjustment. Bring a cool drink for the lady. Quickly, now!"

Slowly, Darcy's dizziness ebbed and her eyes fluttered open. She was embarrassed to discover the comforting voice belonged to none other than Rory Collins. Reginald and several others had gathered and were observing her with a mixture of curiosity and alarm.

"She's normally of very sound stature. I don't know what's gotten into her," Reginald blustered.

Even though Honor was experiencing Darcy's queasiness, she frowned with disgust at the way Reginald spoke about her as if she were livestock.

"Perhaps it's just the excitement of reaching your destination after the long journey," Rory volunteered.

Reginald nodded, accepting this logical explanation. "Darcy, you wait here while I go and register. Once we have settled into our lodgings, you can take a rest."

Still shaky, Darcy nodded in agreement. When the bellman returned with a glass of cool, sweet tea, the small crowd dispersed. Only Rory stayed behind.

"Try a sip of this," Rory urged, his brow wrinkled with concern.

Once the cool drink refreshed her, Darcy realized how much attention her unstable behavior had elicited, and flushed.

Rory observed the color in her cheeks and brightened. "There now, that's better. The beautiful pink color is returning to your complexion!"

Darcy groaned, even more embarrassed by his inaccurate assessment of her condition.

Understanding flashed in his hazel eyes. "Don't worry your pretty self about this silly incident. The spirit of the tropics enters the soul of every person who comes here. For some, like you, that moment is so powerful it causes a physical reaction." He winked and smiled, revealing straight, white teeth and dimples on either side of his square chin. "Now the tropics will always be a part of you. I predict you will discover as I have, that your soul will yearn for frequent doses of warm winter sunshine and sweet tea for the rest of your life."

Rory's joke eased the tension. Darcy returned his smile and soon they were chatting like old friends. Neither saw Reginald become engrossed in conversation with another gentleman near the front desk.

Eventually, Reginald made his way back to where they were seated. "I apologize for the delay, my dear."

Darcy glanced up, startled by his apology. She had been so engrossed in her conversation with Rory that she didn't realize her husband had been gone longer than anticipated.

Reginald continued, "I know we only just arrived, but a business acquaintance has invited me to join him on a brief fishing excursion and I don't want to pass up the opportunity. Unfortunately, we depart first thing in the morning, but I shouldn't be gone more than two or three days."

"Mr. Loughman," Rory interjected, "since Mrs. Loughman isn't yet acquainted with the other guests, perhaps she would enjoy taking a golf lesson while you're away on your adventure. I'm offering instruction here at the Tampa Hotel for a few weeks, before relocating to the new Belleview Hotel." Lowering his voice, he added, "It might be a pleasant distraction and besides, it would be good for her to become familiar with the game before you move over to the Belleview, since so many guests already know how to play golf."

"I suppose if she has an activity to keep her amused in my absence, she will be less upset about me leaving her alone so soon after our arrival." He gave Rory an appreciative wink. "Splendid idea, my good man."

Darcy gulped, unable to comprehend how Reginald could approve of her spending time with another man, unescorted. She managed to mumble her thanks to Rory before following Reginald and the bellman down the corridor, toward their suite.

Reginald complained the rooms were small, but Darcy was delighted by everything from the oak canopy bed to the three electric lights and private balcony. "Why, the toilet is just next door and will only be shared with the guests staying in the two suites across the corridor," she marveled.

Reginald smoked his pipe and read a newspaper while Darcy worked with the hotel staff to unpack and store their trunks, and then pack a small valise for Reginald's upcoming fishing excursion. When she finished, they ventured down to the dining hall.

Darcy was so in awe of her glamorous surroundings, she barely touched her food. Reginald, on the other hand, ate ravenously and then announced it was time to retire, as he would be meeting his fishing companions early the following morning.

Darcy wanted to explore the grounds, but said nothing. Honor understood she remained silent because she was afraid that if she annoyed Reginald, he would remember to confine her to their suite while he was away.

Neither Darcy nor Honor realized Reginald mistook Darcy's unusual silence for anger about being left alone. Hoping to avoid a quarrel, he woke at the crack of dawn, dressed quietly and let himself out of the room without waking her - or so he thought. Darcy feigned sleep until she heard the door to their suite close behind him. Then she sprang from bed, a bird let loose from its cage.

Without speaking to Honor, Darcy dressed and strolled to the lobby, stopping frequently to admire artwork from all around the world. Once outside, she roamed the grounds, watching the hotel come to life. Honor felt Darcy's tantalizing sensation of freedom that no words could express.

Lost in the ecstasy of the morning, Darcy was startled to hear someone call her name. She turned and saw Rory striding toward her, as if he were a part of the marvelous daybreak. He was the most beautiful creature Darcy had ever seen. Certain she was simply imagining his approach, she closed her eyes and tried to recall the feel of his muscular arm across her back and the sound of his deep, reassuring whispers in her ear.

Rory's voice jerked her back to reality. "How are you feeling this morning, Mrs. Loughman?"

When Rory smiled, Honor felt Darcy's knees go weak. She mumbled a greeting.

"If you're available, I thought we could start your golf lessons this morning."

As if suddenly struck dumb, Darcy bobbed her head up and down in response.

"Wonderful! We can get started right away," Rory

continued.

Darcy was torn. She longed to be near this man, but was frightened by a host of new sensations that threatened to engulf her. Flustered, she struggled to find her voice.

"I don't know what to wear to play golf... and I don't have a playing stick," she stammered.

Rory gave her another brilliant smile. "You can use my golf clubs this morning, and if you enjoy the game, you can purchase a club or two from the hotel shop later. As for your attire; you'll need to remove enough petticoats so that you can see the golf ball when it's placed on the ground near your feet." He cleared his throat. "I'll meet you in the lobby in a quarter hour, and escort you to the south lawn for your first lesson."

Darcy flushed, suddenly aware she hadn't heard a word Rory said after he mentioned removing her petticoats. Honor concentrated on the words *lobby* and *fifteen minutes*.

Without acknowledging Honor's presence, Darcy nodded to Rory and repeated her exact words. "Lobby. Fifteen minutes."

Chapter 26

Honor followed Darcy to her suite, trying unsuccessfully to continue communicating with her mind. While Darcy removed her petticoats and rolled her hair into a tight bun, Honor contemplated the issue. Finally, she concluded that just as Darcy could only share her memories when Honor was daydreaming or asleep, Darcy could only hear Honor's thoughts when she was likewise daydreaming or asleep.

When they returned to the lobby, Rory was there waiting. He watched her advance toward him. Her dress, now minus its petticoats, revealed a slim figure and hips that swayed back and forth in a smooth, even gait.

They walked to the make-shift golf instruction area, chatting about the new hotel and then about Rory's life and his hopes and dreams for the future.

When Darcy got married, she had stopped dreaming about her own future; and began to fantasize about leading different lives. Listening to Rory, she now imagined what it would be like to be his love interest. Accidentally making her private thoughts known, she asked, "Where would we settle down when it was time to start a family?"

Rory was amused at her horrified expression and playfully countered, "Well, I guess we would have to consult your husband about that!"

"I meant *you*... where would *you* settle down," she sputtered, blushing furiously.

Thankfully, at that moment, two gentlemen broke into their conversation, with questions for Rory about the unfinished golf course at the Belleview Hotel, the proper stance, and other golf minutia. Darcy was grateful for the interruption, which allowed her a few minutes in which to compose herself. By the time Rory turned his attention back to her, she resolved to pretend the awkward exchange never happened.

"So, one's shoulders should be parallel to the target when standing over the ball?" she asked, mimicking one of the other golfer's queries.

Rory followed her lead, resuming his role as her golf instructor. "Let me show you the proper golf swing before you attempt to strike a ball."

He demonstrated the correct swing several times. "Note the way the club follows an imaginary arc, ending over my shoulder," he coached as he swung.

Although his behavior was strictly professional, Darcy's imagination refused to abate. She watched the muscles of his body flex and imagined how it would feel to be cradled in his strong arms.

"Now you give it a go." Rory handed her the club and placed a ball on the ground.

Darcy wrapped her fingers around the handle, fascinated to be holding something that moments before, had been covered by his large, sturdy hands. She could still feel the warmth of his grip on the club as she awkwardly attempted to emulate the swing she had watched him perform so flawlessly.

After her swing, she was amazed to see the ball was still lying on the ground in front of her feet, exactly where Rory had put it. She looked up at him, puzzled.

"That happens when you don't swing correctly," he explained. "Let me show you." He moved around behind her and placed his hands on top of hers. Then he moved the club in a smooth arc. "Don't take your eyes off the ball."

Honor watched as Darcy tried to focus on the lesson. With Rory so close to her, she could barely remember how to breathe. Darcy worried Rory could feel her quivering.

His breath was warm against her neck and goose bumps flowed down Darcy's body in waves. Instinctively, her head rolled slightly to the side, exposing her neck more fully to him.

"Look at the ball," he instructed, his voice catching as he quickly stepped away from her. "And try to swing the club."

Darcy's swing was clumsy, but she managed to make contact with the ball, rolling it forward several feet. She glanced up, surprised to find Rory already trotting after it.

Keeping his back to her, he picked up the ball and shifted his gaze to the sun. "Florida has truly wonderful weather. This winter sunshine should help the new Belleview golf course thrive."

Darcy's momentary confusion at Rory's odd behavior gave way to understanding. He was trying to hide the fact that he too, had become aroused when they touched. To help ease the tension, she pretended nothing was awry. "Yes, outstanding weather... simply marvelous."

Rory tossed the golf ball back to Darcy. "Place the ball at your feet and try again."

By the time the next student arrived for a lesson, the unsettling interaction had dissolved into friendly banter and Darcy's golf swing was improving.

"Shall we meet again tomorrow for another lesson?" Rory asked hopefully.

"That would be lovely," Darcy agreed. She turned and walked back to the shade of the hotel porch, to enjoy a glass of sweet tea and sort out her emotions.

Honor felt voyeuristic and uncomfortable, unsure if Darcy remembered she was still sharing her thoughts. As if reading her mind, Darcy turned and spoke to her.

"Sitting here in the comfort of this rocking chair, watching married couples stroll through the gardens together, I try to imagine myself enjoying Reginald's company in this manner. But I just can't." She bowed her head, watery eyes closed, lips pressed tight together.

When she finally lifted her chin, it was with unexpected resolve. "I must stop thinking like a child, wishing life could be more than it is. My husband is a good provider. I should be grateful to him, instead of behaving like a wanton woman as soon as he is out of sight." Contrite, she vowed, "It's time to put away these romantic notions of mine. Tomorrow, I will remember my place and make amends." She sighed, "If only golf lessons weren't so stimulating..."

Honor was engulfed in swirling clouds of fog. When it dissipated, she was lying next to a sleeping Darcy. After watching her toss and turn a few seconds, Honor closed her eyes. She was instantly transported into Darcy's dream world. The images were fuzzy and cracked around the edges, reminding Honor of an old damsel-in-distress movie clip, but Darcy's emotions were vivid. She was terrified.

Reginald was pulling her along behind him through a forest, tethered on a rope as if she were a pet. Deep in the gloomy woods, he stopped at a gnarly oak tree, whose branches dripped with gray Spanish moss. Ignoring her protests, Reginald tied Darcy to the tree and walked away, oblivious to the red, beady eyes of predators in the thicket.

As soon as he was gone, huge black birds with dangerously long beaks and sharp talons swooped in, taunting Darcy as she tried in vain to pull herself free from the tree. Wolves slunk out from the thicket and began to circle her, growling.

Just when Darcy was about to be devoured, Reginald reappeared. Oblivious to the danger, he untied Darcy and led her to another tree. No matter how hard she tried to explain what was happening to her in his absence, Reginald ignored her. He tied her to another tree and left, chanting, "There now. Be a good girl, Darcy. Don't embarrass me."

Honor wanted to help, but how? She concentrated on a single thought. "Wake up, Darcy!"

Darcy awoke with a start. Still agitated from her

nightmare, she got out of bed, pulled a robe over her gown and walked out onto her balcony. The chilly night sky was clear, but the nearly full moon was too bright to see many stars. She studied the hotel grounds, admiring the pools of moonlight reflecting on crushed white shell garden paths. Then, in the shadows below her balcony, she thought she saw Rory sitting on a bench, watching her. Rattled, she retreated to her room, unclear where reality ended and imagination began. Regardless, her heart pounded at the possibility that Rory was nearby.

When Darcy fell back to sleep, she returned to her dream. Again, Reginald tied her to a tree, but when he left, Rory materialized and released her. Free from her bonds, Darcy grew wings and took flight.

For Honor, the entire night evaporated in mere minutes.

When she woke, Darcy finally acknowledged Honor. "I believe I associated my new found freedom with Mr. Collins, when in fact, his presence was only coincidental. I will correct our relationship today."

At noon, Darcy dressed for her second golf lesson and left her room, firm in her resolve to set things back on a proper course with Rory. She sipped tea on the lobby porch, waiting for him. When at last she saw Rory approaching, Darcy intentionally averted her eyes, and concentrated on the antics of a bee, hovering on a nearby flowering bush.

When he cleared his throat to gain her attention, Darcy glanced up and spoke, using her most formal tone. "Ah, Mr. Collins, is it time for my golf lesson already? I seem to have lost track of the hour."

Rory raised his eyebrows, surprised and disappointed their friendly relationship had taken a step backward, but he followed her lead. "I understand, Mrs. Loughman. Florida often seems to have that effect on visitors. Now... for today's lesson, I thought we would try to play a few holes of golf along the river bank. With practice, I believe you could master the fundamentals of the sport before your husband returns."

"You're too kind."

"Shall we get started, then?"

Darcy rose from her seat and fell into step beside him, ignoring her rapid heartbeat and sweaty palms.

Once they began playing, Darcy found it easier to keep up the pretense, focusing all of her attention on learning the skills of the game. She turned out to be a natural athlete, which both surprised and delighted Rory. For her part, Darcy was thrilled to find something at which she could excel. After each good shot, she turned to Rory to share her triumphs, enjoying his encouragement and genuine admiration.

More than once, Darcy overheard other golfers comment about her lucky shots, while making excuses for their own poor attempts. Each time, she noticed Rory biting his lip to keep from laughing. When one of the men interrupted to request a lesson, she was startled to realize how much time had slipped by.

"Mrs. Loughman, if you would like to keep practicing until after this gentleman's lesson, we might play a bit more before the sun sets."

"I would enjoy that very much," she replied.

Chapter 27

When Rory finally returned to her side, Darcy was alone, practicing her putting on a flat area of crushed shells, very near the river's edge. Dusk had already begun to settle. "Let's work on your putting a little while longer and then I'll escort you back to the hotel to join the other guests for dinner," Rory suggested.

"Splendid. I fear I am too tired to swing any other club," Darcy joked.

With the sun setting, Rory taught Darcy how to look at the contours of the ground to determine the path the ball would take as it rolled toward the cup. After he demonstrated the correct stroke, she would place her own ball down and putt from the same location. As she improved, he moved the ball farther from the hole.

"Tell me what you think the ball will do," he coached, helping her line up a long putt.

She squinted in the dim light. "It will roll to the right about four inches," she replied.

He smiled and nodded his approval. She stood over the ball and swung the putter in a smooth pendulum motion. Together they watched as the ball rolled twenty feet and dropped into the cup.

Ecstatic, Darcy whooped, "yes!"

She spun around and without stopping to think, gave Rory a joyous hug. He returned her affection, proud of her accomplishment. Neither of them expected what happened next.

The instant their bodies crushed together, it was as though a match had been struck, transforming their exuberance into passion.

Rory moved his arm to cradle her head and bent his lips to hers, offering a tender kiss. Darcy's willing body pushed even closer to his, urging him to kiss her more deeply. She was confused by the experience. As a married woman, she had been kissed and knew what the hungry embrace of a man could lead to, yet this was the first time in her life that she felt the same desire.

Using all the strength he could muster, Rory broke away from her lips and stared into her smoldering green eyes. "If you wish, I can take you back to the hotel immediately. We would never have to speak of this again."

Darcy could barely breathe. "I don't think I have ever wanted anything in my life more than your next kiss. Please don't withhold it from me."

A small cry escaped Rory's lips as he swept her into his arms and carried her off the putting green, down a rise and into a large canvas tent with a thatch roof. Darcy stared at Rory with silent amazement, wondering how he had been able to instantly produce a private dwelling for their use.

"This is a foul weather hut, used to protect guests who get caught out here in one of our frequent thunderstorms," Rory explained.

The full moon poured through the tent opening, bathing them in its white light. He gently set Darcy on her feet and moved to the back of the musty tent, where an army cot leaned against the wall. He righted the little bed and then paused, avoiding eye contact.

Darcy understood. Like her, he was torn between his conscience and his desire. She drifted silently to the cot and sat down, making her choice known. She began pulling the pins from her hair one by one, allowing her curls to tumble freely around her shoulders. His lustful gaze excited her. She held her hand out to him, beckoning.

Struggling to maintain control, Rory knelt before her and rained gentle kisses along her neck and nibbled her ears. Darcy unbuttoned his shirt and stroked his lean, muscular chest. She could feel his pounding heart beneath her trembling fingertips.

Rory moved his shaking hands to the long row of tiny buttons on the front of her blouse. His thick fingers fumbled unsuccessfully at the task until Darcy stopped him, giggling nervously.

Rory watched as her nimble, practiced hands unfastened one button after the next until her blouse fell away. He eyed her breasts for a long moment, bathed in moonlight and tipping over the top of her corset; then slid his fingers inside to touch her nipple.

Darcy's chest jerked involuntarily, arching toward him, but he pulled his hand away. Without taking his eyes from her, he stood and began to undress. Darcy followed his lead and removed the rest of her own clothing.

The tiny cot was so narrow; he carefully lay down directly on top of her. When she felt his bare skin press against hers, it was as though every nerve in her body reacted, sending delightful, tingly sensations in every direction. He lifted the right side of his torso enough to allow his hand to slide over her breast and linger there, fondling her nipple and massaging her ample bosom. Her breath came in short gasps and her entire body began to undulate, as if every fiber of her being wanted to melt into his. She parted her legs and moaned when she felt him move into position between them. He hesitated only a moment before pushing himself into her welcoming body.

She cried out with pleasure, shocked at how wonderful his hard body felt as compared to Reginald's sagging skin and semi-limp member. It was as though one of her daydreams had finally come true and she was determined to relish every moment.

They moved together in perfect rhythm. It was ecstasy. Suddenly, Darcy's muscles stiffened and her toes curled as if electricity was flowing from where they were joined, all the way up her body, causing stars to burst behind her closed eyelids. Darcy had never experienced the rush of a climax before and was nearly overwhelmed by the experience. Her excitement thrilled Rory until he couldn't hold back any longer. He drove deep inside of her and released.

Still pressed under Rory, listening to his ragged breathing, her tears of joy ran unchecked. She was all at once, dazed, exhausted, peaceful, and completely sated.

And she was in love -- madly and passionately in love. Of course, she knew a future together with Rory was impossible. She was a married gentlewoman. He was the hired help. She caressed his naked body, trying to memorize every detail of their time together. Every touch. Every sound. Every smell. Every taste. She knew the memories of this night would have to last her lifetime.

Rory was first to speak. "Please believe me when I tell you I have never before felt such desire for a woman. I want to keep you pressed against me for the rest of my life."

Darcy sobbed, "If only wishing could make it so. But one cannot alter reality. There is nothing we can do to change our lot in life."

His voice hoarse with emotion, Rory whispered, "My life will be miserable without you."

They kissed over and over again, until their parting could be postponed no longer.

Devastated, Darcy pushed him away. "We have to go back now. It will be morning soon and Reginald could return within hours."

They dressed in silence by the brilliant moonlight and began to trudge slowly toward the hotel. As they drew near the massive building, they stopped behind the shelter of a giant oak tree to share a last kiss and tight embrace. The tears that welled in Darcy's eyes spoke the words she could not say.

Rory nodded his understanding. "I know you belong to him, but I will always love you without reservation. Please know that I will never be far from you, and that I will never ask you for anything more than you can give. If I live to be a hundred, I will never know a night so bright, feel a touch so soft or share a love so perfect."

Darcy held him close and whispered, "He will never own my heart. This I give to you tonight and for always."

Chapter 28

The fog engulfed Honor, catching her off guard. An instant later, she woke up in her hotel room. It was morning and the air still cold from her spirit visitors. She was aroused from watching Darcy and Rory's rendezvous and was happy to find Josh lying beside her, still naked from the night before. She rolled on top of him and began kissing the side of his neck, while moving her hips in a slow circle.

Without opening his eyes, Josh wrapped his arms around her. His voice still husky with sleep, he mumbled, "If this is a dream, I don't want to wake up... and if it isn't, I want to wake up this way every morning."

Honor didn't respond with words; she used unbridled passion.

***

Later, as they sat in bed munching their way through a room-service pastry basket, Honor told Josh everything she had witnessed the night before. "Do you remember what Margaret said about how a spirit can sometimes connect with a person when they have something in common? Well, I think Darcy might identify with me because we both had unhappy marriages and then discovered love with a better man."

"A better man? I like the sound of that." Josh winked, then swung his legs over the side of the bed. "Seriously, I think you need to be patient, like Margaret said. Now, come on and get up! We need to grab a shower and get ourselves over to your mom's house. You know, we'd already be over there, if you hadn't taken advantage of me in my sleep," he teased.

Honor giggled. "Poor guy. Like you tried so hard to fight me off."

Josh laughed. "I wasn't complaining...just stating facts, that's all."

They were working hard, cleaning out her mother's storage room, when Honor's cell phone rang. It was her company's attorney, Leon Goldstein, returning her call from the day before.

"Leon, our conversations are confidential, right?"

"Of course," he assured her.

"Okay, I need your advice. I heard a nasty rumor about William and some shady financial records at Soft Fix. Is that something I ought to investigate on my own, or should I involve the authorities immediately? Also, I'm considering ending my partnership with William by dividing the company in half."

Leon cleared his throat and spoke slowly. "Honor, you need to understand that I am corporate counsel for Soft Fix. I'm also William's personal attorney - not yours. That being said, I don't believe you have the legal authority to force a division of company assets. You should hire your own attorney to explain the company's structure to you and clarify your obligations to the firm, as outlined in your non-compete agreement."

Honor was baffled. "I don't understand, Leon."

"When you and William were first establishing your company, I recommended you each hire legal counsel, but you declined, opting to waive that right," he reminded her.

"What has that got to do with this situation?"

"Honor, my advice is to hire an attorney to review your contractual documents, and then have him contact me." Leon ended the call.

Anxious, Honor tried to remember back to when she first launched her fledgling company with William. They possessed distinctly different skills, so William said it would be best if she had total control over technical operations and software design. She would hire who she wanted, negotiate salaries, develop policies and procedures - everything. He said he would use his skills to manage the rest of the business—the office management, marketing and financial operations—using the same ground rules of independent control. It had seemed very reasonable to her.

Honor quickly brought Josh up to speed. "There was a lot of paperwork involved in setting up a corporation. I vaguely remember William saying he didn't think it was necessary to pay two lawyers to do the same work. He suggested I waive my right to independent counsel and let his attorney, Leon, handle everything. William called the waiver a formality, and because I hate reviewing financial paperwork, I signed it and never looked back." She shook her head. "Stupid, stupid mistake. All this time, I believed Soft Fix was a fifty-fifty partnership, but I actually have no idea how William structured the business."

"Try not to worry. I'll bet my brother James knows some good contract lawyers who can get this straightened out. We can talk to him when we pick up Cody this afternoon."

They got back to work on the cluttered storage room, but Honor couldn't keep her mind off her escalating problems. Needing a few minutes to herself, she wandered into her mother's bedroom and sat down on the floor of the closet, hugging her bended knees.

"Mom, it looks like I might have made a big mistake going into business with William. I can't believe I was so gullible."

Honor dropped her head against her knees and squeezed her eyes shut to hold back angry tears. For an instant, she felt the sensation of her hair being smoothed back from her face, the way her mother had comforted her when she was a child. Then it was gone. Before she had time to contemplate the experience, Josh appeared in the doorway.

At the sight of her teary eyes, he dropped down beside her without a word and wrapped his muscular arms tightly around her.

"I was so stupid to trust William," she began, haltingly.

"Shhhhh... stop saying that. You're not stupid. He may have taken advantage of your trust, but everything is going to work out just fine. You'll see."

Honor wasn't convinced, but she began to relax in the safety of his arms.

They decided to call it a day and go pick up Cody. And since first impressions tend to be lasting, they agreed not to tell Josh's family about their recent experiences with the spirit world.

When they arrived at James and Lisa's house, Cody came running out to greet them. He jumped from the porch into Josh's open arms and immediately began recounting every detail of his visit, without seeming to take a breath.

Lisa, who was standing in the open door, laughed. "That child sure is a talker!"

"Yes he is!" Josh agreed. "Lisa, this is my girlfriend, Honor."

Cody interrupted. "Honor is my girlfriend too, Daddy."

Josh laughed. "No way, Cody... you find your own girl." He stepped over to Honor and kissed her cheek.

Cody stretched his little arms toward Honor, signaling for her to take him, which she did. He laid his head on her shoulder and with his pouty lower lip stuck out, repeated, "She's *my* Honor, Daddy!"

Josh chuckled at his son. "Okay, Pal, you win. We'll share her."

Cody's smile instantly returned to his face. Lisa laughed again, extending her hand to shake Honor's. "Nice to meet you, Honor. It looks like you get two for the price of one!"

Honor thoroughly enjoyed the evening. Even though Josh and James teased each other about everything under the sun, it was obvious theirs' was a loving family. Honor was fascinated by stories of growing up with the rest of the Js and learning that all of them now earned a living in the construction industry.

"It's nice to know the Js can provide one-stop shopping for all my home repairs," she commented.

"You bet. Hey, James, wait till you see her house. It's an amazing 1900 Queen Anne Victorian. The floors need to be refinished and it needs paint inside and out, but mostly it's in great shape. The hand-carved cornices on the crown molding and the inlaid staircase are top-shelf."

"Josh is assessing how much work needs to be done before I put Mom's house on the market. You're welcome to stop by anytime."

"Yeah, James, that's a good idea," Josh said. "I'm toying with the idea of buying it as an investment property and sure would appreciate a second opinion."

James didn't hesitate to volunteer his help. "Let's get started at eight o'clock tomorrow morning. We should be able to knock out the repairs in no time."

A sudden wave of melancholy washed over Honor, as she realized she was running out of reasons to stay in Florida. Her thoughts turned to Chicago, reminding her of the problems that loomed ahead there. "I could also use your help finding a good attorney."

James raised his eyebrows, curious.

Honor briefly recapped her suspicions about William and her unsettling conversation with Leon Goldstein.

James gave a low whistle, a trait he had in common with Josh. Recognizing the family quirk, Honor giggled, despite the circumstances.

Lisa understood Honor's reaction. "The whistle -- I know. Wait until you meet the other Js. They have so many similarities, it's almost creepy sometimes."

Josh pretended to be offended. "What's so weird about eleven men all looking and acting exactly the same way? You guys are just jealous." Lisa and Honor laughed and the conversation resumed on a much lighter note.

When the evening was drawing to a close, Cody wobbled into the dining room and crawled up into Honor's lap. Worn out from his busy day, he snuggled against her and she instinctively began rocking him and stroking his hair back from his face. Cody closed his eyes and relaxed into sleep. Honor kissed the top of his little head, enjoying the maternal instincts the young boy elicited from her. When she glanced up, everyone was watching her.

Lisa explained in hushed tones. "Cody never lets anyone but Josh hold him when he's tired, hurt or upset."

Honor glanced at Josh, who was nodding his head in agreement.

"Yeah, this is definitely a first," he agreed.

Chapter 29

Honor was relieved Josh didn't seem to be upset by his apparent loss in stature. Rather; he seemed to enjoy the sight of his little boy, asleep in her arms. She returned his smile.

As they were preparing to leave, James wrote down Sarah Jacobs's phone number and handed it to Honor. "Sarah is the attorney most of us Js use to handle our contract issues. She really knows her stuff. I hope she can help you."

Honor accepted the recommendation gratefully and climbed into Josh's truck.

Soon they were back at the hotel, but this time, Honor wasn't ready to say goodnight. "Why don't you and Cody spend the night in my suite?" she suggested tentatively. "As a matter of fact, I would love it if you guys stayed with me until I return to Chicago. I mean, the suite is huge and you could save money…"

"Honor, you don't have to convince me. I'd love the chance to spend more time with you. But I will insist on sharing the hotel expenses."

"How macho of you," Honor teased.

They picked up a few things from Josh's room, opting to finish their move to her suite in the morning. Again, they tucked Cody into the bed in the small parlor that adjoined Honor's bedroom and quietly closed the door.

They talked for a long time that night, letting the conversation drift easily between topics ranging from the spirits haunting the hotel to family stories and Honor's options regarding her company… anything that came to mind.

Honor's last thought before falling asleep with Josh that night was that although they had been too busy talking, and then too tired to make love, she felt closer to him than ever before.

***

Honor was no longer surprised by the fog. She hoped to find Margaret waiting for her at her parlor table, ready to explain the meaning of her recent encounters. Instead, she found herself back with Darcy and Rory.

It was just before dawn when the couple sneaked into the Tampa Hotel through the servant's entrance and quietly ascended the shabby wooden stairs closest to her room.

Rory checked to make sure the coast was clear, and then turned to Darcy. "More than anything, I want to pull you back into my arms, but I know you belong to the world that exists on the other side of this door and I must let you go." With a heavy heart, he ushered Darcy into the guest corridor and quickly closed the service door behind her.

Darcy stared at the little door, wondering if Rory was still on the other side, just out of reach. Finally, she turned away, knowing he was right.

Honor could feel Darcy's racing heart as she fumbled with her room key. She opened the door to her suite, praying Reginald hadn't returned earlier than expected. She stepped inside, listening carefully for his breathing. There was only silence. Sighing with relief, Darcy turned on the light and ran a bath. She removed a large hat from its box and carefully folded her clothes, still ripe with the scent of their love-making, into the folds of tissue paper. She closed the lid, tied the silk bow and returned the box to the shelf of her closet.

Honor recognized the box instantly. It was the one she discovered in her mother's closet, still filled with Darcy's clothing.

Darcy interrupted Honor's thoughts to explain. "This is the

only proof I will ever have that for one night of my life, I was loved as a woman should be loved."

Honor's heart broke for Darcy as the familiar fog descended, pulling her away from this scene and into another. They were still in Darcy's hotel room, but now it was mid-morning.

Honor heard a loud commotion in the hallway and then Reginald banged through the door, coughing uncontrollably. He didn't notice Darcy was still in bed.

She rose quickly to help her husband unload his fishing gear and valise, while listening to him recount the adventures of his trip.

"Damned fine fishing, but sleeping on the boat in the damp air got to me. Feel my head and tell me if I have a fever. And you best lay out my bedclothes."

When Darcy put her hand to Reginald's forehead, he finally noticed that she was still wearing her own bedclothes. He knit his eyebrows together, surprised.

"You were awake, weren't you?" Without waiting for her to respond, he continued, "Getting a bit lazy while I was away? Never mind. Just get dressed and get me a hot toddy. Did I tell you I caught a monster of a fish the first day out? We feasted like kings! It's getting harder to keep up with the young bucks, though."

When Reginald changed into his nightshirt, Darcy couldn't help comparing his physique to Rory's. Consumed with guilt, she shifted her gaze to the floor.

Reginald experienced another coughing fit and when it finally ended, he moaned, "I want to sleep a while, so I need you to keep the hotel staff at bay. Come on, Darcy. Move along and get me something to soothe my throat. Can't you see I'm in pain, woman?"

It was obvious to Darcy that her husband had already been drinking something much stronger than a hot toddy today. She assumed he had been using whiskey to soothe his throat and was certain he would be asleep long before she returned with a warm drink from the kitchen. Nonetheless, she dressed and went to fetch it for him.

"Just as well," she whispered to Honor. "Sitting quietly at his bedside will give me some much-needed time to think."

Memories of the next few weeks passed by in seconds. Honor was aware Reginald continued to suffer with a severe cold and that Darcy stayed indoors, caring for him. She left Reginald's side only long enough to bring him soup and whiskey-laden tonics to help him sleep.

While sitting in a chair by his bed, pretending to read her book, Darcy daydreamed about Rory. She replayed their illicit evening together over and over in her mind, wanting to remember every detail, despite the fact that she was literally sick to her stomach with guilt for having been untrue to her marriage vows.

Sometimes she pretended that she and Rory were happily married, but her fantasies were usually interrupted by Reginald's coughing and swearing, and his demands for her attention. Each time Darcy was jarred back to reality, her heart ached anew.

Unfortunately, as Reginald's health began to improve, Darcy's own well-being seemed to take a turn for the worse. Soon it was she who was in bed, sick.

Reginald, afraid of becoming re-infected, stayed out of their room and away from Darcy as much as possible. He spent his days hunting and fishing, and whiled away his evenings sipping whiskey, smoking cigars and playing cards with the other gentlemen guests of the hotel.

When Reginald returned to their room each night, the smell of whiskey and tobacco would sour Darcy's stomach, but she faithfully helped him to bed, secretly happy that he was afraid to get too close to her.

By Thanksgiving, Darcy was over her cold, but since she'd had no appetite for weeks, her eyes had grown dull and her face gaunt. Honor sat on the side of her bed, sensing her overwhelming sadness. Watching her spiral deeper into depression was unbearable. Finally Honor didn't care if talking would result in leaving this awful memory. She leaned close and whispered, "Darcy, don't give up hope. Reginald is so much older than you; it is certain you will be a widow one day. Then you can leave New York with Rory and start over somewhere far away from there."

Darcy was so deeply immersed in misery that not even Honor's words seemed to faze her. She cried, "I'll never have that opportunity. My days are severely numbered, even as we speak. My sinful deeds will soon be known to all."

With tears in her hollow green eyes, she stared right through Honor. "I am carrying Rory's child in my belly."

Honor was shocked at the revelation. She didn't have any words to offer that would help Darcy...not in the Victorian society in which she lived. Suddenly, Honor remembered that Margaret Plant said she helped Darcy on her darkest day. Could the dark day in question be the one when Darcy's pregnancy became known?

Honor wondered if she should risk speaking again, but before she could decide, she was distracted by a bell tolling in the background. The sound seemed to be growing steadily louder. Honor was engulfed in fog and woke in her own bed.

Chapter 30

It was Josh's cell phone. They had overslept and James was calling, reminding Josh they were supposed to meet him at her mother's house fifteen minutes ago. Josh sprang from bed, brushing his teeth and dressing at breakneck speeds.

Groggily, Honor organized a mental checklist. "Take the house key. You guys get started and I'll join you in a little while, after I call James' attorney to schedule an appointment. I can get Cody dressed and fed and bring him with me, if you move his car-seat into my rental car."

"Sounds like a plan, but how about I just take your car and leave you my truck?" Josh stopped, sensing something was wrong. "Is everything alright?"

"Last night's trip into the spirit world was, um... troubling. But it's too long a story to tell with James waiting for you."

Josh sat down by her. "He can wait if you need to talk."

Honor smiled at the sweet gesture. "Don't be silly. I'm fine. We'll catch-up later."

Josh stood. "Okay, if you're sure."

"I'm sure."

With that, Josh grabbed her keys from beside his, gave her a quick kiss goodbye, and dashed out the door.

Honor laid back on her pillows, thinking about Darcy's predicament and wondering what she was supposed to learn from all this. She thought she had solved the mystery of her association with Darcy. After all, she and Darcy had both fallen in love after they had been married to someone else. So why was Darcy's spirit continuing to visit her, sharing such private and painful memories?

Honor drifted back to sleep, and was thrilled to find the older versions of both Margaret and Darcy sitting at the parlor table in her room. Excited to learn the answers to her questions, Honor sat down with them.

Sadly, Margaret was just about to speak when Cody started waking up. As Honor fell back through the fog into her own bed again, she heard Margaret say, "You are only beginning to learn what you need to know. Be patient."

Moments later, Cody was at her bedside, complaining about the cold. She oriented herself as quickly as possible, then reached down and grabbed him, pulling him under her covers while tickling him, making him squeal with delight.

"Tickling should warm you up! Let me know when you're warm and I'll stop!"

"I'm warm! I'm warm!" he howled.

She hugged him as he calmed down. "Your Daddy is already at my mom's house with Uncle James, and we're going to meet them there after breakfast."

"I want pancakes," Cody announced, without missing a beat.

Honor tickled him again. "You're going to turn into a pancake if you're not careful!"

Honor dressed Cody in Spiderman-adorned clothes, from his underwear to his tee-shirt. "Who taught you so much about Spiderman?"

"I don't know," he replied absently.

Honor decided to pursue the question from a different angle. "I thought your mommy, Amy, taught you about using spider webs to keep the bad dreams away when you slept."

"Uh-huh... ghosts can't bother me under a web."

Honor continued to gently pry. "What else does your mommy say?"

"She can't move to Florida, but she said I shouldn't be sad because she'll keep watching over me from heaven." After a moment, he added wistfully, "but I don't think she'll be able to sing me Happy Birthday from there."

Without a moment's hesitation, Honor promised, "If she can't, then I'll sing it to you twice, Cody. Once from me and once from her."

Cody brightened. "Two Happy Birthdays...one from Mommy Amy and one from Mommy Honor." Honor was startled to hear him call her *Mommy*, but she liked the sound of it.

The new "Mommy" title was still fresh in her mind when the waitress asked what her *son* would like for breakfast. Cody grinned when she winked at him. "He'll have pancakes," she said.

***

By the time Honor and Cody arrived at her mother's house, the two men had nearly finished their survey of home repair recommendations.

Cody ran to Josh, shouting, "Daddy, did you know Honor can drive your truck?"

Josh reached down for his son. "Well, good morning to you, too! Do you think Honor drives as good as Daddy?"

"Yeah," Cody replied.

Josh started to tickle him. "What? Are you sure about that?"

Cody squealed with laughter. "No! You drive better!"

Josh set the still-laughing child back on his feet. "That's more like it." Then he held his hand up in a tickle-threatening claw at Honor. "And what about you? Who do you think drives better?"

Honor grabbed his hand and kissed him hello. "Why don't we call it a tie?"

"Sure... use your womanly wiles on me to win the argument, see if I care." Josh pulled her close and kissed her again; more deeply.

James turned to Cody. "Are they always so mushy?"

"Yep... all the time," Cody frowned, shaking his head.

James joined in, shaking his head in mock disgust.

Turning back to the couple, James got down to business. "Honor, my brother was right. This home is a beauty, but it does need some work."

He and Josh walked her through the house to show her their repair and remodeling recommendations. Honor was impressed with how much Josh knew about vintage home restoration. Some of the rooms just required a fresh coat of paint, but the kitchen and bathrooms called for major renovations. Also, the wood floors needed to be refinished, the pool deck would have to be replaced and the entire yard required landscaping.

Just as they finished their summary, Sarah Jacobs returned Honor's phone call. In her message earlier that morning, Honor had requested that Sarah contact Leon Goldstein on her behalf.

Sarah wasted little time on pleasantries. "Leon's sending me copies of all relevant documents via overnight mail, but in the meantime, he faxed me the corporation structure summary and your non-compete agreement." She paused. "I'm sorry to have to tell you this, Honor, but from what I've read so far, the structure of your corporation is so biased in favor of your ex-husband, that Leon should have been ashamed of himself for allowing you to participate in the process without legal representation. Frankly, the terms of your non-compete agreement are some of the most onerous I've ever read."

Honor's heart sank.

Having delivered the worst of the news, Sarah softened. "This is serious, but I don't want you to become disheartened. When corporate paperwork is so obviously full of ill-intent, it can actually be easier to get a judge to side with the plaintiff than when the wording is more or less evenly weighted. I need some time to study the detailed documents when they arrive, but would you be available to meet with me later this week?"

Numbly, Honor agreed, the reality of her situation finally beginning to sink in. She hung up and told Josh and James about Sarah's findings.

Josh hugged her close. "I know things look bad right now, but I'm sure everything will work out."

"My brother's right. If anyone can find a way out of a contract dispute, it's Sarah," James encouraged.

Determined to shake off her increasing sense of dread with regard to Soft Fix, Honor nodded and changed the subject. "About the renovation; I know all the Js are in the construction business, but I'm not sure who does what. I mean, do they handle all the types of work I need to have done?"

"James, you know more about what everyone does than I do... you tell her."

James nodded and began, "Well, you already know that Josh and I are general contractors, but where I specialize in new construction and additions, Josh here prefers renovating old houses. Personally, that kind of work makes me crazy, because you never know what kind of damage you're going to find when you open up an old wall." He nodded at his brother. "But Josh has a real knack for being able to tell if the basic structure of a house is solid or not."

Josh smiled at the compliment.

"I'm the oldest of the Js, named after my Dad. The second oldest, John, is an architect. Like Josh, he prefers restoring historic homes and buildings. You can bet he's going to want to work on this project! He's really good, but you can't tell him that, because his head is big enough already." He and Josh shared a brotherly laugh.

"Next in line is Jacob. He handles landscaping, outdoor lighting and installs pavers." James turned to Josh. "Everyone wants paved driveways and decorative retention walls these days. Jacob says pavers account for over half of his work this year."

Josh raised his eyebrows. "You know, I've seen a lot of

paving work since I've been back in town, but I had no idea the industry has grown that much."

Honor interrupted. "Before you go off on a tangent, who's next in line?"

"Okay, let's see...where was I? Oh yeah, next are Jeff and Jeremy, the twins. They're in business together. They build swimming pools, decks, and irrigation systems." He turned to Josh. "I swear those boys are happiest when they're hip deep in dirt, installing a job."

Josh nodded. "You know, it makes sense, given the way they kept their room when we were growing up."

"You're right!" James chuckled. "Anyway, next is Jesse, who's a plumber, and then Jerrod, who's an amazing electrician." Again, he turned to Josh. "You should see the automated theater room he just designed for an estate in Indian Rocks."

"Sounds interesting."

"It's spectacular. Remind me to tell you about it later." Shifting his attention back to Honor, James continued, "Next in line is Justin, who, like the twins, prefers to work outside. He specializes in gutter system and screened enclosure installations, but he also does rescreening work...especially after an active hurricane season. A few years ago, he formed a partnership with a contractor who installs emergency power generators. They dubbed themselves the *Storm Chasers*, since they get so much work after a good storm blows through." He grinned. "Oh yeah...I almost forgot. You'll love this, Josh... his partner's name is Joel Jenkins and they call him JJ!"

When their outburst of laughter subsided, James rubbed his chin, trying to remember where he left off. "Hmmm...let's see. Next there's Joseph, who's an independent framer and dry wall hanger. Then, of course, there's Josh here. He's the only one of us who ever left Florida. But, hallelujah, he finally figured out what a mistake he made and has agreed to move back here where he belongs! Finally, there's Jason, the baby of the family. He does concrete foundation and block work. And that's it...that's all the Js."

Puzzled, Honor studied Josh. Why didn't he tell James that he decided to move to Chicago? And why was he avoiding making eye contact with her? Then she understood. It was simple. He had changed his mind. Not that she could blame him. After all, why wouldn't he want to live close to his wonderful family? It would be good for Cody, and Josh could work year-round in this weather. Still, she was reeling. His decision meant she would soon be returning to Chicago alone. Their relationship had just been a vacation fling after all.

Chapter 31

Honor could hear Josh and James talking about bringing their brothers over to check out the house, but she had retreated into her painful, private thoughts and was no longer listening.

Josh tried to put his arm around her shoulders, but she pulled away; accusations shooting from her eyes. How could he have led her on this way -- letting her think they had a future together? Her eyes fell on Cody and she felt as though someone was twisting a knife in her chest. She wasn't going to be his mommy after all. When would she ever learn? First she trusted William with her life's savings and then she trusted Josh with her heart. How would she survive another loss? She needed to get away to clear her head. Right now.

"You know what?" she stammered. "I totally forgot that I have to do some work back at the hotel. One of my clients has a software design problem. Um, I should have handled it before I left. Tell you what... you guys stay here and finish what you're doing and I'll catch up with you later, okay?"

It was an obvious lie. James glanced from Honor to Josh, not comprehending what had gone wrong so quickly.

Josh tried to hold her again, his eyes begging her to understand. Clearly, he was hurting, too, but Honor couldn't worry about him right now. It was all she could do to keep herself from falling apart. She turned and walked quickly toward the door, fighting back her tears.

Outside, she wrenched her car door open and flopped down into the driver's seat before realizing she was still holding the keys to Josh's truck, not her rental car. She cupped her face in her hands, shaking her head in despair. "Now what?" she moaned.

Honor was startled by the sound of Josh's tender voice outside her open window.

"Don't cry," he pleaded.

She looked up to find him holding her car key. Wordlessly she handed his keys through the window and made the exchange.

"Please don't go, Honor. I love you."

She clenched her jaw, silently fighting back the tears.

Josh continued. "It's not what you think. I just need a little time with my family. Construction will be shutting down for the winter in Chicago pretty soon, so I figured I would just stay here for the season. It's only a few months."

Without answering, she shakily inserted her key into the ignition and started the engine. The anguish on his face stabbed at her heart. "You should have told me," she muttered.

"I know... I was going to. I just couldn't find the right moment. I guess I was afraid you would misunderstand and I just made things worse. I'm so sorry, Honor. Please come back inside."

She shook her head. "I need a little space right now, Josh."

"You're upset with me. I get it. But I know that what we have -- the love I feel for you—it's the real thing, Honor. So, if staying in Florida for the winter means losing you, then I'm on the first flight to Chicago. Okay?"

Honor nodded, but didn't attempt to speak. She didn't know what to believe.

"Are you okay to drive?" he choked hoarsely.

"I'll be fine."

He nodded and took a step back from the car. "Can I call you tonight? Maybe we could go to dinner and talk? I could get a sitter for Cody."

Honor shook her head. "I don't know. I need some time alone. I'll call you later."

She put the car in reverse and backed out of the drive.

***

As soon as Honor stepped into the hotel, a sudden wave of exhaustion swept over her. Groggy, she opened the door of her suite and was both saddened and oddly comforted by the sight of Josh and Cody's things lying around. She lectured herself, "What the heck's the matter with you? Last night, you asked Josh to move in because you wanted to spend as much time with him as possible, and today you're ready to end your relationship. You make absolutely no sense at all. So what if he changed his mind about moving to Chicago. I mean, how dumb would it be to end things with him now, just because they might not last forever?"

Honor yawned, now barely able to keep her eyes open, let alone think coherently. The hotel staff hadn't serviced the suite yet, so she hung the 'Do Not Disturb' sign on her door and lay down on the bed, still rumpled from the night before. She held Josh's pillow to her face and breathed in his scent. "Now I understand why you kept those clothes in a hatbox, Darcy," she murmured, as sleep overtook her.

Honor floated peacefully in the fog, as if adrift in a stream. When the clouds parted, it took a moment for her to recognize the lobby of the Belleview Hotel. The air smelled of fresh paint and roses. In an alcove near the windows, a band entertained guests with a waltz, while eager hotel staff bustled through the crowd, serving drinks. A train whistle blew nearby, reminding Honor hotel guests often arrived in their private Pullman cars on the tracks just outside the hotel.

She marveled at the magnificent spectacle until she noticed Margaret Plant, standing in a receiving line near the door, talking to a middle-aged couple. Honor edged closer until she could hear the conversation. "I'm pleased we are finally wintering in a location that lives up to its advertisement," the woman said. Her husband agreed. "It's splendid to be among the first guests in what I'm sure will be a long and happy life for this establishment," he said.

It dawned on Honor that she was witnessing the grand opening of the hotel. Fascinated, she gawked at the lobby, amazed that many aspects of the room hadn't changed in over a century. Just then, Darcy and Reginald walked through the front door, clad in black, traveling clothes.

Reginald's proud demeanor as he entered the building with Darcy on his arm, told Honor he hadn't yet learned her dark secret. Darcy was still quite trim at three months pregnant, but Honor wondered how much longer she would be able to hide her growing belly from her husband.

Honor remembered reading that the hotel opened its doors on January 15, 1897. She was so excited to be witnessing this event first hand, she had to resist the urge to go exploring. Instead, she stood by Reginald and Darcy as they moved forward in the receiving line. When they reached Margaret, she extended her hand and Reginald lifted it for a perfunctory kiss.

Margaret smiled unenthusiastically. "Hello, cousin. I trust your journey across the Bay was without incident?"

"It was delightful, cousin. I must say, your husband has outdone himself with this newest venture of his. I feel as though only a few hours ago we were living in a castle in Tampa, and now a short boat and train ride later, I find myself in a Swiss chalet, but surrounded with sunshine instead of snow. Yes, indeed, your husband is to be commended. Well done, I say. You must be very proud of him."

Continuing to smile, Margaret withdrew her hand, but both Honor and Darcy recognized the contempt beneath the surface of her one-word response: "Quite."

Darcy curtsied politely. "Madam, with all due respect to your talented husband, I'm sure this exquisite décor reflects your decorating skills and wish, therefore, to congratulate you on a superb establishment."

Margaret softened. She nodded to Darcy with a sincere smile. "Thank you, Madam Darcy. Your observation is accurate. The Belleview has been a joint effort, requiring both my husband's talents and my own."

Oblivious he had offended his cousin, Reginald turned and strode toward the front desk register. Darcy glanced at Margaret apologetically, curtsied again and then started after her husband. Honor followed them, while attempting to take in the unfolding spectacle around her, as if watching a three ring circus.

Suddenly, Darcy stopped short. Honor followed her gaze across the room, instantly understanding her reaction. Rory Collins was standing next to a distinguished-looking gentleman. Several other men clustered around them, listening intently to a story the older man was telling. Honor wondered who could command such rapt attention from so many. She didn't have to wait long to find out.

Reginald rejoined Darcy, a bellman in tow. "Darcy, this good man will escort you to our suite, so you can begin getting us settled in for the winter. I'll be up directly, but first want to pay my respects to the great Sir Launcelot Cressy Servos."

In response to her quizzical expression, Reginald almost gushed with excitement, "He's a world-famous golf course architect and he's designing a nine-hole golf course right here at the Belleview Hotel. The course won't be finished until next year, but he's decided to open a few of the holes for this inaugural season."

Darcy avoided looking in Sir Servos' direction, for fear of catching Rory's eye. Struggling to keep her true emotions hidden, she forced a smile and managed to feign a calm appearance. "Take your time, sir. I will endeavor to have us settled by supper time." She turned and followed the bellman down the corridor, relieved to have escaped notice.

Honor glanced back at Rory Collins. It was instantly evident that Darcy had not gone unnoticed. The expression on Rory's face was the quintessential picture of desire, love and heartache.

Chapter 32

Just then, a thin layer of fog gathered around Honor, but she wasn't pulled from the scene. Instead, as she continued to watch the grand opening through the veil of mist, a voice began to fill her thoughts.

"Rory told me he wasn't able to keep his eyes off me from the moment I arrived."

The scene in the lobby blurred in the misty background and people moved as if in slow motion. Honor concentrated on the voice. It belonged to Darcy, but now she sounded like an old woman.

"He said he looked everywhere for me in the days and weeks after our night in the tent. Rory hoped I would make an excuse to see him; perhaps to take another golf lesson. He stood for hours beneath my balcony, hoping to catch a glimpse of me when I came out to enjoy the stars. But I never did. He said it was as if I had disappeared from the face of the earth."

Honor shook her head. If Reginald hadn't been so busy kowtowing to Sir Servos, he surely would have noticed Rory sneering at him with contempt.

At that moment, the fog thickened and engulfed Honor, pulling her away. When it dissipated, Honor was standing beside Darcy. She was holding her special hat box, while a maid busied herself unpacking the three steamer trunks. Darcy carefully stored her secret treasure in the closet, hoping the maid hadn't noticed she was unusually possessive with the box.

As soon as the two of them were alone in the closet, Darcy

spoke. "I anticipated crossing paths with Rory sometime during our stay at the Belleview, but I wasn't prepared for this event to occur so soon." Her hands were still shaking from the surprise encounter. "I haven't seen Rory since the night we made love by the river, but I constantly dream of running away with him; escaping this unhappy life forever."

Her confession was interrupted by a knock on the hotel room door. When the maid answered, Darcy froze at the sound of Rory's voice.

"I have a message for Mrs. Loughman and I am to wait for her reply."

"Very well. Wait there." The maid closed the door and brought the note to Darcy.

Darcy tried her best not to let her excitement show. With trembling fingers, she pulled the note from the envelope and read, *'Please join me on the south portico after dinner this evening, to discuss unfinished business. Respectfully yours, R.'*

Darcy walked to a nearby table, dipped a pen in ink and wrote, *'I will try. Warm regards, D.'* She slipped her response into the envelope and handed it to the maid, who in turn, cracked open the door and passed it back to Rory.

As the door closed, the familiar fog rolled in, but Honor had only a moment to be curious about the next memory. The mist cleared as abruptly as it had formed, leaving Honor dizzy and trying to focus in the darkness that now engulfed the hotel property. In the light of a gas lamp, she was able to make out Rory's figure standing still as a statue at the end of a winding path. Honor surmised it was the South Portico.

Darcy approached him and held out a nervous hand. Rory took it and bestowed a light kiss. The air between them was thick with desire, but they held their distance; each fearing the forbidden attraction.

Rory finally spoke. "Until tonight, I believed longing for you was the worst pain my heart could ever experience. But watching you walk through that door this evening on the arm of another man, looking even more beautiful than I remembered, well—that was agonizing."

"I understand. You see, I dread each sunrise because it means I have to leave you behind in my dreams and wake to the reality that I am married to another."

"Is that why you hid yourself from me? You regretted breaking your vows?"

"I have no regrets. Reginald was ill when he returned from his trip and by the time he was well, I myself had become indisposed. When my health finally returned, I summoned the courage to look for you, but you had already gone."

Rory's jaw dropped. "I left only because I believed you wished it so. I've spent weeks working for Sir Servos, hoping in vain to forget my love for you."

Darcy shook her head. "Whatever are we to do?"

"I watched your husband tonight, fawning over Sir Servos, intoxicated by his celebrity. Only a buffoon would choose to spend time with an old man over you. It's as if he's willing to exchange the diamond in his grasp for fool's gold." Rory's disgust was palpable. "A man who doesn't value his treasure doesn't deserve to keep it."

"Tonight I am glad Reginald is fascinated with Sir Servos. His desire to spend the evening playing cards with the gentleman is the reason I am able to be here with you."

"The card game was my doing," Rory confessed. "You see, Sir Servos and I have played cards almost every night since I arrived here. I suspected your husband wouldn't be able to resist an opportunity to spend time with the famous golfer, so I told Sir Servos I wanted to walk the new golf course to make sure it was ready for play. When I asked Reginald if he could take my place at the table, he became as giddy as a school girl." A sly smile played at the corners of Rory's mouth.

"Being with you makes me feel as giddy as a schoolgirl myself." Darcy glanced down and gently placed her hands around the small bulge on her abdomen. "Actually, we're both in high spirits."

"Both?" Rory's expression quickly changed from confusion to understanding.

The fog had begun collect, but just before Honor lost sight of the couple, they locked together in a tight embrace. She smiled at the young lovers, now certain the lesson Darcy was trying to teach her is that a brief separation doesn't necessarily signal the end of a relationship.

Memories started flashing in front of Honor in rapid sequence, reminding her of a strobe light. Rory and Darcy were meeting secretly at every opportunity, often hiding in one of the private rail cars, stored behind the hotel. When Reginald was traveling, Rory would sneak Darcy out through the servants' tunnels. A few times, she even dared to slip out while Reginald slept.

Finally the memories stopped whizzing by and Honor, feeling as though she had just disembarked a roller coaster, found herself in a Pullman car with Darcy and Rory.

Darcy was worried. "Reginald hasn't demanded his husbandly rights since we arrived in Florida, so my adultery is bound to soon be discovered."

"We'll be in California, living as husband and wife before that happens. But we haven't yet saved enough money for our journey. Sir Servos is fond of me and is recommending my golf lessons to all inquiring guests, so it shouldn't be too much longer now."

Darcy smiled and then laid an ivory brush, comb and mirror set on the table. "Here are some more of my belongings you can trade for pearls."

Local oyster shuckers were well-known for their bartering business, trading pearls for items of interest. Like gold, pearls could be used as alternate currency during their journey.

Rory admired the pieces. "These are beautiful. I promise to buy you new ones once we are settled in California." He reached into his pocket and pulled out a small, black velvet pouch. "Take this. Our savings will be safer in your keeping than on my person." Rory gave Darcy all the money he had earned, along with three pearls from previous bartering sessions.

The mist returned and once again, memories started flashing by. Each time Darcy returned to her room, she added precious funds to the velvet pouch, hidden in a small compartment at the bottom of her special hat box.

The next time the mist cleared to show Honor a full memory, it was dark and the couple was just inside one of the servant's tunnel entrances, concealing Darcy's identity beneath a long, black hooded cloak.

"Our blissful time together evaporates so quickly," Darcy lamented.

Just then, one of the hotel workers entered the tunnel. Darcy quickly looked away, covering her face with a gloved hand. The man gave Rory a knowing wink and a smile, assuming he was sneaking a prostitute in for one of the gentlemen guests. Rory nodded in conspiratorial agreement.

When the man was out of earshot, Rory muttered, "I detest sneaking around like this."

"I, too, hate the lies, but soon this life will be behind us."

Rory nodded. "And we'll never have to say goodbye again."

They shared a tender kiss and moved down the dark corridor to a worn wooden staircase, lit by a single bare bulb protruding from the wall. When they reached the third floor, Rory removed the cloak and Darcy slipped into the hallway near her room.

Honor could feel Darcy's heart racing as she opened the door, even though Reginald's snores could have concealed the sound of a trumpeting elephant entering the room. Thankful there was a door between their sleeping chambers, Darcy quickly drifted off to sleep, dreaming of California.

Chapter 33

She woke to the sound of Reginald's morning coughing binge and rose to help him prepare for his day. He announced, "One of the lads is taking me hunting for an alligator this morning."

Darcy gasped.

"Don't worry. We'll have guns, so it won't be any more dangerous than joining you and the other ladies for tea."

"I doubt that. Our most dangerous activity is needlepoint."

Reginald chuckled and left the room in good humor.

After a nap, Darcy strolled down for her daily ritual - tea with the ladies. A terrible storm was brewing, so they met on the west porch instead of the south garden. She took a seat, absently listening to Cora Austen read from a novel about the Civil War.

Suddenly, a bolt of lightning split the sky right overhead, followed immediately by a loud clap of thunder. A few ladies squealed with fright and moved their chairs away from the edge of the porch as the rain began to pelt down.

"Have you noticed how fast the weather changes in Florida?" Cora commented. "This morning the sky was bright blue and the sun was shining, but you would never know it by looking at it now. And the truly amazing thing is that it will probably be perfectly clear again this evening!"

Darcy and the other ladies nodded in agreement, continuing to watch the storm from the safety of the large porch. Cora resumed reading from the novel.

Darcy was daydreaming, unaware how long she had been watching the rain, when one of the ladies' husbands, whose name she could not remember, walked out onto the porch to address his wife and the other members of the group.

"I'm afraid I have troubling news. A short while ago, a bolt of lightning struck out on the golf course, killing a man and giving General Peterson the scare of his life."

Several ladies gasped and the man's wife gushed, "Do tell! What happened?"

Feeling quite important to be sharing news that commanded the rapt attention of every lady on the porch, the short, stout man continued with his story. "I hope I don't upset your gentle sensibilities with my recounting of this event, but apparently, the General had hoped the storm would hold off until he was able to play a bit of golf, so he had headed out with the golf instructor."

Terrified, Honor turned to face Darcy, who was barely breathing. She felt Darcy's blood run cold. Darcy could hear her heart beating so loudly, she was worried the other women would hear it as well.

Not Rory, Darcy prayed silently. *Please God, not Rory!* Desperately, she waited for the man to announce who had been killed.

The man continued, dragging out the details of the story for effect. "The General said the rain was just beginning to come down and they were thinking about quitting, but he wanted to play one more hole before retiring to the hotel. The instructor was giving the General some pointers on the tee box, demonstrating the arc the golf club should take, and just when the club was high above his head --"

The pudgy man demonstrated a golf swing using an imaginary club to create a more vivid picture of the event for his audience before finishing with a flourish. "A bolt of lightning hit the club and killed the boy instantly."

The man paused dramatically and then added, "Thank God, the General was standing a bit away, so as to observe the motion of the club, or he might have been killed as well. He said he was standing near enough to the unfortunate Collins fellow, that the electrical charge caused every hair on his body to stand on end! "

Darcy was afraid she was going to begin screaming and wouldn't be able to stop. She could hear blood rushing in her ears and felt faint. Honor had no idea what to do for her.

Elizabeth Grant speculated, "Why, I myself took a golf lesson earlier this week with Mr. Collins. But for the grace of God, I could have been the one that was with him today."

Cora replied, "But Elizabeth, unlike those men, you would have had the sense to come in out of the rain before the lightning began!"

The irreverent remark broke the somber mood and the ladies began to giggle. Even the man had to shake his jowls and smile at the macabre joke before concluding his story.

"Fortunately, Collins wasn't a family man, so at least there is no widow or orphans to worry about." He casually consulted his pocket watch. "I best rejoin the men in the library now. You ladies have a nice day and let this be a lesson. Stay indoors whenever you see lightning on the horizon."

Darcy felt as though she was floating outside of her body. Surely this was just a bad dream and she would wake at any moment.

In the distance, someone said, "Goodness, you just never know when you're living the last day of your life. I had an acquaintance in St. Louis who died a few years ago when a horse suddenly bucked with no warning, throwing him to the ground right on top of a stone. He died instantly, leaving a wife and five small children to fend for themselves."

A few of the women clucked and shook their heads with empathy; then began telling other stories about close encounters with death.

Darcy stared at her hands, her mind racing. She was afraid to meet anyone's gaze, for fear they would see the truth in her eyes. All at once, she felt a woman's strong arm on her elbow, guiding her to her feet and towards the door.

It was Margaret Plant. "There now, Mrs. Loughman. I think this dreadful weather and shocking news might have been a bit much for you. You seem to be suffering from a touch of the vapors. Let's go inside. Ladies, if you will excuse us...."

The morbid conversation barely missed a beat as Margaret and Darcy made their exit. Darcy was somewhat aware of the conversation fading away as they walked down one of the long corridors of the hotel. Honor cried as they walked, experiencing the same indescribable pain that Darcy was feeling.

Once they were safely tucked away in a quiet corner, Margaret began, "There now, Mrs. Loughman. No good would come from those ladies learning how familiar you were with the dead golf instructor, now would it?"

Darcy stared at Margaret incredulously, still trying to comprehend the events of the morning. She fumbled, unable to form a complete sentence. "How... When... Pardon me?"

Margaret shrugged. "I know many things. Now tell me... how big is the tangle in your ball of yarn? I can help you straighten it out, but I need to know everything." She paused. "Do you want my help?"

"Yes," choked Darcy, as the first of her alligator tears began to fall. "I loved him so. We were going away to be a family. We were leaving in a few weeks, before my belly begins to swell." She looked at her stomach and then raised her horror-filled eyes to meet Margaret's; the reality of her plight finally beginning to sink in.

When Honor felt herself falling into the fog and leaving this memory, she finally began to voice her horror, "No, no! Not now! Please no! This can't happen!"

She woke to the sound of someone pounding on her door. Fighting to orient herself, she realized Josh was calling out to her. She sprang from the bed and yanked the door open.

Josh's face was contorted by fright, but Honor was unable

to speak about what she had just witnessed. She fell into his arms, sobbing so hard she could barely catch her breath. Josh held her tight as he stepped inside.

The room was so cold that Josh thought he might actually be able to see his breath. Without letting go of his grip on Honor, he kicked the door closed and pulled her over to the bed. He wrapped the down comforter around her shoulders and sat rocking her, letting her cry until she was finally able to gain enough control over her emotions to tell him what had happened.

When she finished, Josh gave one of his low whistles and tried to comfort her. "I know it was horrible, but remember -- all those things happened over a century ago." He stopped short when the look on her face told him that for her, no time had passed at all. Just a few minutes ago, she witnessed the death of a man and the heartbreak of a woman in the year 1897. Honor's connection with Darcy was so strong now that she felt Darcy's agonizing pain as if it were her own.

Honor closed her eyes and rested against Josh's strong shoulder. "The more I discover about Darcy, the less I understand what I'm supposed to learn from her." She thought for a moment. "Maybe she's trying to teach me that you never know how much time you have with the person you love, so you'd better treasure every moment."

Josh kissed the top of her head tenderly. "Hard teacher, but good lesson."

Chapter 34

Honor was surprised to learn that she had slept for only a few hours. It didn't seem possible that she had seen so much of Darcy's life in such a short time. Once she was calm and the room had warmed up, Josh ventured, "I suppose you're wondering why I was at your door when you woke up."

"I'm glad you were there, but yes, the thought did cross my mind."

"I know I was supposed to wait for you to call me, but after you left your Mom's house, I told James why you were upset and then I sort of spilled my guts to him about everything. He made me realize how much I stood to lose if you decided to end our relationship. He offered to watch Cody for a while, so I could come over and talk things out with you."

"And here you are."

"Yep. And here I am."

"Okay... talk."

"Well, the most important thing I want to tell you is that I haven't changed my mind about us. I just figured you've got a lot to do when you get back to Chicago, so instead of being underfoot, Cody and I could stay here with my family and I could oversee the renovations on your Mom's house." He bit his lip. "James said I was stupid to tell him my plans before talking them over with you. I'm really sorry about that. This is new to me, but I'm learning. So, if you need me to go to Chicago with you, I'm there."

Honor considered his apology. "I was hurt when I learned you changed your plans. I mean, Chicago would be easier if I knew I was coming home to you every night, but you're right. We need to take things more slowly and have faith everything will work out."

Josh nodded and smiled hopefully. "So, we're okay then? We've made it through our first fight unscathed?"

Honor returned his smile. "Yeah... we're okay for now, but you better stay on your toes. You never know how many gorgeous guys are out there, secretly hoping to meet a divorcee who's being haunted."

Josh laughed. "Sure, but how many of those guys can offer you a huge, instant family like Cody and the Js?"

"Yeah, I guess that does make you special."

Josh chuckled, but then his smile faded. "It scared the hell out of me when I came to the door and heard you screaming."

Honor shuddered, remembering Darcy's agony. "I'm sorry I scared you. But can you imagine the pain she was going through; hearing the man she love died and not even being able to react to the news? It was horrible. And it made me realize no one knows how many precious moments they'll get." Honor paused. "Do we have enough time to move the rest of your things into my suite before we go back and pick up Cody?"

Josh whooped, "Oh yeah... we'll make time for that!"

***

After settling in and notifying the front desk of the change, they drove back to her mother's house to rejoin James and Cody.

James was reviewing paperwork in the kitchen, while Cody watched a DVD in the living room. When Cody spied them walking through the door, he ran to them, hugging first his father and then Honor. "I'm glad you're back. We were so worried about you!"

Josh glanced at James, his eyebrows raised in an unspoken question.

James put up his hands and shook his head. "Don't look at

me. I didn't say anything. He came up with that all on his own." Then he teased, "I actually thought you might be gone a while longer, but I guess some of us take more time making up with their women than others." He smiled at Honor. "You were too easy on him... you should have made him suffer a while longer. Otherwise, he'll think he can get away with anything."

She giggled. "Thanks, coach... I'll remember that next time."

With mock panic, Josh gasped, "Next time? You really think there's going to be a next time?"

When their laughter died down, James told them he had been working on a few ideas for the remodel and thought he had come up with a way to add some modern features to the kitchen without losing its antique charm.

While the brothers huddled over the new sketches at the kitchen counter, Cody pulled Honor with him into the living room. His coloring materials were scattered on the floor in front of the DVD player. He picked up his latest drawing and showed it to her. Honor couldn't make it out, so he patiently explained it was a picture of her, sleeping in bed with a web above her. "I colored you safe so you don't have to be scared when you sleep anymore."

Honor marveled over the boy's intuition. "Thanks, Cody. This is beautiful. It's definitely refrigerator quality artwork."

They showed the drawing to Josh and James, who were duly impressed, and then Honor proceeded to tape it to the refrigerator.

"Grandma says you need to stop worrying so much," Cody admonished Honor.

James had already turned his attention back to his design sketches, but Josh overheard Cody's comment and stared at his son in disbelief. Honor shook her head at Josh, signaling him to stay quiet.

She smiled at the boy. "She said that, did she? Well, I guess she's right. It isn't good to worry too much. Did she say anything else, Cody?"

Cody thought about it. "She said she's going away soon."

Josh remained stone quiet, listening intently, as Honor questioned, "She's going away?"

Cody nodded. "Yep, but she said not to be sad because she's like a snowman."

Honor wasn't sure she had heard him correctly. "A snowman?"

"Uh-huh. She's gonna melt, but she won't really be gone because snowmen melt into water, and water makes carrots grow and then when it snows, you use the carrot to make a nose on a new snowman and everything just keeps on going."

Josh glanced at James, who was still absorbed in his work and completely oblivious to the conversation. He returned his attention to his son.

"Anything else?" Honor asked.

"Nope," Cody shrugged. "But I'm hungry!"

Honor laughed. "You know, I'm hungry, too. How about you guys?"

She caught Josh's attention and mouthed the word, "later."

He nodded his understanding.

James looked at his watch, surprised to find the day had evaporated so quickly. "Wow...nothing for me, thanks. I have to get home. James Junior has tee-ball tonight and I don't want to miss it. You guys want to come?"

Josh answered for the three of them. "Maybe next time."

"Okay, but you don't know what you're missing! Those games are a riot." James picked up his sketches. "I'll take these over to John in the morning to get his architectural input."

"That would be great. Thanks." Josh bumped his shoulder against James in what passed for a hug goodbye. "Have fun at JJ's game."

Once James left, Honor suggested, "Why don't go we to Clearwater Beach for dinner? There's a little place I know called Frenchy's and I have been dying for one of their grouper sandwiches."

Cody put out his lip and pouted. "I don't like grouper!" Then he turned to Josh and asked, "What's grouper?"

Josh laughed. "You don't know what it is but you're still sure you don't like it? Don't worry about it, buddy. I'll bet they have fried shrimp for you little guys."

"They sure do," Honor agreed, "and they have fried Oreos, too."

Now it was Josh's turn to ask, "What's a fried Oreo?"

Honor grinned. "About a billion calories - and worth every one of them! Trust me, you'll both love this place."

***

They decided to take in a Clearwater Beach sunset before dinner. Honor and Josh sat on an abandoned cabana bench, pulled off their shoes and let their toes play in the bone white sugar sand, while Cody ran down to the shallow water's edge to play. Mesmerized, they gazed at the horizon, enjoying the salty breeze as the sun turned into an orange ball, painting the sky with streaks of pink and purple.

Josh noticed Cody was talking to himself.

"He's not just pretending someone's there, is he?"

Honor shook her head.

"It's not an imaginary playmate. He's talking to a real somebody that I just can't see." Josh watched his son closely, then asked, "Can you see spirits when you're awake like he can?"

"No, but there was that time in the closet. I mean, I didn't see anyone, but I heard a voice. And even though I haven't actually seen or heard my mom, I sometimes feel her presence when I'm at her house." Honor buried her toes in the sand. "Don't forget, this is all new to me, too."

"Yeah, but you know more than I do, and I want to learn."

"Well, according to Margaret, sensitive children can see lots of spirits, but adults usually block them out unless the spirits share a bloodline, or they experienced similar life-altering events. Even then, adults have to be asleep before a spirit can connect long enough to share an important memory. Margaret says spirits hope the living can benefit from their experiences."

Honor frowned. "But so far, I don't know what connection I have with Margaret or Darcy, let alone what they're trying to teach me. It's so frustrating! Sometimes I want to go to sleep and not wake up until I figure everything out, but other times I'm sort of afraid of what I might learn."

Josh listened while keeping an eye on Cody. He nodded at Honor to let her know he understood her quandary; then turned and called out, "Stay out of the water, Cody. Don't get your clothes wet!" Without missing a beat, he returned his attention to Honor. "Why don't you just ask them to answer your questions?"

Honor smiled, admiring Josh's ability to pay attention to her and Cody at the same time. "It doesn't work that way. To share a memory, the spirits first have to pull as much energy from the environment as possible and then focus really hard. If I talk, it shatters their concentration and the memory is lost."

Josh nodded thoughtfully. "So that's why it's always so cold when they're around... they absorb all the heat energy from the room!"

Honor nodded. "I think that's exactly right."

"Well, they better hurry up or you'll have to go back to Chicago without learning what they want to teach you."

Honor winced at the reminder. Soon, she would be miles and miles away from Josh and Cody. She changed the subject.

"Look... the sun is just about gone. Watch very carefully and we might get lucky enough to see a green flash for a second just before it disappears."

Although the sunset was beautiful and the purple afterglow sky was exquisite, there was no green flash. While they were collecting Cody and their belongings, Josh commented, "I think the whole green flash thing is just a myth."

"No it's not. I've seen it," Honor insisted.

"First you get me to believe in spirits and now a green flash? What's next?" Josh teased.

Chapter 35

When it was evident Josh thoroughly enjoyed his grouper sandwich, Honor joked, "Thank goodness! Frenchy's Cafe has been one of my favorite restaurants since I was a little girl. If you didn't like it, I'm afraid I would have been forced to dump you."

Wide-eyed, Cody exclaimed, "I like Frenchy's too, Honor... so you don't have to dump me, either!"

Honor grinned, watching the two of them share the last bite of a fried Oreo and memorizing this perfect moment. She couldn't remember ever being this content.

Later that night, after they tucked Cody in, Honor and Josh lay in her bed, talking softly.

Honor tried to downplay her grave concerns about her business. "I have an appointment with that attorney, Sarah Jacobs, tomorrow. I'm sure she'll be able to straighten out this situation with William."

Josh saw through her phony optimism. "Honor, no matter what happens, I sincerely believe you'll land on your feet."

"You're right. If William takes Soft Fix from me, I'll just start another software business down the street."

Josh had been cuddling against her comfortably as they talked, but now he slid his hand down and pulled up her pajama top, sucking her nipple into his mouth.

She took a sharp breath, melting into the sensation. "So... you're... changing the subject then?" she moaned.

"Yep." He rolled on top of her, kissing away any further conversation.

A few minutes later, Josh suddenly stopped; his body rigid.

"Damn. We can't do this. I don't have any protection."

Her voice thick with passion, Honor whispered, "It's okay."

He pulled back slightly, searching her eyes. "Are you sure?"

She nodded and slid her fingers around his penis, moving him into place between her legs. He needed no further encouragement. Hungry for her, Josh plunged himself into her welcoming body, moaning at the sensation of his bare skin rubbing against her wet, velvety core.

Honor gritted her teeth, forcing herself to stay quiet so as not to wake Cody, but exercising this restraint was difficult. Her body writhed beneath him, as if using movement instead of words to express herself. Her hips bucked up against him, trying to take him into to her as deeply as possible.

Honor knew her rapid movements would make it difficult for Josh to last much longer, but she took guilty pleasure in his erotic agony. With every push, he took her soaring to heights her body had never experienced with other men. Finally embracing an overwhelming desire to feel him come inside of her, Honor arched her back and tensed her pelvic muscles. "Now!" she hissed through her clenched jaw.

Josh didn't hesitate. He tossed his head back as he released; a small cry escaping his lips with his final exploding thrusts. Then he collapsed on top of her, shaking with exhaustion.

They clung tightly to one another until their breathing slowly returned to normal.

"I love you," Josh whispered. He rolled to her side and pawed lazily at her, pulling her up to rest against his shoulder. He was clearly worn out and ready for sleep.

"Does this mean you're changing the subject again?" Honor teased.

He chuckled without opening his eyes. "Nobody likes a smart ass."

Honor propped herself up on an elbow. "Well, as long as we're changing the subject, what would you think about me buying out my sisters' shares of my mom's house so that we can renovate it together?"

Josh rallied, pleasantly surprised by the suggestion. "I'd like that a lot."

They began discussing remodeling possibilities, but soon their conversation slowed and they drifted off to sleep.

The temperature dropped. Realizing she was heading for the spirit realm, Honor wondered who she was going to encounter. More relaxed with the process now, she allowed herself to float through the fog. Drifting into memories still made her feel nauseous, but not as much as when she tried to resist the swirling mist.

When the fog cleared, she was sitting beside Darcy on the bed of an unfamiliar room in the Belleview Hotel. Margaret sat opposite them on a chair, engrossed in conversation with Darcy. Neither of the ladies acknowledged Honor's arrival.

"Darcy, you have to face some very unpleasant truths. Reginald is my mother's cousin and I know he fancies himself as an aristocrat. If he learns you're pregnant with another man's baby, he'll likely banish you without a second thought."

Darcy flinched, pain and guilt etched upon her face.

Margaret softened. "I know these harsh words compound the incomprehensible tragedy that has befallen you. But we must make a plan and do it quickly. If Reginald discovers your secret, you will lose all means of support and your family name will be ruined. You would have no one to care for you in your delicate condition, let alone harbor a bastard infant."

Margaret paused, allowing the gravity of her situation to sink in. "You must know that you cannot keep the baby."

Honor's jaw dropped. Darcy's eyes flew open wide as though she had been kicked in the stomach, but she did not protest. She knew Margaret spoke the truth.

Darcy's voice was choked with desperation. "I cannot abide letting the child come to any harm, even if it ruins me. The babe is the only proof that Rory Collins lived and that he loved me."

Margaret nodded her consent. "Agreed. Your child will live a good life. We will see to it. But it can never know that you are its mother."

Darcy gave Margaret a stiff nod.

With the grim understanding in place, Margaret began laying out a plan for Darcy and her unborn child.

"The first thing we must attend to is concealing your belly for the rest of the winter season. We'll start by making some petticoats that are full on the sides and in the back, but flat in front, to give the illusion of proportion. Also, you'll take to wearing a muff tied around your waist. I'll make a point of telling you how much I like the fashion when we are amongst the other ladies. I'll even wear a muff myself on occasion."

Margaret laughed ruefully. "I have no doubt the rest of the ladies will start wearing muffs shortly after we begin. In fact, I won't be the least bit surprised if muffs become the fashion rage by the end of the season."

Darcy managed a weak smile.

"The next part of our plan requires us to convince everyone we have become fast friends. The Plant name is respected in the highest levels of society, so Reginald will be thrilled by our association. I'll meet with him and offer to take you under my wing as my protégé. I'm already scheduled to voyage to Europe at the conclusion of the winter season, so I'll invite you to be my traveling companion. Then I'll spend the spring and summer collecting artwork for the Belleview Hotel, while you rest. By mid-summer, you'll give birth in Europe and return to your husband shortly thereafter with your reputation intact."

Darcy listened in awe as Margaret laid out the plan; then addressed the obvious omission.

"And what of the infant?"

"We have a few choices available to us. The simplest plan is to bundle the child in a basket along with a donation and leave it on the steps of a church, thereby tasking the clergy to find a home for it."

Honor was certain Margaret had used this plan successfully several times in her former life, but Darcy's response was instantaneous and non-negotiable. "This child is a precious gift. It is Rory's legacy. Abandoning it is not an option."

"As you wish. I suppose I can find a family in Europe that would be willing to raise the child as their own - for a fee. They would never see you, so your identity would be protected. Once it's grown, you might even make its acquaintance—albeit, anonymously."

Numb, Darcy nodded her agreement. "Yes, it would be a comfort to know what becomes of the child."

Honor felt tremendous pity for Darcy, but before she had much time to dwell on her sad state of affairs, the fog folded around her.

When the clouds parted, she saw Reginald and Darcy sitting at a garden table together. Honor drifted into a chair next to Darcy.

Reginald read a newspaper while Darcy stitched needlepoint in her lap. From time to time, Reginald would read a brief passage out loud from paper, adding his dole commentary about the item. Darcy feigned interest, but was clearly suffering through the visit.

Honor was just beginning to wonder why she had been brought to this mundane memory, when Margaret approached and greeted the couple affectionately.

Reginald's famous cousin and her wealthy husband had all but ignored him since his arrival in Florida, so Reginald glanced around to see who might be observing this intimate encounter. It was immediately obvious to the ladies that he was too flustered to extend the proper courtesies.

Darcy stepped in. "It's a beautiful day, Madam. Would you like to sit with us for a while?"

Chapter 36

Margaret smiled at Darcy. "Why thank you, a visit would be lovely."

Reginald beamed and composed himself. He jumped to his feet and pulled a chair out for his cousin.

"I'm unusually parched today," Margaret commented.

Darcy recognized her cue. "I too, would appreciate a libation. I'll fetch one of the servants to bring a cool pitcher of sweet tea for the table."

Margaret smiled. "That would be delightful."

Darcy got up and left the two sitting at the table. Margaret watched her walk away before speaking. "Cousin, when I first learned of your marriage, I was not convinced marrying someone so young was a wise course of action. But now that I have come to know Darcy, I must say, I have changed my mind."

Reginald looked surprised, but pleased none the less. "You've spoken with Darcy?"

"Ah, yes. Her insights often catch my attention during our afternoon teas. I find her intelligent and she possesses uncommonly good taste in art and décor. It's a shame wasn't able to gain more experience entertaining before she was married, because I think she has the ability to become a first rate hostess for your household."

Instantly attempting to take credit for any valuable abilities Darcy might possess, Reginald stammered, "Yes, indeed. I try to keep her abreast of current events. Why, only this morning, I was reading from the paper and telling her about..."

Margaret interrupted, "Yes, yes, I'm sure you've tried to help her along, but I think it might behoove her to spend more time with me as my protégé, learning social graces as only a knowledgeable woman can teach them. As I said, she shows promise and we are, after all, cousins, are we not? In return for my tutelage, perhaps Darcy could assist me with hosting the annual 'Masters of Industry Ball,' in New York next year. It might serve as a belated 'coming-out' party, to introduce her to society."

Reginald gulped and nodded enthusiastically, beside himself with glee. Margaret could tell he was already envisioning a significant rise in his social ranking.

Though he tried to appear calm, Reginald's voice almost squeaked with excitement. "I believe I can arrange for Darcy to spend more time with you during the balance of our winter here. Of course, my personal situation will suffer without her at my side, but I will make this sacrifice for her benefit. As a matter of fact, I may be able to remove myself from her concern by accepting a few invitations to participate in extended hunts and fishing excursions."

Margaret forced her smirk into a smile. "Then it is settled."

As the memory began to fade back into the fog, Honor had to bite her lip to keep from giggling at the way Margaret pulled Reginald's strings like a talented puppet master. She relaxed and floated away, wondering how many memories were still hiding within the folds of the heavy, swirling mist. She didn't have to wait long to see the next one.

The fog dissipated to reveal Margaret and Darcy, deep in conversation at the parlor table in Darcy's hotel suite. Honor got the impression the two women were no longer just pretending to be friends, but had instead developed a close bond.

Margaret clucked, "My dear, Darcy, I'm more concerned about your future than I am about this current crisis."

"Yes, being a man's third wife is an unenviable position," Darcy agreed. "If I had borne him a son, things might be different. But as it is, when Reginald passes on, his sons will inherit all of his property and I will have to rely on their generosity for my survival." Darcy winced at the idea.

"His sons will inherit everything *except* your personal possessions," Margaret corrected. "It's true you can't change the sad fact that Reginald's sons will inherit your home, and when they do, they will most likely either move you into small quarters within the bowels of the house, or they will expect you to leave altogether." Margaret leaned toward Darcy, lowering her voice. "But there *is* something you can do to prepare for that eventuality. You can build a nest egg, with which you can live out your days in comfort."

"A nest egg?" Darcy lamented. "How do you propose I manage this feat, when I have no means of income? When Rory and I were making plans to run away together, we sold some of my personal trinkets, but they yielded very little profit and I own nothing else."

Margaret shook her head at her friend. "Darcy, you are a very intelligent woman, but you lack confidence in your ability to outwit the men in your life. These things I am teaching you are things I have already accomplished for myself, as have several other ladies with whom I have become acquainted over the years."

Margaret now had both Darcy's and Honor's full attention.

"The key to survival is remembering that society is like the current of a river. If you fight it, you won't get very far; but if instead you learn to float with the current, it can carry you a long way."

Darcy knitted her eyebrows together, trying unsuccessfully to understand Margaret's analogy.

Margaret smiled patiently. "You are learning everything necessary to become the envy of your peers. Soon you will set the standard for proper social behavior and you will utilize your wonderful creative abilities when entertaining. All the ladies who know you will begin to crave invitations to your parties and those who don't yet know you will hear about your events and seek you out. Your status will influence and elevate your husband's place in the social standing of your community."

"I understand what is expected of me, but cannot comprehend how that will help me build a nest egg."

"It's simple, really. You must immediately develop an affinity for fine jewelry, clothing and art and let Reginald know these things bring you joy. When he realizes you are responsible for bringing him the social recognition he has always sought, he'll want to keep you happy. Each time he gives you an expensive gift, you will reward him with public recognition for his generosity. The more you socialize, the more your jewels and finery will show off his wealth to those he wishes to impress."

Darcy smiled, beginning to understand the methodology.

Margaret continued, "Also, if Reginald upsets you or wants you to help him with additional social obligations, allow him to demonstrate his regret or appreciation with jewels. He will quickly learn that expensive gifts are an easy way to gain forgiveness and cooperation."

"But what if Reginald doesn't oblige me in this manner?"

Margaret laughed at her naiveté. "He will. All men are the same in this regard. Once Reginald learns that gifts not only keep peace at home, but also make his peers envious and his competitors wary, he will gladly spend as much as he can afford."

Darcy nodded thoughtfully.

Pleased with her pupil's grasp of the lesson, Margaret continued. "Many women in society are as concerned about their own futures as you are about yours. And some of us have discovered our goals are more easily obtained when we secretly cooperate with one another."

"But how can I help others obtain what I myself do not have?" Darcy queried.

"By building a force of allies. For instance, if you see another woman wearing a new piece of jewelry in a social setting, you compliment her in front of her husband. You admire his good taste and his ability to select jewels of obviously high quality. That woman, in return, will do the same for you. And so it goes. Men use social gatherings to build their self-esteem and impress business competitors, while intelligent women use them to build personal wealth."

For the first time in her life, Darcy began to believe she could influence her own destiny.

Margaret advised, "You also need to build a social gathering circle."

"A social gathering circle?"

"Yes. You're aware that services of certain clothing designers, caterers, florists, and musicians are more highly regarded by affluent society than others, are you not?"

Darcy nodded; concentrating on Margaret's lesson.

Margaret lowered her voice again. "Well, the reason many of these establishments are sought out on a regular basis is that the business owner provides a discrete cash payment to the hostess for selecting them."

Shocked, Darcy blurted, "bribery!"

"No, not bribery," Margaret clarified. "Incentive. A social gathering circle provides positive benefits to all involved. For instance, many of the businesses I utilize are operated by women. When it becomes known that I patronize their shops, they become far more successful than they might have otherwise. And the more sought-after the shop owner's products become, the more prestige my husband reaps when I am able to secure their services."

"I suppose that makes sense." Darcy hesitated. "Margaret, as you are Henry's second wife and have borne him no children, have you acquired a nest egg of your own?"

Margaret gave her a sly smile. "Even if Henry left me nothing at all, I could live quite comfortably for more than a hundred years. Never forget this important lesson. An intelligent woman with allies can accomplish anything."

As the fog rolled in, Honor floated away willingly, pleased with what she had just witnessed. Margaret had managed to manipulate the very protocols that were meant to keep Victorian women subservient to men. By doing so, she had accumulated enough personal wealth to protect her from an uncertain future. And now she was teaching other women to do the same.

Honor shook her head in admiration. She could hardly wait to get back to her own time, so she could tell Josh what she had learned. But instead of waking up in bed, the fog parted to again reveal Reginald and Darcy at the little table in the Belleview Hotel garden.

Honor was confused. Why was she being shown the same memory she had visited earlier that evening? Just as before, Reginald read a newspaper while Darcy worked on a needlepoint project. But almost immediately, it became clear this was a different day in more ways than one.

Chapter 37

Over the top edge of his newspaper, Reginald saw Margaret approaching their table. Pretending not to notice she was within earshot, he lowered the paper and spoke to Darcy, his voice dripping with honey. "There's an article in the Gazette about a group of artists called *Ten American Painters*. They'll be exhibiting some of their work in town, week after next. This might be an excellent opportunity for me to help you further your education in the arts."

Before Darcy could respond, Margaret interrupted. "Good afternoon, cousin. I'd like a word, please. As you know, I'm counting on Darcy to assist me in hosting the Belleview's first ball, but I'm concerned her wardrobe is lacking the formal attire she will be expected to wear as my protégé. Might I suggest a local seamstress and jeweler to prepare her for the heightened role she will soon occupy in society?"

Reginald shifted in his chair and cleared his throat, uncomfortable discussing feminine matters.

Darcy came to his rescue. "I'm sure Reginald would enjoy seeing me adorned in a more stylish fashion, but I fear I lack the expertise necessary to achieve the desired results. If you wouldn't mind too terribly, we would greatly appreciate your assistance in selecting a dress and jewelry worthy of my position at this prestigious event."

Reginald shot Darcy an approving glance for taking the lead in the conversation.

Margaret gave a curt nod. "Yes, I'd be willing to accompany the two of you on a day-long shopping excursion. Unless, of course, Reginald would prefer to simply fill your purse, allowing us to tour the shops at our leisure."

Honor was certain a man's man like Reginald would gladly hand Darcy a large sum of money, if it meant he would be spared from spending an entire day shopping. As the mist began to gather, she smiled, knowing she had just witnessed the first step in creating Darcy's nest egg.

No sooner had the fog fully engulfed Honor, than it began to dissipate again, revealing a ballroom filled with people attired in formal wear. She was standing next to Darcy, who was dressed in a stylish baby-blue silk gown. The full skirt of the dress was gathered just under her bosom, effectively hiding her belly, while white lace insets in the bodice drew all the men's attention toward her swollen breasts. Her dark curls were piled high and held in place with jewel-studded pins that matched her gold and sapphire necklace and earrings.

Darcy bubbled, "I'm assisting Margaret as hostess of the Belleview Hotel's inaugural Winter Ball. It's so splendid. It's almost as if one of my childhood dreams sprang to life!"

Honor enjoyed watching Darcy glide throughout the Tiffany-windowed ballroom, mingling with guests. Reginald appeared to be in high spirits and genuinely pleased with his wife's transformation into a social butterfly. Honor wanted to stay and enjoy this memory for a while, but soon the swirling fog erased the orchestra and waltzing couples from view.

The next time the clouds parted, Margaret was pouring tea for Reginald and Darcy in one of the hotel's small, private parlors. The tense, quiet atmosphere in the room provided a stark contrast to the lively ball Honor witnessed only moments ago.

Once tea was served, Margaret announced, "I have a matter of some importance to discuss with you, cousin."

Reginald shifted uneasily on the dainty settee. He eyed the delicate cup in his hand with distain, obviously wishing it contained something stronger than tea.

Margaret ignored his discomfort. "As you know, my husband is a busy man. So busy, in fact, that he will be unable to accompany me to Europe this spring, where I intend to purchase additional décor for the both the Tampa and Belleview Hotels."

Reginald nodded. "We successful men must honor business commitments over all else."

"Yes, indeed." Margaret sipped her tea to hide a smirk. It was laughable that Reginald considered himself Henry Plant's equal in the world of business. "Well, it's no secret I value Darcy's artistic opinions and enjoy her company. Therefore, I have decided to invite her to take Henry's place as my traveling companion on this excursion."

Reginald was clearly dumfounded, but Margaret continued, unfazed. "A trip abroad would provide Darcy the worldly experience her education is lacking, and she could shop in the finest stores to complete her wardrobe. By the time she returns home, I dare say she will be able to run your household in a manner that will make you the envy of your peers."

Darcy sat quietly while her husband considered the matter. She knew he was conflicted between the exciting prospect of gaining prestige, and the fear she might embarrass him while traveling without supervision.

Margaret skillfully guided the conversation. "Truthfully, it's just as well Henry's business requires his attention, because this particular trip would be dreadfully boring for any man to endure. Our days will be filled with shopping and our evenings will be spent tutoring Darcy on the arts."

Reginald grimaced.

Margaret lowered her voice and leaned toward Reginald, as if to share a confidence. "When we return and I introduce my polished protégé to our acquaintances within the desirable elements of New York society; consider what grand opportunities might open up for you and your sons."

That did it. Reginald was hooked. "How will I ever thank you for this remarkable gift?"

Margaret smiled. "No thanks are necessary. It's only right that family members look after one another."

Honor smiled as the fog rolled in. She knew the next big step in the plan to hide Darcy's pregnancy had just fallen into place.

This time, Honor fell through the mist and woke with a start, back in her own bed. She glanced at Josh, asleep beside her, and wondered if he was dreaming. Ignoring the chilly air, she slipped out of bed, pulled on her T-shirt, and went to check on Cody.

The boy looked like an angel, almost glowing in the brilliant moonbeams that shone through the window. Honor contemplated the spider web hanging above his bed and wondered if his totem dream catcher was doing its job.

Her thoughts drifted to Darcy. It must have been awful for her being forced to give her precious child away to strangers. She suddenly realized the spirit of Cody's mother, Amy, was also losing her child to a stranger. Amy's frequent visits with Cody over the years demonstrated her devotion, but when Cody moved to Florida, Amy, who had never been there, could not follow. Standing over the sleeping child, Honor decided to find a way to communicate with Amy's spirit and promise her Cody would never forget how much she loved him.

Honor felt Margaret's presence even before she turned and saw her shadowy form sitting at the parlor table. Though not prepared for another waking encounter with a spirit, she quickly composed herself and asked, "Has this all been about Cody? Showing me the precious bond between a mother and a child to help me appreciate this treasure that has come into my life?"

Her response was a raspy whisper. "Yes, in part. But there is more. Much more."

The room was colder now. Instinctively, Honor bent down

to tuck Cody's blankets securely around him. "Do you know what became of Darcy's baby?"

There was no response. Honor shivered, knowing even before she looked back, that Margaret had vanished. "It sure would be nice to get some straight answers around here for a change," she mumbled into the empty space.

She kissed Cody and then crept back into bed, where she snuggled up against Josh as though they were two spoons in a drawer. Without waking, Josh curled his arm around her. Content in his embrace, she fell back to sleep.

***

The next morning, Honor left Josh and Cody watching cartoons and set off for her meeting with Sarah Jacobs.

When the two women were settled in the attorney's small conference room, Sarah began. "I'm not going to mince words, Honor. The situation isn't good."

Honor braced herself for bad news.

"Until I review the company's financial records thoroughly, I can't determine if William has committed any criminal behavior. But I can tell you these incorporation documents don't identify you as an equal partner in the firm, and they grant him a great deal of leeway with regard to how he spends and invests the company's profits."

Honor's jaw dropped. She fought to remain calm. "I don't understand. This has to be a mistake. The money we used to launch Soft Fix was mostly *mine*... and every year, I sign our company tax returns as a *partner*. Besides, if I can prove William's been filing false expense reports with the company, then at a minimum, he's guilty of tax evasion, right? Can't I just report him to the IRS?"

"If we tip off the IRS, they'll likely send an auditor to review your company's suspect tax records. And if that auditor discovers illegal tax documentation, there's a strong possibility you would be held equally liable for any back taxes, fines and penalties that are assessed."

Honor took a deep breath. "So... I don't have equal say-so when it comes to spending our company's money, but I am equal when it comes to responsibility for William's illegal actions? That's just great. It sounds like I might be better off taking half of the assets and starting a whole new company."

"I'm sorry; Honor, but you can't do that, either. You signed one of the most onerous non-compete agreements I have ever seen.' According to that agreement, if you leave Soft Fix, you can't go to work for a competing company and you can't establish a new software business within five hundred miles of Chicago. You also can't do any work for Soft Fix clients, and you can't hire any of your technical staff to come work for you."

Honor gasped, "I can't believe I *trusted* that rat bastard. I *married* him for God's sake! And all the while he was designing Soft Fix in a way that tied me to him like an indentured servant." She pressed her lips tightly together, swallowing a torrent of useless insults. "You know the most ludicrous part of this whole thing? I'm the one who paid the attorney's fees back then. How could I have been so dumb?"

Sarah ignored the rhetorical question. "Honor, I know this information comes as a shock, but don't give up. If there's a way to get your fair share out of Soft Fix, I promise to find it. And I'll let you in on a secret. When the court reviews corporate documents like non-compete agreements, they use a methodology sometimes called the *smell test.* Basically, that means contracts are reviewed to see if they appear to be more or less fair to both parties. None of this paperwork would pass the smell test."

"So you mean there's still a chance I can get justice even though I was stupid enough to give William free reign over everything?"

"Absolutely. Breaking non-compete agreements is one of my specialties." Sarah winked. "And besides, you aren't stupid. Your naiveté might have made you an easy target, but you're still a victim. I'll do my best to convince the judge that William perpetuated fraud against you by the way he designed the corporate structure and the overly restrictive terms of the non-compete agreement."

Sarah opened her calendar. "Let's meet back here next Friday at four thirty. That should give me enough time to review this paperwork in more detail and research Illinois statutes that specifically address non-compete agreements. Meanwhile, it would be extremely helpful if you could get your hands on some company documents that prove William has been misleading you with regard to company expenditures and your role at the firm. I want you to collect as much documentation as you can before we tip our hand."

Honor nodded, her mouth too dry to speak. After leaving Sarah's office, she sat in her parked car trying to figure out the best way to collect financial records without arousing suspicion.

Her disjointed thoughts were interrupted by a call from her assistant, Julie, who proceeded to download a laundry list of conflicts between William and the software designers, along with gossip from within corporate accounting. "When are you coming back?" she whined. "I'm afraid we might lose some of our best people if you don't get back here soon and return some sanity to the bullpen."

Honor's response surprised Julie and herself equally. "I'll catch a flight home Sunday. I need to be back here next Friday afternoon for a meeting with the attorney, but four days in the office might help reassure the techies."

It served no purpose to give Julie more issues to worry about, so Honor intentionally allowed her to assume Friday's meeting was with her mother's estate attorney. "Please make my travel arrangements and call me back with the itinerary."

Chapter 38

Honor caught up with Josh and Cody at the Belleview Biltmore playground. While Cody played in the sandbox, Honor brought Josh up to speed regarding the day's events, and then recounted her experiences with the spirits from the night before. Josh listened closely until she was finished.

"Maybe Margaret is trying to teach you the same thing she taught Darcy."

"What's that?"

"Whenever a man tries to dominate a woman, she can always count on the combination of her wits and her girlfriends to outmaneuver him."

"If only I were a smarter woman with a lot more friends."

Josh cupped her shoulders firmly with his large hands and gazed into her eyes. "Honor, I truly don't understand how you can be so wickedly smart and not see it. And you make friends easily, so how many you have is entirely up to you."

Honor blushed. "You always manage to make me feel better. I sure wish you were going to Chicago with me!"

Josh pointed to her cell phone. "I'm right there on speed dial, whenever you need me." At that exact moment, her phone rang.

Giggling, Honor answered and got her flight information from Julie, just as Cody ran back to the porch.

"We're going to Chicago?" Cody bubbled enthusiastically.

"Not us. Just Honor," Josh corrected.

Out came Cody's bottom lip.

"Don't worry, Cody. I'll only be gone for a few days. And

I'm leaving a special camera and my laptop behind so we'll be able to talk and see each other on our computers."

His lip retracted as quickly as it had appeared, his blue eyes beginning to sparkle with excitement. "I want to talk on the computer! Can you go to Chicago right now?"

Honor and Josh laughed at the rapid mood swing.

"Sorry, I'm not leaving until Sunday. But before I go, could you do me a favor and sit next to your Daddy, so I can take a few pictures to keep me company on my trip?"

Honor snapped pictures until Cody put a stop to it, complaining, "My face hurts from smiling too much."

She laughed, shaking her head. Then, as she knew it would, the weekend melted away.

***

On Sunday, Josh wanted to accompany Honor to the airport, but at her insistence, they said their goodbyes in the hotel lobby. She wanted to return her rental car and besides, she needed the quiet drive time to make a mental list of what she needed to accomplish in Chicago.

It was a good plan, but her mind wouldn't cooperate. No matter how hard she tried to focus, Josh and the spirits filled her thoughts all the way to Tampa International.

Check-in was a breeze without luggage, so Honor stopped at one of the terminal shops to purchase a notebook, still hoping to formulate her list. But when inspiration finally struck, it was not a list that materialized, but a journal.

She wrote: *Before I looked at them closely, I thought they were alive, sitting at the parlor table, chatting. Then I noticed they were strangely attired. Not Halloween night strange; just out of date. And then it slowly sank in. They weren't exactly what you would call "solid"...*

Honor spent the entire flight recording every detail of the past weeks in her new journal. Before she knew it, the plane touched down in Chicago. It was cold and breezy, as if the town was trying to live up to its nickname, *The Windy City*. She hailed a cab and settled back in the seat, trying to stay warm and already wishing she was back in Florida.

When she walked through the door of her condo, she expected to be comforted by the familiar surroundings, but instead, she felt lonely. After only a few minutes, she telephoned Josh. "I just wanted to let you know I arrived safely and I miss you already!"

"Then you should catch the next flight back."

"Yeah, right."

"I'm only half-kidding," Josh insisted.

"I wish I could. I can hardly wait to see your face tonight, even if it's only on my computer screen. I'll call at eight o'clock, so I can say goodnight to Cody."

After they hung up, Honor was restless. She walked from room to room, objectively appraising the spacious condo, trying to decide where she could put her mother's grandfather clock. The earth-tone rooms were tastefully furnished, but other than a few pictures of ancestors that had been chosen more for the decorative value of their frames than for their familial connection, the condo décor was rather impersonal.

"What this place needs is a refrigerator art gallery," she mused. She pulled her camera from her purse and wistfully clicked through the pictures. "I really miss you guys," she whispered.

Her stomach grumbled, reminding her she hadn't eaten since breakfast. Still talking to Josh and Cody's images, she confessed, "You know what else I miss? Chicago style pizza— and that's an itch I can scratch right now! Then afterwards, I can run by the office to have a look around."

Satisfied with her plan, she grabbed her keys and headed out into the cold evening. She enjoyed sliding behind the wheel of her faithful old BMW and hearing the purr of its engine, but after driving only a few blocks, she was already complaining. "I haven't missed this city traffic one little bit!"

She counted herself lucky to find a parking spot only a half block down from Giordano's Pizza. Outside the restaurant, a street vendor was selling toys. She paused to search his table for something Spiderman-related and was pleased to find a large package of stickers. There were several images of Spiderman in various poses, as well as some webs and several of the superhero's archenemies. Honor grinned, realizing she could name several of the villains and wondered if Cody would be impressed. She paid for the stickers and then followed the heavenly scent of hot pizza inside.

After gorging herself on a delicious stuffed slice, Honor checked her watch and realized with a start that she had forgotten about the time difference. She only had one hour before she was supposed to call Josh and Cody. She turned up her collar against the chill of the wind, and walked another block down the street to her office. Soft Fix was deserted this time of night, so she had to punch in a security code to open the door. The sense of unfamiliarity was even stronger here than it had been at her condo. She headed down the hall to her office, turning on a few lights along the way.

When she flipped on the light in her office, Honor groaned at the mountain of paperwork that covered every inch of her desk and conference table. Honor knew her assistant liked to use her office furniture as extra work surfaces whenever she was away on business, but Julie usually made sure everything was cleared off before Honor returned.

"Well, Julie," she mumbled, "It's pretty obvious you thought you had until tomorrow to hide your mess."

The words sparked an idea. "Wait a minute. No one expects me to be here tonight. I wonder if anyone else planned to clean up in the morning."

She glanced around, wondering what she should be looking for and wished she had been more attentive during their weekly business meetings. She had never even tried to learn the coded language of the financial spreadsheets and reports. In fact, unless the topic of a meeting directly involved her area of expertise, she usually spent her time answering email on her Blackberry.

Now disgusted with her own ignorance, Honor remembered William always handed out weekly financial reports *during* the meeting—never before. And he always insisted that everyone drop them into the recycle bin on their way out of the conference room when the meeting was over. She had admired that habit. It promoted recycling while at the same time, discouraging employees from becoming office pack rats. Now enlightened that William may have had more sinister motives, Honor rethought his methodology and realized it was a brilliant way to keep anyone from scrutinizing the details of his reports.

Angry about the potential deception, Honor went to the main conference room, pulled the lid from the paper recycling bin and looked inside. She was thrilled to find it hadn't been emptied for several days. She didn't know if any of the discarded reports contained valuable information, but decided to utilize the more-is-better approach to collecting evidence and sort it out later. She rifled through the contents, collecting samples of several different types of reports. She noticed some reports had been issued to specific people and had notes written in the margins. She took all the reports for comparison.

Honor made it back to her own office just in time to plug in a spare camera from her desk drawer and place the call to Josh and Cody, using Julie's desktop computer. Predictably, Cody led the conversation, showing Honor a few pictures he had drawn and telling her everything that had happened in her absence.

"Daddy put his shoes on the bed, so I told him he better take them off or I was going tell on him," he announced.

Honor could hear Josh in the background. "Sure... rat me out. I'm only your flesh and blood."

Cody protested, "I didn't tell on you, Daddy. I just told her that I was *going* to tell on you if you didn't take your shoes off the bed."

Honor laughed at the little boy's logic.

She remembered the Spiderman stickers and held them up in front of the camera for Cody to examine. She named some of Spiderman's enemies, intentionally getting a few of them wrong, so Cody could correct her. He did so, patiently reminding her which movie every nemesis had been in and what villainous super powers each possessed.

Josh finally intervened. "Okay, that's enough Spiderman trivia for now. It's time for you to say goodnight to Honor."

The little boy's face grew serious. "Honor, you can use some of those spider web stickers over your bed until you come back home."

Honor thanked him, touched by his generosity almost as much as the fact that he called their hotel suite *home*.

Josh moved Cody aside and came into view, "Where are you? That isn't your condo, is it?"

"I got restless and decided to come to the office for a while."

Josh's eyes darkened with concern. "I don't want to sound overprotective, but are you sure you should be alone in downtown Chicago this late at night? I sure would feel better if I knew you were safely locked inside your condo."

Honor smiled reassuringly. "Don't worry. It's a good neighborhood. I work late pretty often and I've never had any trouble."

Josh looked unconvinced.

"I'm not going to stay too much longer. Would you feel better if I called your cell when I get home?"

"Much better."

They touched hands on the computer screen and ended the call. When the screen went dark, Honor stared at it for a long moment, thinking ahead and wondering how she was going to make it through the long winter months without Josh and Cody.

Chapter 39

She went back to her desk and began rifling through the paperwork stacks; taking anything that looked like it might demonstrate differences between the financial documentation William had been providing to her, versus the company's actual expense and revenue numbers. She also made copies of a few expense reports that were on her desk awaiting approval, returning the originals to the stacks, just as she had found them.

Honor placed the results of her reconnaissance efforts into a cardboard box and prepared to head back to her condo. As she was leaving her office, she noticed what appeared to be a project schedule on one of the four chairs that surrounded the small conference table. Assuming Julie had prepared it for her review, she tossed it into the box, intending to study it later that evening.

When she arrived back at her condo, Honor carried the box of paperwork to her dining room table and left it there, unopened. She took a shower and then called Josh to say goodnight.

Josh confessed, "I laid your nightshirt on your side of the bed and have been sitting here watching TV with it. But I've noticed it isn't quite the same as when you're here in person."

Honor giggled, picturing him lying in bed. "If I were there with you, I doubt I'd still be wearing my nightshirt."

"Touché."

Honor dropped onto her bed. "Seriously, Josh... I really miss the feel of lying next to you with your arms wrapped around me. I kept wishing you were with me in the shower earlier."

Josh groaned. "Now you're just torturing me."

Honor feigned innocence. "Oh, really? I'm sorry. I certainly didn't mean to upset you with images of me in a steamy shower; squeezing a sponge over my soapy breasts and letting the bubbles run down my belly."

Josh gave her a low whistle.

Emboldened, Honor continued to tease. "And I better not tell you I'm pretending you're here with me right now, rubbing this lotion on my skin...running your hands all over my naked body."

Josh moaned. "You're cruel!"

But he didn't say he wanted her to stop. So she didn't...

When they finally said goodnight, Honor relaxed into her soft pillows. She still missed being with Josh in person, but had to admit the phone sex had been wildly erotic and quite satisfying. "Maybe we'll be able to make it through those lonely winter months after all."

She drifted off to sleep, wondering if the spirits would be able to visit her here and if not, then what would fill her dreams?

Chapter 40

Honor's sleep was fitful and filled with nightmares about William's deception. She missed the blissful, rested feeling she had when she awoke from visiting with the spirits at the Belleview Biltmore.

Groggy, she shuffled into the kitchen and opened the coffee canister. "Empty. Damn." She glanced at the magnetic shopping list on her refrigerator. "Yep, there it is: Buy coffee." She settled for a cup of tea and called Julie to let her know she was planning to be in the office at ten o'clock.

Julie answered in a hushed voice. "Honor, I'm glad you called. I came in extra early to um... tidy up a bit before you got here." She lowered her voice even more. "When I opened the door to your office, William was in there, going through some stacks of paperwork on your desk. I almost had a heart attack! It was obvious I caught him by surprise, but I played it cool and just casually asked if I could help him with anything. He said he was retrieving an expense report that needed to be corrected before you signed off on it."

Honor was confused. "But why wouldn't William just send one of his clerks to pick it up?"

"Exactly!" Julie exclaimed in an excited whisper. "I knew he was lying, but I didn't know what to do. I just stood there, pretending I believed him. He asked me if everything I had saved for your review was on top of your desk, and I assured him it was. I could tell he wasn't happy with my answer, but it was the truth. He said the report he was looking for must still be in his own department and then he walked out."

Julie paused; still shaken by the encounter. "Something weird is going on here, Honor. I'm positive William was looking for something, but there's no way it was an expense report. I sure am glad you're back. Maybe you can get to the bottom of this mess."

"I'm not really *back*. I'm only in Chicago for a couple of days. When I return to Florida on Friday, I plan to stay there at least through the Thanksgiving holiday."

"I know...just wishful thinking."

Honor decided against confiding to Julie that she had been at the office the night before and had taken a box of paperwork home with her. She didn't want Julie to have to lie if anyone else questioned her about missing items.

The hot tea hadn't satisfied her morning caffeine craving; so Honor stopped at Intelligencia, her favorite coffee shop, on the way to the office. She figured it would be easier to snoop around if William believed she was still in the dark about his questionable business practices, so she bought a large, house-blend coffee for herself, Julie and William, just as she had done so often in the past.

The Soft Fix lobby was bustling with morning activity. Amid the polite greetings, Honor noticed a few employees eyeing her and she wondered if they knew William had been playing her for a fool all this time. She strolled toward her office, smiling at everyone, hoping to appear more in-control and self-confident than she actually felt.

Julie jumped up from her desk to wrap Honor in a welcome-home hug, almost spilling the hot coffee in the process. Other than being slender and about the same height, the two women looked nothing alike. Julie's thick auburn hair was cut in a short bob that curled under her chin, forming a tidy frame for her dainty, porcelain features and deep brown eyes. She looked like royalty, but her personality revealed her streetwise upbringing.

"Tell me all about your trip," she begged, "especially the

hot, sexy parts."

Honor laughed and then feigned shock at the amount of paper stacked upon her desk.

Julie protested, "I planned to move everything to your conference table this morning, but William's visit threw me off my game. And it's not as bad as it looks -- the piles are all tagged and prioritized."

Honor glanced around skeptically.

Julie offered a compromise. "Okay, I'll clear everything off your desk while you tell me about that hunk you discovered in Florida."

Honor laughed again. "Down, girl! First I want to say 'hello' to William."

Julie lowered her voice. "Are you going to tell him you want to split the company in half?"

"No. That idea is 'on hold' for a while. First, I have to figure out if William has been running our financial operations legitimately or not."

Julie nodded. "Okay. You know I'm behind you no matter what, but if you do decide to split the company in two, I think you should relocate your half down south. I would love to live in sunny Florida!"

"I'll bet you would, but unfortunately, our customers aren't located in Florida." Honor started for William's office, teasing over her shoulder, "When I get back, it sure would be nice if I could see my desktop."

                         ***

As Honor pushed through the double doors underneath the gold lettered sign that read 'Corporate Finance Department,' she suddenly realized how little this portion of the office had interested her in the past. She hoped William wouldn't be able to sense that she wasn't as naïve as she had been a few weeks ago.

The odd looks she had received in the lobby were nothing

compared to the ones she was getting from the finance staff. She ignored their stares and walked straight to William's office. She stopped in his half-open doorway and held the cup of coffee out toward him to catch his attention.

William was having a discussion with his assistant, Ben Dugan, and from the looks of it, he was not at all pleased with the young man. When he caught sight of Honor, he stopped talking and turned on one of his award-winning smiles.

Honor recoiled, remembering how she had been drawn to that smile at the beginning of their relationship. She hid her contempt behind her own smile, hoping he wouldn't notice.

"Too busy for coffee?"

"Not at all. Come on in, Honor. We were just finishing up. Ben, you go find that misplaced document and we'll resume this meeting over lunch."

Summarily dismissed, Ben headed for the door, with a look on his face that said he was relieved to be getting out of there. He mumbled, "welcome back," as he passed Honor, but didn't wait for a response.

After he was gone, Honor asked, "trouble?"

"Nothing serious. Now, please tell me your mom's estate is all wrapped up and you're ready to jump back into work with both feet. We've missed you around here!"

Honor handed him his coffee and sat down in one of the chairs opposite his desk. "Not exactly."

William's smile faded. "What does that mean?"

"I've decided to remodel my mom's house before selling it, so I'll be spending some more time in Florida. I plan to head back down in a few days to celebrate Thanksgiving and I'll probably spend most of the holiday season down there."

William appeared confused. "Honor, I'm disappointed you made such a big decision without consulting me first."

"We're divorced, remember?"

"But I still want what's best for you. Remodeling that old house will cost you a fortune. Besides, you belong here in

Chicago. Your team needs you."

"I'm not deserting my team, William. As a matter of fact, Ellen and I designed a complicated patch last week, using our cell phones and the Internet to collaborate. It worked great and proved my team can operate with equal efficiency, whether I'm in Florida or here in Chicago."

Once William understood Honor planned to maintain the status quo at Soft Fix, he relaxed. Honor breathed a sigh of relief, too. Obviously Leon Goldstein hadn't told William about their conversation. The longer she could keep him in the dark about that, the better.

She changed the subject. "You look tired. How's your baby girl?"

"Fine, but I wish she'd start sleeping through the night." William stifled a yawn.

"Get used to not sleeping. Before you know it, she'll be talking your ears off and running you ragged."

William's eyes narrowed. "Since when did you become an expert on kids?"

"I've been spending time with a single father I met in Florida. He has an energetic four-year-old-son."

"You need to be careful, Honor. Florida is full of con artists, scheming to take advantage of trusting women with money. That guy could be trying to get his hands on your bank account."

Honor fought to keep her emotions in check, angry that William had the nerve to question Josh's motives. She took a deep breath and breathed it out slowly before answering. "He's not a con artist. Come on, William. You knew I'd eventually start looking for someone else to share my life with, right?"

The wounded look on William's face registered a mix of sadness and surprise. Clearly, he had *not* considered the possibility that Honor would find someone new.

Chapter 41

Though she should have been used to it by now, Honor was startled by William's incredible arrogance. She wanted to tell him that Josh was superior to him in every way imaginable, but she knew it was smarter to remain non-confrontational.

"Good grief, William. You're remarried. You have a child. Are you really so selfish as to not want that kind of happiness for me, too?"

Without waiting for his reply, she stood. "Listen, I have to run. I need to meet with my engineering staff to make sure I'm up to speed on all the active projects. I'll catch you later."

By the time Honor got back to her office she had cooled down somewhat. Seeing that Julie had cleared the paperwork from her desk, relocating all of it to her small conference table, improved her spirits even more.

"There's my desk, she joked. "I knew it was hiding under there somewhere."

"Very funny," Julie retorted.

"I've decided to call an impromptu staff meeting. Please pick up a box of bagels from next door and let me know as soon as everyone's assembled in the conference room."

While Julie attended to that task, Honor sat down at the table and began sorting through a stack of phone messages Julie had pulled from her Blackberry and deemed *High Priority.* Several customers had left messages asking to speak directly with her, so she closed her office door and began making calls.

She was appalled to discover William had reached out to them in her absence, telling them not to worry that she was out of town because the vast majority of the design work was handled by her staff these days. He even attempted to convince some of them that all software designers possessed relatively equal skillsets, and so were interchangeable—like pieces on a checker board. Fortunately for Honor, most of their clients knew better and were calling to acknowledge her extraordinary talent and to offer her their allegiance.

At first, Honor was confused, but then she remembered William's inflated ego. She hissed under her breath, "He thinks he's holding all the cards. By calling our customers and giving the credit for my conceptual designs to my team, the rat bastard thinks he can push me out without losing any customers."

By the time Julie called to say everyone was assembled, Honor was seething. When she entered the conference room, her senior project managers, Pete Cross and Ellen Christianson, led the others in a comical version of the *wave*. The warm gesture improved her mood significantly. Laughing with her team, Honor felt at home for the first time since arriving in Chicago.

When everyone settled down, Honor announced, "I'm going to be spending more time in Florida, so it's important that we learn to function as a team, regardless of physical location."

There were several groans at the thought of her leaving again.

"Come on, guys, let's list the problems you had while I was away and then improve our long-distance work processes."

Pete snarked, "I think I speak for all of us when I say the majority of our problems would disappear if you simply took William with you any time you travel."

Honor chuckled. "Was he really that bad?"

The team hurled a barrage of unflattering descriptors ranging from "village idiot" to "dictator", indicating that yes, William's behavior had been unbearable.

Honor allowed them to vent their frustration. Afterwards, they focused their attention on finding solutions to non-William-related problems they might encounter while she was in Florida. They established a local chain of command, protocols for addressing customer issues, and effective methods of collaborating on projects long-distance.

"And another thing -- Mr. Peaches and I miss our weekly bagels when you're out of town," Ellen complained.

Several of the others nodded in agreement.

"I wouldn't dream of depriving your bird of his bagel," Honor giggled. "I'll ask Julie to place an order every week, whether or not I'm around."

To Honor's amusement, the entire group gave her a standing ovation.

"Let's adjourn on that note. I'll be here the rest of the week, so let me know if you think of any other issues that need to be addressed."

After the meeting, Honor dug into the next stack of paperwork on her office table, marked *Project Status Up-Dates*. Soft Fix couldn't issue final invoices until they were completed, and from the looks of the pile, a good deal of revenue was currently tied up waiting for this important process. Honor meticulously combed through each of the projects, whining about the fact William's staff didn't use computerized forms.

If Honor was able to check all the items off the list for a given project, it was sent to accounting for final invoicing. Those that were not completely finished stayed with her, so she could make work assignments the following day.

Honor was amazed when Julie interrupted her to ask if she needed anything else before she left for the day. She had been so busy, she barely noticed the hours slipping by. As if her stomach just realized the time of day as well, it growled.

"You know what? Instead of staying late, I think I'll take this work home with me. I need to grab a bite to eat."

Julie raised her eyebrows. "Wow, I'm impressed you're

willing to leave the office at a reasonable time for a change. I'd be more impressed if you left the work behind, but I won't ask for miracles. I'll grab a file box and help you pack up."

Honor placed a large stack of paperwork in the box, along with a spare laptop and a few office supplies.

"I guess that's enough for one evening."

Julie shook her head. "I should say so! You know, you really need to think about getting a life. All you ever do is work."

Honor smiled, remembering the phone sex from the night before. *If you only knew*, she thought, as she hefted the box.

Julie and Honor were surprised to see William milling around in the lobby, blocking their exit.

"Hey, Honor, what do you have there?"

Honor knitted her eyebrows, annoyed by the intrusion. "It's just some work I'm planning to finish at home this evening."

William reached into the box and pulled out a sampling of its contents, reviewing the items as if to verify she was authorized to remove them from the building.

Honor paled with anger. "What the hell do you think you're doing?"

When William's eyes met hers, his smug, impersonal stare reminded Honor of a customs official, assuming he had the right to search her belongings, as he saw fit. Wordlessly, he continued thumbing through the paperwork.

Honor slammed the box to the floor and grabbed the paperwork back from him. She threw it back into the carton.

Apparently satisfied that she wasn't trying to sneak any unauthorized materials from of the building, William tried to make light of the situation. "Don't be so touchy. I'm just kidding around." He turned on his heel and headed back toward his office, calling over his shoulder, "Have a nice night and don't work too hard."

William was either unaware or unconcerned that Honor's

eyes were shooting lightning bolts at his back.

Julie whispered, "I don't know what he's looking for, but whatever it is, he thinks we have it. I sure wish I knew what *it* was."

Honor wished the same thing, but was encouraged by the fact that *something* was making William nervous. She checked her watch. "I have to be home by seven thirty to call Josh, but do you have time for a quick drink?"

Julie nodded. "I'll make the time."

The two women walked down the street to a small, cozy pub, seated themselves in a back booth, and ordered two glasses of chardonnay. Honor wasted no time. "I want you to tell me everything that has happened while I've been gone."

Julie teased, "only if you tell me all about Josh."

"Sounds fair, but you first." Honor agreed.

Julie took a deep breath. "First of all, I swear I didn't say anything to anyone about your plan to split Soft Fix in half, but I think William suspects something is going on. I thought I could get the scoop if I made friends with some of the people in the accounting department. Since everyone knows software engineers aren't exactly *social butterflies*, I told Ben Dugan that I was lonely on my side of the building while you were in Florida. He's always been nice to me, so I asked him to lunch."

"Good idea. If anyone knows what William is up to, it would be his right-hand man."

"That's what I thought, but he became evasive whenever I tried to talk to him about the details of his work. And when I asked him if he knew that William had a girlfriend before it became public knowledge, he looked very uncomfortable and changed the subject. I'm sure he knows more than he told me, but I was afraid if I pressed him too hard, he would become suspicious of my motives, so I backed off. We just talked about music and stuff for the rest of our lunch hour. He's really interesting."

"Well, thanks for trying."

Julie frowned. "Ben hasn't called me for a repeat lunch date, so I don't know where we stand. I mean, he's still pretty friendly when we see each other in the hallways or at the copier, and last week he even helped me hang that new bulletin board on your office wall. But now he acts like he's uncomfortable around me. I think something happened and he feels bad about it."

"You like Ben a lot, don't you?" Honor observed.

"Maybe, but I'm not sure. Most of the time Ben seems sweet and honest, but over the past few days, both he and William have gone into your office, saying they were looking for first one thing and then another. But don't worry, Honor. I planted myself by the conference table next to the door and watched them every minute. They were never in there alone -- well, not until this morning."

Honor smiled to show her appreciation, encouraging Julie to go on.

"I saved you a copy of the report from every meeting while you were gone and had them in stacks on your desk." She frowned. "But I think I should have kept them hidden, because after I came in this morning and found William in your office, I checked your desk and noticed that they were all gone."

"I stopped by the office last night and took some paperwork home with me," Honor admitted. "But I haven't had a chance to review any of it yet."

Julie rolled her eyes.

"I'm sorry I didn't mention it, Julie."

"That's okay. You know, William knew I would be back in the office today. I'll bet that's why he was snooping around in here so early this morning. He probably would have confiscated those reports if you hadn't already grabbed them, so I'm glad you took them."

"Yeah, now if only I knew how to search them for incriminating information, things would be wonderful. God, I hate looking for proof that William is guilty of illegal activity, but I guess his behavior tonight killed any lingering hopes I was harboring about him being an honest business partner."

"Okay, enough about that. It's your turn... Tell me about this new guy, Josh."

Honor smiled. "It might sound corny, but I think I may have found the prince in my fairytale."

She told Julie about Josh's large family of J's, his desire to renovate her mother's old house, and Cody's obsession with all things Spiderman, but was careful not to mention her spirit encounters.

Julie grinned. "I've never seen you like this. You actually light-up when you're talking about them."

Honor checked her watch again, returning the smile. "Speaking of my boys, I need to get home so I can talk to Cody before he goes to sleep."

Julie smirked. "I know I've said it before, but really... who are you and what have you done with my boss?"

Chapter 42

By the time she got home, Honor barely had a moment to kick off her shoes before placing her computer call to Josh and Cody. They had been waiting for her, and were happy to see her face appear on their monitor.

Honor set her laptop on her dresser and aimed the camera directly at her face, so she could wiggle out of her work clothes and into her sweats, while listening to Cody tell her all about his visit to the local Primate Sanctuary.

"Bobo could throw kisses and Mongo smokes cigarettes, even though he shouldn't. And we had to stand way back from George and Gracie, because they're old and grouchy and they like to throw their poop and other gross stuff."

Honor wrinkled her nose.

In the background, Josh coached, "Show her how the apes talk to one another, Cody."

Honor laughed out loud as Cody made monkey faces and ape sounds.

"And you know what, Honor? Monkeys can swing on branches like Spiderman, but they don't use spider webs."

Honor teased, "Is there any topic of conversation that doesn't remind you of Spiderman?"

When it was finally Josh's turn to talk, he moved close to the microphone and lowered his voice. "Okay, I know I couldn't see anything, but just knowing you were changing your clothes was all it took to turn me on. You really need to get back here."

Honor chuckled. "Down, boy. Now, what have you been up to besides watching apes throw crap at people?"

"Actually, I helped my brother John work on some architectural designs for one of his vintage restoration projects. In return for my free labor, he's going to take a look at the sketches for your mom's house this weekend. How about you? How are you sleeping without spirits invading your dreams?"

She smiled. "Not as well as you would think. Guess I don't like sleeping alone."

"Me neither. Good thing I didn't have to."

Honor raised her eyebrows, giving him a you-better-explain-quickly look.

Josh laughed. "Cody got into bed with me last night. He said it was quieter in our bed. Apparently, some of the 'invisible people' were having a conversation at the parlor table by his bed and he couldn't sleep."

"Is Cody okay? He wasn't frightened, was he?"

"No, he was fine... more annoyed by the noise than anything. When Cody told them you were in Chicago, they said to remind you to build your social circle. Any idea what that means?"

"I'm not sure. I'll think about it and let you know if I figure it out."

As soon as they said goodnight, Honor shut down her computer and got busy reviewing the financial reports she and Julie had discussed earlier that evening. She hoped it would be easy to spot evidence of William's wrongdoing, but it wasn't. She finally gave up, hoping Sarah Jacobs would have better luck deciphering the columns of numbers. She turned her attention to the task she did understand; updating project close-out reports. She worked her way through the entire stack before falling asleep, exhausted.

Chapter 43

Honor slapped the buzzing alarm clock, silencing it as she tried to clear the sleepy cobwebs from her mind. As soon as she remembered she was in her condo, an unexpected wave of disappointment washed over her.

She closed her eyes and pretended Josh and Cody were living in Chicago with her. She sat up smiling, but as she tried to visualize them here, her mood darkened. They would be miserable, cooped up inside all winter with no family nearby. Gradually, she realized she couldn't ask them to move here. If she wanted her relationship with Josh to survive, she would have to commute—assuming, of course, she was successful in forcing William to do the right thing and divide the company in half with her.

Honor reached for the tablet and pen she kept on her bedside table, determined to outline a plan of action before the growing list of disheartening challenges could overwhelm her. Without conscious thought, she drew a tight circle on the page and then traced over it again and again. The image reminded her of Margaret's admonition to build a social circle. Honor stared at the doodle until her goal finally became clear.

I must form a circle of business allies to help me reveal William's dishonest business practices.

***

When she arrived at Soft Fix, Honor pushed the door open with her box of finished paperwork.

"Good Morning," the receptionist purred.

Normally, Honor would have simply returned Debbie's greeting and walked on past, but not today. Smiling, she stopped and put the box down, pretending to rest her arms while assessing the young, southern Kim Basinger look-alike.

"Debbie, you're witnessing the end of an era. I'm going to stop taking so much work home with me."

"I'll believe it when I see it," Debbie giggled, tossing her blond curls. "But you really should spend more time enjoying life."

Honor smiled again. "How about you, Debbie… are you enjoying life?"

If Debbie thought Honor's behavior was odd, she didn't acknowledge it.

"I guess so. I have a new boyfriend. He's a bicycle currier, but he's real smart. He's going to school at night to earn a degree in architecture."

Honor nodded her approval. "He sounds ambitious."

"Yes, he is. He's been trying to talk me into enrolling, but I'm not cut out for college."

Honor coaxed her to continue. "But I doubt you want to be a receptionist forever, either."

Debbie shook her head. "No. Don't laugh, but I'm actually thinking about applying to the police academy."

"What's stopping you?"

"I don't know."

Debbie liked to project a dumb-blonde persona, but Honor knew better. Debbie was unflappable, even when the lobby was busy and the switchboard was lit up like a Christmas tree. And she always seemed to know everything that was going on throughout the office.

An idea suddenly popped into Honor's mind.

"Well, I think you should look into it. You would make a great detective."

Debbie cocked her head, intrigued. "Really? What makes you say that?"

"Because you know everything about everyone around here, and most of it you learned by piecing together clues. For instance, how did you know George Avery was quitting his job before he turned in his resignation?"

Debbie stared at her, confused by the question.

Honor tried again. "Seriously... think about it and tell me, step by step, how you figured it out. What clues tipped you off?"

Debbie bit her lip, thinking. "Well, first of all, he received a couple phone calls which he asked me to transfer from his cubicle to the conference room. His need for privacy struck me as odd. Then he came to work all dressed up and went out to lunch without Greg, who had been his lunch buddy every day since he started working here. I knew something was up, but I didn't put two and two together until he told me he was expecting a letter from a delivery service. He said it was very important that I let him know as soon as the letter arrived. When the delivery came, I checked the return address label and saw it was from a competitor of ours, so I was pretty sure it was a job offer. I told him his letter was here and he practically ran to the lobby to get it. I saw him hide the envelope in the middle of a stack of folders he was carrying, so I asked, 'When do you start your new job, George?'"

Debbie paused to giggle at the memory. "You should have seen the look on his face when he realized I knew what he was up to!"

"You see what I mean? You have natural instincts for detective work. You're able to figure out all kinds of stuff, even though you're stuck out here in the lobby by yourself most of the time. How do you do that?"

Debbie sat up straight in her chair. Honor knew she was hooked, and began to reel her in.

"You know, if you're game, we could try an experiment to prove you have what it takes to become a great detective."

Debbie bobbed her head in agreement.

Honor smiled. "During the next day or two, you write down three office secrets you think you've uncovered. Then we'll get together and I'll tell you if your powers of observation led you to the correct conclusions. If you do well, I'll help you check into police academy requirements."

Debbie's face lit with excitement. "I'll take that challenge."

Honor picked up the box of paperwork, pleased with her first attempt to make an ally who could help her learn some of William's secrets. It was time for step two.

In her office, Honor retrieved the project files that were ready for invoicing from the box, along with a small bag of gourmet doughnuts she purchased earlier that morning.

As she walked past Julie's desk, her assistant asked, "Don't you want me to take those to the accounting department for you?"

"No, thanks. I want to say 'hello' to the accounting staff and apologize for creating so much work for them to do."

Seeing the disappointment on Julie's face, Honor flashed a knowing grin. "Don't worry -- if I see Ben, I'll put in a good word for you."

Julie blushed. "What? I don't care about..."

Honor raised her eyebrows, daring Julie to deny she had a crush.

"Okay, but *please* don't be too obvious about it."

Honor laughed and continued on her way. At the end of the hallway, she opened the double doors to the finance department and almost ran into William's assistant. Honor didn't like Yvonne and knew the feelings were mutual. They exchanged tight, insincere smiles without speaking, and Honor headed directly for the senior accountant's office.

Helen Ellis was so short that if she didn't wear her gray hair piled in a bun on top of her head, she might have been completely hidden by the piles of work on her desk. Her dark-circled eyes widened when she noticed Honor standing in front of her.

"Are you lost or something?" Helen quipped over the top of her wire-rimmed glasses.

Honor smiled disarmingly. "I have a lot of work to go over with you, but first, look... I come bearing gifts!"

Aware she had a weakness for pastry, Honor handed the doughnuts to the plump, middle-aged woman.

"Bribes aren't necessary," Helen said as she pulled one of the doughnuts from the bag. "But thanks just the same."

Honor moved a chair next to Helen and went through the projects one by one, pointing out unusual billing charges and other significant factors. While they worked, she tried to observe the rhythm of the department. She noticed Yvonne kept a vigilant eye on her through the open door. A few people started to come into Helen's office, but when they spotted her with Honor, they turned on their heels and walked away.

Honor decided the majority of the finance employees were jumpy, but she wasn't sure if they were hiding something or if they were simply surprised by the unusual sight of her in the midst of their territory.

When they finished, Honor got up to leave. "Don't hesitate to call me if you have any questions," she offered. "And please tell your co-workers they need to get used to seeing me in here, Helen. I plan to make it a regular practice going forward."

Helen cocked her head, her curiosity evident. "Okay." Her lips curved into a smile. "And thanks again for the bag of calories."

Chapter 44

Just as Honor pushed one of the double doors open to exit the department, Ben Dugan entered through the other one. Honor smiled. "Hey, Ben - I wanted to thank you for helping Julie hang up the new bulletin board in my office. It looks great!"

"No problem," he mumbled. "I was happy to help out."

Trying not to sound like a match-maker, Honor ventured, "Julie told me she has really enjoyed your company during the past few weeks. You know, she's a real people-person, and when I'm not around, she feels isolated in our department, surrounded by nothing but serious engineering geeks. It's nice that she has a close friend like you."

Ben blushed, revealing his attraction to Julie. To avoid embarrassing him, Honor said, "Speaking of my engineering geeks, I guess I better get back to them."

As she stepped through the doorway, Honor glanced over her shoulder and saw Yvonne making a beeline to Helen's desk. She shook her head. "What a busybody."

Back in the engineering department, Honor distributed assignments to various project managers for completion, and then she sat down with Julie to go through a few of the other stacks of paperwork, which still seemed to dominate every corner of her office. She was determined to make sense out of the financial reports, and with that objective in mind, she began to highlight everything on the reports that she didn't understand. She was hard at work when she heard a knock on her door. She looked up to find William standing there, trying much too hard to appear casual.

"I heard you were meeting with Helen Ellis this morning. What's up?"

Honor was positive Yvonne had called him immediately after debriefing Helen, but chose not to let on. "I've decided to take a more 'hands-on' approach to the financial side of project management, so you'll probably be seeing me on your side of the building more often."

William couched his objection behind one of his broad smiles. "Come on, Honor...why mess with a good system? I like things the way they are."

Honor was undeterred. "I confess I was never very interested in your end of the business, William. But now that I'm traveling more, I realize I need to understand our finances so I can resolve issues over the phone and comprehend the reports Julie sends to me." She plastered an innocent look on her face. "Actually, I'm just following your lead, William. While I was away, you called our customers to assure them everything was under control because we're interchangeable. That's great, but for your statements to be accurate, we both need to understand our total operation."

William paled, realizing his plan to entrench himself in her department had backfired.

Honor pretended not to notice William's discomfort. She waved her hand at the mountain of paperwork, stacked on her table. "I was planning to ask Helen to help me understand this stuff, but if you think that would be too much extra work for her, I can just take a class in financial management at the college annex. I'm sure I could get one of the professors to spend some time with me after class, helping me decipher all these reports."

William stammered, "No need for you to get outside help. I can teach you myself. But let's take things slowly, okay? After all, you're pretty busy right now, handling your mother's affairs and keeping up with technical stuff, right?"

Honor could tell William was beginning to hit his stride in

his sales pitch. "And, you're right. I talked to a few of our customers about minor technical issues while you were away, but it didn't take me long to realize how easy it was to get in over my head. It's difficult to step back and forth across the aisle between finance and technology. In fact, the more I think about it, the more convinced I am that we should just keep things the way they are. After all, this company is our baby. We make an unstoppable team when we put our separate skills together, right?"

Honor wondered how many times she had heard William spout that worn-out refrain over the years. Unmoved, she persisted. "I'm tired of not being able to understand our financial operations, William. If you want to teach me about them, that's fine, but please don't try to discourage me."

William's wide smile reappeared, undaunted. "Okay... it sounds like your mind is made up. Let me know when you want to get started and I'll try to clear some time on my calendar. But please keep in mind that we're getting close to the end of the year and that's a busy time for me. Perhaps in January..."

Honor interrupted. "I know there are a lot of financial issues that have to be handled at the end of the year, but that's my point, William. I don't understand any of them and that needs to change."

William nodded stiffly, and then checked his watch. He pretended to be amazed at the time. "I've got to run. We'll talk more about this later." With that, he disappeared from her doorway.

Honor trembled. She didn't usually stand up to William on non-technical issues. Proud of herself and flush with adrenalin, she decided to check on Debbie, to see if she had given any thought to the detective challenge.

When Honor entered the lobby, Debbie flipped her notebook closed and cried, "No peeking!"

Honor was delighted to find she was taking the challenge

seriously. "Okay, I'll wait. If you're free tomorrow night, I'll take you out for dinner and you can show me what you've come up with."

Debbie patted her notebook confidently. "It's a date. I think you'll be impressed. In fact, you should probably start checking into police academy classes right now."

Honor chuckled. "I think I'll wait till tomorrow."

Still smiling, Honor turned and walked back to her office, wondering if her attempt to create a circle of allies might actually have an impact on Debbie's long term career plans. "Wouldn't that be something?" she mused under her breath.

At the end of the workday, Honor decided to take the freshly highlighted reports home with her and compare them to the reports she gathered from the conference room on her first night back in Chicago.

Julie stepped in as she was packing up. "Wow, I'm impressed... you're leaving the office on time two nights in a row! You really are turning over a new leaf." Then she noticed the stack of paperwork in Honor's arms and chided, "You know, simply changing the location of where you're working isn't actually the same thing as leaving work."

"I know, but with Josh and Cody so far away, there really isn't much else for me to do."

Julie nodded. "I can understand that. At least you finally have something more important in your life than work. That's encouraging."

Chapter 45

When she arrived home, Honor phoned in an order for Chinese food and laid the highlighted reports on the floor, side by side with those she had pulled from the conference room trash bin. She wasn't sure what she expected to find, but hoped the reports with handwritten notes would help her understand the report's content, and perhaps identify irregularities. Toward the bottom of the box, she found a few items that, like leftover socks in a laundry basket, didn't have a highlighted report match. She set these items off to the side and concentrated on the reports that she could compare. When she reviewed the first report against its mate, she was disappointed to find no differences whatsoever. She tossed the un-highlighted copy into the trash and started comparing the next set of reports.

Soon, loud knocking interrupted her concentration. "Yen's Chinese Cuisine," a voice called from the other side of the door. Honor paid for her dinner and then resumed her review, using her chopsticks simultaneously as eating utensils and pointers.

She found a few cryptic notes in the margins of the third report, but didn't have any idea what they meant...something about referencing an account schedule. She stuck a post-it flag next to each note, hoping to make sense of them later. She finished comparing the reports just in time to call Josh and Cody.

It quickly became obvious that for Cody, the novelty of talking to Honor on the computer had worn off. He barely said hello before asking, "Did you buy me something today?"

"Not today, Cody. Sorry."

Disappointed, he turned his back to the computer screen and asked, "Can we go get ice cream, Daddy?"

"Knock it off, Cody. We're talking to Honor because she's far away, remember?"

Cody turned back around and yawned. "When are you coming home, Honor?"

Honor knew he was too young to understand concepts of time beyond "now" and "later", so she cooed, "Pretty soon, Cody. I miss you so much I can hardly wait to get back to Florida."

Josh picked Cody up and took his place in front of the monitor. Much to Honor's surprise, instead of trying to squirm out of Josh's grip, Cody rested his head against his Daddy's muscular shoulder and closed his eyes. Honor shot Josh a questioning look.

"Sorry Cody's so cranky. We were running errands today, so he didn't get his nap."

"I know exactly how he feels. I've had a long day, too. In fact, I wish I was the one sleeping on your shoulder right now."

"I'm not sleeping," Cody protested, raising his head.

Josh frowned and ignored his son's comment. "Tell me about your day, Honor."

Honor outlined her plan to develop allies and her decision to learn more about the financial aspects of her company.

The comforting hum of the computer and familiar cadence of grown-up conversation in an otherwise quiet room proved too much for Cody. He laid his head back down and let his eyes drift closed. Josh put his finger against his lips, warning Honor not to say anything about him falling asleep, least he wake again.

Honor nodded her understanding and smiled at the peaceful child. Then she told Josh about the cryptic notes she had discovered on some of the reports, referencing an account schedule.

"Account schedules are kind of like decoder rings for

reports."

"What do you mean?"

"Say there's an item on a report called *Overhead Expenses* and there's a dollar amount next to it. An account schedule would detail what specific items make up that number-- like rent, office supplies, printing, or whatever. If you reviewed an itemized overhead expenses report and found that some of the items listed as company expenses were actually William's personal expenses, then you would be able to prove that William was mishandling the company's funds."

Honor nodded, listening carefully.

"Now, I'm no expert, but I think if William's hiding personal expenses in business accounts, that's tax fraud and if he's convicted, he could go to jail."

"Okay, then," Honor said. "I'll get a copy of the account schedule from the finance department tomorrow and begin looking for unusual expenses."

"Keep in mind that if William is misappropriating company money, he probably keeps two separate account schedules... one that appears to list legitimate expenses, but contains inflated costs to cover up missing funds, and a second schedule that lists real expenditures."

Honor narrowed her eyes. "How do you know all this stuff?"

Josh laughed. "Don't worry, not from personal experience. I watch a lot of TV cop shows."

"Good. I was getting worried," Honor joked.

"Another thing... if he's keeping a double set of books, I doubt his whole staff knows about them. It would be too hard to keep them a secret. The real schedule is probably carefully protected against prying eyes. On the other hand, keeping books is a lot of work, so William probably isn't doing the accounting himself. That means somebody in that department knows what's really going on. You just have to figure out who it is and get them to confess."

"Is that all? Okay then... I'll take care of it tomorrow!"

Josh chuckled. "I didn't say it would be easy. But those notes you found in the margins could be important. They might help Sarah Jacobs determine which financial documents she should subpoena and, if things get nasty, who should be deposed... or maybe even prosecuted."

"I think I'll go by Federal Express and ship this stuff to Sarah tomorrow, instead of waiting until I get back to Florida."

"Good idea."

Honor told Josh about her plan to develop allies, including her bet with the receptionist, Debbie.

"Okay, now it's your turn. Tell me about your day. What errands were you handling that kept you-know-who from taking an n-a-p?"

"Actually, I was working on the engineering drawings for your mom's house with my brother, John."

"Cool!"

"Yep, and that's not all. I got in touch with my realtor in North Carolina and told her I was ready to list my house for sale. She seems to think it will sell quickly - something about homes in that area being considered hot properties. Anyway, it means I need to fly up there and pack up our stuff. And since I can't afford to stay at the Belleview Biltmore for the whole winter, I need to start looking for an apartment."

Honor wanted to tell Josh about her plan to commute between Chicago and Belleair, but decided it would be wiser to take things one step at a time.

"You and Cody are welcome to live in my mom's house while it's being renovated," Honor offered.

"Wow. Thanks, Honor." Josh murmured, obviously touched by her generous offer, "It would be nice to save on rent for a few months, but I think it might be too dangerous for Cody."

"Obviously, I still have a lot to learn about kids," she observed.

Neither of them wanted to stop talking, but eventually they

hung up and Honor dragged herself to bed, conjuring a plan to defeat William. She had grown more self-confident in Florida, but knew she must hide this fact from William a little bit longer. It would be easier to collect evidence if the rat bastard wasn't prepared for her to mount a serious challenge against him.

She fingered the five pearls on her necklace until she fell asleep, still strategizing.

***

Honor woke up early, eager to continue pursuing her plan. She slid the highlighted reports into a large envelope, along with the rest of the paperwork she had collected on her first night back in Chicago. She addressed the package to Sarah and dropped it off at Federal Express on her way to the office.

When she arrived at Soft Fix, she stopped by the reception desk. "Hi, Debbie. Are you still free for dinner after work?"

"You bet!"

"Would it be okay with you if I invite Julie to go with us? I want to get both of your opinions about a new business strategy I'm considering."

"It's fine by me as long as you don't mind her learning my three office secrets. You're still paying for dinner, right?"

Honor chuckled. "Yep. See you after work."

When Honor asked Julie to join her and Debbie for dinner to discuss a new business concept, Julie was puzzled.

"Debbie... Debbie who? You don't mean ditzy receptionist Debbie, do you?"

Honor indulged her with a smile. "You know I always suspected she was faking that 'dumb-blonde' routine, and now I'm positive it's an act. Debbie's actually a very intelligent woman."

Julie looked dubious. "If you say so... I guess I'll go; but mostly because my only other dinner option is a crappy, microwaved turkey pot pie."

"Gee, thanks."

The two women engulfed themselves in their work as the day melted away unnoticed. Late in the afternoon, Honor decided to revisit the finance department.

When she pushed through the heavy double doors, Yvonne forced her grimace into a smile. Honor returned the fake smile, and then walked over to the accountant's office, went inside and closed the door.

She put Helen at ease with a cheerful greeting. "Good afternoon. I just stopped by to make sure that you have everything you needed from me in order to get those invoices out."

"As a matter of fact..." Helen began, reaching for a stack of paperwork.

While Helen rifled through invoices, Honor sat down and casually glanced around the tiny office. She spied several pictures of a small, red-headed boy scattered throughout the space, but sadly, she had to admit she knew very little about Helen's personal life and had no idea who the child was.

Hoping to expand her circle of allies, Honor cooed, "What a cute little boy! Is he about five years old?"

Helen glanced up and smiled at one of the boy's pictures. "That's my grand-baby, Eli. He'll be six years old in December."

"I'm dating a guy who has a four year old son. Tell me, is Eli crazy about Spiderman?"

Helen gave her a knowing smile. "Yeah, most little boys are. Actually, I think Eli likes almost every superhero they feature on the Cartoon Network."

"I have to confess that until recently, I didn't even know there was such a thing as a Cartoon Network."

Helen laughed. "I know what you mean. What's your little guy's name?"

"Cody. He's super-intelligent and he has the most adorable smile I've ever seen." Honor paused, recalling Cody's aloofness the previous night. "But I'm a little concerned he's going to forget me while I'm away."

Helen knitted her eyebrows. "Why would you think that?"

"Well, when I first got back to Chicago, Cody was really excited to talk to me over the computer, but last night he seemed bored with me."

Helen nodded. "Don't worry about it. Little boys are like rubber balls, constantly bouncing from one thing to another; never stopping unless they're asleep. The secret is to have something interesting to show him every time you call... or you can watch a few cartoons before you place your call and then tell him what happened to the bad guys. You'll regain Cody's interest in no time."

"Really? Thanks, I'll give it a try."

Honor didn't want to push her relationship with Helen too far - too fast, so she turned her attention to the stack of invoices. "Now... let's see if I can answer your questions so we can get these things processed and out in the mail."

Honor was able to field every one of Helen's questions, which impressed the accountant. Obviously, she wasn't used to working with managers who understood the nuts and bolts of billing for technical work.

Once the invoices were complete, Honor stood. "I have to get back. I still have a pile of work on my own desk."

Helen glanced around her office at the stacks of paperwork still covering most flat surfaces. "I know exactly what you mean. Good luck."

As Honor left the finance department, she noted several curious stares, in addition to Yvonne's contemptuous glare. She smiled at everyone - except Yvonne.

Chapter 46

That evening, Honor, Julie and Debbie left the office together and shared a cab to one of Debbie's favorite restaurants. Honor was pleasantly surprised Debbie had selected Pisano's, a cozy Italian restaurant, furnished with high-backed, dark mahogany booths that were dimly lit and draped with heavy red curtains to provide each table a great deal of privacy.

Debbie raved, "Everything on the menu is great, but their specialty is spaghetti and marinara meat sauce, baked inside a bread bowl, with mozzarella cheese melted on top. It isn't a dish for people who count calories, but it's delicious."

Honor and Julie accepted Debbie's recommendation and ordered three spaghetti bowls and a bottle of Chianti for the table.

After a few minutes of light conversation, Honor turned to Julie. "You may not know it, but Debbie is very perceptive. In fact, she has figured out all kinds of office secrets, simply by paying attention to little details that most of us overlook and then putting clues together. I challenged her to uncover three secrets that most people at the office don't know about." She smiled at Debbie. "Okay, now - amaze us with your discoveries."

"Well, for starters, I know you're sleeping with someone in Florida, and that he has a little boy."

Honor shot an accusing glance at Julie, who shrugged her shoulders. "Don't look at me...I didn't say anything."

Debbie giggled. "Julie didn't give you up. I figured you were dating someone new when I saw you walk into the office on your first day back. A woman pays more attention to her clothes, hair and make-up when she's dating and you were doing all of that. Also, you looked more relaxed than I've seen you look in months, so I figured you had either taken up yoga or you were getting laid... and like I said, you were all dressed up."

Julie laughed and nodded. "You're right about the man, but what makes you think he has a little boy?"

"Well, one of the guys went into your office the first day you were back, and later he made a wisecrack about some Spiderman stickers he saw on your desk. So I put two and two together, and bam, I deduced your Florida boyfriend must have a young son. Am I right?"

Honor smiled. "Okay, you got me. What else have you figured out?"

"I know that Yvonne has the *hots* for William."

"Aw, come on," Julie protested. "You're guessing. How could you possibly know something like that?"

"By keeping my ear to the ground, that's how. Yvonne would do anything for that man." Grinning, she added, "And she probably has, if you get my drift."

Honor and Julie stared intently at Debbie, waiting for her to explain her deductive logic.

Debbie obliged. "Yvonne tried for ages to break up your marriage to William. She was always making comments about how you guys were mismatched from the beginning and how William deserved a woman who understood him, and stuff like that. I'm telling you, she was absolutely giddy when you guys announced that you were going to divorce. She was walking on air, trying to listen in whenever people were talking about it. She kept asking everyone if they had heard the *inevitable news*. I think she believed she would finally have an opportunity to make her move. She probably envisioned her and William as the perfect couple, running the company together. But then, shortly after you announced your divorce, we all learned about his girlfriend, Sherri, and their baby. I honestly thought Yvonne might slit her wrists. The day the news leaked out, she actually had to leave the finance department several times and come out to the lobby to cool down. She was muttering under her breath, calling Sherri obscene names and everything."

Debbie nodded solemnly. "These days, Yvonne says stuff to undermine William's relationship with Sherri every chance she gets. I think in her fantasy world, William will wake up from the Sherri trance any day now, and realize that his one true love is none other than his faithful old sidekick, Yvonne."

Honor shook her head to clear it. "Everything you say makes perfect sense and actually helps explain Yvonne's nasty attitude, but wow... I never suspected a thing. Are you sure about this?"

Debbie nodded. "She hides her feelings pretty well most of the time, but yeah, I'm positive."

Honor considered Yvonne's role in the break-up of her marriage and quickly realized she probably owed the woman a debt of gratitude. After all, if her marriage to William hadn't ended, Josh and Cody would never have become such a precious part of her life. She noticed Debbie was watching her carefully, chewing on her lower lip and wondering if she had said too much.

Honor smiled and Debbie relaxed. "So far, so good. Now what's the third thing?"

Debbie had saved her juiciest revelation for last. "William pays for Sherri's car insurance with company money, and maybe some other stuff, too."

Honor's jaw fell open and Julie's fork clattered to the table. As calmly as she could manage, Honor asked, "How do you know that?"

"I'm friends with the new accounting intern, Mixed Metaphor Melody. I gave her that nickname because, well... for obvious reasons. Anyway, right after you left for Florida, Melody came storming into the lobby to vent. She tells me, 'I guess it's true - when the cat's away, the water goes over the dam!'" Debbie giggled. "I laughed at her mangled metaphor, and told her that it's supposed to go 'when the cat's away, *the mice will play.*'"

Debbie suppressed another giggle. "Anyway, Melody was upset because, while she was filing some paid vendor statements, she noticed the amount we were paying for our fleet vehicle insurance seemed inappropriately high. She hoped to impress William with her attention to detail, so she reviewed the statements carefully and discovered what she thought were errors. When she showed the statement to William, he yanked it away from her and told her she wasn't being paid to work on things that didn't concern her. A few minutes later, he slammed a huge stack of employee time cards on her desk and told her to review every one of them for overtime pay errors. Melody knew he was punishing her with busy work. She told me she might not be 'the sharpest note in the drawer'," Debbie giggled again, "but she knew the company's fleet vehicles were cargo vans, and it didn't make sense that we were insuring a Jaguar and a Porsche."

Debbie paused to take a breath. "Hell, Melody was so pissed, I was even afraid to correct her metaphor to either '*the sharpest knife* in the drawer' or 'the sharpest note *in the stanza*'. Anyway, after she calmed down, I told her to keep her mouth shut because paid intern positions aren't easy to come by."

Debbie and Julie turned to Honor, waiting for her response. Blood was pounding in Honor's ears, but she hid her rage.

"No, I didn't know about this, but you can bet I'll be looking into it PDQ."

"PDQ?" Debbie repeated.

"Yeah—pretty damn quick. And tell Melody not to worry— her job is safe." Honor clenched her jaw, determined not to let knowledge of William's actions spoil the evening. She held her wine glass up in a toast. "Congratulations, Debbie... you did very well."

The topic of conversation changed when their gourmet spaghetti bowls arrived at the table, a combination of top shelf dining and comfort food. Julie ordered a second bottle of Chianti.

The time was right for Honor to disclose her new goal. She wondered what Debbie and Julie would say if she told them a spirit from the 1800s visited her while she was sleeping in Florida and advised her to build a social network. She opted for a version of the plan that wouldn't leave them questioning her sanity.

"I think if the two of you were given the opportunities you deserve, you would enjoy tremendously successful careers in whatever industries you choose," she began. "Unfortunately, it's difficult for women to find support along the path to their dream jobs. In fact, sometimes it seems as though people intentionally put obstacles in the way, making it almost impossible to keep going. I'd like to change that." She turned to face Julie. "Debbie is interested in pursuing a career in law enforcement, so I told her I would help her look into the police academy."

Julie glanced at Debbie, surprised by her career choice.

Debbie nodded. "I think I'd be good at solving crimes."

"I can see that," Julie said. "One day, I'd like to be in charge of operations for a big company, but I doubt it will happen. I had to quit college in my junior year."

Honor hesitated, but she knew if her social circle was going to succeed, its members would have to trust each other with their secret goals and strategies. She took a leap of faith and announced, "I think William has been embezzling a lot more than car insurance from our company. He's very smart, but if I can prove that's true, maybe I can force him to split the business in half, or buy me out so I can start a new company in Florida."

She smiled at their stunned faces. "I think each of us is more likely to reach our goals if we band together to help one another."

Debbie nodded slowly. "I'm in."

With eyes like saucers, Julie affirmed, "Me too. How do we get started?"

Honor pumped her fist. "Great! Well, first and foremost, we agree to watch one another's backs and keep each other's confidences. At the same time, we agree to look for opportunities to help each other achieve our goals. You know how the early settlers circled their wagons for the protection of the group? Well, our circle would help protect one another's dreams and aspirations. And we'll keep an eye out for new members: women who are serious about wanting to achieve worthwhile goals and who would be willing to help support the other members of the group."

Without going into detail, Honor explained how social circles had been used by women for more than a century to build successful coalitions.

Julie lifted her wine glass. "Here's to the first meeting of 'The Wagon Circle.' May each of us watch out for one another, help one another, and cheer for one another when we reach our goals."

Honor beamed as they clinked glasses.

"'The Wagon Circle' sounds too ancient," Debbie noted. "Let's shorten it to 'The Circle'."

"Okay. To '*The Circle*,'" Julie agreed as they toasted once more.

They hashed out some of The Circle's basic principles and pledged to make themselves available if another member wanted to discuss an issue or particular course of action.

"And offers of assistance have to be specific," Honor insisted. "For instance, I promised to help Debbie find out about the police academy. But I should have told her exactly how I can help. Like, I can her help fill out the police academy application and write her a letter of reference."

Julie added, "Two of my cousins are police officers. I can introduce you to them, and ask them to give you some pointers."

"Exactly!" Honor enthused. "I'll bet we can find lots of ways to support one another."

At closing time, they took a cab back to the office, where they reluctantly parted ways, each of them still excited about The Circle's potential to have a lasting impact on their lives.

Driving home, Honor contemplated Debbie's disturbing revelation earlier that evening. "I swear I'm going to uncover every single one of William's rotten secrets, starting with this fleet vehicle insurance scam."

Chapter 47

Honor's mind was spinning by the time she arrived at her condo. Because of the late hour, she fought the urge to call Josh and tell him everything that had transpired that day. Frustrated and unable to relax, she finally made a cup of hot tea and turned on her laptop. Working always helped her unwind.

She started outlining a few ground rules for The Circle, but the moment her fingers touched the keyboard, ideas began to flow, one right after another. By the time Honor was tired enough to shut down her computer and go to bed, she had completed the entire framework for the new organization, including bylaws, an enrollment application questionnaire, and even a simple database to store all of the member's information.

Satisfied with her accomplishments, she drifted off to sleep, still thinking about The Circle. She didn't know if the group would ever become a successful social circle, but she hoped it would at least encourage a few women to follow their dreams.

***

Honor wasn't asleep very long before her alarm clock went off, but she didn't mind. She got ready for work in a rush, still excited about The Circle and eager to share the newly written bi-laws with Julie and Debbie.

As she drove to Soft Fix, self-doubt crept into her thoughts, triggering an avalanche of uncertainty. By the time she reached the office, she was questioning the entire concept. What if she was the only one who still believed The Circle was a good idea in the harsh light of day? She hesitated outside to steel herself; then entered the lobby, prepared for the worst.

Debbie was at her post behind the receptionist desk, engaged in a spirited discussion with the accounting intern, Melody. When they spied Honor, Melody rushed over to her and, without so much as a "good morning", began pleading her case in hyper-speed.

"Please let me join... I need The Circle. I have a great head for numbers, but I'm a total disaster when it comes to composing reports or writing business letters, and without writing skills, I'll never qualify for promotions into management, and if you let me join The Circle, I could help someone learn about accounting and in exchange, she could teach me to write, and it would increase my career potential forever. You know...like they say, 'Teach a man to fish and he laughs best for a lifetime'!"

Stunned, Honor shot a glance at Debbie, who was holding her hand over her mouth to keep from laughing at her friend's enthusiastic use of yet another badly mixed metaphor. Honor regained her composure and then spoke to Melody as though she were trying to calm a puppy. "Okay... okay. Settle down. You're in. Perhaps someone can help you with your speaking skills, too."

Melody's confused expression was too much for Debbie, who burst out laughing.

Honor shook her head. "Actually, I developed some guidelines for The Circle last night and I'd like to get some feedback. Could the two of you join me for lunch?"

Melody squealed with delight and Debbie nodded her assent, still giggling.

Julie was just as excited about The Circle as the others, giving Honor's self-confidence a much-needed boost, and restoring her sense that the social circle could provide real value, beyond helping her collect proof of William's crimes.

"Why do I have to wait till lunch to see the bi-laws?" Julie whined.

"Because I'm returning to Belleair tomorrow and I think our morning would be better spent improving our telecommuting work processes."

"Good point. Damn."

They installed a camera on Julie's computer, so they would be able to see one another when they were talking throughout the day. They also created new directories on the company's computer network, so they could easily transmit files back and forth between them, avoiding the paperwork nightmare that had developed the last time Honor was in Florida. During a brief lull in their work, Honor decided to confide in Julie and tell her the real reason she had come back to Chicago.

"Years ago, I was duped into signing legal documents, giving William total control of Soft Fix. It doesn't appear to matter that we used my money to finance the start-up, or that I've poured my heart and soul into this company since the beginning. Unless I find evidence of illegal activity, I won't have any leverage to force William to admit I'm his equal partner. And, as if that isn't bad enough, I can't even quit Soft Fix and start over on my own, because William has me hog-tied with a non-compete agreement."

Julie was stunned. "I don't know what to say, Honor. It's not right. I mean, this place is your whole world!"

"Well, it was my whole world for a long time, but not anymore. I have a chance for a new beginning with Josh and Cody and I want to make the most of it. I figure that no matter what happens, I'll be fine as long as I keep the two of them at the center of my universe. Besides, things could be worse. I mean, William still believes I'm in the dark about all of this, so he won't suspect that I'm looking for evidence to use against him. I'm going to pretend to work as though nothing has happened and hope if I give him enough rope, he'll hang himself."

Honor suddenly broke into a grin. "Besides, now that I don't have any incentive to work crazy hours to keep growing the company, I might actually be able to take some time off and enjoy my life for a change."

Julie's face was still etched with concern. "Well, I must admit, I agree with that part. And I'm thrilled you finally found someone who makes you happy. But Honor... losing your life's work..."

"Wait a minute. Don't think for a minute I'm giving up on Soft Fix without a fight. I'm calling my attorney today to tell her that William's using our fleet vehicle account to pay for his wife's car insurance, and then I'm going to keep searching for more evidence. Now, let's get back to work."

Honor spent the rest of the morning meeting individually with the senior members of her engineering team to review new processes, aimed at making her telecommuting less of a burden on them. She saved her meeting with Ellen Christiansen, the only female senior engineer, for last.

As their meeting was ending, Honor suggested, "Ellen, if you can force yourself to leave Mr. Peaches in his cage for an hour or two, I'd like you to join Julie, me and a couple other ladies for lunch. We're forming a woman's group to provide mentoring alliances."

"Thanks for the offer, but I don't usually get along with other women. They think I'm weird, and I think they're insecure and whiney."

Honor snickered at her blunt assessment. "I understand your point of view, but I think you'll find this group is different. Each member is intelligent, ambitious, and is pursuing challenging career goals, just like you."

With a little more coaxing, Ellen agreed to meet her in the lobby in fifteen minutes and join the group for lunch. Honor was pleased. She considered Pete Cross and Ellen to be her peers when it came to work ethics and software development expertise. But more than that, they were her friends and in recent years, she felt closer to them than to her siblings.

As Honor walked back to her office, Charity, Patience and Chastity flashed through her mind, causing her a twinge of guilt. She had been dodging her sisters' phone calls for weeks, mostly because she was trying to avoid telling them she was communicating with spirits of the dead, including their mother.

"They wouldn't think I'm so crazy if they experienced a few spirit encounters for themselves," she muttered. The fleeting thought instantly crystallized into a plan of action. She wrote a quick list of activities necessary to carry out her fledgling plan, then gathered her notes about The Circle and joined the others in the lobby. When the eclectic group headed out together, several people took notice, including the always-lurking Yvonne.

To avoid running into their co-workers, the group took a cab back to Pisano's Restaurant, and requested a booth in the back. Debbie ordered antipasto salad, garlic bread-sticks and Italian wedding soup for everyone, while Honor briefly explained the concept of The Circle to Melody and Ellen.

Then Honor opened a folded sheet of paper and announced, "Last night I wrote five basic principles to govern The Circle." She cleared her throat and began reading, "First: *An intelligent woman can accomplish anything, as long as she has motivation and allies. We agree to be one another's allies.* Second: *To get, we must also give. So we agree the help we provide others must equal or surpass the help we receive from the group.* Third: *We agree that all goals we pursue and all help we provide must be legal, but..."*

Honor glanced up, *"being creative and looking for loop holes will be encouraged."*

The group chuckled and nodded their approval.

Honor continued, "Fourth: *We agree we will never undermine the efforts of another member in the pursuit of a goal* and Fifth: *All new members must be sponsored by an existing member, who agrees to serve as her mentor and teach her principles of The Circle."*

Julie interjected, "And if a member doesn't obey these principles, her sponsor should have the authority to revoke her membership in The Circle."

"You don't think that's too strict?" Honor asked.

Debbie spoke up, "I think it's good. The rules should say we support one another, but we also police one another."

"I like it, too. It'll keep the wolves in cheap clothing out of the hen house." Melody said.

To everyone's amusement, Ellen cocked her head and asked, "Should I be concerned that I understood Melody's point?"

Chapter 48

Honor passed around copies of the new member application form. "Remember, The Circle is no place for modesty or insecurity. Goals can be as outrageous as your imagination allows. But they should also be real goals that you are willing to work hard to achieve. And one more thing: Please keep The Circle confidential until we work out all the details." Secretly, Honor reasoned the fewer people who knew she was developing allies, the better."

Everyone agreed to complete their applications by the following Monday and send them to Honor in Florida, where she would be busy perfecting The Circle's data base system. Honor was enjoying the discussion, but because the group had attracted attention when they left work, she insisted they return to the office on time.

As soon as they entered the building, Honor noticed William milling around the lobby trying, but not succeeding, to appear nonchalant. He sauntered over to them.

"So, where have all you ladies been?"

Honor gave him one of her sweetest smiles. "I took a group of employees from various departments to lunch, to discuss how we might better support one another in the future."

Debbie smiled at Honor's misleading remark as she turned to hang her jacket on the nearby coat rack. Then she strutted to the reception station, her tight skirt drawing William's attention until she disappeared behind the desk.

Still distracted, William turned back to Honor. "Um, when are you going back to Florida to finish up?"

William's subtle attempt to continue directing Honor's life irked her. "I'm leaving tomorrow afternoon, but as I already told you, I won't be *finishing up* anytime soon. I'll be telecommuting for a while."

William glared at her, displeased, but Honor stood her ground, drawing strength from her new allies. "Don't worry, William. As your partner, I'm still committed to taking excellent care of our customers. The work processes my engineering team and I put in place should allow us to coordinate seamlessly on technical assignments. But as I mentioned the other day, I need to understand our corporate finances better, so I can keep up when attending meetings virtually. For starters, I need some tutoring on a few financial reports. Do you have some time to help me… or could you loan me Ben for a while this afternoon?"

William's eyes narrowed, but he flashed a broad smile. "Gosh, I'm swamped today, Honor… and so is Ben. Maybe we could go over some things when you return."

William's smile used to charm Honor, but these days it held all the appeal of an oil slick. She started to respond, but he took her arm and skillfully maneuvered her away from the group.

When he spoke, his voice was almost a whisper. "Honor, even though we're not married anymore, I still care about you and have only your best interest at heart. You know that, right?"

He didn't wait for her to respond. "So listen to me. You don't belong in the Retirement Capitol of the USA, shacking up with some beach bum. You belong in Chicago…here with your Soft Fix family… where you fit in."

Honor despised William for attempting to conceal his self-serving motives behind a false sense of concern for her welfare. She gently removed his hand from her arm, struggling to hide her true emotions.

"Thanks for your concern, William, but I'm fine…really.

And listen, since you and Ben are both busy today, perhaps one of your other finance employees could help me out this afternoon. I don't need much... just an overview of our weekly financials, and maybe a key that shows what items make up each of the numbers on the reports."

William paled, his smile now a sneer. His voice boomed. "You're being ridiculous. We don't have time for this. Besides, you know we've always kept the technical and financial divisions separate because *you can't grasp the principles of strategic marketing and finance* and I gave up trying to teach you!"

Honor shrank from him, her resolve crumbling into embarrassment. Was that the truth? Frantically, she recalled how she had tried to learn everything about the business in the beginning. Learning about corporate finances was like trying to learn a foreign language and William teased her relentlessly. Before long, she stopped trying; opting to focus all of her attention on the technical side of the business, where she could shine.

With his back turned, William didn't see Debbie stand up behind the reception desk. She struck a boxer's pose, encouraging Honor to fight back. Her demonstration of support was exactly what Honor needed to regain her voice.

"William, I'm determined to overcome my aversion to corporate finances. I want to be able to help out whenever you're away, the same way you've been able to help run the technical division while I was in Florida. You always say, 'You and I need to trust in each other one hundred and ten percent, and trust in outsiders zero percent.' But how can you trust me when I don't actually understand how our business operates?"

William scowled, frustrated by Honor's uncharacteristic persistence.

"Maybe the new intern, Melody, could work with me a little bit today."

"God, Honor, give it a rest already," William snapped. "I

told you that my division is really busy this time of year." An instant later, his insincere smile reappeared. "I'll try to free Melody up, but no promises, okay? And meanwhile, I want you think about what I said." As he walked away, he called over his shoulder, "You belong here."

Debbie gave Honor a thumbs-up sign and answered the phone.

Honor smiled at her; but as she watched William disappear down the hallway, she knew it would be a tremendous challenge to outsmart him.

Back in her office, Honor considered whether William was cocky enough to keep records of his illegal activities on the company's computer network. Paper records might be easier to keep hidden, but manual bookkeeping was also a lot more work. William tended to be lazy, so it was likely that he would take the easier route as long as he believed she would never catch on.

Honor perked up at the thought. Although she hadn't worked on the company's computer network recently, she still had all the passwords necessary for backdoor access to everything. She could log into the system and pull out all the information Sarah needed to prosecute her case.

That is, provided she could figure out what she was looking for and where to find it.

Honor pushed open the doors to the Corporate Finance department, ready to begin her quest. She approached Ben Dugan with what she hoped was an exaggeration rather than an out-right lie. "Hey, Ben, William said he'd try to free-up Melody's schedule for an hour or so, to work with me on some stuff." She paused and wrinkled her nose. "Uh oh. From the look on your face, I'm guessing he forgot."

"He didn't mention it, but sure, Melody can help you for the rest of the afternoon. She's just reviewing old timesheets, and that chore can easily wait."

As Ben escorted her to the intern's cubicle, Honor hoped

for Julie's sake that he wasn't involved with William's crooked activities. She pushed the worrisome thoughts from her mind and focused on the task at hand: how to make the most out of her time with Melody.

Once Ben was out of earshot, she asked, "Melody, can you print me a copy of our financial account legend... you know, a report that itemizes the content of each account?"

"Hmmm. I'm not sure that report exists...at least I haven't seen anything like that. What if I print out a report that lists all the account numbers and their titles? From there, we might be able to figure out what each account contains. Would that help?"

"That sounds like a great place to start."

Melody tapped her keyboard a few seconds and a report began to print. While they waited for it to finish, Honor ventured, "Debbie said you've been assigned grunt work as punishment for asking questions about fleet vehicle costs. Care to fill me in on the details?"

Melody nodded and whispered conspiratorially, "I have sort of a photographic memory for numbers, but since I'm the lowly intern, I get stuck with most of the boring filing. To keep from going stir-crazy, I started reviewing everything before I filed it. That's when I noticed the fleet vehicle insurance premiums seemed too high to be accurate. I decided to dig into it and called the vendor to see why they were charging such high premiums for a few cargo vans. Well, the insurance agent told me our fleet included a Porsche and a Jaguar, which he assumed were company perks for you and William. I know you drive a BMW, so I asked Ben about it. He didn't know the answer, but said he would ask William. The next thing I know, William takes my insurance file and says he'll handle the matter himself. When I asked if I had done anything wrong, he smiled and pretended he wasn't mad, but I could tell he was totally pissed. Then he said I had a good eye for detail, which would be helpful in reviewing time cards and *presto*." She pointed to the large stack on her desk. "I've been watching the parking lot ever since, to see who drives what. William drives a Porsche, but I still don't know who drives the Jag."

"William took the file?"

"Yeah, he took everything. But remember my photographic memory?" Melody smiled. "Since William was acting so weird, I decided to write down the key information while the details were still fresh in my mind." She opened her desk drawer, retrieved a thin file, and handed it to Honor.

Just then, Ben returned, obviously agitated. "I'm sorry, Honor, but I forgot I need Melody to work on something for me for the rest of the day. I don't know how it slipped my mind, but it's really important."

Honor smiled and stood, knowing very well that Ben had been sent by William to stop her from learning any key financial information. With her hands behind her back, she discreetly lifted the report from Melody's printer.

"No problem, Ben. Unfortunately, Melody and I were just getting started, so I guess my education will have to wait. What's the critical project you need her to work on?"

Ben looked down at his shoes. "Just some finance stuff...deadlines...you know. Uh...Melody, I'll be right back with the, um...project." He turned on his heel and walked away.

Honor didn't buy his routine, but apparently Melody did.

"Ben is a great guy, but he's always forgetting stuff like that. He's not much of a planner, which makes it hard to work for him. He's always shooting from the seat of his pants and then the rest of us have to scurry around getting stuff done at the last minute."

Honor laughed. "Melody! If Ben doesn't plan things in advance, then you say '*he shoots from his hip*' or '*he flies by the seat of his pants*', but trust me... what you said he does is a whole different kind of problem."

Melody thought about it for a second, then her eyes widened. "Yeah, I guess that would be pretty bad."

Chapter 49

Honor was still giggling over Melody's goof when she passed by Helen's office and caught her curious eye. She decided to stop to say hello, and shared Melody's unfortunate mixed metaphor. When they finally stopped laughing, Honor reminded Helen, "I'll be leaving for Florida tomorrow afternoon. Do you need anything from me before I go?"

"Nope. I got all those invoices out already. By the way, how are things going between you and Cody?"

"I'll find out tonight. I'm taking your advice about keeping him interested in our conversations. I'm going to buy a Spiderman coloring book on the way home, so we can talk about the characters on each page. I'll let you know if it works."

Honor left, still clutching the folder containing the accounting report and Melody's information. She suspected the Jaguar belonged to *Miss Barely Legal*, William's child bride, but she would have to wait until she returned to Florida to confirm that hunch.

The day was evaporating. She met with her engineering team to finalize their long-distance work routines. At the end of the meeting, Pete Cross spoke up. "Quit worrying so much, Honor. I know I speak for the whole group when I say we're fine with you telecommuting -- that is, as long as you never forget your Blackberry again."

Honor grinned. She had developed an extraordinary team of engineers. No matter what happened, no one could take that accomplishment from her.

***

When she left the office that night, Honor dashed across the street to a drugstore and began searching the low children's book shelf for a Spiderman coloring book that Cody didn't already own. While she was stooped down, she caught sight of William coming into the store, and he was not alone. He and Yvonne strode down the aisle opposite where Honor was crouched, without noticing her.

She heard William's seductive voice ask, "Ribbed for her pleasure or cherry-tasting?"

Yvonne tittered like a schoolgirl, completely smitten by William. "Why not both?" she teased.

William laughed and they headed for the counter to pay for the condoms.

Honor sat down on the floor, repulsed. When he had asked her for a divorce, William claimed it was because he found his soul mate. But here he was, cheating on Miss Barely Legal only a few months after she had given birth to his baby. It crossed Honor's mind that Miss Barely Legal had herself, knowingly bedded a married man, and in terms of karma, *what goes around, comes around.* But she felt sorry for the girl, nonetheless.

She picked out a coloring book and walked to the check-out counter, where a friendly, elderly woman was operating the register. "I'll bet your little boy is going to love this."

Honor didn't correct the woman. "I'm sure he will... he loves anything with a web on it. Listen, that man and woman who just left...do they come in here often?"

The clerk glanced toward the exit. "I've never seen the woman before, but the guy has been a regular for years. He does pretty well with the ladies... always seems to have a new one hanging on his arm. Personally, I don't get it. He must have a lot of money or something. Why? Do you know him?"

"I thought I did," Honor mumbled.

She left the store and stopped for a slice of pizza before going home. Though she tried to focus on savoring the Chicago deep-dish slice, her mind insisted on replaying the scene between William and Yvonne. Feeling gullible and foolish, she wondered how many times a similar scenario had played out while she was still married to the rat bastard. She was thankful those days were over.

Suddenly she realized how much she wanted to be in Florida, talking to Josh and feeling his arms around her. She wanted to rock Cody to sleep. She wanted to visit with Darcy and Margaret in her dreams and thank them for teaching her the value of developing allies and standing up for herself. And she didn't want to sell her mother's home when the renovations were complete. With her thoughts clear, she decided, "It's time for my sisters to learn about my new life."

At her condo, she poured a large glass of wine and curled up in a comfortable chair. Her first call was to her sister, Charity.

"Hi, Cherry. Brace yourself. I've decided to start commuting between Chicago and Belleair, and I want to buy-out your share of Mom's house."

"What? Are you crazy? You have the perfect life... a beautiful condo in a fantastic city, plenty of cash and no obligations. I *dream* about leading your life. And why would you want to spend any more time in sleepy old Belleair than you absolutely have to?"

"Because..."

"Wait a minute...this decision to uproot your life involves a man, doesn't it?"

"Well, I am seeing a special man, but my decision really has more to do with some stuff I learned during my stay at the Belleview Biltmore Resort. It's about living my own life and keeping my priorities straight."

Cherry interrupted again. "What is it about that place? Mom had to stay there every couple months to 'get her fix,' and now you're talking the same way she used to."

"About that...did you ever hear Mom talk about spirits

haunting the Belleview Biltmore?"

"Yeah," Cherry replied cautiously.

It wasn't the answer Honor expected. "Really? What did she say?"

"It happened one summer while you were at camp and Chase was staying with Grandma. Mom decided to take me with her to the Resort for one of her weekends. I remember being all excited about having a sleep away with Mom, just the two of us. She told me the hotel was haunted, and if I was lucky, I would see a few ghosts. I thought she was joking. Anyway, the whole weekend, Mom insisted we take long naps in the afternoon and go to bed early. I remember being really bored. Every time we woke up, she asked me if I saw any ghosts in my dreams, and she seemed disappointed that I didn't. It was all pretty creepy, if you ask me. I just went with her the one time, which was fine with me. Why are you asking me about this, anyway?"

"Just curious."

"I seem to remember Mom took Chase with her one weekend, too. You know, I should think about taking each of my girls on special sleep-away trips. We could…"

"Listen, Cherry, the reason I called is to see if you would like to come down to Florida for a visit before the renovation gets underway. I'm inviting Patty and Chase, too."

"That sounds like fun, but I'll have to take a look at my calendar to see if I can get away. You know, the girls keep me so busy…"

"This is important to me. Try to work it out and let me know tomorrow, okay?"

As soon as they hung up, Honor dialed Patience's number. A recording invited her to leave a message.

"Hi, Patty. We have lots to talk about. I've decided to buy Mom's house and I'm hoping to get all of us girls together in Belleair for a few days real soon. Call me as soon as you get this message and I'll fill you in on the details. Love ya!"

Lastly, Honor called Chastity, the easy-going baby of the family, who was in favor of Honor keeping the old family home.

"That's cool. I didn't like thinking about other people living in our house," Chase said. "What will you do about your company in Chicago?"

"Things are up in the air, but for now, I'll telecommute. I'll know more soon," Honor hedged. "In the meantime, I'm staying at the Belleview Biltmore for a little while longer, and I'm hoping to talk you, Cherry and Patty into coming down for a few days... sort of a Macklin sisters' reunion before the remodeling gets underway. Are you game?"

"I wouldn't mind coming down, as long as we all stay at Mom's house and not that hotel."

"I'm intrigued. Why would you rather sleep in an empty house than at a luxury Resort?"

"Didn't you ever hear the story about my weekend there with Mom?"

"No... tell me."

"I was just a little kid, and I know it's silly, but I had some nightmares there, and they scared me so much that I never went back."

"What did you dream about?" Honor coaxed.

"It doesn't matter. I just think the hotel is creepy and would rather not stay there, okay?"

Honor was certain Chase's nightmare was actually an encounter with the spirit realm, but decided to wait until Chase was in Florida before revealing her own experiences there.

"No problem... we can stay at Mom's, but I want to introduce you guys to the new man in my life, Josh, and his little boy, Cody."

Chase squealed, "Yippee! I'm so glad you're finally over William." She hesitated a moment, then confessed, "I guess it's okay to tell you now. William hit on me the last time I came to visit you in Chicago."

Honor cringed. "Why didn't you tell me?"

"I didn't want to mess up your marriage."

"Well, I'm sorry that happened to you. I saw him slipping around with his assistant, Yvonne, earlier tonight, so he probably cheated on me a lot."

"Yuck, he's with Yvonne? That bag of bones? Wonder what he's up to? I mean, men like William are all about using women. His kind runs after young girls to use their bodies, but you have to wonder...what's he using Yvonne for?" Chase clucked her tongue. "Watch your back, Honor. He could be trying to gain Yvonne's loyalty so she'll manipulate company records or lie for him. I've seen women like her do some crazy shit for men."

"I hope you're wrong, but thanks for the warning. I have to run, but I'll try to call back tomorrow to lock in a date for our reunion."

When they hung up, Honor poured herself another glass of wine, fetched the coloring book and then dialed Josh and Cody on her computer. Helen's idea about using the book to hold Cody's attention worked perfectly. They discussed each of the Spiderman characters and which crayons Cody would choose to color their costumes. Then he showed her his scraped elbow.

"I forgot I wasn't supposed to run by the pool and I fell down," he explained.

"Aw, poor Cody. If you put your elbow on the computer screen, I'll kiss it and make it better."

After her kiss, Cody inspected his scrape and declared, "Kisses don't work over the computer."

Honor pretended to be shocked. "That didn't work? Well when I get back to Florida tomorrow, I'll have to kiss it right!"

Cody grinned at the news of her return and nodded his agreement.

Off-screen, she heard Josh say, "Okay Cody, it's time for bed. Say 'goodnight' to Honor."

Cody mumbled his farewell while climbing off the chair,

then Josh's face appeared on her monitor, his blue eyes sparkling.

"Hey, did I mention my whole body hurts? I'm think I'm gonna need lots of kisses all over."

Honor laughed. "I'll bet."

He gave her a wink. "Bye for now. I'll call your cell after I get Cody to sleep."

Honor decided to see how much of her packing she could get done before Josh called and was pleased with her efforts. By the time the phone rang, she was packing the last of her things—some sexy lingerie.

She told Josh everything that had transpired over the last two days, starting with forming The Circle and ending with Chase's warning that William might be using Yvonne to help hide his criminal activity.

Josh whistled. "Wow. Busy couple of days, huh? For what it's worth, I agree with your sister. William does seem like the kind of scumbag who would take advantage of a woman like that. But even together, they're no match for you. I mean, look at what you're capable of. You just created a whole organization in a single night!"

Honor blushed. "Give me a break. It's not an *organization*. It's a little group."

"Well, maybe it's a little group right now, but all you have to do is give it a catchy motto and it could go national."

Honor giggled. "A catchy motto?"

"Sure—something like - '*In the circle of life, we're the part that comes after the Girl Scouts and before the Red Hats.*'" He chuckled. "Well, you'll think of something better."

"Yeah, right."

"What can I say? I expect big things from you."

Chapter 50

Honor secured her condo and car, then threw her bags in the taxi and headed to the office to get a bit more done before her flight to Florida.

In the lobby, Debbie handed her a completed membership application form for The Circle. "I figured you could use my application to get started on the membership data base."

Honor grinned. "This is great. You're officially *Member Number One.*"

As she approached her office, Honor noticed Julie talking in hushed tones with Ben Dugan. Not wanting to interrupt, she awkwardly mumbled "good morning" and slid by the couple. She pulled out her desk chair and plopped down, pretending to be completely engrossed with Debbie's application form.

The moment she sat, Honor heard paper crumple on her chair. She lifted herself up and pulled out a wrinkled document that had been left on her seat. It was a report very similar to the one Melody had printed out for her, except this one had the same kind of cryptic notes in the margins that Honor had found in the conference room recycling bin her first night back in town.

Honor puzzled over the pages of the report, trying unsuccessfully to understand what the notes meant, until Julie walked in and closed the office door behind her.

"Ben is going to quit his job," Julie blurted. "He said William has flipped out and is trying to cover up all kinds of bookkeeping entries. He's making changes to the histories of several accounts and threatening the jobs of anyone who questions his directives. Ben thinks William is afraid of what you're going to find... or what you may have already found."

"I get the same feeling...William's hiding something and I'm getting close. The problem is I still don't have a clue what it is." Honor held up the report. "Did you leave this on my desk chair?"

"Nope." Julie walked around to Honor's side of the desk so she could read the report over her shoulder. "I think those notes are in William's handwriting," she observed.

"I agree, but can't make out the notes. This word looks like it might be *Duncan* and that one might be *Bay*... or maybe *Boy*...or *Buy*. And these notes over here look like they might be acronyms...*KFHG* and *SMLI*. I just can't make heads or tails of it."

Further review of the report was pointless, so Honor hid it in her purse, away from prying eyes. After bidding farewell to her staff, she walked down to see if she could spot any unusual activity in the finance department, using the pretense that she was there to say goodbye to Helen.

Seeing nothing out of the ordinary, Honor stepped into Helen's office. She was on the phone.

"Later?"Honor mouthed.

Helen raised her pointer finger, signaling "one minute," and quickly wrapped up her conversation. "Don't worry... something will come up. Listen, I have to go now. We'll talk later. Love you!"

Helen returned the phone to its cradle and explained, "I don't usually take personal calls at work, but that was my daughter, Wendy. She's the mother of this little guy in my pictures. Her company has just been bought out and they are laying off the entire administrative staff. Her worthless ex-husband hasn't been in the picture for over a year now, so if she doesn't get a new job pretty quick, she might lose her home."

"Gee, I hate to hear that."

"I guess she and Eli could move back in with my husband and me, but our home is so small...there really isn't any yard for my grandson to play in, and we live on such a busy street." Helen shook her head. "I'm sorry. I shouldn't be bothering you with my personal problems when I know you have a plane to catch. What can I do for you?"

"Don't apologize. I just stopped by to thank you. Your suggestion about the coloring book worked like a charm on Cody."

Helen smiled. "No problem."

"Now, about your daughter...what kind of work does she do?"

"She's an administrative assistant to one of her company's Vice Presidents. She's really smart. Wendy was in her junior year of college when she got pregnant and had to drop out. She wants to go back and finish her business degree when Eli gets a little older, but it's hard for a single mother to juggle so much."

"Did Wendy inherit your work ethic and penchant for accuracy?"

"Absolutely."

"Good. We don't have any openings here at Soft Fix, but we have a few customers that might have an opening. I'll make a few calls before I head back to Florida."

Helen's eyes moistened. "I didn't expect that...thank you so much."

"You don't need to thank me. I've come to believe that women should do more to help one another. I'll let you know if I come up with any good leads."

She started to leave, but then thought to ask, "By the way, Helen, do you know if we have a customer named Duncan?"

"I don't believe so. Why?"

Honor didn't want to tip her hand. "It's nothing. I just found the name written on a scrap of paper in my office and couldn't recall why I wrote it down." She pulled out one of her business cards and wrote her personal cell phone number on the back. "Have Wendy e-mail me a copy of her resume, and tell her to call me at this number, if she has any questions."

"I'll do that right now. Thanks again."

Honor walked to the back of the department to check on Melody. She was reviewing another huge stack of timesheets. When she saw Honor, Melody grumbled, "I'm trying not to complain, but man this job is boring. I hope William forgives me soon."

Honor sympathized, "Hang in there, kiddo."

"Wait a minute," Melody brightened. "I have something for you. I decided to get my application form done before you left. You know, the early bird gets the worm... um, not that I mean The Circle is a worm or anything."

Honor grinned. "I understand. Debbie completed her application, too."

She glanced down at the *goals* section of Melody's form and saw that, in addition to the writing and public speaking goals they had discussed, Melody added: "Earn My CPA."

"Ambitious goals, but I like them," Honor observed. "They embody the first principle... An intelligent woman can accomplish anything, as long as she has motivation and allies."

Melody nodded with enthusiasm and wished Honor safe travels.

As Honor made her way toward the exit, she noticed Yvonne working on some files at a long table. Yvonne gasped when she saw Honor approaching. She slipped off her cardigan and tossed it over the files.

Subtle, thought Honor, wondering what Yvonne was hiding. She tried to think of Yvonne as a victim, but still couldn't resist the urge to challenge her.

"Hey there, Yvonne. I saw you and William going into the corner drugstore last night as I was leaving the office. What were you guys up to?"

Yvonne's facial expression resembled a deer caught in the headlights of an on-coming car, but she didn't spew forth a sexual confession, as Honor half-hoped she might.

She sputtered, "Oh yes...the drugstore...uh, we just needed a few office supplies, like rubber bands and paper clips. We can get them at the drugstore for about the same price as the office supply stores, and we don't have to buy such huge quantities there."

Honor couldn't let the lie slide that easily. "Really? I thought William used interns to run those kinds of errands."

"Um, he does... but they were too busy doing... other things."

"I'll have to remember to tell William about the adorable young, blonde intern I just interviewed. She seemed eager to please, and I'll bet she would be happy to stay after hours and help out whenever he needs something from the drugstore."

The look on Yvonne's face was priceless. A part of Honor wanted to drag out the conversation, twisting the knife a few more times, but she decided against it and made her exit.

As she walked back up the corridor, Honor thought about Yvonne's pathetic situation. How often did she lie for William, and what was she hiding? Had William made enough pillow-talk promises that she was willing to risk her career to alter the accounting records that Ben refused to change?

Repulsed by this possibility, Honor considered turning around and demanding to see what Yvonne was doing. The only thing that stopped her was her fear that she didn't know enough about financial recordkeeping to figure out what was amiss. She opted to discuss her concerns with Sarah Jacobs and follow her recommendations.

Honor said goodbye to a few more people and then headed for the airport. Once again, she spent the entire flight writing in her journal; this time adding entries about The Circle. Writing helped pass the time, but more than that, she liked the idea of leaving something in her own handwriting for future generations to discover, just as she had come across the journal of Darcy Loughman in her mother's kitchen cabinet.

While waiting to deplane into Tampa International Airport, Sarah called.

"I won't keep you, but something's come up and I can't make our appointment tonight. Can we reschedule for tomorrow morning at ten?"

"No problem. Actually, I'm happy not to have to rush over to your office right now."

Honor hung up and boarded the shuttle between the airside and the terminal, just as she had done several dozen times in the past.

But this time, her arrival at the terminal would be different.

This time, Josh and Cody would be waiting for her.

Chapter 51

Honor heard Josh's voice before she saw him. He was calling after Cody while at the same time, trying to catch a helium-filled Mylar balloon before it rose too high for him to reach. Then she caught sight of Cody, running to her full-tilt. She bent down to catch him up in her arms and hugged him close as she walked toward Josh. Cody was holding onto her so tightly that she had to turn sideways to give Josh an awkward hug and kiss.

Josh laughed. "He missed you."

Honor replied, "I guess so! How about you?"

Josh licked his lips. "Me too. I plan to show you how much later tonight." He held up a bouquet of flowers for her while still wrestling with the uncooperative balloon. "Hey, Cody... you forgot to hold onto your present for Honor."

Cody released his death grip and reached for the string that was tied to the floating Mylar balloon. "We bought you presents to make you happy you're home."

Honor smiled at him and then at the red and silver *I Love You* balloon. "Why, thanks Cody. But truthfully, I missed the two of you something awful, so just seeing your faces was enough to make me happy."

By the time they took the escalator down to the baggage claim area, Cody was growing heavy in Honor's arms, but she didn't put him down. It was sheer joy having his little arms wrapped around her, with his cheek resting on her shoulder. She exchanged loving glances with Josh over the top of Cody's head, wishing nothing more from life than to experience a few thousand more moments, just like this one.

Once Honor had unpacked her things at the Belleview Biltmore, she and Josh took Cody down to the playground to burn off some energy before bed. They sat together on a double-wide Adirondack chair, watching Cody play in the sandbox.

Honor gazed into Josh's blue eyes. "I didn't realize how much I missed you until I saw you in the airport."

Josh tucked one of her curls behind her ear, and then let his fingertips slide over her cheek to trace the outline of her lips before lifting her chin for a tender kiss. "I'm so damn glad you're back. I was worried you wouldn't want to leave Chicago."

"You have nothing to worry about. Don't you know you take my breath away?"

Josh swallowed hard. "I think it's time for Cody to get his bath and hit the hay."

Honor nodded in agreement.

"Cody! Come on, buddy - play time is over for the night."

After his bath, Cody decided he wanted Honor to be the one to read him a story and tuck him into bed. She obliged, but when she finished the story, he begged her to read another.

"Hey, Josh, why don't you read the next story, while I hop in the shower? I think it's our bedtime, too." Honor licked her lips and gave him a seductive wink.

Josh cleared his throat. "Pick a short story, Cody...a very short story!"

When Honor walked out of the bathroom, clad in a pink lace baby-doll nightie and thong underwear, Josh let out a soft wolf-whistle. He flipped back the comforter and pulled her into bed with him as soon as she was within reach.

His voice was gruff with passion. "Christ...you just get better and better. You look incredible."

***

Honor snuggled with Josh, relishing the tranquil afterglow

and amused at how quickly he had fallen asleep after making love. She wondered if she would have an encounter with the spirit realm her first night back -- or for that matter, ever again. She whispered, "Margaret, I hope we still have a connection. I want to tell you about my new social circle and learn what happened to Darcy."

Honor dozed in and out of sleep, enjoying the simple pleasure of Josh's hard, lean body resting against hers. Finally, the fog started to swirl around her, thick and damp. Honor relaxed, letting the fog take her away.

When the clouds began to dissipate, Honor had no idea where she was. It was difficult to get her footing and the air was cold and misty. As the haze continued to lift, she recognized the outline of a ship's bow and saw Darcy on the deck, leaning against the railing. As she gulped in air to settle her stomach, Honor realized Darcy was attempting to do exactly the same thing.

"I've never been on a ship before and I'm not adapting to the conditions very well," Darcy moaned. "Perhaps my delicate condition makes the rocking more difficult to endure..." Her words trailed off, as she gulped more of the cold night air and then slid onto a nearby bench. "Thus far, I've spent most of the journey on this deck, where the effects of seasickness are less pronounced. Margaret makes excuses for me, least the other passengers take note of my growing belly and begin to suspect my condition."

She pointed to a woman, walking across the deck towards them. "And she sends her accountant, Hannah, to see to my needs."

As the woman drew closer, Honor's memory clicked. Margaret's accountant, Hannah, had been a child prostitute. Margaret saved her life the night she was almost beaten to death in a brothel.

Honor guessed Hannah was about twenty five years old now, and she still walked with a bit of a limp. Hannah sat by

Darcy on the bench and placed a tray between them. Lifting off a cloth, she revealed a small bowl of stew, some crackers and a cup of hot tea. Darcy gratefully accepted the tea, holding the cup in her hands to warm them, but she looked warily at the stew and crackers.

Hannah encouraged, "I know you don't feel well, but you must eat. Starving yourself isn't good for the babe."

Darcy avoided eye contact with Hannah. "What has Margaret told you about my situation?"

"Margaret knows I can be trusted and she thought you might appreciate the company of a woman who has dark secrets of her own."

Darcy nodded. "She's an insightful woman."

The two sat quietly while Darcy nibbled at the stew and crackers.

Finally Hannah interrupted the silence, hoping to cheer Darcy. "Take heart. This wretched journey will soon be over."

"The end of the journey might relieve the vapors, but it will also mark the onset of new tortures that I will be forced to endure," Darcy lamented.

Hannah tilted her head quizzically.

Unable to stem a tide of emotion, Darcy wept, "God is surely punishing me for being unfaithful to my marriage vows. And the worst of my punishment is yet to come. After I suffer childbirth, I must abandon the babe -- the only evidence that Rory ever lived. To the world, it will be as though he and our love never existed. I alone will ache for him every moment of every day for the rest of my years."

Large teardrops rolled unattended down Darcy's cheeks. "Alas, I can think of no greater retribution than what God has in store for me."

Hannah soothed, "I do not pretend to know God's plan, but I learned long ago that no one can tell a heart whom it is to love. A heart doesn't care about wedding vows or social circumstance, and it doesn't consider consequences. A heart can bedevil the mind until nothing else matters except what it desires, and it can convince the purest soul that all will work out in the end, even when this is far from the truth. When reality is laid bare, the heart often shatters."

Hannah rubbed Darcy's hands, warming them. "But I know from experience that one can survive heartbreak. The pain may seem unbearable for a time, but when your mind finally regains control of your heart, you will come to realize you made the best decision for yourself and for the infant. That's when you'll discover a glimmer of hope still lives within your broken heart, and with hope, all things will become possible once more."

Honor's eyes welled with tears. She was amazed that Hannah was still capable of such compassion after her ordeal. Honor was so lost in the moment, she didn't notice the folds of fog gathering until they were swirling around like a tempest. Knowing it was useless to resist traveling to the next memory destination, she relaxed and allowed herself to be carried away.

Chapter 52

When the fog cleared again, Honor was surprised to find she and Darcy were sitting exactly where they had been during the last memory, except now the sun was shining and the ship's deck was alive with people bustling about. Darcy stared out to sea, ignoring Honor's presence.

Honor glanced around, fascinated by the other passengers. She tried to imagine being in Darcy's situation during a time when strict rules of society controlled every aspect of life. She wasn't sure how long she had been day dreaming when Hannah's arrival snapped her out of her daze.

Hannah curtsied. "Good morning, Mrs. Loughman."

Honor supposed that in the light of day, social status could not be ignored on the ship's deck, the way it had been when it was dark and deserted. Darcy glanced up at Hannah, nodding her head without comment.

"May I sit with you and have a word?"

Darcy motioned to the bench next to her. Hannah pulled a book from a deep pocket in her skirt, looked around to make sure no one was within earshot, and sat, laying the book beside her.

"I was thinking about what you said last night and believe I may be of assistance."

Darcy studied Hannah, curious.

"You said that the worst part of your pain was that once the baby was gone, no memory of its father would exist. I understand this sorrow more than you know. When I was a child of eleven, I lost both my parents, whom I had loved and whose loving attention I had taken for granted. When they were gone, my sister, Marie, and I were left alone, with no relatives to provide for us. We were placed into an orphanage, which was run by dishonorable individuals."

Darcy protested, "This child will not be placed in an orphanage."

"I understand, but please, allow me to continue."

Darcy nodded.

"I tried to care for my younger sister the best I could, but the work at the foundling home was hard and the provisions scarce. We children battled for food and water, with the strongest and most determined surviving. The caretakers of the facility watched us fight over scraps of food as if observing dogs fighting over bones in an alley."

Darcy gasped, but said nothing.

"I was not very strong, but I was motivated to feed my sister, so I fought hard and we survived for a time. We endured a summer and most of the following winter before Marie became gravely ill. I was desperate to save her."

Hannah paused, momentarily overcome with the pain of her memories. She balled her fists and coughed, then continued. "One of the girls was friendly with a man who tended the grounds. In return for allowing him to become personal with her, the girl was given enough bread and meat to live without having to fight the others. I decided that, for the sake of my ailing sister, I would try to establish the same kind of relationship with the man. Much to my dismay, the other girl revealed my intentions to the man's wife. Later that same week, I was loaded onto a wagon and taken away from my sister. I will never forget the look on Marie's face as I was being pulled from her. I remember telling her to be strong and promising that I would come back for her. She looked so frightened."

Darcy reached over and patted Hannah's shoulder, unconcerned whether other passengers observed the comforting gesture.

Hannah swallowed hard and smirked. "I was told that my wish to become a whore had been granted. I was taken to a brothel and sold to the filthy man that ran the establishment for a few dollars. He took me to a room and..."

Hannah paused again, searching for words that would convey the brutal rape she had suffered at the man's hands. Finding none, she spat, "He took me to a room and showed me exactly what his customers expected of me."

Hannah glanced at Darcy. Seeing pity in Darcy's eyes, rather than judgment, gave her the strength to finish her story.

"Because I was young and pretty back then, I was allowed to work in one of the parlor rooms, which were a bit nicer than the common rooms, and were visited by wealthier clientele. I lived that life until I was nearly beaten to death one night."

Hannah hung her head. "After I healed, I came to live with Margaret and tried to find my sister. But it had been three years and no one at the orphanage remembered what had become of Marie. She probably died soon after they took me away from her. Still, a glimmer of hope remains in my heart that she was adopted by a kind family. I fantasize that she has been looking for me ever since, and imagine our joyful reunion. But in case she is already in heaven, I also pray that God will be merciful and forgive me for my sinful past... in the hope we can be reunited in heaven."

Honor bit her tongue to keep from screaming, "Forgive you for what? It's the men who abused you as a child who should be seeking God's forgiveness!"

Hannah glanced up, touched to see Darcy dabbing her teary eyes with a handkerchief.

"Now, now there. Don't cry for me. These things are in my past, not my present. I told you my story only so that I could make you understand that I survived my heartache by finding strength in my memories and keeping a spark of hope alive in my heart."

Hannah picked up the book and studied it. "I purchased a journal much like this one and filled it with recollections of my family. Memories of my mother and my father...of Christmases with presents... laughter and warm cocoa... the taste of my mother's pie and the feel of her soft kisses on my forehead...my father's voice as he read from the scripture and the sweet smell of his pipe...my sister's blue eyes and rosy cheeks...the puppy I named *Ebony* because his coat was so black and shiny..."

Hannah held the book out to Darcy. "The memories I captured in my journal give me comfort, even my darkest hours. Whenever I begin to doubt my family ever really existed, I read my book and am reassured. I remember that I was blessed to have been loved by them, even if it was only for a while."

Darcy reached for the journal with shaky hands.

Hannah's tone was deliberate, but tender. "Write everything in this book...your journal. Write about meeting this young man of yours. Include every detail of him and all the plans you made together. Put into words the love you have for your baby and the life you hope it will live. Do it now, while your memories are sharp and you still know them to be true. Then, on dark days, when you are not certain this part of your life ever existed, you can read this book and remember."

Hannah stood and pulled a pen and bottle of ink from her pocket, placing them on the bench beside Darcy. "Please believe me. Do this and that spark of hope in your heart will survive, come what may."

Darcy glanced from Hannah down to the journal. When she lifted her eyes, Hannah was already walking away. Gingerly, Darcy opened the book and stared at the white page for a long time. Then she unstopped the bottle of ink, dipped her pen and began to write, "I longed for a world so different than the one I inhabited..."

Honor's jaw dropped open. Darcy was writing the very journal that she had found in the bottom her mother's kitchen cabinet. She was baffled. How in the world had her mother come into possession of Darcy's journal?

As the fog began to roll in, draping around Honor and pulling her into its folds, she tried desperately to connect the dots, and wondered if her possession of the journal was the bridge connecting her to Darcy.

When at last she stopped tumbling through the fog, Honor's nausea was overwhelming. She had to take several deep breaths before the sick feeling began to subside. Finally, she was able to take in her surroundings.

They were in a hotel room, but the floral wallpaper in autumn hues, gas lamps and dark, missionary-style furniture combined to create a vastly different ambiance than the light and airy Belleview Biltmore. From the damp air and bustling city street sounds outside, Honor deduced they were in England.

Darcy was almost hidden behind a stack of books at a small wooden table, where she sat alone, writing in her journal. She lay down her pen, closed her ink and stood to stretch.

Honor gasped at the size of her abdomen, which had grown tremendously since the last memory. She knew Darcy must be very close to delivering the baby, and wondered if Margaret had already found a home for the infant.

Darcy picked up the top book from the stack, flipped it open, and read a passage out loud. Then she closed the book and paraphrased the passage as if in conversation with an invisible acquaintance. "Did you know Master Charles Worth finds inspiration for his elegant gown designs in historic portraiture?"

She thumbed through several more chapters, reading and then paraphrasing various passages. "Lord Leighton is a brilliant artist. Why, his most recent painting, '*Flaming June*,' brings to mind the work of Michelangelo." And then, "Emily Childers' paintings impressed Lord Halifax so greatly that he commissioned her to restore royal art treasures."

Darcy continued until she heard familiar voices in the hallway. She flung open the door and Hannah and Margaret entered, laden with packages. After exchanging greetings, Hannah unwrapped one of the packages, revealing a small bolt of lace. She proceeded to describe not only the tatting pattern, but the entire purchase process, including imageries of the street, the shop and even negotiations over the price paid. When Hannah finished, she gave the lace to Darcy, who then repeated the entire description while rewrapping the package.

Hannah opened the remaining parcels one by one and discussed the purchase of each piece of art or fabric in minute detail. Following each description, Darcy would repeat the story and rewrap the item.

Margaret unwrapped the final bundle, which contained a book and a tin.

Darcy groaned. "Another book? I don't think I can memorize one more word."

"If you hope to convince everyone you spent the summer season shopping with me in Europe rather than resting in a hotel suite, you must absorb everything," Margaret reminded her. "And chin up... this is a picture book about European architecture, and the tin contains a stereoscope, along with photograph cards of several famous structures. I think you'll find them most interesting."

"I'm sure I will, but might we please take a respite?"

Margaret nodded. "You've been working hard. Let's take our supper in the city this evening."

Darcy was revitalized by the offer and rushed to change into loose fitting clothing that would conceal her belly.

Hannah yawned. "I'm too tired to go out."

"How is it that I'm heavy with child, yet have more vigor than you?" Darcy teased.

"Perhaps it is because I walked miles today while you sat comfortably, with your feet propped up," Hannah shot back.

Honor marveled at how the passage of time had changed

Hannah and Darcy's relationship. In the memories she had witnessed earlier in the evening, they were strangers on the deck of a ship. Now they seemed more like sisters.

"Suit yourself, Hannah," Margaret interrupted. "Let's be off, Darcy. It will soon be dark."

Chapter 53

Honor tagged after Darcy and Margaret, excited to see London at the end of the nineteenth century. The day was just coming to a close when they stepped out of the hotel onto an uneven cobblestone walkway. A nearby shopkeeper was busy sweeping his stoop, but stopped long enough to tip his imaginary hat as they passed by. Horse-drawn carriages splashed through muddy potholes, clamoring for space in the narrow street. A man dressed in a top hat and tails walked by on stilts, carrying a small torch for lighting street lamps. People were beginning to gather at several outdoor bistros along the street, creating a light, festive atmosphere.

Honor was so distracted by the incredible panorama that she had to catch herself from tripping over jutting cobblestones time and again.

Margaret and Darcy selected a small terrace restaurant and were seated at a wrought iron table, lit by a miniature hurricane lamp. The waitress brought each of them an order of meat-pie and a glass of wine, the apparent fare of the restaurant for the day.

Amused, Honor wondered how customers would react in her world if, instead of letting them choose from a menu, the server just brought them an order of whatever the cook decided to prepare that afternoon. The sound of Margaret's voice recaptured Honor's attention.

"I found a family in a nearby farming community who will accept the babe with no questions asked, in exchange for a small dowry."

Darcy sneered. "I find it ironic that, had I possessed a dowry when I was a girl, I wouldn't be in this unfortunate position."

"It's no use dwelling on what might have been," Margaret clucked. "I found a discrete jeweler who is willing to buy some pieces of your jewelry collection. So when the time comes, you should be able to assemble the required dowry."

"Please tell me about the family."

"They have a few children. I counted three, but assume a few more were likely out working in the fields. The farmhouse has three rooms, so they'll have no problem making space for another child. And they own goats, so there will be plenty of milk for the infant."

"I don't want my child treated as a servant."

"Calm yourself, Darcy. Farm children work hard, but it's a good life. I'm sure your baby will be fine."

"Can I meet the family?"

Margaret shook her head. "It's not a good idea. The less the family knows about you, the better chance our plan has of succeeding. You have to trust me, Darcy. I negotiated several discrete adoptions in my former occupation and find it's best that I alone handle the transaction."

Darcy was miserable, but nodded her head in somber agreement.

An instant later, Honor was engulfed in fog and pulled away from the memory. Her heart broke for Darcy, though she knew there was nothing she could do to change the sad situation.

When the mist cleared, Honor was standing in a dark room. She could hear muffled sobs nearby, but couldn't see anyone. She edged toward the mournful sounds, feeling her way in the darkness.

Across the room, she heard rustling and suddenly the flame of a hurricane lamp blazed, illuminating the entire room. Honor shielded her eyes while they adjusted to the light, but through her fingers, she saw Hannah approaching the bed where Darcy lay.

Hannah placed the lamp on a nearby table. "Are you in pain, Darcy? Is the babe coming?"

"No," Darcy sniffed. "I'm sorry to have awakened you. I just can't seem to stop mourning what might have been."

Hannah sat on the edge of the bed and gently patted Darcy's back.

"There, there. Everything will be fine...you'll see."

Darcy shuddered, breathing in short gasps between sobs. "No, it won't."

Hannah lifted the quilt and slid into the bed. She wrapped her arms around Darcy and cradled her as she wept, gently brushing away her tears and smoothing her hair.

"I wish you had known Rory," Darcy choked between sobs. "It's distressing that his entire existence resides only in my memory. Knowing I'll never feel his loving embrace again breaks my heart. And failing to look after his child feels like a mortal sin."

"Darcy, I hope you won't be angry with me, but when you and Margaret went out for dinner, I read your journal. I know it was wrong, but I wanted to understand your pain."

Honor sensed mixed emotions bubbling inside Darcy. She didn't approve, but she didn't push Hannah away either.

Hannah continued, "I told you that Margaret saved me from almost certain death, but I didn't tell you the beating that almost ended my life came from the man I loved... whom I thought loved me. With one beating, he killed my dreams, our babe, and rendered me unable to have another child. And then Margaret had to pretend my death to protect me from further harm."

Hannah swallowed hard to quell the lump that was forming in her throat. "When Hannah Johnson was buried, so were my memories... both good and bad. I could never speak of them again."

Darcy gasped. "Hannah, my dear friend...I am so sorry. I must sound like a fool to you, crying over a lost love when I still have a home to go back to, and have never felt the back of any man's hand upon me."

"I thought nothing of the sort. I simply wanted you understand that until now, I have had to bear my losses alone, but neither of us has to do that anymore."

There was a long silence as each woman thought about the other's life.

Finally, Hannah spoke. "Even on my happiest of days, I never experienced anything like the love you wrote about in your journal. I wish you and Rory Collins could have had the life you planned together."

"Rory's love was a great blessing, even if only for a short while. I wish you could have known true love as well."

"Yes, how different my life might have been..." Hannah's voice trailed off.

Darcy and Hannah lay quietly together, lost in thought.

More than anything, Honor wanted to wake up right now, so she could hold Josh and Cody tightly to her, and never let them go.

All at once, Darcy became animated. She struggled into a sitting position on the side of the bed, babbling about a solution to all their problems. Hannah tried to comprehend the abrupt change in her mood.

"I know what to do now! Everything will be alright. Rory's memories will be yours and his child will be yours as well!"

Hannah knit her eyebrows together, trying to grasp Darcy's plan, but she was already on her feet, running to wake Margaret.

Like Hannah, Margaret was confused at first, so Darcy repeated her plan until Margaret was wide awake and nodding in agreement.

"Hannah always wanted a baby more than anything in this world. This would be a magnificent gift to her, Darcy."

"It will be as much a gift to me as to her. Rory's memory will live on through his child and I will be at peace, knowing the woman raising our child possesses strength, integrity and compassion. Hannah will be an excellent mother."

Hannah was stunned at the turn of events. For the next several hours, the three women worked out the details, turning *Hannah* into *Hannah Collins*, the widow of a young golfer named Rory.

The trio decided Hannah and the baby would move from Florida to New York, where no one knew them. Once there, Margaret's social circle would be utilized to furnish Hannah with bookkeeping customers, thereby generating enough income to support her and the child.

"I will always be there to help you," Darcy promised Hannah. "I'll start by giving you the dowry I had planned to pay the farming family for adopting my baby. And I'll write down every detail I can remember about Rory, so that one day, you can tell his child all about him."

Hannah hesitated. "Dearest Darcy, though I am overjoyed at the prospect of becoming a mother and replacing my true past with Rory's tender love story, I feel I am taking everything from you."

"You take only my burden. I will be ever content knowing the love Rory and I shared did not die, but simply transformed like a butterfly, into something even more beautiful."

As Honor faded into the thickening fog, she heard Hannah promise, "I swear to you, Darcy, you will never be sorry. I will be a good mother to your child."

This time, Honor woke in her own hotel room. Purring, she rolled over to Josh and spooned into the curve of his back. As she drifted back to sleep, she vowed to appreciate every moment with Josh and Cody, never forgetting the fragility of life, the strength of love or the magic of tomorrow's possibilities.

Chapter 54

"Where there's smoke there's bound to be fire, Honor," Sarah Jacobs said into the phone.

She was pleased Honor had uncovered evidence that William was charging the company's fleet vehicle account for personal coverage.

"It's a good start. If we're able to prove he regularly abuses his financial authority, that's called a pattern of fraudulent behavior. It'll be easier to convince a judge that you were a victim of intentional fraud, perpetrated by William, once we have established his pattern."

Honor felt less positive. "Were you able to decipher the acronyms on the Soft Fix financial reports I sent you? I was hoping they represented common legal terms or financial jargon."

"No, they don't mean a thing to me, but I do have some good news. The report you found lying on the chair in your office is actually a detailed list of Soft Fix's accounting files. File names usually indicate what types of documents are contained in them, so I'm working my way through the list, trying to determine which files might be significant. Once I figure that out, I'll have you access some of the more interesting files on your company's computer network for closer review."

They agreed to meet the following week to assess their progress.

Meanwhile, Josh was thrilled with Honor's decision not to sell her mother's home and rolled out the draft renovation plans for her review.

"I opened the primary living space to improve flow and modernize the interior, but I was careful to preserve your home's Victorian charm."

Honor nodded. He took pride in his work and it showed. "These are impressive, Josh, but can you design one of the rooms to serve as an office for me? It looks like I may be telecommuting quite a bit."

"How about the big bedroom across from the master suite?"

"But that's Cody's room."

Josh paused. "Cody has his own room here?"

Honor was perplexed. "Of course he does. He's been taking his naps in there every time we're over there and he seems to like that room."

Then, Josh's real question dawned on her. She realized she had told him she intended to buy out her sisters' interest in the house and wanted him to remodel it, but they never discussed living there once the remodeling was complete.

Her eyes flew open. "Oh Josh... I'm so sorry. I thought you understood. I shouldn't make assumptions about such important things. I was hoping this would be our home... yours... mine... Cody's... don't you want..."

Before Honor could finish her thought, Josh pulled her close and kissed her hard.

"Hell, yes, I want." He kissed her again and then pulled back. "Listen, I know we planned to spend Thanksgiving here with my family, but what would you think about a change in plans? As much as I love spending the holiday watching football with my brothers, I think we should spend our first Thanksgiving in North Carolina, packing up my house there."

Honor wasn't used to such spontaneity and her mind was spinning. "But we already accepted James and Lisa's invitation. Won't they be offended if we renege?"

"With so many of the Js in attendance, the three of us won't be missed. Besides, when my brothers learn the reason I'm missing the family dinner is because I'm packing to move back to Florida, they'll be ecstatic. I think we should put my furniture into storage and find a furnished apartment to live in until we get the remodeling finished."

Honor stammered, "I guess I'm game... if you're absolutely certain it will be okay with Lisa."

"Is something else bothering you?"

Honor screwed up her face. "Yes there is. I can't believe I brought so many clothes back from Chicago and I still don't have the right wardrobe with me! I have the coat I wore to the airport, but none of my other warm clothes."

Josh laughed. "I'm sure we can find something for you to wear. I thought you were worried about me suggesting that we get an apartment together. You know, if you think we're moving too fast, I would totally understand. It's just..."

Honor cut him off. "I am absolutely ready for that step, Josh. I must admit, I'm a little sad to think about leaving our grand hotel suite to move into an apartment, but I can't think of a happier reason to leave the Belleview Biltmore than to begin a life with my two guys."

Josh's blue eyes twinkled. "Okay then... why don't we fly up day after tomorrow? The whole trip shouldn't take more than three days. I'll call and have movers deliver one of those huge storage cubes to my house for us to pack my stuff into."

"We need a checklist. Hold on while I grab some paper and a pen."

"Don't bother. In the time it takes to write everything down that needs doing, I could have already done most of it."

Honor gasped. "*Everything* has to go on a checklist. Without one, won't you worry we're forgetting something? Besides, don't you want the satisfaction of checking stuff off when it's finished?"

"Umm... no and no."

"Life together is all about compromise, you know."

"Okay, you do the list and I'll do the stuff."

After Honor completed her list, she called the office to check-in and was surprised to hear, "Thanks for calling Soft Fix. This is Melody. How can I direct your call?"

"Hi, Melody. Why are you covering the switchboard? Where's Debbie?"

"One of Julie's cop cousins agreed to let Debbie experience a typical day in the life of a police officer by riding along with him for a shift. It was sort of last minute and Debbie couldn't find anyone to fill in for her, so I volunteered. Truthfully, I hate answering phones, but it's cool to know I'm helping Debbie reach her goal."

"Well, I'm impressed you're following the principles of The Circle. Can you transfer me to Julie?"

Julie also was busy with The Circle.

"I know we're supposed to be keeping things confidential, but this morning Ellen Christianson decided to sponsor her first new member -- a young computer technician named Becky Adams. They met at some computer conference and she was impressed by the girl's potential, but thinks she needs guidance. I hope that's okay because she already gave me Becky's completed application. Are you making good progress on The Circle's database design? It looks like we're going to need it real soon. Anyway, I scanned all the completed applications I've collected and just sent them to you via e-mail."

Honor opened Julie's e-mail as soon as they hung up and began reviewing the applications. She was delighted to read Becky Adam's reason for wanting to join The Circle.

"I'm tired of hearing about strangers who have accomplished amazing things," she wrote. "I want to meet real, successful women and see first-hand what opportunities are out there so I can become one of the people who achieves amazing things."

Included in her list of "Strengths/Contributions", Becky wrote that she could help set-up and run a members-only blog or computer chat-room for The Circle. Honor was intrigued by her ideas and called Becky to discuss them.

"Would you be willing to fly down to Florida for a few days, right after the long holiday weekend? You could stay in one of the extra rooms in my apartment at the Belleview Biltmore Resort."

Becky squealed with delight.

"Was that a *yes*?"

"Absolutely!"

Honor laughed. "I can't tell if you're more excited about the project or the idea of spending a few days in the warm Florida sun, but I'll have Julie make your travel arrangements."

Next, Honor called a few business contacts in Chicago to see if they could use a good administrative assistant. Three of them were willing to take a look at Wendy's resume. Honor e-mailed their contact information to Wendy's mother, Helen, and then got back to work on The Circle's system software.

Now that Honor had several completed applications to work with, she was able to tweak the operating system to make it more beneficial and easier for members to use. As usual, when she was working on software development, the hours flew by.

All at once, the absolute silence of the suite caught her attention. Josh had taken Cody with him to James and Lisa's and the hotel suite seemed empty without them. Honor realized she was beginning to find it difficult to remember a time when they weren't part of her life. She decided to close down her software project for a while and called the airline to book their flights to North Carolina. Afterward, she checked the item off her list with a flourish.

Since Josh and Cody still hadn't returned, she idly opened her e-mail to scan for important messages. She came upon an item with the subject heading, "Acronyms". Curious, she opened the message and read:

DUN—Duncan Street - Sherri's place

JOY—Johnny O Yachts
SML—Sherri's Medical & Life Insurance
MIN—Minton Motors
KFH—Keep From Honor

Honor recognized these acronyms. They were among the cryptic notes she had discovered in the margins of a few financial reports. She tried to figure out who sent the e-mail, but the sender was anonymous and the address did not accept reply messages.

Excited, she called Sarah Jacobs, but got her voice mail. She left a rambling message and forwarded the e-mail to her. Then she re-read the list.

The idea that William and his lieutenants used a special code specifically to keep information away from her was particularly infuriating.

"No wonder his staff looks at me so strangely. They probably think I'm an idiot for not realizing what was going on right under my nose."

Her thoughts were interrupted by Josh and Cody's return.

They speculated about who might have sent her the e-mail and how the information could help uncover William's criminal activities until Cody blurted, "I'm starving."

Honor beamed at the child and stood. "This turned out to be a great day. Why don't we celebrate by going to Frenchy's for dinner?"

"Sounds great," Josh agreed, heading for the door. "While we're at the restaurant, I'll fill you in on the moving tasks I've accomplished so far."

Honor stopped short. "Oh, my gosh—I almost forgot my checklist! We need to compare notes and check stuff off."

Chapter 55

As she fell asleep that night, Honor tried to concentrate on Margaret, picturing her sitting at the table in her hotel suite. To her happy amazement, she was seated at the table with Margaret only a moment later.

"Would you care for tea?"

"Yes, please."

While Margaret fussed with the tea, Honor asked, "How am I connected to you and Darcy Loughman?"

"Tell me, have you learned anything of value from our memories?"

"Yes, but you didn't answer my question."

"Darcy's story is not mine to tell. She alone will decide when to answer your questions."

Honor knew it was no use arguing. After all, Margaret had over a century of experience keeping secrets. She changed the subject.

"I followed your example and developed a social circle. Actually, I started off trying to make allies who would help me dig up dirt on William, but the group has already outgrown that motive. Now it's a support network for women trying to pursue challenging career goals."

"I would have thought women would have taken control of the world by now."

"No, we're still struggling to achieve equality with men."

Margaret shook her head. "Ah, well... perhaps circles like yours will change things so we won't be having this same discussion in another hundred years."

"I hope so." Honor took a sip of her tea, wondering if Margaret's spirit would still be here in a hundred years. "Margaret, my mother's spirit is still in her house."

"Well, now, this is surprising news. I always thought Faith Macklin would travel the lighted path immediately. Perhaps since her departure was so unexpected, she decided to linger here long enough to say farewell to her loved ones."

"Her loved ones... you mean my sisters?"

Margaret nodded. "And you. Many spirits want their loved ones to know they still exist, even though they are no longer alive."

"But she hasn't connected with me -- only Cody."

Margaret clucked. "You think it's easy for spirits to connect with the living? Even after all these years, I can only communicate with a fraction of the living and spirits with whom I would like to make contact. You can't expect your mother to acquire abilities in a few months that I have taken decades to learn."

"I'm sorry. I didn't mean to offend you."

Margaret softened. "I forget how little you know. Let me explain." She waved a hand toward Cody's sleeping form. "As I mentioned before, this boy is a particularly sensitive medium. It's rare for a child to possess the ability to communicate with weak spirits like your mother, but his gift allowed him to make a connection. She's very lucky you brought him to her home."

"How did Cody become a medium?"

"When children are young, they're easy to contact, but communication with them seldom renders satisfactory results. As they grow, most children learn to attribute spirit visits to bad dreams or overactive imaginations. Eventually, they eliminate the possibility that spirits exist from their reality, and contact becomes impossible without a connection. In Cody's case, I suspect a spirit visited so often, the spirit realm remained a part of his reality."

"Will he become less sensitive as he grows up?"

"His future is impossible to ascertain, but if his gift is nurtured, it might remain with him throughout his lifetime."

All at once, Honor was seized by an overwhelming sense of urgency. Cody had said her mother's spirit would be leaving soon. It was up to her to get her sisters to Florida in time to say goodbye. Her thoughts were so distracting; Honor didn't realize she had slipped into the thick fog until she woke with a start, in her bed.

She decided to check on Cody. He was sleeping peacefully, with a slight smile on his lips, like he hadn't a care in the world, and no idea he was a spirit medium. Honor vowed to continue nurturing Cody's special abilities, a process she was certain had begun with frequent visits from the spirit of Amy, his mother.

***

Early the next morning, Honor's cell phone rang, waking her. "Hello?" she mumbled through a yawn.

Sarah Jacobs was too excited to notice. "Let's schedule a meeting with William and his attorney ASAP before they figure out we're in possession of incriminating information."

Honor struggled to clear the cobwebs from her thoughts. "Whoa, Sarah. The meeting will have to wait until after the holiday weekend. Josh and I are leaving for North Carolina tomorrow."

"Okay. But could you come by my office this morning? I'd like to discuss the implications of this e-mail before you leave town."

"Sure. I'll be there in an hour" Honor hung up and stumbled to the shower.

Twenty minutes later, Josh leaned against the bathroom doorframe, watching her with interest as she applied her make-up. "I'm glad I'm not a woman. I think I'd poke myself in my eye if I tried to put that stuff on."

"I'm glad you're not a woman, too... but for different

reasons," Honor smiled, enjoying the fact they had become so comfortable around one another. "What's on your schedule for the day?"

"My brother John wants to bid on a big vintage home renovation project and he asked if I could help him work-up the cost estimate this morning. After that, I need to make a trip to the laundry mat."

Honor kissed him on her way out of the bathroom. "Want to meet back here in time for dinner?"

"Sounds like a plan."

When Honor arrived at Sarah Jacobs's office, she was escorted to a conference room, where Sarah was reviewing Soft Fix financial reports.

"Thanks for coming in on such short notice. I'm still working on these, but I definitely found irregularities we need to investigate. Pull up a chair and look at this."

She pointed to a line item on a report titled "Lease and Operating Expenses."

"Usually companies list operating costs individually... you know - rent, phone, postage, janitorial services, etcetera. But look here, William combines all of those things into a single entry on this report. Well, I called your building manager to find out the cost of your monthly rent and other costs associated with leasing your space, and the numbers he provided aren't even close to William's total."

Sarah flipped through her notes. "By my calculation, William's number is inflated by about five thousand dollars per month."

Honor's jaw dropped open. "Five thousand a month?"

"Yeah, and the abbreviation DUN is scribbled next to that line. According to the decoder e-mail you received, that means *Duncan Street - Sherri's place*. So, I think your ex-husband is paying for some woman's home and utilities out of your company profits."

"Mistress turned second wife," Honor hissed. "That's

probably her old place."

Sarah paused. "Anyway, now that I know what to look for, I'm certain I'll find other fraudulent expenses hidden throughout these financial reports." She leaned back in her chair. "Before we knew about these codes, I requested detailed financial reports through your company's attorney. William may try to destroy evidence contained in those records before making copies, but I don't think he'll be able to hide what he has done."

"I'm positive he's shredding evidence. His top employee has decided to quit his job over this, and I think I saw his assistant tampering with files. I can recover electronic files from our computer back-up system, but not this paper stuff."

"Actually, the reports we already have are perfect. They contain notes in his own handwriting and he doesn't know we have them. But before we meet with William and his attorney, you need to be very clear about what you want at the end of the day, and how far you are willing to go to exact justice from this creep."

"I don't understand."

"I suspect felony crimes have been committed here. I think we can keep your name out of the fray by proving that, although you are a partner, you were duped and didn't profit in any way from the criminal acts."

Honor nodded, paying close attention.

"But if we keep digging and turn our suspicions into facts, we may be compelled to report the crimes to the police and the IRS. Once that's done, the matter is out of our hands. William will be processed through the legal system like any other criminal...and so will anyone who conspired to help him perpetrate or hide the crimes."

Honor sucked in a long breath, scared for Ben and Helen... and even pathetic Yvonne.

"Let me think about it."

She left Sarah's office, stunned at the extent of William's

corruption and sad that he had become so entangled in his self-spun web of greed and deceit, that he had lost sight of what was truly meaningful in life.

She was torn.

For the first time in many years, Honor didn't feel obligated to protect William. But if she didn't, some good people's lives might be ruined.

She worked for the next several hours, trying not to think about it. Then she called her sisters to ask them to come to Florida the first weekend in December to officially transfer the deed of their mother's home to her, and spend a last night in the house before the workers began the renovation. She was thrilled when they all agreed.

Chase joked, "Wow, Patty and Cherry are coming without their husbands and kids in tow? This should be fun: the *Macklin women ala carte.*"

After Honor hung up the phone with Chase, she decided to drive over and tell their mother's spirit about the upcoming visit.

She unlocked the front door just as the grandfather clock struck the hour, the nostalgic sound of its chimes filling the otherwise empty foyer.

"Hi, Mom! I'm home!" she called out as she walked to the kitchen. She sat on the floor, her legs crisscrossed, and talked about The Circle, her upcoming trip to North Carolina, and William's apparent fraud before finally getting to the purpose for this visit.

"Mom, Margaret Plant said you're probably still here because you want to say goodbye to us girls before following Dad down the lighted path, so I wanted to let you know that Cherry, Patty and Chase are coming to Belleair to close on the house week after next, and we're all going to spend the night here. They don't know you're still around or that I've become aware of the spirit realm. I figure it will be easier to tell them everything when we're together."

Honor rose to her feet and prepared to leave. "I still have a lot to do before we leave for North Carolina in the morning, so I'd better get going."

She paused, her hand on the doorknob. "Mom, I understand that you want to go be with Dad. I really do. But I'm going to miss you so much...I sure wish you could stay."

Tears welled in her eyes as she felt the gentle sensation of her mother brushing the hair back from her face.

"Yeah, I love you, too." She stepped onto the porch and closed the door.

Chapter 56

Josh and Cody were at the hotel when she returned. Cody was glowing with excitement about the upcoming airplane ride and the fact that Honor was going to see his *'real bedroom.'* She listened with mock excitement equal to his own, laughing at his unbridled enthusiasm.

Josh shook his head. "He's been going full tilt all day...no nap. I expect him to crash any minute now, so we better get some food before he hits the wall."

Although they made a valiant effort to hurry, Cody fell asleep with his head on the restaurant table, halfway through his meal. Josh and Honor finished their dinner, exchanging amused glances with several passersby who couldn't help but smile at the sight of the tuckered-out little boy.

Honor told Josh about her visit with Sarah Jacobs. "What do you think I should do?"

Josh folded his arms across his chest. "I understand your concern for the people who work for William, but you need to be careful not to wind up in trouble yourself."

"I know. I need to start thinking like Margaret and find a creative way around the rules."

Josh did not smile. "This is serious. They're not rules, Honor. They're laws, and they're major laws at that. You really need to be careful."

Honor nodded. "I will. I promise." She smiled. "On a lighter note, it looks like you're going to be meeting all three of my sisters when we get back from North Carolina."

She explained their plans to close on the house and then

stay overnight there.

"Sounds terrific. I promise to make myself scarce during your sleepover—right after I pry all of your embarrassing childhood secrets out of them, that is."

Honor giggled. "I guess that's fair, since I've already heard most of yours."

They went back to their room and tucked sleeping Cody in for the night, then packed for their trip and snuggled together in bed.

"Did I tell you a few of my friends are going to come over to help us move the heavy stuff into the storage cube?"

"Define 'heavy stuff.'"

Josh chuckled. "Don't worry. You only have to fill up the boxes. We'll move them all." He hesitated. "I guess we'll take Amy's stuff to Good Will."

"You still have her things?"

"Yeah. I didn't need her room, so it was easier just to keep her door closed."

Honor wondered if keeping Amy's belongings had made it easier for her to stay and visit Cody. She coaxed, "Tell me more about Amy."

"What do you want to know?"

"I'm not sure... just tell me everything you can think of."

Josh cleared his throat. "Well, she wasn't nearly as beautiful as you are."

Honor lifted her head from Josh's shoulder and frowned at him. "I'm not looking for reassurance, Josh. Just tell me about *her*. What was her last name? What did she look like? How did you guys meet? That sort of thing..."

Honor lay back down on his shoulder.

Josh took a deep breath and let it out slowly. "Her name was Amy Douglas, and she had short brown hair, blue eyes and a great sense of humor. She worked for a flooring company and we met when she stopped by one of my project sites to check on an installation. We hung out with mutual friends a couple times and then one night, after too many beers, we wound up in bed together. We tried going out a few times after that, but we both knew that we weren't really clicking together, so we just sort of stopped calling one another. A few months later, she called out of the blue and said she needed to talk to me. She came over and told me she was pregnant and that I could be as involved or uninvolved as I wanted to be, but she was going to keep our baby. And presto... my life changed forever."

"Uh huh—Then what?"

"Well, I wasn't thrilled about her being pregnant. I mean, who wants to have a baby with someone they don't love? But the idea of being a dad grew on me pretty fast. Then, when she was about six months pregnant, she developed preeclampsia... high blood pressure, and her doctor told her she was going to have to take it easy until she delivered. She had to quit her job and couldn't afford to pay her rent. I owned my house, so I suggested that she could move into one of my guestrooms until she was ready to go back to work. She moved in that weekend. I panicked. I remember thinking, 'Now what have I done?'"

Josh kissed the top of Honor's head and she looked up at him. She could tell he was trying to read her reaction.

"It must have been hard trying to care for Amy without getting stuck in a situation you didn't bargain for."

Josh nodded. "Exactly. At first, I was sort of walking on eggshells in my own house. Then one night another girl I was interested in called. Amy answered the phone and told her that she was my platonic roommate. Given the fact that she was pregnant with my child, this might sound strange...but after that, we were exactly what she said we were: platonic roommates. We had fun together, decorating the nursery and talking about names for the baby and stuff like that, but for the most part, we led separate lives."

Honor reached up and kissed his cheek, then snuggled back into her favorite position against his shoulder.

"Amy was pretty concerned about the preeclampsia. Since

her folks were dead and she was an only child, she brought home some forms for me to sign, making me her medical representative and the legal guardian of our child in the event that something went drastically wrong during the delivery. I thought she was being overly dramatic, but I signed the papers to ease her mind, and boy, am I glad I did."

Josh took another deep breath. "Things were fine until Amy got restless one afternoon and drove herself to the store to buy a few books. On her way back home, a truck ran a red light and smashed into the driver's side of her little car. The next thing I know, I get a call at work saying there had been a car accident and that a card in Amy Douglas' wallet listed me as her emergency contact. They told me she had been taken by helicopter to a level one trauma center and that I should get there right away. She wasn't wearing a seat belt. She complained they were too uncomfortable with her belly being so big and all..." Josh swallowed hard.

"You don't have to go on if this is too hard to talk about."

"Thanks, but you should know the whole story."

He swallowed again.

"When they finally let me see her at the hospital, there were tubes and wires all over the place. The doctors said Amy would never regain consciousness, but miraculously, the baby was doing okay. They wanted to increase his chances of survival by giving him a little more time in her womb before performing a cesarean section. As her medical representative, I agreed to let them keep her on life support." His voice faltered.

Honor patted Josh's heart, wishing she could take away his pain.

"A month went by like that. Amy lying in the hospital on life support—a human incubator. It was horrible. I knew she was brain dead, but a part of me couldn't accept that. I went there every day and sat by her bed, talking to her about everything from stuff at work to how the interviews with nannies were going."

Honor hugged him, hoping to give him strength.

"One Sunday morning, a couple of doctors were standing in her doorway when I arrived. I knew something was wrong even before they said anything. They told me Amy's heart rate was becoming unstable. They were worried about the baby and recommended delivery as soon as they could book an operating room. Since I was her medical representative, the decision was up to me."

Josh's arms tightened around Honor.

"I signed my consent and asked if I could stay with her. The doctor said I could watch the birth, but because they were worried about the baby, he said I would have to leave the O. R. immediately, if anything went wrong."

Josh combed his fingers through his hair.

"You must have been scared."

"Yeah. I kept talking to Amy throughout the surgery, telling her she was very brave to hang in there taking care of our son and stuff like that. A part of me was still hoping she would hear me and just, you know...wake up." Josh paused again.

"Jesus, Honor, when I saw the doctors pull this tiny baby out of her body, it was the most amazing and terrifying moment of my whole life. I just held my breath, waiting for him to cry while they looked him over. It seemed to take forever, but then he let out this pitiful little wail, and I just knew he was going to be okay." Josh rubbed his eyes.

"I remember the details like they happened yesterday. The doctor said, *'time of birth...5:29 p.m.'* It was great. I told Amy, *'Look what you made. That's Cody Douglas Lancing over there. Can you hear him hollering?'*"

He shook his head. "What happened next was surreal. A machine that was right next to my ear started beeping really loud. I jumped backward and banged into something. Someone said, 'get him out of here,' and a nurse took me by the arm. I was confused, but let her lead me out of the operating room. She told me not to worry, but I didn't believe her. I knew Amy was dying and they didn't want me to watch it happen."

Josh choked up and Honor felt a shiver run through him. She clung to him as he continued his story.

"The nurse told me to go to the surgical waiting room at the end of the hall, but I couldn't make my feet move. My mind was racing and I felt numb all over. I noticed the sounds from the alarm had stopped. Everything was quiet. I opened the door and went back inside. I knew Amy was dead, but it still didn't seem right to leave her alone. She had been so alone most of her life. There was a lot of blood on the floor and no one was hurrying anymore. The nurse tried to push me out of the room again, but I told her it was okay... I knew Amy was gone. One of the doctors nodded at her and she let me in. Someone covered Amy with a sheet, except for her head, and I went to stand by her side. She had a peaceful expression on her face and I couldn't take my eyes off of her. It was incomprehensible to me that she was no longer alive. The doctor told me he had pronounced her dead at 5:39 and I remember thinking that our son had been born exactly ten minutes before she died." Josh swiped at his tears.

"They let me stay with her for a few minutes, to say goodbye. I just kept looking at her, feeling sad that her life had been so short and empty, and that she had been denied the satisfaction of holding the baby that she had been so excited about bringing into this world. I felt guilty about how little I knew about her and I wondered if she would have wanted me to call anyone except the people she worked with to let them know she was gone. The nurse came over and told me it was time for me to leave Amy, so she could take me to the nursery to hold my baby boy. It's funny, but I had forgotten he was out. I looked toward her belly and it was so flat..."

Josh shuddered, as if that memory was almost too painful to touch, even now. "I thanked Amy for giving me a son and promised to take care of him. Then I bent over, kissed her forehead and said goodbye. Like I said, it was surreal. The nurse took my arm and led me away. And the next thing I know, I'm holding Cody and feeding him his first bottle. I've never been so happy or sad in my life. It was weird to be both at the same time."

"Well, I think the way you're raising Cody is a tribute to Amy."

"Thanks. I really can't imagine my life without him anymore."

Josh's breathing leveled out and a few minutes later, he was asleep, emotionally exhausted.

Honor lay awake, thinking about Amy's spirit. Eventually, she drifted to sleep and the chilly fog swept in around her.

Chapter 57

The mist parted to reveal Darcy and Hannah, still at the hotel in London. They sat at the table, chatting like sisters, discussing how different their lives would be in New York, now that they were part of Margaret's social circle.

"Think of all the people we'll meet and..." Hannah stopped mid-sentence. "Darcy... these people in New York... what if some of them met Rory during his travels and know he didn't have a wife or child?"

The thought sent a chill up Darcy's spine. Gossip from such a chance encounter could expose their charade. A sudden stabbing pain in her abdomen caught her off guard. She sucked in a breath and bent forward, her hands balled into fists.

Hannah was scared. She reached out for her friend, but Darcy waved her away.

"Don't worry. It was but a twinge. I'm feeling better already."

Honor suspected Darcy was in labor. She wished Margaret was here.

"Why didn't I consider the possibility someone would know Rory? He passed out calling cards to nearly everyone he encountered, and he...oh!"

Darcy wasn't able to ignore the next contraction. She doubled over until the pain ebbed.

Hannah jumped to her feet. "Come, Darcy. We need to change you into a dressing gown before the pains worsen."

She helped Darcy change and get into bed.

"I must fetch Margaret now. Keep your wits about you. I'll

return presently." Hannah darted from the room.

Honor drifted into the folds of the familiar fog and watched through the haze as time zoomed past. When the mist receded, Darcy was still alone in the hotel room, writhing in pain with each contraction, her hair soaked with perspiration.

All at once, the door burst open and Margaret rushed in. "How close are the pains?"

Darcy moaned, "Close. Very close."

Margaret crossed over to the dresser. She withdrew an egg timer from a velvet bag and used it to determine Darcy's pains were a little more than three minutes apart.

"You're doing fine," she comforted.

Margaret poured a basin of water and carried it to the bedside. She wet a small rag, dabbed it gently against Darcy's forehead.

"Where's Hannah?" Darcy sobbed.

"She'll be here soon. She went to fetch the doctor."

Just then, a new contraction caused Darcy to cry out. Margaret held her hand and murmured soothing reassurances until the pain passed.

Darcy was miserable. Between contractions, she told Margaret about her new concern that Hannah would come into contact with an individual who had actually known Rory.

"It might be wise to give the baby another name besides Collins."

Margaret listened, her eyes filled with compassion. It was evident that giving Rory's child a different name was painful for Darcy to consider.

"I've watched you and Hannah grow very close over the last months. At times I find it difficult to believe you didn't know one another before we came to Europe."

Darcy nodded, then winced as a new pain flooded her body. Margaret dabbed Darcy's face with the cool, wet cloth, waiting patiently for the contraction to end.

"You and Hannah have already blended your memories

together, and are going to blend your futures together in New York. So, why not blend your names together as well?"

At first, Darcy was confused. "Blend our names together?"

"Yes, blend Collins and Johnson together into a new name like Collinson or Johncollin..."

"Oh, I see. Yes, that's a superb idea."

Margaret's idea calmed Darcy's fears, while at the same time, providing an activity to distract her from her labor pains.

Finally, Hannah returned with the doctor in tow. "I'm so sorry to have taken so long, but the doctor was, um, *indisposed* for a time," she fretted.

The doctor let out a loud belch and Honor realized he had been drinking.

A young servant followed behind Hannah and the doctor, carrying a pot of coffee. She poured a cup for the doctor, and then looked around, uncertain what to do next. She looked positively relieved when Margaret waved her away. Without a moment's hesitation, she scooted out the door, leaving the coffee pot on the table.

Margaret narrowed her eyes and took a long, hard look at the doctor. She planted her hands on her hips and demanded, "Are you too drunk to deliver a baby?"

"Madam, I've delivered dozens of babies while in much worse condition than I am in at the moment."

Margaret's voice was icy. "If you seek to comfort me by providing knowledge that you are often drunk while working, you have failed miserably."

The doctor wasn't humiliated or angered by her remarks. He gave her an amused smile and then sauntered over to where Darcy lay moaning in great distress.

He lifted one of Darcy's hands and placed it on his palm. He began to rub it gently with the fingertips of his other hand while looking directly into her eyes. "There, there, sweet lady. Your pain will be over soon."

His technique calmed Darcy instantly.

"May I have permission to look beneath your gown?"

Darcy nodded.

He gently laid her hand down and moved to the foot of the bed. Once he finished his examination, he announced, "Your baby will soon be here."

Without altering his relaxed demeanor, he ordered Hannah to bring several towels and hot water. Hannah ran to do his bidding while Margaret stood at Darcy's side, arms folded across her chest, watching the doctor's every move.

The doctor picked up the mug of coffee, drinking deeply of the bitter brew. Afterward, he turned to Margaret. "Where's the lady's husband during this crucial time?"

"He was killed in an accident several months ago."

Honor wasn't sure the doctor believed her.

When Hannah returned, he tied a rag loop to both sides of the headboard and then pulled one of Darcy's hands through each loop.

"Hold on tightly," the doctor instructed. "This will give you added strength when it's time to push your baby out."

He tucked some towels beneath Darcy's lower body before taking another long drink of coffee. Then he bent Darcy's knees and braced his hands against them. Once everything was in place, he instructed, "Take a deep breath and push with the next pain."

Darcy did as she was instructed, straining with the effort over and over again, as she endured several more contractions. Honor couldn't feel Darcy's contractions, but she experienced the panic that was welling up inside her tormented body.

Margaret and Hannah took turns dabbing the wet cloth against Darcy's brow.

"Just a little while longer Darcy...there's a brave girl," Margaret murmured.

"You're doing wonderfully, Darcy," Hannah added.

Darcy was becoming exhausted. Margaret, Hannah and Honor were worried, but the doctor didn't seem to share their concern. He just kept telling Darcy she was doing fine; encouraging her to take deep breaths and push harder.

The doctor studied the women, especially Margaret. Suddenly, a look of recognition lit his features. He was about to say something when Darcy let out a painful howl.

"Ah, your baby is beginning to show itself. This is good. Keep pushing."

"I can't push anymore," Darcy wailed, exhausted.

The doctor ignored her pitiful protests. Alternating between encouragement and commands, he persuaded her to push even harder.

Honor moved to the foot of the bed and watched with fascination as a patch of the baby's dark hair became visible. With a few more pushes, the baby's head was out and resting in the doctor's hand. He gently coaxed one shoulder out and then whoosh...the rest of the baby slid out into the world and began to cry.

The doctor announced, "You have a fine daughter, my lady, and she has a strong pair of lungs to boot!"

He handed the baby to Hannah while he quickly delivered the placenta, then tied off and cut the umbilical cord. The doctor cleaned up the mess, while Margaret helped Darcy change into a fresh gown and settle into bed. Hannah washed the baby's perfect little body and swaddled her in a blanket.

Darcy was physically and emotionally spent, but smiled when Hannah gently laid her newborn daughter in her arms. Darcy stared at the magical bundle in her arms and whispered, "Welcome to the world, Hope Marie Colson."

Hannah gasped. She understood the name immediately. The child represented the spark of hope Darcy kept alive in her heart, the memory of her own lost sister and a surname that merged the Collins and the Johnson families forever.

Darcy smiled. "Do you like her name?"

Hannah bobbed her head up and down, gleeful, but too choked with emotion to find words.

Honor staggered back and sat heavily into a chair, finally grasping her connection to these women. Hope Marie Colson. She had just witnessed the birth of her great grandmother.

Chapter 58

Honor stared at Hannah and Darcy, trying to grasp the fact that Darcy was actually her great-great grandmother by birth, and Hannah was her adoptive great-great grandmother. She shook her head in amazement. No wonder she resembled the portrait of Darcy Loughman.

The doctor turned away from the women, smiling, his work almost complete. He walked over to the small table beside Honor, opened his bag and pulled out a blank birth record. He uncorked a bottle of ink and began to fill out the record, repeating the baby's name out loud as he wrote, "Hope Marie Colson."

When he asked the father's name, Hannah quickly responded, "Rory Collins Colson."

The doctor nodded and continued to write without looking up. "And the mother's name?"

The women exchanged uneasy glances, aware the doctor had heard them using their correct names throughout the evening.

Darcy set her jaw and proclaimed defiantly, "Hannah Johnson Colson!"

Hannah interrupted. "That's not quite right... the mother's name is Hannah Darcy Johnson Colson."

The doctor didn't look up or question the fact that Darcy didn't seem to know her own name. He simply finished filling out the form, then dated and signed it with a flourish.

Hannah sat down on the side of the bed and Darcy, eyes brimming with grateful tears, handed the baby to her.

The doctor packed his things back into his bag and Margaret walked him out.

At the door, she held out a small pouch of gold coins. "Remember, this sum pays for your services and your silence."

"You don't remember me, but you saved my reputation when I was a young man. I was involved in a barroom brawl that led to a man's death. You sent me to Europe and suggested that I think of a way to make up for the life I took. I became a doctor, but the memory of that night continues to haunt me. It's why I drink so much. But unless I am mistaken, my actions tonight allowed you to help another lost soul."

Margaret nodded. "Three souls, actually."

"Then perhaps I have atoned for the life I took after all."

"Perhaps." Margaret smiled.

The doctor took one more look at Hannah, Darcy and baby Hope, then pushed the pouch of gold away and stepped into the corridor.

Margaret nodded with pride and closed the door.

Honor watched as Hannah rocked the baby. It was odd. She had just watched Hope's birth, yet she already knew her whole life's story. She knew Hope would grow up and attend college in New York and would march in the Suffrage protests until women won the right to vote. She would become a successful business woman and would marry a forward-thinking man named Geoffrey Pickery. Honor possessed a framed photograph of them, taken on their wedding day. Together, Geoffrey and Hope would raise and educate twelve children, one of whom was Honor Pickery-Bond, Honor's grandmother for whom she was named. Hope would live long enough to spoil all of her grandchildren, including Honor's own mother, Faith Bond-Macklin. And she would give each of her descendants a few pearls from a necklace that had belonged to her mother.

Suddenly irritated, Honor wondered why her mother had never told her about all of this family history. She reached for the pearls hanging on the gold chain around her neck, wondering who had owned the original necklace: Darcy or Hannah.

The swirling mist engulfed Honor as soon as she touched the pearls. She woke up, grateful to be back in her own time. She needed time to process everything she had just witnessed. She started to wake Josh, but he was sleeping peacefully and since they would be flying out early the next morning, she thought better of the idea. Instead, she pulled out her journal and scribbled down her family tree, identifying Rory Collins as her great, great grandfather, and both Darcy Loughman and Hannah Johnson-Colson as her great, great grandmothers.

Honor didn't realize she had fallen back to sleep until the alarm clock buzzed. She rolled over and hit the snooze button. The room was chilly, as it always was after an encounter with spirits, and she was hoping to doze until it warmed up.

Awakened by the alarm, Cody burst into their room and climbed onto the bed, perplexed that they were still sleeping.

"Did you forget we're going for an airplane ride today?"

Josh moaned and rolled away, covering his head with his pillow.

Undaunted and bubbling with enthusiasm, Cody continued, "Can I bring my Spiderman movies? What color is our airplane? Can I sit by the window? I'm hungry..."

Unlike Josh, Honor couldn't tune-out the nonstop chatter. She rubbed her eyes. "Okay, you win. I'm up. Just give me a minute to brush my teeth."

Once she and Cody were dressed and Cody was settled in front of the TV, she woke Josh again.

"I know you're tired, but wait till you hear what I learned about my family's history last night..."

***

They checked-in at the airport and decided to have breakfast before their flight. Cody was so excited, he was difficult to restrain. A business woman seated at the table across from theirs kept throwing aggravated glances their direction. Honor wondered how many times she had been on the other end of this exchange—the childless traveler using pointed stares to beseech a parent to get her child under control. Now that she was experiencing what it was actually like to travel with child, she made a mental note to be more tolerant in the future.

Once they were in the air and Cody's fascination with his junior pilot wings finally wore off, he fell sound asleep. Grateful, Honor and Josh resumed their conversation from that morning.

"It's weird to think my family was invented to conceal a love affair."

Josh frowned. "I think you've got it backwards. Darcy wanted her love story out in the open and giving it to Hannah allowed that to happen. She was an amazing woman."

"Actually, she still is." Honor smiled. "First, she opened my eyes about true love, and then she taught me that being a parent isn't about biology, it's about taking a child into your heart. I have a lot to thank her for."

Josh kissed her. "So do I."

The pilot's voice came over the sound system, announcing they would be landing in fifteen minutes. Honor woke Cody, knowing he wouldn't want to miss their arrival. An instant later, he was wide awake and chattering as though he had never fallen asleep. Honor laughed and enjoyed the rest of the flight through his enthusiastic eyes.

***

They rented a car at the airport for the drive to Josh's house. Fall had come late to the area, so most of the trees along the roadside still boasted brightly colored leaves. Honor enjoyed the majestic views, but as they neared their destination, her stomach tightened with apprehension.

Even if Josh wasn't convinced, she knew Amy's spirit visited Cody on a regular basis. Honor had formulated a plan to help Amy to move on, but she didn't know if it would work and she was debating whether or not to discuss it with Josh.

They turned off the highway onto a narrow, two-lane road, running alongside a clear, bubbling brook. Gold and burgundy maple leaves blanketed the ground as though festooning the path to the *For Sale* sign, posted at the curb. Two red brick columns marked the entrance to the matching brick driveway. As they pulled in, the large Craftsman-style home came into view, featuring a steep pitched roofline, light yellow siding, forest green shutters and covered porch, complete with wooden bench swing.

As they walked up the three stairs to the front door, Honor noticed the porch swing moved slightly. She wondered if it was Amy, or simply her imagination working overtime.

Cody pulled at Honor's hand, wanting to show her his bedroom.

She knelt down. "I'll tell you what. If you let your Dad give me a tour of the house, I promise we'll play in your room next, okay?"

Cody agreed and dashed off to his bedroom.

As they walked from room to room, Josh pointed out his favorite features, including intricate crown molding and beautifully refinished hardwood floors.

"Wow, Josh, this is gorgeous. I can tell you really poured yourself into this restoration. Are you positive you want to sell it and move to Florida?"

Josh took her into his arms. "Honor, this is a nice house, but it was a project, not a home. I actually feel more at home at the hotel with you than I ever felt living here."

Honor beamed. "Well then, where are those packing boxes?"

"You read my mind." Josh laughed. "As soon as I sign some paperwork at the moving company, they'll bring us a storage cube and packing materials. It shouldn't take long. Would you rather wait here with Cody or ride along with me?"

"I think I'll wait here. I promised Cody I'd hang out in his room for a while and I don't want to disappoint him."

"Okay, then. I'll be back shortly." He gave her another hug. "I love you. I can't tell you how glad I am that you're here with me."

"Aw, you're just trying to butter me up so I'll work harder. You know, I've been thinking. Between my mother's house and this one, I think we have spent more time packing than we have dating!"

"You're probably right, but I'll make it up to you. I promise." He winked, grabbed his keys and ducked out the door.

Chapter 59

Honor wasn't surprised by the décor in Cody's room. Images of Spiderman adorned his bedspread and were featured in posters on all four walls. Spiderman action figures, along with his various nemeses, lined his shelves and over-filled his toy box. A Spiderman lamp sat next to his bed, and a large, rope spider web hung over it, to keep out the bad dreams—and ghosts.

Honor sat on the floor as Cody showed off some of his favorite action figures. She pretended to examine each one with interest, while secretly trying to sense Amy's presence in the room. Finally, she decided to put her plan into motion.

"Hey, Cody, come sit with me for a minute."

Cody crawled into her lap, still holding a Spiderman figurine.

"Sweetie, is your Mommy here right now?"

Cody shrugged. "She doesn't talk to me when people are here."

Honor nodded. "I get that, but just in case she is listening right now, I'm going to talk to her and I think she might be able to hear me better if we're sitting together, okay?"

"Okay."

Honor felt a bit foolish, but took a deep breath and began, "Amy, my name is Honor Macklin and I love Josh and Cody. We've come here to pack up their belongings so they can move to Florida, where we plan to live together."

Cody joined in. "I like Florida, Mommy. Honor's house has a swimming pool!"

Honor continued, "Amy, I know you love Cody and I'm sure you wish he would continue living in North Carolina, so I'm sorry for the pain this decision must be causing you. But I promise I won't let his memory of you fade away."

"Honor's going to sing me two 'Happy Birthdays', one from her and one from you, Mommy."

Honor smiled at Cody and kissed the top of his head. "You bet I will!"

She didn't know if Cody could feel his mother's presence any more than she could, but decided to keep going.

"I want to help Cody remember you as he grows up. I promise to make sure he knows that you loved him so much that you postponed your eternal journey to stay with him as long as you could."

Honor hugged Cody a little tighter. "Amy, we're only going to be here a few days, but I'm hoping you can visit Cody while he's sleeping and tell him all the things you want him to know about you. When he wakes up, I'll write it all down, so that your memories will never be forgotten."

Honor looked into Cody's blue eyes. "Do you understand what I want you to do?"

"Sure. You want me to tell you what Mommy Amy says."

Honor nodded. She hoped Amy heard and understood what she was trying to do.

"Amy, you may already suspect this, but Cody is extremely sensitive to the spirit world. We're going to try to nurture that in him as he grows up. So if you want to stay in this world and see Cody from time to time, please tell him about a public place you like to go, and we'll try to bring him there to connect with you sometimes."

Then, remembering Hannah's words to Darcy, Honor added, "And whether you choose to stay here or travel down the lighted path, I promise you that I will do my best to be a good mother to your child."

Once again, Cody chimed in. "I love Honor, Mommy! She

reads me stories and hangs my pictures on her refrigerator and buys me pancakes."

His words warmed Honor's heart. She had no idea if Amy heard anything either of them had said, but she was satisfied with her effort. To break the somber mood, she raised her hand into a claw and teased, "And she tickles him!"

Cody squealed with laughter. They played in his room until they heard a big horn blast in the driveway.

"It sounds like Daddy is back with the truck!"

By the time they got their coats on and went outside, the driver had backed the truck into the driveway and was separating the storage cube from the truck bed. Soon he drove off, leaving Josh and Honor alone to pack.

Cody kept himself amused, playing in the packing materials while they worked in the living room, kitchen and then Amy's old room. Honor was surprised that Josh had left the room exactly as it was when Amy had occupied it.

"I didn't need the space and I felt bad giving her stuff away," Josh explained, "but I guess everything in here can go to Goodwill."

"We should keep her mementos. They might be important to Cody one day."

"Good point."

They wrapped her personal belongings and keepsakes carefully in a box, which Honor labeled *Amy Douglas.*

Later, when they tucked Cody into his bed, Honor kissed him goodnight. "Don't forget to listen carefully if Mommy Amy comes to visit."

Josh cocked his head, curious.

Honor winked at him. "I'll explain later."

Josh kissed his son goodnight and turned out the light, pausing at the door. Honor rested her head against his shoulder and he wrapped an arm around her.

"Are you doing okay?" she whispered.

"I'm fine," he said. "It just hit me that I won't be tucking

Cody into bed here anymore. That seems strange, but not sad. I'm looking forward to living in Florida."

They turned and walked down the hallway to Josh's room.

"So, what are you and Cody up to?"

As they undressed for bed, Honor told him about her attempts to contact Amy.

"I doubt it worked, but it would be cool if Amy could say goodbye to Cody and move on, knowing he'd always remember her."

"I doubt Amy can communicate like the spirits at the hotel can, but it's nice you're trying to do that for Cody. It's no wonder I love you so much."

Honor slid between the cool sheets, thankful she had remembered to pack her flannel granny-gown. Josh pulled her close to him and kissed her; then kissed her again, more passionately.

Honor gently pushed him away. "Not tonight, okay? Amy might be watching."

"Seriously?"

"Yeah, sorry. I'll make it up to you when we get back home, okay?"

"I'll hold you to that."

Josh turned on the bedroom TV and Honor curled up on his shoulder. She didn't remember falling asleep, but suddenly Cody was at her bedside, whispering in her ear.

"Wake up, Honor."

She glanced at the clock and groaned. Five o'clock. Groggy, she swung her legs over the side of the bed. "It's too early to wake up, Cody. Let's get you back to bed."

She picked him up. "Your skin is freezing. Did you kick off your blanket?"

Yawning, she carried him back to his room and turned on the light. His room was freezing cold. Honor's eyes flew open with understanding. She gasped, her heart pounding. Amy really had been here.

"Mommy Amy said I have to tell you everything before I forget," Cody mumbled.

"Okay, but first let's warm you up."

Honor wrapped a blanket around Cody and carried him to the cozy living room, grabbing her oversized purse from a table along the way. She sat on the couch with Cody on her lap, then reached into her purse and pulled out a small tape recorder.

"Okay, Cody, tell me everything you can remember." She pushed the record button.

Honor was astounded by Cody's vivid memories of the visit. He repeated a few stories from Amy's life and talked about which of his personality traits were most like hers, including the fact that she had always been sensitive to the spirit realm.

When Cody grew quiet, Honor prompted, "Did she say anything else?"

He yawned. "She said she can't come to Florida, so she's going to follow the bright light to heaven. She can watch over me from up there, because angels can go anywhere they want to." He yawned again and closed his eyes. "And she said to tell you to write down your promise and don't ever forget."

"My promise?" Honor asked, momentarily confused. Then she remembered. "I won't forget."

She glanced at the clock. It was almost six. Cody had fallen asleep, so she carried him back to bed, tucked him in and kissed his forehead.

Next, she retrieved a new journal from her purse. On the first page, she penned, "*The Memoirs of Amy Douglas; Angel Mommy.*" Then she played back the recording and transcribed Cody's words to paper. When she was finished, she ended the journal with, "*I, Honor Macklin promise Amy Douglas that I will be a good mother to her beloved child, Cody Douglas Lancing.*"

Honor closed the journal and stretched, tired, but happy with what she had accomplished. When Josh woke up, he found her in the kitchen, rummaging through boxes, looking for coffee mugs.

She smiled at the sight of him. "I made a pot of coffee. I think you're going to need some caffeine before I tell you how I spent the morning!"

Chapter 60

When they finished packing, Josh drove Honor and Cody to Granny's Kitchen for a traditional Thanksgiving feast. Honor was delighted with the country atmosphere of the historic barn-turned-restaurant. The hostess escorted them past a magnificent Thanksgiving buffet and three carving stations to a table close to the dance floor, where a bluegrass band was getting ready to play.

A young server approached, clad in a red-checked blouse and blue jeans; her blonde hair in braids. "Welcome to Granny's traditional Thanksgiving. I'll take your drink orders and then you can help yourselves to the buffet. But before you eat, Granny asks that you join hands and tell each other one thing you're thankful for this year."

They filled their plates and returned to their table, noticing most guests were honoring Granny's tradition. Once they were seated, they too, joined hands.

Honor spoke first. "I'm thankful to be spending Thanksgiving with my guys."

Josh's blue eyes glistened. "I am so thankful you came into our lives."

They turned to Cody, who was hungrily eyeing his plate. "I'm thankful they put little marshmallows on the sweet potatoes."

***

The next day, three of Josh's friends came over to help pack the storage cube. Although moving the heavy furniture and boxes was hard work, they joked and told stories throughout the afternoon, creating a light-hearted atmosphere.

When they finished, Josh called to have the container picked up, and then treated the guys and their wives to drinks and dinner at a nearby tavern restaurant. The pleasant evening ended with everyone promising to stay in touch.

Josh's house was empty and their flight was early the following day, so they decided to stay at the airport hotel. Cody claimed he wasn't tired, but he fell asleep on the couch moments after they checked into their suite. Josh retrieved a blanket from the closet and tucked him in, then joined Honor in bed.

"Your friends are fantastic," Honor remarked. "Are you sure you won't regret leaving here?"

Josh laughed. "It's a little late to be asking that question, don't you think?"

"Well, I didn't realize how much you're giving up until now."

Josh shook his head. "Here's the thing. All of my friends are married and raising families these days. Being around them just kept reminding me how alone Cody and I were, and how much I missed my family in Florida. Then you came into the picture, and the decision to move became a no-brainer." He smiled. "You aren't having second-thoughts about changing your life to include us, are you?"

Honor's eyes flew open. "Absolutely not! I'm still amazed you chose me, when you could have your pick of women."

Josh shook his head. "Jesus, Honor. How did your self-image become so distorted?" He brushed her dark curls back from her face. "Every time I see you coming toward me, I think to myself, *'Josh you are one lucky son of a bitch.'* Honor, you're beautiful and sexy and brilliant. People are constantly drawn to you, hoping you can fix whatever problems they have...and you never let them down. And as if that isn't enough, you're wonderful with my son." He lifted her chin. "Do you need me to go on? Because I could list a dozen more reasons why I love you... your sense of humor... the way your body fits mine so perfectly... your beautiful green eyes... those black curls..."

Honor giggled to hide her embarrassment. "That's exactly how I feel about you."

"You love my black curls?"

"Oh stop it... you know what I mean. Don't you think it's kind of miraculous that we met at a time when we were both ready for a permanent relationship?"

"Miraculous. Good word." Josh agreed. "Speaking of relationships, what's your plan for dealing with William?"

"Sarah's writing a letter, demanding legal recognition of the fact that one half of Soft Fix's assets belong to me. If William agrees, I'll have nothing to worry about."

Josh whistled. "You think he'll concede without a fight?"

"No." Honor winced. "And I'm definitely the underdog in the fight. Sarah isn't sure I have legal standing to sue, because even though we used my money to start Soft Fix, William's the sole owner on paper." Honor chewed her bottom lip. "Fortunately, Sarah says he can only enforce my non-compete agreement for two years after we separate, but unless William would be willing to repay the money I invested in Soft Fix, I wouldn't have enough capital to start a new company."

"If you can prove he's a crook, that would give you leverage, right?"

"Maybe, but he's really smart and he suspects I'm up to something, so he's already hiding the evidence. I'm probably screwed, and I have no one but myself to blame."

"Honor, I just don't get it... you're one of the smartest women I have ever met, but whenever we talk about that jackass, you turn into someone I don't even recognize. It's your company. William's cooked the books. Your technical staff thinks he's an idiot and at least some your customers can't stand him. And oh yeah, you know he's cheating on his new wife. And yet you lay there telling me you're at his mercy.

Honest to God, Honor...if this was any other problem in your path, you would have already figured out how to resolve it. You'd be checking stuff off a list and you'd be well on your way to taking back what's rightfully yours. I don't understand why you're handling things so differently, just because the battle is with William."

Honor was stunned by Josh's frank assessment of her situation, but she knew his observations were accurate. William gained the upper hand in their relationship in the beginning, when she had been terrified about investing all of her savings to start a new company. Back then, she questioned every decision she made, no matter how minute the issue. Conversely, William seemed to know how to handle every problem with ease. At the time, she had been grateful to turn things over to him. The echo of his words still rang in Honor's memory: "You just focus on creating great software and leave the rest up to me."

After Soft Fix was up and running, Honor tried to become more engaged in the daily operations by speaking her mind at company meetings. William often scoffed at her naïve ideas in front of everyone and suggested she leave the complicated financial decisions to him and his staff. Embarrassed by her ignorance, Honor spoke up less and less. Over time, she stopped trying, accepting William's assessment that she was incapable of handling the business side of their operations.

Josh's voice brought Honor back to the present. "Hey, where did you go?"

Honor shook her head, clearing away the unpleasant memories. "Sorry... you got me thinking, and you know how dangerous that can be."

"Listen, Honor, I'm sorry if I stepped over the line. I should learn to keep my mouth shut."

"Don't apologize... you're absolutely right. I was just trying to figure out how that rat bastard gained so much control over me and more importantly, how I'm going to put a stop to it."

Josh grinned at her. "There's the woman I've come to know and love. Now I almost feel sorry for the guy... he doesn't stand a chance."

***

In the morning, they dressed and walked the short distance to the airline counter, once again struggling to control Cody's boundless energy. When they arrived at their gate, Cody ran to the window overlooking the tarmac, and began carrying on a conversation with someone Josh and Honor couldn't see.

"At least he's not running around, driving everyone crazy," Josh commented as they relaxed into nearby chairs.

"And we did agree to encourage his psychic gifts," Honor added.

"Would you mind if I took advantage of having an invisible babysitter long enough to read the paper in peace?"

"No problem. I'm going to make a few calls, but I can keep an eye on him... on them... whatever."

Honor called Sarah Jacobs for an update.

"I sent the demand letter via express delivery yesterday, so William should receive it this morning. We need to set-up a meeting with him and Leon Goldstein ASAP. You never know, William might do the right thing and concede."

"That would take a miracle."

"Well, if he challenges your ownership, we'll use the meeting to begin negotiations. It's in our best interest to settle this out of court, where your legal standing won't come into question."

"I understand. Call me back once you set the date for the meeting."

Next, Honor called her assistant, Julie.

"Honor, I think I'm spending as much time managing The Circle as I am doing my regular job."

"Gosh, I'm sorry..."

Julie interrupted, "That wasn't a complaint. I love the new

challenge! It's giving me a little taste of what it would be like to reach my goal... you know... becoming the Chief Operations Officer at a major corporation." Julie laughed. "Hey, tell Josh I'm using his description of our membership... *'the perfect organization for women too old for Girl Scouts and too young to wear Red Hats.'*"

Honor protested, "Oh, that's just great! Now Josh will know I tell you *everything*."

Josh looked up at the mention of his name. Honor winked and smiled at him. He shook his head, amused, and returned his attention to the sports section.

"Well, Mark Sutton called and when I told him you had gone back down to Florida, he asked if you were still planning to leave Soft Fix. I pretended I didn't know anything about it and to change the subject, I told him about *The not-so-top-secret-anymore Circle*."

"Really?"

"Yeah, and he seemed very interested. He said The Circle sounded like a terrific organization for his daughter. He liked the idea of her associating with women who were actually taking steps to make their dreams come true, rather than simply listening to lectures by college professors. He asked me the cost of initiation fees and annual dues. I didn't know what to tell him, so I told him you were still in the process of putting that together. Was that the right thing to say?"

"I'm not sure. I guess I didn't plan on The Circle growing like this. I'll discuss it with Sarah Jacobs and get back to you."

Before hanging up, Honor asked Julie to transfer her call to Helen Ellis in Accounting. Helen answered on the first ring.

"Hi, Julie, what's up?"

"It's Honor. I just wanted to check to see how your daughter's job search was going."

"Um, thanks. Wendy already interviewed with one your contacts and has a second interview today. She thinks she might get a job offer by the end of the week."

Honor couldn't put her finger on it, but even though the news was good, Helen's voice sounded strained.

"Is everything okay, Helen?"

Helen lowered her voice. "Yvonne gave strict orders. Finance employees aren't supposed to talk to you. The receptionist is supposed to route your calls directly to her extension."

"I didn't go through the switchboard. Julie transferred my call to you."

"That explains how you got through. According to Yvonne, she's better equipped to personally handle your requests for assistance from our department."

"*Oh, really?*"

"Listen, I feel terrible about this, Honor. I'm willing to break the stupid rule, as long as you don't tell anyone."

"Thanks, but I don't want you to do anything that will jeopardize your job, Helen. I'll play along with Yvonne's scheme...but I do want you to do two things for me. First of all, let Julie know if Wendy lands the job. And second, be very careful not to let Yvonne or anyone else talk you into doing anything illegal. If this situation winds up in the hands of the police, I don't want you to get burned."

"I promise to watch my P's and Q's. You be careful, too."

As disturbing as her phone call to Helen had been, Honor had to make one more call before they boarded their flight.

She dialed Becky Adams' number to confirm the young computer genius was still flying down to meet with her about developing a website and blog for The Circle.

"Are you kidding?" Becky gushed. "I packed my suitcase a week ago! Are you sure you have room for me in your hotel suite? Do you have time to discuss some conceptual ideas right now?"

Honor chuckled at her enthusiasm. "Yes, I have room. I have to board a plane right now, but I'm looking forward to meeting you and discussing your concepts tomorrow!"

Chapter 61

She and Josh took advantage of the gate attendant's offer to allow those traveling with small children to board early. Once they were settled in their seats, Cody told them about his new spirit acquaintance.

"In his day, pilots had to crank a propeller to start the plane."

Honor asked, "So what does your new friend think about these big jet engine planes?"

"Ace says they aren't that special...computers pretty much run them. Pilots nowadays never even feel the wind on their faces and, boy, oh boy, they don't know what they're missing!"

Honor smiled; certain that had been a direct quote. "What else did you talk about?"

"I told Ace that Spiderman can feel the wind on his face because he shoots out spider webs and flies from one building to the next one like this..." Cody pretended to shoot webs from his hands.

"What did Ace think of Spiderman?"

"He said he'd like to meet him and buy him a whiskey."

Josh laughed. "I wonder if Ace understood that Spiderman isn't a real person."

Honor giggled at the thought.

When the plane taxied away from the gate, Cody waved wildly out the window.

"Goodbye, Ace! I'll watch for you in the clouds!"

Honor was startled. "Can Ace fly, even without his old plane?"

Cody nodded. "Yes... but only to the places he flew in his day. He said it sure would be nice if he had flown to faraway places, instead of just flying the mail back and forth between here and crappy Cincinnati."

Honor choked back a laugh. "Cody! You mustn't repeat bad words that other people say."

"What's a bad word?"

Honor spent the next ten minutes trying to explain the difference between *good words* and *bad words* to Cody; thoroughly entertaining Josh, who pretended to be completely absorbed in a magazine article.

Honor was relieved when the flight attendant finally brought the conversation to a close by offering them peanuts and a drink.

She poked Josh in the ribs. "Thanks a lot for all your help there."

Josh smiled innocently. "Gosh, I'm sorry... I didn't realize you needed my help. You seemed to be doing fine on your own."

"Yeah, yeah...you know what they say about payback, right?"

Just then, Cody let out a loud belch that brought disapproving looks from several people sitting around them.

Honor's jaw dropped, embarrassed by the child's lack of manners. But instead of chastising him, she batted her eyelashes at Josh. "Your turn."

Josh narrowed his eyes at her in mock anger, but then addressed Cody firmly. "Cody! What do you say when a burp slips out?"

Cody, unfazed by the rebuke, paused from his drink long enough to mumble, "Excuse me."

Josh grinned at Honor. "All done. Hey, I like this Mommy and Daddy taking turns thing... especially since it's your turn again."

Honor protested the obvious disparity, but without

conviction. In her heart, she loved being *Mommy.*

***

It was dark by the time they arrived at the Belleview Biltmore. Much to their delight, the staff had decorated the resort for the holidays while they were away, transforming it into a winter wonderland, despite the warm temperatures. Rows of small pine trees, sparkling with white lights, lined both sides of the driveway to the entrance, where twelve-foot tall toy soldiers stood guard. Just inside, a huge Christmas tree, decked with gold and burgundy velvet ribbons, antique ornaments and artificial candles, filled the center of the lobby. Enormous swags of decorated pine garland were scalloped along the entire length of the main corridor. Still more garland was looped along the handrails of the grand staircases. A mechanical Santa sat in his gift-filled sleigh near the elevator, waving to passersby.

When at last Josh opened the door to their suite, another surprise greeted them: a Christmas tree stood in their living room, decorated with strings of red bubble-lights and silver garland.

Honor spread a blanket and pillows on the floor by the tree while Josh put on some music and made microwave popcorn. As they snacked, Honor told Cody a story about a magical forest, where fairies hung strings of popcorn on the trees to feed birds throughout the long, cold winter. Mesmerized by the story and the bubble-lights, Cody soon fell asleep. Josh carried his son to bed and then returned to the blanket to cuddle with Honor and reminisce about their favorite Christmas memories.

Josh rose up on his elbow, just high enough to be able to see Honor's face in the glow of the flickering lights.

"Tonight...being here with you...this is definitely going on my list of favorite holiday memories."

Honor purred. "I believe I promised you a special night

when we got back here."

Josh required no further prompting. He stood up and pulled off his shirt and jeans.

The red lights dancing across his skin had an erotic effect on Honor. When he knelt down to unfasten her jeans, she stopped him and patted the blanket, signaling him to lie down. Once he had done so, she stood between his legs and began to sway seductively with the music, stripping her clothes off slowly. As she stepped out of her panties, Josh sat up and kissed her inner thighs. When he teased her with his tongue, Honor felt her knees go weak. She allowed him to pull her down to the floor, where the bubble lights continued to cast soft, flickering pools of red light along the length of their bodies.

Honor craved the riveting sensation of Josh's body merging with hers. He rolled on top of her and she opened her legs, waiting for him, breathless. She was not disappointed. The hard floor beneath her seemed to increase the intensity of his thrusts and she moaned with pleasure. He extended his arms, pushing up off of her while continuing to plunge in and out with almost reckless abandon. Unable to cling to him in this position, she arched her back and squeezed her breasts hard, licking her nipple as she climaxed. She heard Josh gasp at the sight of her pleasuring herself, just before he exploded into her.

Trembling, Josh lowered himself onto her. She caressed his back, relaxing as the room came back into focus.

Suddenly shy, Honor confessed, "I've never done a striptease before."

"Then it was a first for both of us. No one ever danced for me before." He rolled to her side and let his fingertips glide slowly back and forth over her breast and down her abdomen. "Yep, this holiday memory just moved up to number one on my list."

She giggled and then stifled a yawn. "I love this, but I think we should move into our bedroom before we fall asleep here on the floor."

"Yeah... Cody waking up and finding us naked on the floor is a Christmas memory we can all do without."

"Oh my God... I hadn't even thought of that possibility." Honor immediately rolled herself in the blanket and struggled to her feet. "Come on, help me pick up our clothes."

Josh chuckled. "You look like a human burrito. Don't worry; I've got this." He snatched up the clothing and followed her to their room.

Once they were in bed, he ventured, "You know, between Becky getting here tomorrow and your sisters coming in for the weekend, you have a busy week ahead of you. What would you think about me starting our search for an apartment?"

Honor gave a contented sigh and closed her eyes. "That would be outstanding."

Chapter 62

Honor didn't realize how much she had missed her visits with the spirits, until the thick mist cleared and she was standing beside Darcy, near a small sapling on the side lawn of the Belleview Biltmore. In this memory, Darcy was several years older than the last time Honor had seen her.

When Darcy spoke, her voice was tinged with sadness. "I believe this tree was a gift from Rory -- a symbol of our love. I come back to the Belleview every winter and sit here, where I can remember our time together and talk to him about our beautiful daughter."

The base of the tree forked into two trunks. Several feet off the ground, the two trunks folded back together and then split apart again, reaching for sun. Even higher, the two trunks branched out in every direction and were covered with bright green leaves and purple flowers.

Darcy pointed to where the fork in the trunk had grown back together. "I wept here the year I lost Rory. The next year when I returned, I found this waiting for me."

Honor moved closer and without thinking, exclaimed, "Why, the tree grew in the shape of a heart!"

Instantly, she regretted speaking, but it was already too late. The fog rushed in and carried her away. At the edge of the mist, Honor watched Darcy's memories of her visits to the heart-tree race by until she became an old woman.

Just before Honor woke up in her own bed, Darcy's voice filtered through the mist. "Over the years, I've watched countless wedding ceremonies take place beneath the branches of our heart-tree. I dare say Rory would be pleased to know his gift to me played a role in so many love stories."

***

The next morning, Josh took Cody to James' house so Honor and Becky could concentrate on their project. While Honor waited for Becky to arrive, she wrote about her recent spirit visits in her journal. Her entries were almost up to date, when she heard loud clatter in the hallway outside of her suite. She opened the door to find a young woman struggling to collect scattered papers from the hallway floor.

The girl looked up at Honor, distraught. "Um, I'm Becky. You're Honor? Nice to meet you."

"Nice to meet you too, Becky. Listen, I know you're eager to get started, but I think you should come inside first. It'll be easier to work at the table than on the hallway floor."

Relieved to learn Honor had a sense of humor, Becky confessed, "This is so embarrassing. When I let go of my suitcase to knock on the door, the stupid thing fell over and dumped my portfolio."

"You have a portfolio? I can hardly wait to see your work."

Becky relaxed and finished collecting the contents of her folder. Honor helped her roll her troublesome suitcase into an extra bedroom. Afterward, they sat at the large table in the main parlor to review Becky's ideas for the website and blog.

"Your graphics are innovative and the website is user-friendly," Honor praised. This is exactly the fresh look I was hoping for."

"Thanks. Once the website is set-up, I figure you could post an article on the blog once a week and maybe invite professional women from various fields to guest blog sometimes."

Honor was impressed. "Becky, how would you like to set up *The Circle's* website and links to its membership database and blog? It would be a temporary job and it wouldn't pay much, but it would be good work experience... and you would be spending some of the winter in Florida."

Becky jumped at the opportunity.

"Great," Honor said. "I'll call my attorney and have her draw up an employment contract."

Becky's knowledge of Internet technology, combined with Honor's ability to design cutting-edge system software, proved to be a perfect combination of skill-sets. They were still working when Josh and Cody returned that evening.

Following introductions, Josh ventured, "Cody and I ate an early lunch, so we're ready for dinner, if you're interested in joining us."

Becky and Honor looked at each other and then laughed, realizing they had been so engrossed in their work, they had forgotten to break for lunch.

Becky stood. "You don't have to ask me twice. I'm starving."

***

Later that evening, when Josh and Honor were finally alone, Honor lamented, "I love working with Becky, and I'm enjoying this challenge, but I'm worried. *The Circle* is growing so fast, it's taking up a lot of my time already. And if William agrees to split Soft Fix in half, I'm going to be overwhelmed trying to make my half succeed. If he decides to buy me out instead, I'll be swamped starting a new company from scratch and won't have time for *The Circle.*"

Josh listened attentively before he spoke. "Honor, haven't you considered that *The Circle* might actually turn out to *be* your next business?"

The question caught Honor off guard. "No, I guess I haven't. I was just inspired by Margaret Plant to form a network of women who could help one another achieve their goals...a sort of *girls' club* to help even the playing field with the *good old boys' club* that so many women encounter in the business world."

"Why can't it do that and be a profitable business, too?"

"Julie suggested charging initiation fees and annual membership dues."

Josh nodded. "Yeah, and I'll bet some of your members would pay extra fees to consult with career counselors."

Honor nodded enthusiastically. "Or attend web conferences... and I could sell advertising space on the site, too."

The longer they talked about it, the more possibilities Honor could visualize. "Maybe Julie could help out on part-time basis, too. I think I'll talk this over with Sarah Jacobs tomorrow."

Freshly inspired, she pulled out a notebook and began to formulate a checklist. Josh knew her well enough by now to realize that Honor would be absorbed with this new task until she fell asleep, so he kissed her cheek and rolled over to the other side of the bed.

Later that night, when Honor heard Margaret's familiar voice beckoning from the parlor table, she was thrilled. She wanted to know more about her family history and why it had been kept a secret.

She rushed to the parlor, but when she realized Darcy was sitting at the table with Margaret, Honor stopped dead in her tracks. After all, she had had very little success talking directly to Darcy thus far.

Margaret motioned her to sit. "Hello, darlin' girl. Do you remember Darcy here? Come say hello."

Honor smiled at the older version of Darcy. "Hello, Grandmother."

Darcy's eyes brimmed with tears. "How I have longed for my descendants to know the truth. Giving up my daughter was best for all concerned, but a selfish part of me always wanted to trade places with Hannah...to raise my child and hear her call me '*Mother*.'"

Honor was puzzled. "If you wanted us to know about you, why didn't my mother tell us about the adoption long ago?"

Darcy glanced at Margaret and then cast her eyes down, wringing her hands in her lap.

Margaret spoke for her friend. "Darcy never spoke to your mother or grandmother. Her story was not mine to tell, so I said nothing to them, either. You are the first in your line to learn the true origins of your family."

"Why is that?" Honor asked.

Margaret continued patiently. "Darcy was never able to make contact with a living being before. I suspect she was able to connect with you because not only are you her blood relative, but you brought her long-lost journal and hat box here. Also, I suppose there are many similarities between your life and hers... your unhappy marriage, your new love, your willingness to adopt the child of another..." She trailed off.

Honor contemplated the magnitude of these revelations, feeling privileged to have been the one to finally connect with Darcy. Suddenly, she remembered the family pearls. Turning to Darcy, she asked, "Did the original pearl necklace belong to you?"

The fog swept in immediately and Honor cursed herself for being too inquisitive. She expected to wake in her own time, but this was not the case. Instead, the clouds parted to reveal an unfamiliar, but elegant Victorian bedroom.

Honor gulped air to calm her nausea, while taking in the scene. A woman was sitting on the edge of the bed talking to another, who was buried underneath a mountain of quilts.

When Honor approached the end of the dark sleigh-bed, she realized Darcy was the woman under the blankets and Hannah sat next to her.

Hannah was pleading, "You mustn't talk that way, Darcy... you'll be well again in no time at all."

"If so, you can return it to me. Now, please go and fetch it from the closet."

Dutifully, Hannah rose and opened the closet door. When she returned, she was carrying a large hat box. Honor recognized it instantly. It was the same hat box that was currently sitting on a table in her hotel suite, still filled with the clothes Darcy was wearing when she first made love to Rory Collins.

"Open the ribbon for me, Hannah. Quickly, now!"

Hannah untied the bow and lifted off the lid.

Darcy raised a weak hand and pulled the clothing to her face. She closed her eyes and breathed in the old, familiar scent of her true love, Rory. A single tear rolled down her wrinkled cheek. Then, reluctantly, she set the clothing aside and reached back into the empty box. To Honor's surprise, she lifted a false bottom from the box, revealing a stack of cash and several pieces of jewelry, including a beautiful pearl necklace.

Darcy gave the money and jewelry to Hannah, who tucked it into a small, velvet bag, and then slipped the bag into a deep pocket within the folds of her skirt. Moving quite rapidly, Hannah then layered Darcy's old clothing underneath her own. When she finished dressing, she placed a hat into the empty box and retied the ribbon.

Darcy was pale and tired, but still gave Hannah a satisfied smile.

When they heard footsteps approaching, Hannah picked up a tablet from a nearby table, and began discussing financial accounts for the residence. Honor was puzzled, but soon the reason for the masquerade became apparent.

Chapter 63

A stern man entered the room, with an equally fierce nurse trailing behind him. He looked down his nose at Hannah before he turned and addressed Darcy. "That's enough now, madam. You needn't be concerned with household affairs any longer. You need your rest."

He turned to Hannah. "Going forward, you'll report to my wife, Millicent –the new Head Mistress of this household."

Hannah's eyes darted to Darcy, certain this was the last time she would see her dear friend and benefactor. With her lips pressed tightly together, she nodded goodbye.

Confident her secrets would be kept safe, Darcy's eyes twinkled. "Goodbye, Mrs. Colson. Be well and give my best wishes to your daughter." Then she turned to the man and protested, "Arnold, you remind me so much of your father, Reginald when you issue commands that way..."

Hannah picked up the hatbox and turned to leave the room, but Arnold glimpsed her in the corner of his steel grey eyes. "Stop there woman... what do you think you're doing?"

Hannah froze, terrified.

Darcy intervened. "Leave her be, Arnold. She's done nothing wrong. I gave her an old hat that she admired. Obviously, I won't be needing it anymore. It's a small gift to thank her for her years of dedicated service to me."

Arnold gave a curt, respectful nod in Darcy's direction, but still stalked over to Hannah. "Allow me?"

He took the box from her and untied the ribbon. He lifted the hat from the box and turned it over in his hands, checking the lining to make sure Hannah wasn't stealing anything from his stepmother's room. He then felt around inside the empty box. When he turned it upside down, the lid of the secret compartment clattered to the floor. Arnold's look of triumph quickly turned to curiosity when nothing fell out of the compartment.

Darcy lied, "That hat box was made to hold a hat and store gloves in a compartment underneath, but the gloves were lost long ago." She shifted her gaze to Hannah. "I do apologize for my stepson, Mrs. Colson. He tends to be suspicious of everyone."

Darcy directed her next comments at the nurse. "Help Mrs. Colson put her gift back together and see her to the door."

After first glancing to Arnold for approval, the nurse did as she was asked. When Hannah left the room, the nurse and Arnold followed after her, still concerned she might try to slip some valuables into the big box on her way out.

Once they were alone, Darcy spoke to Honor. "That's the last time I will see my beloved Hannah. But I will rest comfortably, knowing my darling Hope is attending a university for young women in Connecticut, recommended by my dear friend, Margaret Plant."

Her voice wavered as her life's light began to fade. "Hope will have opportunities I never dreamed possible..."

The swirling fog returned, carrying Honor away from Darcy's last memory.

When the swirls of mist cleared, Honor was back at her parlor table with Margaret and Darcy. It was as though she never left, except Darcy was much more translucent than before.

Honor could tell sharing her last memories had taken its toll on her great-great grandmother. She didn't dare waste a moment. "Grandmother..." she cooed.

Darcy looked at her with sad, tired eyes.

"Would you like to hear about your family...your

descendants, I mean....yours and Great-Great Grandfather Rory's?"

Despite her weakened condition, Darcy smiled and nodded. She paid rapt attention as Honor told her about the family, including its tradition of naming all the girls after positive qualities and virtues, which Darcy started by naming her baby *Hope*.

Darcy clapped her hands together with glee.

Honor smiled and continued, "Your love affair has produced close to one hundred descendants to date, including many successful business men and women, doctors, teachers, and other noble professions. My cousin, Bliss, is poised to become a professional golfer, just like Great-Great Grandfather." Honor fingered her necklace. "And all of us women still wear your pearls."

Though exhausted, Darcy beamed in amazement, her eyes filled with tears.

Honor continued. "My three sisters, Charity, Patience and Chastity, are coming to visit at the end of the week. I know it isn't mine to tell, but please, may I share your story with them?"

Darcy considered the request, then nodded her consent.

"Thank you, Grandmother. I'll make sure they understand the sacrifices you made so that our lives could be better than your own."

Darcy smiled and then turned to Margaret. "Dear, dear friend. You know I haven't stayed in this world for the same reasons as you. Though I glean no joy from this existence, I feared my lighted path would end at the gates of hell because of my sinful behavior."

She glanced at Honor before continuing. "But now I know it was my destiny to meet Rory and for everything to unfold exactly as it did. A magnificent lineage resulted from our union, so I am no longer afraid to face what waits for me beyond this world. It is time for me to go and find Rory and Hannah, and share with them the joy of our legacy."

Margaret swallowed a lump in her throat. "Goodbye, my friend. Perhaps we'll meet again one day."

Darcy nodded. Without another word, she smiled at Honor and then faded from sight.

Honor wasn't sure what she had just witnessed. Confused, she searched Margaret's face for an explanation.

Margaret poured a cup of tea. "Your connection to Darcy taught you the truth about your heritage and at the same time brought Darcy the peace she needed to move along on her eternal journey. Nothing more was to be gained by her remaining in this time and space."

She paused and dabbed her eyes with her handkerchief. "You must remember everything you witnessed and never forget that you come from a long line of intelligent women who were able to overcome unimaginable obstacles in order to lead a life beyond what society dictated. Their essence abounds in the blood that flows through your veins, demanding that you too, achieve the extraordinary."

Tearfully, Honor stammered, "I won't ever see my grandmother's spirit again?"

Margaret spoke tenderly, as if comforting a child. "You won't share her memories the same way you experienced them in these past weeks, but you will always keep her in your heart. And who knows what lies ahead after this life is finished? Never be concerned about temporary absences from those you love, darlin'. This life of yours will pass in the blink of an eye. Live it without regrets and don't waste a single moment of it pining about things beyond your control."

"It's just that I have so many questions about her life after she returned to New York."

"Ah, well, perhaps I can answer some of your questions." Margaret took a sip of tea and smiled. "When Darcy first returned home from London, Reginald's son, Arnold, and his family were still visiting. His shrew of a wife waxed-on about the difficulty of obtaining quality domestics in Connecticut, so Darcy generously insisted they take Ella home with them. She told me she relished the notion of Ella cleaning up after their monstrous children and listening to Millicent's whining for the rest of her days."

Margaret and Honor giggled at Darcy's final triumph over the wicked housekeeper.

"Darcy ran her household with the precision of a Swiss time piece from that point forward. She became her husband's pride and joy and was known as a superb hostess, keeping company with prestigious politicians, business magnates and even royalty." Margaret smiled at the memory of her friend. "In fact, she was held in such high esteem by New York society that her stepsons didn't dare treat her poorly following Reginald's death."

"And Reginald never learned her secrets or realized she manipulated him to build her personal wealth?"

"No. He remained blissfully ignorant and happy with their marital arrangement. I'll show you."

The fog swirled around, carrying Honor back through time. When the mist began to clear, she was standing in the foyer of the house where she had first seen Darcy as a child bride being chastised by her husband, Reginald.

While Honor fought to rid herself of the nausea that always accompanied trips into a spirit's memory, she noticed the atmosphere in the house was quite different than it had been during her previous visits. The chandeliers were lit, casting a bright and cheerful glow around the room. A band played in the large ballroom down the hallway, where many people were gathered. Honor was standing next to Margaret and Henry Plant, who had apparently just arrived at the festivities and were being greeted by their hosts, Darcy and Reginald Loughman.

Both couples were lavishly dressed. Henry beamed at Darcy, who looked truly radiant in a royal blue gown with a corseted middle and low-cut neckline. "My dear, you are more beautiful every time I see you."

Darcy smiled and laid her hand against her throat, which was adorned by a stunning, triple-strand pearl necklace. She batted her eyes and leaned toward Henry, exposing even more of her voluptuous breasts. "Thank you for the compliment, sir, but I'm sure the beauty you noticed is this magnificent necklace that my dear Reginald surprised me with just this afternoon."

Both men stared hungrily at her breasts as they pretended to admire the necklace.

Margaret winked at Darcy, amused. "My dear cousin..." she said, "your business must be flourishing for you to present such a luxurious gift to your wife."

Reginald's chest puffed with pride, but he feigned modesty. "I can't complain...no, can't complain at all."

Henry sniffed. "Yes. The market is quite bullish as of late."

To fuel their sense of competition, Darcy returned Margaret's compliment. "Why, Madam Margaret, your gown is exquisite!"

Margaret replied, "How kind of you to notice. When you attend our holiday gala next month, perhaps I will have something new to show you, since that gathering follows our wedding anniversary."

Henry nodded at his wife's subtle reminder.

Honor was amused at the way the woman used their husbands' competitive egos to their own benefit and wondered what Henry could buy Margaret that would out-shine Reginald's gift of pearls.

Pearls!

Honor spun around and stared at Darcy's necklace. She was certain that, four generations later, she was wearing five pearls from that very same necklace.

Chapter 64

Just then, the fog closed in and pulled Honor from the scene, returning her to her seat at the parlor table.

"What did Darcy do with all her jewelry?"

Margaret chuckled. "Darcy sold pieces of her collection each time Hannah and Hope needed additional funds, replacing some of them with paste duplicates. When it became obvious that she was dying, her step-sons beseeched her to reveal the location of her hidden jewelry collection, but she refused to tell them. She became conveniently senile in her last days and said she couldn't remember where her jewels were hidden. Why, I do believe those men searched every nook and cranny of that house for years, looking for her missing jewels!"

Honor chuckled at the thought of the greedy heirs searching for a jewelry collection that no longer existed, but then her smile faded.

"It's incredibly sad that Darcy's entire life was devoted to caring for a husband and step-sons she did not love, so that she could finance a family who didn't know she existed."

Margaret clucked. "A life dedicated to anonymous service is the most honorable of existences. My friend deserves your admiration, not your pity. Tonight she left this realm glowing with satisfaction, knowing the result of her selflessness was the creation of an astounding legacy. Darcy's blood spawned generations of remarkable women, and now it flows through your veins. You must make the most of the spec of time allotted for your life. Like your ancestors, you, too, can accomplish extraordinary things, but there's no time to waste."

Honor nodded, thinking about her family. "Margaret, since Darcy didn't share a connection with my mother, how did you come to know her?"

Margaret paused, reflecting on the past. "I think my close friendship with Darcy made it easier for me to connect with her relatives. But the true link between Faith Macklin and me was our mutual love of the stock market."

Honor's bewildered expression caused a sly smile to spread across Margaret's face. "Faith and I both loved the rivalry of the business world and we were drawn to the stock market because it was a forum in which we could compete with men on equal footing. When Faith came here to the Belleview to attend a lecture about investing and stayed over for a night, we connected."

"She never mentioned it."

"She tried to tell you, but you weren't receptive to her discoveries about the afterlife."

Honor groaned, remembering how dismissive she had been of her mother's quirky ideology.

"Faith and I enjoyed great visits. I always hoped she would connect with Darcy, but in the meantime, we spent our evenings together developing investment strategies, which she would later implement and track. We enjoyed a rather successful run in the market, if I do say so myself."

Honor was puzzled. "You thought my Mother invested money in the stock market?"

"Well, you inherited a stock portfolio, didn't you?"

Honor shook her head, dumbfounded.

Margaret knitted her eyebrows. "Then she must have maintained a false profit leger, so we could pretend to invest in the stock market without any real risk." She sighed. "Too bad. Well, it was fun, even if it was just a game. I'll miss my visits with Faith."

Both women grew quiet, lost in their private thoughts. Honor noticed the mist beginning to swirl around her.

Just before she disappeared into the fog, Margaret said, "Any life worth living involves taking *real* risks. When you won't risk losing what you have, you stand almost no chance of acquiring something even better. That new enterprise of yours could inspire countless women to take the risks that are necessary to realize their dreams."

Honor heard a noise coming from another room in the suite and turned toward the sound. She felt herself falling through the fog and wasn't surprised to find herself back in her own bed when she opened her eyes. She listened for a moment, then got up, put on a robe and crept in to check on Cody. He was sleeping peacefully.

While Honor gazed at him, she thought about her visit with the spirits. She was sad that she would never again share Darcy's memories, but prayed that her great-great grandmother would find peace at the end of the lighted path.

Suddenly the hair on Honor's neck stood on end. She whirled around, sensing that she was not alone. She balled her fists, ready to attack anyone who might try to harm Cody.

Then, somewhere in the darkness, she heard Becky say, "Ouch!" and realized her guest had gotten up to go to the bathroom and was innocently stumbling back into her bedroom, unaware that anyone else was awake at this hour.

When she heard Becky close the door to her room, Honor took a deep breath, unclenched her fists, and tried to calm her heart rate. While she waited for the adrenalin to slowly dissipate, she bent over and tucked Cody's blanket under his chin, then kissed his cheek. Like Hannah before her, she may not have given birth to her child but Cody was hers now, and Honor knew she would have given her life to protect him.

She returned to bed and curled her chilly body into the warm curve of Josh's back. When she slid her arm around him, he captured her hand and held it in his own. She smiled and closed her eyes.

***

Honor woke to the sound of cartoons and Cody's voice, telling Becky about Spiderman's run-in with one of his arch enemies. She pulled on a thick robe and shuffled into the parlor.

As soon as he spotted her, Cody called out, "Mommy's awake!"

Honor stifled a yawn. "Good morning, you two. Where's Josh?"

"He said he had to get to a jobsite early, so I told him to leave Cody here with us." Becky rubbed her hands together. "You know, this old hotel needs some work on the heating system. I woke up in the middle of the night and this suite was freezing!"

Cody nodded in agreement. "The invisible people make it cold."

Honor decided to use Josh's old explanation for Cody's unusual outbursts. "Cody has a lot of invisible friends. I guess he thinks they mess with the thermostat at night."

Becky smiled broadly at Cody's imagination and played along. "They do, do they? Well...we'll have to put up a sign saying 'please don't change the temperature in this room,' won't we?"

Cody, satisfied the problem had been solved, went back to watching cartoons. Honor showed Becky her systems design checklist and in no time, they were back at the dining room table, bouncing ideas off each other.

Eventually, Cody came into the parlor and announced, "I'm hungry."

Embarrassed, Honor realized that she had momentarily forgotten Cody was even in the suite. *Some mother*, she chided herself. "I'm sorry, Sweetie. Sometimes I get busy and forget to eat, so I'm glad you reminded me."

Cody admonished, "Daddy says I have to eat so I can grow up to be a big boy."

Honor smiled at Josh's quote. "He's absolutely right. Just give me a minute to get cleaned up and we'll go out for breakfast. You know, Cody, when we move to a regular house, you're going to discover I make great pancakes."

The thought of moving to a new home spurred Cody's imagination and he followed Honor to the bathroom, listing everything that would be different once they moved. He chattered away the entire time she was brushing her teeth. Finally, Honor interrupted him.

"Okay, Cody... you need to scoot and close the door, so I can take my shower."

Obediently, Cody walked to the bathroom door and closed it, but to Honor's astonishment, he remained in the bathroom with her.

She laughed at the misunderstanding and tried to explain. "Uh...Cody...you need to leave the bathroom while I shower."

"Why can't I talk to you while you're taking a shower?"

Flustered, Honor said the first thing that popped into her mind. "Because girls aren't supposed to take showers when boys are in the room."

His quick mind immediately countered, "But you came in here when my Daddy was in the shower."

Honor tried to dodge the comment. "That's different." As soon as the words escaped her lips, she knew what he was going to ask next.

"Why, Mommy?"

Honor smiled at the sound of her new name, wondering how long it would take her to get used to it. She took him by his hand and led him to the door. As she opened it, she explained, "It's about privacy, Cody. But I'm not ready to have that discussion this early in the morning, so you're just going to have to take my word for it. Now scat!"

Cody put out his bottom lip. Honor smiled and tried another tactic. "Do you think you could draw a picture for Becky while I'm in the shower?"

His lip retracted instantly, all signs of upset gone as quickly as they had appeared.

As he left the bathroom, he yelled, "Becky... I'm going to draw a picture for you!"

From elsewhere in the suite, Honor heard Becky answer, "Great, Cody. Why don't you come sit here at the table with me?"

Honor closed the door, then leaned against it and shook her head over the embarrassing encounter. She made a mental note to ask Josh how he thought they should approach the privacy subject with Cody. There were so many things she had to learn about being a mother. Feelings of anxiety began to blossom, but as she stepped into the warm shower, she recalled Margaret's words. *'Darcy's blood spawned generations of remarkable women, and now it flows through your veins'.*

Honor thought about her female ancestors. All of them had been wonderful mothers and now their blood was flowing through her veins. The thought calmed her, although she couldn't help but wonder if any of them ever had to deal with a child as inquisitive as Cody.

Chapter 65

The rest of the week, Honor struggled to divide her time between Soft Fix and The Circle. Soon it was Friday and she was waving goodbye to Becky as the airport shuttle bus pulled away from the hotel curb.

"See you after the holidays," she called. She checked her watch. In just a few hours, her sisters were scheduled to arrive for a meeting at the title company, where they would sign ownership of their mother's house over to Honor, in exchange for a large chunk of her retirement savings.

Honor wasn't thrilled about leaving her posh suite to spend the night on air mattresses, but Chase refused to stay at the Belleview Biltmore, and Patty and Cherry thought it would be fun to spend one more night in their mother's home before the work crews started the renovation. With no time to waste, Josh cleaned the grill, while Honor and Cody shopped for groceries and a second air bed.

When Chase's cab pulled up, Honor raced out to greet her baby sister with excited shrieks and hugs. Chase was heavier than Honor and wore her dark hair in a short, straight bob, but they both had green eyes and possessed similar facial features.

Cody hid behind his father's legs while Josh paid the cabbie and retrieved Chase's overnight bag from the trunk.

Honor introduced Chase to Josh, and she hugged him, too. "I've never heard my sister speak so highly of any man before."

Josh blushed and mumbled, "Good to meet you, too."

"And that's Cody," Honor pointed.

Cody continued to hide behind Josh.

"I think I have something for you in my purse, Cody," Chase teased. She rifled around in her large handbag, knowing she had Cody's full attention. "My sister said you like some superhero, but I just can't remember which one it was."

Cody stepped out from behind Josh; his eyes glued on her purse. "Spiderman," he said.

Chase smiled. "That's right, Spiderman." She pulled a Spiderman action figure from her bag. Excited, Cody practically snatched the toy from her.

Josh prompted, "What do you say, Cody?"

Cody gushed, "I don't have this one!"

Josh prompted him again.

"Thank you," Cody mumbled. He allowed Chase to give him a hug.

"Come on inside." Honor suggested, "Cherry and Patty are going to meet us at the title company, but we have time for a drink before we have to leave."

"A cold beer sounds great." Chase stopped in the foyer and looked around. "Wow, it's strange to see the house so empty."

"You know, it's not too late to change your mind about sleeping in our suite at the Belleview Biltmore."

Chase pretended to shiver. "No thanks...I had a bad experience there when I was a kid."

Josh and Honor exchanged a bewildered glance as they moved into the kitchen.

"You can't make a statement like that and expect us to let it slide," Honor prodded as she opened three beers.

Josh nodded in agreement.

Chase rolled her eyes. "No fair. Josh just met me and he'll think I'm a kook!"

"Try me. I've heard some pretty bizarre stuff since I've been with your sister."

Chase took a swig of beer before conceding. "For some reason, our mother liked to spend a weekend at that hotel every couple months, right Honor?"

Honor nodded, "That's true."

"Well, one summer, while I was still too little to go to sleep-away camp with my sisters, Mom decided to take me along with her. I remember we sat in huge wooden rocking chairs on the porch and ate ice cream. It was great having our mom to myself."

"Sounds nice," Honor commented.

"At first it was. But that night, Mom was tired and wanted to go to bed early." Chase paused to take another drink of beer. "I guess I fell asleep and had a scary dream, but it was so unbelievably real, I still remember it."

Honor coaxed, "Tell us about the dream."

"I dreamed that I woke up in the middle of the night and saw a ghost. I was scared and heard Mom talking in the next room, so I got out of bed and ran toward her voice. But when I came around the corner, I froze. Mom had turned into a ghost, too! She was sitting at a table sipping tea with another ghost, and acting as if being transparent was just as normal as can be. I ran back to bed to hide under the covers, and when I jumped in, I thought I found Mom's body!"

Chase shuddered at the memory. "She was just asleep, of course. I started to cry and she woke up. When I told her I had a nightmare, she hugged me and said everything was fine, so I should go back to sleep. I plastered myself against Mom and tried to sleep, but I could still hear the ghost voices in the next room. Anyway...I never forgot that night and I guess the hotel brings back that scary memory." She took a long drink. "So, now you think I'm crazy, right?"

Honor shook her head. "Chase, I don't think you were dreaming. I've had several similar experiences at the hotel. When Patty and Cherry get here, I'll tell you guys about them."

Chase cracked, "Oh goody... an old fashioned sleepover, complete with ghost stories!" Changing the subject, she asked, "What time is the closing?"

Honor glanced at her watch, startled at how quickly time

had evaporated. "Actually, we should get going right now." She stood and reached for her keys. "Josh, do you have everything you need for the barbeque?"

Josh nodded. "Sure do. You guys take your time. I turned up the heat on the pool, so we're going for a swim while you're gone."

Honor gave him and Cody a quick kiss and then she and Chase rushed out the door.

Cherry and Patty were already at the title company when Chase and Honor arrived. Both sisters had dark hair, but their eyes were light brown and they had inherited their father's longer nose. Cherry's hair was pulled back in a knot, held in place with a clip, while Patty embraced her curls with a short, carefree cut.

It was great to be together, even if they did have to sign a mountain of paperwork. The closing was completed without a hitch and soon they were on their way back home. Except now, it belonged to Honor.

***

After everyone had been properly introduced, Honor put Cody down for a nap and Josh started supper. The autumn weather was perfect, so they all sat outside and amused Josh with stories from their childhood, while the foil-wrapped potatoes, carrots and onions roasted on the hot grill.

As the sun sank lower, the temperature dropped, making it easy for Honor to recruit indoor kitchen help. The sisters prepared the side dishes and then sat on the living room floor, drinking beer and reminiscing.

Patty remarked, "I think Mom would be happy to know the house is staying in the family."

"Speaking of Mom," Honor confessed, "I need to tell you guys something. Her spirit is still here."

"I feel her, too!" Chase interrupted.

"Really?" Patty questioned.

Cherry shook her head. "Nonsense. You guys are letting your imaginations get the better of you."

Just then, Cody shuffled into the room, rubbing his sleepy eyes.

"Hey there, little guy...did you have a nice nap?" Honor reached out and pulled him onto her lap.

Still tired, he yawned and curled up comfortably, resting his head against Honor's shoulder. Immediately, she noticed his skin was cold. She tensed. "Is everything okay, Cody?"

"Grandma came to visit while I was sleeping."

Honor knew her sisters wouldn't understand what Cody was talking about, but she decided to let him tell her about the visit and then explain everything to her siblings afterward.

They listened, fascinated as she urged, "What did Grandma have to say, Cody?"

Cody rubbed his nose, still trying to wake up. "Grandma said she's glad everyone's together and happy. Now she can go join Grandpa."

"Grandma said she's joining Grandpa?"

Cody nodded. "Yeah. She's been lonely without him."

More awake now, Cody sat up straighter in Honor's lap. "She said she wants to leave before the carpenters start tearing down walls. I tried to tell her how much fun it's going to be, but..." he shrugged, unable to understand how anyone could find the prospect of home remodeling less than awesome.

Honor encouraged him to continue. "Did she want you to tell us anything else?"

Cody screwed up his face, concentrating. "She said she loves everybody and when we get really, really, *really* old, she'll be waiting for us at the end of the lighted path." He paused and then added, "And she said to remember her favorite saying... the one on the sign that used to be in the kitchen...about laughing."

"I remember that sign. It said 'Live well. Laugh often. And love much'."

Cody nodded. "Yep, that's it." He clambered to his feet, now wide awake. "I'm thirsty, Mommy. Can I have some juice?"

Honor smiled. "Sure you can, Sweetie...let's go to the kitchen and I'll show you where that sign about laughing used to hang."

She glanced at her sisters, who were staring open-mouthed at the two of them. She wasn't surprised. Even though she accepted the fact that Cody was a medium, she was still amazed by his ability to form a bridge between the living and the dead.

Looking over the kitchen island into the living room, she could see her sisters whispering to one another, but she couldn't make out what they were saying.

She handed Cody a drink box. "Daddy should be just about finished cooking our steaks—are you hungry?"

Cody nodded enthusiastically.

"Why don't you go check on Daddy to see what's taking so long?"

Needing no further encouragement, Cody ran towards the door to the back yard.

Honor called after him, "Walk! Don't spill your drink." Then she took a deep breath and walked back into the living room to face her sister's questions.

They fell silent as Honor approached. She sat down. "Okay, I know that was pretty strange..."

Cherry interrupted. "Strange? That's an understatement, don't you think? I mean...Cody just called you '*Mommy*' for goodness sake!"

Honor laughed, "Mommy? That's the part that caught your attention?" Her laughter became contagious. They all laughed so hard, they didn't even hear Josh and Cody come in the room.

Josh asked, "What's so funny?"

Before Honor could explain, Cody interjected, "I know why they're laughing, Daddy... Grandma told them they were supposed to laugh a lot."

His explanation sent them into new fits of laughter. When they finally calmed down, Honor suggested they postpone the rest of their discussion until after dinner, hinting she had a lot to tell them about their family's history.

Chapter 66

Josh rubbed his stomach as he carried his empty dinner plate to the kitchen. "I'm stuffed. I think it's time for Cody and me to head back to the hotel, so you girls can talk about us without worrying about hurting our feelings."

Chase laughed. "You don't know us very well yet, but believe me...you being here won't stop us from talking about you."

Honor giggled. "Well, we only have two air mattresses, so unless two of you want to sleep on the floor, they need to go back to the hotel."

Chase turned back to Josh. "Like I was saying, drive safely and we'll see you tomorrow!"

Honor walked Josh and Cody out to the truck and kissed them both goodnight.

"I'll call you in the morning, but don't wait on us for breakfast. I have a feeling we're going to stay up late and then sleep in."

Josh teased, "I would expect nothing less from girls at a slumber party. But seriously, I'll miss you tonight."

"I'll miss you too."

Honor gave him one last kiss, then waved goodbye as the truck backed out of the driveway. She turned toward the front door and caught her sisters spying on her through the front window. Amused, she walked to the kitchen and opened a bottle of wine.

"Okay, let's hear it...what do think of my guys?" Honor filled four wine glasses.

Patty drooled, "Josh has ten brothers? Man, if I wasn't a happily married woman, I'd be seriously considering moving my practice back to Florida."

Chase reached for a glass. "I never pictured you as a mother, Honor...but you seem to have taken to the role like a duck to water."

Cherry clucked, "Josh seems terrific and Cody is adorable, but is it wise to take on an *instant family* a year after your divorce? I mean...you could be rebounding because William became a father."

"I'm not rebounding," Honor responded without hesitation. "I love Josh because he makes me laugh and I feel safe when I'm with him. He believes in me and respects my opinions. He even understands when I get absorbed in a project and totally ignore him. And I admire every aspect of his life. Just thinking about him makes me smile." As if to make her point, Honor's lips curved into a smile. "And I don't miss anything about William... and I do mean *anything*!"

She wiggled her eyebrows up and down to make sure they understood she meant his physical attributes. Her sisters laughed.

"And as for Cody...well...he's been gone for a half an hour and I miss him already. His mind is amazing and he has an incredible vocabulary. He's only four years old and he can already spell his whole name. And you guys have to admit, he is the cutest little boy you could ever ask for. Oh, and on top of all that, he's a spiritual medium!"

Honor stopped to take a sip of wine.

"Yessiree," Chase repeated, "like a duck to water... she even brags like a mother."

Laughing, the sisters clinked their wine glasses to toast Honor's new relationship.

They inflated the air mattresses in the living room, and settled down facing each other, with Honor and Chase on one mattress and Cherry and Patty on the other.

Honor decided it was time to tell her sisters about their mother and the spirits of the Belleview Biltmore. She began, "Love and motherhood aren't the only life-changing experiences I've had recently."

She told them about discovering Darcy's journal in the kitchen cabinet and the antique hat box in the closet. She summarized her encounters with Margaret, Darcy, Hannah and the rest of the spirits. When she shared the details of Rory's death and Darcy's selfless decision to allow Hannah to raise Hope, her sisters were teary-eyed. She explained the origins of the Colson name and the pearl necklace. Lastly, she revealed, "Mom never encountered the spirits of our relatives at the Belleview Biltmore, but she did visit with Margaret every time she stayed there."

Chase murmured, "Then I wasn't dreaming. Mom was talking to a transparent lady that night."

"Yep," Honor confirmed.

Cherry's eyes widened. "Didn't it scare the bejesus out of you to be around all those dead people?"

Honor considered her question. "I don't think I was ever scared. At first I was confused, but once Margaret explained what was going on, I was fascinated. In fact, most nights I could hardly wait to go to sleep. Now that Darcy has moved on, I doubt I'll have any more encounters and that makes me a little sad."

Patty smacked her hand on the floor. "Oh my gosh... remember when my Larry decided to trace the genealogy for both sides of our family? He tracked his relatives back almost to the Revolutionary War, but on our side, he got stumped at Rory and Hannah Colson. Now it all makes sense. He couldn't find a record of their births or marriage because they made everything up."

"They didn't make everything up... they made everything right." Honor corrected.

"They made our family."

"Speaking of family, do you think Cody really talked to Mom?" Casey asked.

"Yes. He's talked to her several times. He said she wanted to say goodbye to us because once she travels the lighted path, she can't ever come back."

Cherry interjected, "Personally, I would never hang around as a spirit. I believe that lighted path leads to a perfect existence."

"You know," Patty mused, "we were really lucky to have Mom as our mom. She made everything look so easy. Even though there were four of us, I can't remember ever feeling like she didn't have time to help me with my homework or make cookies for class parties. I only have two kids and I can barely manage!"

"All moms feel overwhelmed sometimes," Cherry stated with authority. "I think Mom baked all those cookies as her coping mechanism."

"Well, she sure got good at baking in the process. I wish my kids could have tasted her *banana nut oatmeal* cookies," Patty replied.

"Yum. I loved her *peanut butter kiss* cookies," Chase added.

"And her '*Snickerdoodles*'..." Cherry admitted.

"You know what?" Honor remembered. "I saved Mom's old cookie recipes. I'll make copies for you guys. Who knows? Maybe generations from now, our family will still be baking cookies from the same recipes."

Delighted with the idea, they began calling out the names of their favorite cookies: *chocolate chunk, stained-glass windows, coconut macaroons, ginger snaps, cinnamon snowflakes* and so on.

Honor was the first to notice the temperature in the room was dropping. "I think Mom's here with us right now," she gasped. "When we were growing up, remember how close we felt when we were in the kitchen eating Mom's homemade cookies and talking about everything in the world? Well, I think those memories created a bridge between Mom's spirit and us."

Honor expected her sisters to scoff at her, but no one made a sound.

Finally Patty called out, "I miss you every day, Mom. I always will."

A moment later, Cherry grew wide-eyed. "She *is* here! She just brushed my hair back from my face. I love you, Mom!"

Chase began to cry. "I wish you didn't have to go, Mom. I wish you could stay here forever. I didn't say it enough when you were alive, but I love you."

Honor closed her eyes when she felt her mother's gentle touch. "Thanks, Mom, for everything." She choked back a sob. "I hate to say goodbye, but like Margaret says, I'll see you again 'in the blink of an eye.' Give Daddy my love...and Hannah and Darcy, too."

An instant later, they knew Faith Macklin was gone. The experience had brought them peace, but now exhaustion overtook the sisters. They fell asleep with happy memories of childhood filling their dreams.

***

Honor was the last to wake up in the morning. At first she was confused, but when she heard her sisters talking in the kitchen, the events of the previous evening came flooding back to her. Still groggy, she sat up. "Good Morning," she mumbled.

Chase squealed, "Oh goody! You're finally awake! We decided we want to go out to the cemetery to put flowers on Mom and Daddy's graves today."

Honor yawned, "Okay...but after breakfast, alright?"

"Sounds good, but it's ten thirty and most places stop serving breakfast at ten," Cherry said.

Honor and Patty chorused, "Not at Lenny's Restaurant!"

Cherry smiled. "I haven't eaten there in ages. Do they still give you a little pastry basket to munch on while they cook your breakfast?"

"Yep," Honor confirmed.

Chase was full of energy. "Okay then, let's hurry up and get dressed. Dibs on the shower in the master bathroom!"

Honor teased, "I don't *think* so, little sister...as of yesterday, this is *my* house. That means the big shower is *all mine.* You guys can take turns showering in our old bathroom."

Chase laughed and made a dash towards the master bedroom. Honor chased after her and caught her in the hallway. While they were wrestling, trying to keep each other away from the master bedroom door, Patty waltzed by them. Before they realized what she was up to, she closed and locked master bedroom door.

"Better luck next time!" Patty called, laughing.

Chase ran to the locked door and pounded on it, yelling, "But I had dibs! No fair!"

Honor grinned. "Some things never change."

While waiting her turn for the shower, she called Josh and made plans to meet at the resort pool after they had breakfast and visited the cemetery.

***

Stuffed with an assortment of Lenny's pastries and *"The Best Breakfast in Clearwater"*, which to them meant omelets, scrapple and the house specialty, *Redneck Benedict*, the sisters rolled themselves out of the restaurant and into Honor's rental car.

Honor stopped at a flower shop before driving to the small cemetery. She parked just inside the cemetery gate and winced again at the close proximity of busy roads and a strip mall. But despite its poor location, Honor had to admit the well-maintained grave markers, colorful flowers and lush grass created a peaceful, park-like environment.

They located their parents' tall, granite grave marker with no trouble. It read,

MACKLIN
Andrew 1950 -1990 & Faith 1953-2007
Devoted Soul Mates and Loving Parents
Together For Eternity

They each wanted private time at the graveside, so they took turns wandering through the cemetery, admiring grave markers and epitaphs, some of which were quite old.

Suddenly Patty called out, "Come over here, everybody!"

When Honor drew near, Cherry pointed her finger at the carved epitaph on the headstone. "Last night when you told us about seeing ghosts who revealed all that stuff about our *real* family history, I think a part of me doubted it was true...until now."

Honor's jaw dropped as she read the large stone marker:

DARCY LOUGHMAN
1880 -1938
A Life Well Lived
Rest In Peace

While Patty was taking a picture of the epitaph, Honor walked back to their mother's grave and extracted a few roses from one of the bouquets. She laid the flowers at the base of Darcy's headstone and whispered, "Rest well, Great-Great-Grandmother... you've certainly earned it."

Chapter 67

At the end of the weekend, her sisters flew back to their respective homes and Honor began preparing to leave for Chicago. Over the phone, William Guard and Leon Goldstein had scoffed at the demand letter, but they still consented to a meeting. Sarah Jacobs considered that to be a good sign. She and Honor met to discuss tactics.

"Despite the smoke screens he's put in place to keep his *dubious* financial transactions hidden, I'm confident I can convince a judge that William has been cheating you from the start of your business relationship," Sarah stated. "You say the word and I'll make sure William's prosecuted and convicted of financial fraud."

"Sending William to prison isn't my goal. Besides, if we get the law involved, some good people might get hurt. Let's start by trying to negotiate without threats."

"Alright, then. If William has any conscience whatsoever, I'm confident we have enough evidence to prove the true value of Soft Fix and mediate a fair settlement. If instead, he insists on pursuing criminal behavior, we may have no choice but to report the matter to the police."

Honor nodded, uneasy about the looming confrontation. The possibility of doing irreparable damage to Soft Fix was distressing, but she couldn't let William get away with stealing from her, either. The fact that she couldn't envision an acceptable outcome weighed heavily on her mind.

The night before the meeting, Josh drove Honor to the airport and kissed her goodbye at the shuttle to the gates.

"God, I hate conflict," she moaned.

He held her close, "You'll do just fine, Honor."

She looked doubtful. "I wish I had your confidence. I know there's no way to avoid this fight, but I sure wish it was already over."

"If you get nervous, just think of me and I'll be right there with you...at least in spirit."

"Thanks, Josh. I mean it."

"Call me when the meeting is over, okay?"

"I will, but I wish you could be there to give me a hug. I think I'm going to need one," Honor lamented. She turned and trudged toward the shuttle.

***

They rented a small conference room in a convenient business center for the meeting. William had wanted to meet at Soft Fix, but Sarah graciously refused, suggesting an offsite meeting would assure there would be no disruptions. Truthfully, she hadn't wanted to give William the *home turf* advantage of being in familiar surroundings.

Sarah sat at the table, facing the door, while Honor paced back and forth, playing out every scenario she could think of in her mind. The sound of Sarah's voice made her jump.

"You should sit down now... they'll be here any minute and we don't want to appear nervous."

Sarah gestured for Honor to take the chair next to her and poured two glasses of water. They went over their agenda for the meeting one more time.

"Remember what I said. Don't expect anything to be settled today. We just want to feel them out and let them know we are serious about our demands."

William and Leon arrived together, ten minutes late. They offered no apology for their tardiness. Honor noticed Leon avoided looking her in the eye and wondered if he regretted the part he played in deceiving her.

They exchanged traditional pleasantries as William and Leon sat down on the opposite side of the table. Leon opened his briefcase and pulled out a copy of the demand letter Sarah had sent him.

He cleared his throat. "Let me be blunt. Mr. Guard disputes the assertion that Miss Macklin owns fifty percent of Soft Fix and we are certain the court would support our position, based on legal documentation related to the company's ownership. We also do not agree with your calculation of the company's net worth."

He paused to let their position sink in.

"From the beginning, Miss Macklin has served in a technical support position, while my client cultivated customers and literally ran the entire company. In fact, my client agreed to meet with you today only because of the compassion he feels for Miss Macklin, given their past relationship, and her value as a gifted employee."

Sarah scoffed, "Your claim that Miss Macklin is less than an equal partner is ludicrous. She was the principal investor and has been the company's primary asset since its inception. Also, I'm confident my appraisal of the company's worth is conservative at sixteen million. The settlement figure of eight million dollars or fifty percent ownership is, therefore, perfectly reasonable. Furthermore, if you make the unwise decision to cease negotiations and pursue this matter in court, we will demand a full, independent audit of the company's financial records since its inception."

William interjected, "Come on, Honor. *Partner* is just a word. You earn a damned fine salary and that's what really counts, isn't it?"

Leon put his hand on William's arm, motioning him to be quiet.

Honor glared at William. Sarah cleared her throat, signaling Honor not to respond to the absurd statement.

With the *posturing phase* of the meeting over, Sarah pulled out her own copy of the demand letter, along with a legal pad, and began the true negotiations.

"I suggest we discuss our demands, line by line," she said.

After an hour of sitting quietly and watching the attorneys take jabs at one another, Honor's phone began vibrating in her pocket. She glanced at the caller ID and saw it was a text from Julie that read, "*911.*"

She stood and announced, "I'm sorry, but I have an emergency. Please carry on and I'll be right back." She walked out of the room, aware that three pairs of eyes followed her in disbelief.

"What's wrong, Julie?"

"I'm sorry for interrupting your meeting, but I knew you would want to hear what I just learned. Melody decided to continue investigating the fleet vehicle account and called a phone number associated with that Jaguar our company's insuring. When a woman answered, Melody asked if she knew William Guard. It turns out the woman was William's wife, Sherri, who mistook Melody for some gold digger she suspects is having sex with William. Sherri went bananas and started screaming about her iron-clad pre-nuptial agreement and how if Melody thought she was landing a rich man, she was wrong. Get this: she said if she catches William cheating on her, she'll take their kid and just about everything he owns, including Soft Fix."

"Perfect. I think Sherri just did me a huge favor. I have to get back into the meeting now, but thanks for the info, Julie."

Honor quietly took her seat, her mind racing. Within a few minutes, she had a plan.

"Excuse me, everyone," she interrupted. She turned to William, her face expressionless. "Here's the deal, you rat bastard. You and I are going to sell Soft Fix to Ellen Christiansen and Pete Cross, and split the profits of the sale, fifty-fifty."

William sneered at her with contempt. "What makes you

think I'll agree to that?"

"I have three reasons. I'll jot them down for you."

William's eyes narrowed as Honor scribbled a quick note, folded it in half, and slid it across the table. Much to her satisfaction, William paled as he read it.

"You're bluffing," William bellowed.

"You know me better than that, William." Honor smirked. "Besides, 'partner' is just a word. You can continue to earn a damned fine salary at Soft Fix and that's what really counts, isn't it?" she mimicked.

William's face contorted with rage. "They can't afford Soft Fix."

"Ellen and Pete have wanted to buy partnerships for years." Honor countered, hoping her voice wouldn't falter. "They'll jump at the chance to buy us out. We'll work out a payment schedule and as part of the deal, I'll agree to never divulge *any* information about you or Soft Fix to *anyone*." She paused, wondering why she had cowered before this man for so long. "This is a one-time offer, William. Tomorrow I move on to Plan B. So, do we have a deal?"

Leon threw his hands up. "Whoa...Let's slow down." He turned to Sarah, "I think we should take a fifteen minute break, so we can speak to our clients privately."

"I agree." Sarah nodded.

As soon as the door closed behind Leon and William, Sarah spun around to face Honor. "What did you write in that note?"

"That I know the terms of his prenuptial agreement; that I know he is cheating with Yvonne; and that people go to jail for hiding personal income in company records. It's called tax evasion."

Sarah gasped. "That's extortion, Honor! I can't be a party to this."

"But I didn't threaten William, nor did I claim he committed any crimes. I simply stated some facts and hoped he would read between the lines. I think it worked."

Sarah frowned.

"Look, Sarah, if we sell the company to our top employees, no one loses their jobs. No one goes to jail, and I get to move to Florida. It's a win-win-win."

Sarah considered her arguments. "Wasn't Plan B a threat?"

Honor giggled. "Nope. My Plan B is to continue working for Soft Fix on a long distance basis until I could afford to quit."

A fleeting smile crossed Sarah's lips. "Okay, then. If we're going to do this deal, there will be absolutely no mention of the items in your note from this point forward. Agreed?"

"None whatsoever."

Sarah quickly drafted the terms of their agreement into a memo of understanding. When Leon and William returned, they were almost submissive. Sarah reviewed the document with them and, after some minor tweaking, all four of them signed the memo.

Sarah and Leon made copies of the signed draft and arranged to work together to finalize the agreement the following day. Then he and William left. When they were well out of earshot, Sarah squealed with delight, amazed by their accomplishment.

"Shall we have a drink to celebrate?" Honor suggested.

"I think I'm going to have to settle for a celebratory hug instead. I need to grab a cab back to my hotel so I can get started on the final version of the agreement while all the details are still fresh in my mind."

Chapter 68

When Honor slid behind the wheel of her car, she realized how draining the long day had been. Longing for the sound of Josh's voice, she dialed his cell.

"Is your meeting over?" he queried.

"Yep."

"Well that's perfect timing. Are you hungry?"

Honor was confused. "Now that you mention it, I'm starving. Why?"

"Because I ordered your favorite stuffed pizza here at Giordano's about a half hour ago, and they said it would take about an hour before it would be ready. I planned to bring it to your place to surprise you, but since your meeting is already over, you can just meet me here at the restaurant."

Honor was stunned. "You're in Chicago?"

"Yep...the southern boy is in Chi-Town," Josh laughed.

"I don't understand."

"Well, the more I thought about it, the more I didn't want you to be alone if the meeting turned out worse than you expected. So this morning I dropped Cody off with James and Lisa and took the redeye flight."

Honor's eyes filled with tears as a lump formed in her throat. "You flew here just for me?"

"Well, I've also been craving a good pizza."

Honor rolled her eyes, smiling. She sniffed and wiped away her tears.

Josh misread her reaction. "Don't cry, Honor. Everything will be okay."

"Yes, it will," she agreed. "I'll be right there to pick you up."

***

Honor lit the gas fireplace in her living room, opened a bottle of wine and lay against huge cushions on the floor while they ate and discussed the future.

"I stand to receive eight million dollars from the sale of Soft Fix, over time. I could retire, but I think I'd rather invest it in The Circle. If I work from home, I'll still have plenty of time to bake cookies for Cody. What do you think?"

"I think it's pretty convenient that you waited to tell me you're loaded until after I paid for the pizza."

Honor laughed. "Be serious."

"Okay. I want you to do whatever makes you happy. I'm just thrilled you aren't going to have to commute. How long do you think it will take to wrap things up here and move?"

"Not long."

Josh chewed a bite of pizza and looked around. "It doesn't look like your condominium needs much work before you put it up for sale."

"Yeah, I guess I really never did much to personalize the place."

Josh teased, "Still, you better make a checklist so we don't forget anything."

Glancing around her living room, it dawned on Honor that she had never been truly happy in this room until tonight. She recalled the deep loneliness she felt here, grieving her mother's death and the collapse of her marriage.

"Come back to me, Honor...you're miles away all of a sudden," Josh cooed, interrupting her thoughts.

She gave him a warm smile. "I love the feeling I get every time I realize you're not just a dream."

He grinned, "Good one! You're forgiven." Josh kissed the tip of her nose. "Penny for your thoughts?"

"I was thinking my entire life is completely different from

the one I had so carefully planned out, but I wound up with more than I ever dreamed."

"So, it's time for new dreams—what do you want to accomplish down the road?"

Honor considered the question as she rolled the five pearls back and forth on her gold chain. "Well," she said, "I guess after we restore our beautiful home and create two outrageously successful companies, we could devote our time to raising our son and four daughters."

"What daughters?"

In lieu of an explanation, Honor pointed at her necklace.

Josh smiled. "Sounds like a plan. I figure they'll be named *Darcy, Hannah, Hope* and *Faith*, right?"

She winked at him. "Absolutely. Hey, if we name a couple of them '*Jubilance Darcy*' and '*Joy Hannah*,' we could maintain both of our family's naming traditions."

Josh laughed out loud. "Hopefully, we'll come up with better names than that."

He put his arms around her and pulled her close, gazing at her in the firelight. He brushed a loose curl from her face and murmured, "Wow."

Honor smiled back, remembering the first time he said that to her on the porch of the Belleview Biltmore Resort. The erotic memory was so strong that it took her breath away. She whispered, "Yeah...wow," and leaned forward to kiss him.

They made love on the floor in front of the fire and then fell asleep, wrapped tightly in one another's arms, content and knowing whatever was to come, they would be together.

Epilogue

At first I thought they were alive, the way they sat at the parlor table, casually chatting. Then I noticed they were strangely attired. Not Halloween night strange; just out of date. When I looked closer, it slowly began to sink in. They weren't exactly what you would call "solid."

Honor smiled and closed her old journal. She slid her fingers affectionately across the worn, brown leather cover, caressing its tattered front edge, remembering the journey that now filled every page. Her glance shifted to the table, where a fresh diary lay waiting for her to record the new chapters of her life. Just as she was about to reach for it, there was a knock at the door of her suite.

Ellen Christianson looked worried at the sight of Honor's bathrobe. "Am I too early? I know Julie wanted us bridesmaids to meet at the spa, but that just isn't my style."

"Actually, I'm glad you're here. I feel like I haven't had a moment alone with you."

Ellen sat down on a wide, velvety settee, and accepted the glass of wine Honor offered.

"Did you see the sign in the lobby, welcoming guests to the wedding of Honor Macklin and Josh Lancing? I took a picture of it and sent it to Melody, along with the text, *'All's well that ends well.'* I figure that's a metaphor that not even she can mess up."

Honor giggled. "I'll bet she forwards it to everyone in the Accounting Department at Soft Fix."

"Probably the whole company."

Honor nodded in agreement. "So, can you believe the size

of my wedding party? Since Josh wanted to include all ten of his brothers in the ceremony, I think there are almost as many people *in* the wedding as there are *attending* the wedding."

"I wasn't going to say anything," Ellen teased. "Truthfully, I still can't remember who is who."

"Yeah, I was thinking about making everyone wear name tags. James is the one escorting me down the aisle, and John, who is his new business partner, will be his Best Man and escort Julie. Then you'll be accompanied by Jacob, and the next five brothers will walk with Cherry, Patty, Chase, Becky, and James' wife, Lisa."

"That's only eight."

"His twin brothers, Jeff and Jeremy, are serving as ushers."

Ellen nodded and took a sip of wine. "So what's this I hear about you hiring Ben Dugan as your investment broker?"

"Didn't Julie tell you what happened?"

Ellen shook her head.

Honor smiled. "It's a long story, so I'll just give you the cliffs notes version. When my mother died, I told my sisters to split her belongings evenly among themselves, which they did. But she had always wanted me to have her grandfather clock, so I kept that and a few things they left behind, including a Victorian hatbox. Well, when Josh and I decided to buy my mom's house and renovate it, we called someone to move the clock to storage to keep it out of harm's way during the construction. The movers asked what was in the locked compartment at the base of the clock and I didn't know."

Honor paused to take a sip of wine. "I remembered finding an old key in the bottom of the Victorian hatbox, so I retrieved it and low and behold, it fit the lock. Inside were the keys to a safe deposit box and a post office box, along with a note from my mother, explaining that she started investing in the stock market just after my dad passed away. The two boxes were stuffed with stock reports and paperwork, naming me as co-owner of the portfolio."

"Wow. How much was it worth?"

"A little over five hundred thousand dollars... almost exactly what I had taken out of my retirement savings to buy the house from my sisters."

"Didn't you have to split the money with them?"

"Well, I did offer, but my mother's note said that when she died, she wanted me to keep the portfolio intact. She gave me instructions about getting in touch with a very old friend of hers named Margaret, who shared her interest in the stock market. It turns out they used to get together every month or so to have tea and strategize about their investments, and she wanted me to keep the friendship going. My sisters all agreed to honor our mother's wishes, so now I meet with Margaret at her place every other month, and we decide what we want to buy, sell or trade. It's really pretty interesting. I plan to split the annual dividends with my sisters."

"That's cool. I wish I had that kind of relationship with my family."

Honor nodded. "Yeah... we've grown closer now that our parents are both gone." She paused, trying to remember where she had left off. "Anyway, after Ben left Soft Fix, he went to work for a major stock broker and now he's on my investment team. He's a good guy. I think he and Julie might get serious, if he can transfer to his company's headquarters in St. Petersburg."

Ellen chuckled. "Ah, true love. The only long-term relationship I truly believe in is the one between me and my bird, Mister Peaches." Suddenly remembering it was Honor's wedding day, she added, "except for you and Josh, of course."

"Of course," Honor laughed.

Ellen was relieved Honor had taken no offense. Not wanting to push her luck, she switched topics. "Julie says things are going great with *The Circle*. Since she already met her goal of becoming the Chief Operations Officer of a growing company, she set a new goal...to become one of the top hundred female executives in America."

Honor shook her head. "I wouldn't want to bet against her. *The Circle* is already one of the fastest-growing women-owned enterprises in the country."

"I heard." Ellen shook her head in amazement.

"How are things going at Soft Fix?" Honor asked.

Ellen puffed out her chest. "I'm happy to report the company is rock solid. I'm glad you suggested we promote Helen Ellis to be in charge of the Corporate Finance Department. She runs things by the book. Lots of checks and balances... unlike what I fondly call the '*William-nomics Era*.'"

"That doesn't surprise me."

"Yep. Even though Yvonne and William tried to keep her in the dark, Helen figured out what they were up to. She tried to let you know what was happening without getting herself fired. One day, she was walking by your office when she noticed Ben was helping Julie hang up a bulletin board. He had laid his copy of an important report on your conference table, so she pretended to ask Ben a question while sliding the report from the table and onto a chair, out of sight. When Ben went to retrieve the report, she said she hadn't seen it, and suggested he must have left it back in his office."

Honor recalled William searching her desk the morning she returned to Chicago. "And that night, I picked up the report from the chair before anyone knew I was back, so of course, they never found it. But I didn't know what it was."

"That's right. And when Helen figured out you didn't understand William's codes, she sent you an e-mail to help you understand William's *creative* accounting practices."

They clinked their glasses, toasting Helen.

"This might not be cool to talk about on your wedding day, but you heard William's getting divorced, right?"

Honor nodded. "Yeah... shocking, huh? I heard Sherri found out about Yvonne."

Ellen chuckled. "Yep. After we fired Yvonne, she called

Sherri and told her everything... including the name of the offshore bank where William was hiding assets. Sherri's lawyers are having a field day."

"I guess what goes around, comes around."

"Yeah, karma can be a bitch," Ellen agreed. "You're so much better off with Josh."

"No kidding. I'm so proud of him. Our house was the first project he and his brothers completed together, and it turned out so beautifully that it was featured in a national '*Parade of Vintage Homes*' event. The exposure generated a lot of business."

"Hmm... a great guy with good prospects? Maybe you should consider keeping him." Ellen joked.

"Speaking of that...we should probably start getting dressed for this wedding, don't you think?"

As if they heard their cue, the rest of the bridal party arrived at the suite, all fresh from the spa and chattering happily amongst themselves. Everyone was in high spirits as they dressed in their peach, Victorian Era dresses, complete with hoop skirts, feathered hats and white, lace parasols.

Honor looked positively regal in her silk, high-necked, Victorian wedding gown. Lace and pearl beading accented the design, which followed the lines of her figure. Dark, ringlet curls spilled down her back as if pouring out from underneath her small, feathered hairpiece. Julie attached her lace bustle and handed her three, long-stemmed white calla lilies, tied together with a peach ribbon, to complete her ensemble.

When they had gathered in the staging area, Ellen peeked out at the guests, seated in front of the heart-shaped tree. "What a perfect day for a garden wedding," she commented. "But why is the front row of chairs roped off?"

"The front row is reserved for any spirits of the Belleview Biltmore, who might wish to attend the nuptials," Honor replied coyly.

Ellen was curious. "Ghosts?"

Before Honor could answer, the music started.

One by one, Honor's attendants strolled to where Josh and the groomsmen were waiting under her great-great-grandparent's tree. Cody, dressed in a miniature tuxedo and carrying the ring-bearer's pillow, followed along with the flower girl, James' daughter, Jordan. When the wedding march began to play, Honor took James' arm, and stepped out onto the porch.

She hesitated there, drinking in the pure joy of the moment: the beautiful setting, the large group of well-wishers who had come to share this special day with them, and most of all, Josh. As she started down the stairs, she noticed Cody waving at the first row of chairs and wondered how many invisible guests were in attendance.

She was still smiling at the thought when she returned her gaze to Josh. The look of complete adoration on his face caused her heart to leap as she approached to take her place by his side. She knew the love and devotion they shared would last through eternity, and although she couldn't explain it, she was positive that, no matter where the lighted path had taken them, Rory and Darcy had discovered the same thing.

The End

About the Author

BonSue Brandvik lives with her loving husband near the Belleview Biltmore Resort—the inspiration and setting for her novels. She's a hopeless romantic and an optimist. She believes historic buildings embody irreplaceable echoes of the past and hopes readers will join the campaign to save this grand hotel from demolition. Most of all, she hopes the day will come when the Belleview Biltmore reopens and, once again, welcomes guests from around the world, so all of her readers can experience its grandeur for themselves.

About the
Belleview Biltmore Resort

Built by Henry B. Plant, she first opened her doors in January, 1897. By the early1920s, two new wings had been added, making her the largest occupied wooden structure in the world. For well over a century, she welcomed visitors to step back in time and marvel at the magnificence of her historic beauty. Her guest registers boast visits from USA presidents, British royalty, and countless famous families, sports figures, movie stars and other celebrities.

When developers wanted to tear her down to make room for more condominiums a few years ago, the Town of Belleair, which is literally built around the Resort, came to her rescue by incorporating a historic preservation ordinance into its Town Charter.

Fans of the hotel cheered when a group of investors stepped forward and announced plans to restore the hotel. They closed the hotel in 2009, gutted the interior and began the internal demolition. They planned to replace the entire roof, which had suffered significant damage during the hurricane season of 2004. But when two law suits were filed by neighboring property owners, the renovations were halted until the nuisance claims were resolved. Nearly two years later, both claims were settled in favor of the hotel owners, but by then, the real estate market had collapsed. Investors pulled out and the owners defaulted on the mortgage.

In lieu of foreclosure, the property was sold in January, 2011 for a fraction of its true value.

The new owners are not interested in repairing /renovating the Resort and have expressed a willingness to sell the hotel, golf course and beach property as separate entities, which would be a tragedy for the Resort. They are currently proposing to demolish the hotel to build 80 town homes.

Unless a buyer steps forward soon, this precious and historic property may be lost. Therefore, hotel fans and preservationists are actively seeking a buyer for the property, who shares the goal of saving and restoring the Belleview Biltmore Resort. For additional information, please contact the Save the Biltmore Preservationists at: SaveThe Biltmore.com.